The Midnight Land II
The Gift

E.P. Clark

Helia Press

The Midnight Land II: The Gift
Text copyright © 2015, 2018 E.P. Clark
Cover design copyright © 2021 E.P. Clark
Published by Helia Press
Winston-Salem, NC
Paperback edition 2021
Paperback ISBN: 978-0-9991689-5-0

A Note to the Reader

Presumably if you're here it's because you've already read Part I. I hope so, because otherwise you're going to be really confused. But just to refresh your memory, in Part I our heroine, Slava, left her native Krasnograd to go adventuring above the sunline with Olga Vasilisovna and the rest of her party. After numerous exciting events, they leave the tundra and head to Lesnograd to consult with the sorceresses there about Slava's emerging magical gifts. When they arrive, they discover the city in disarray and all the members of Olga's family at each other's throats. Part I ends with Slava's discovery that a curse has been laid on her sister the Empress, and that ten-year-old Vladislava Vasilisovna, Olga's niece, was the mastermind of the plan. Part II begins immediately where Part I leaves off.

The language the characters speak is essentially Russian, with one important difference: instead of patronymics, characters have matronymics. However, the extensive system of nicknaming is the same.

Distance is measured in versts (pronounced vyorst). 1 verst is approximately 1 kilometer. The gold currency is the chervonets (1 chervonets, 2, 3, 4, chervontsa, 5+ chervontsev—it all makes sense if you speak a Slavic language); each chervonets is worth 200 grosh, which is the coin most commonly in circulation.

Chapter One

"What...what curse?" Slava asked. Her voice was quavering from shock, but Vladislava was so engrossed in her story she didn't even notice, and carried on obliviously.

"The curse was also partly my idea," she said, her voice ringing with pride. "They did a great spell, using Grandmother's blood, and mine too, so that someone of Grandmother's blood would carry the curse to the Empress. But the curse itself was to cause the Empress great harm, so that those closest to her would turn against her, just as had happened to Grandmother, and she would be unable to rule. But when they tried to cast it, Grandmother had a fit, and they told her it was because of the spell, it had gone wrong, so she dismissed all her sorceresses and they laid a curse on her, like you know, and I think on me too, because they blamed me for coming up with the idea, even though the spell going wrong was surely their fault, not mine, and now Grandmother is ill, maybe dying, I don't know. They keep saying she's probably going to die, when they think she and I aren't listening. I've never seen anyone die before, have you? What do dying people look like? Do they look like Grandmother? Is it scary?"

"Most likely," said Slava. "What about the curse on the Tsarina? Was it broken?"

"Probably not," said Vladislava with a shrug of indifference. "Maybe part of it, but it was much too strong a spell to be broken all at once. I wonder how it will come about, don't you? I think they meant her to be betrayed by someone of her own blood. I wonder who that will be, don't you? It would have to be someone of her blood and ours as well. Do you know who that might be? Although Grandmother said we were all fourth-sisters, or something of the kind, so the Zerkalitsy all have Severnolesnaya blood, little as they deserve it. And I wonder how it will happen. They didn't tell me that part, maybe because they didn't know themselves. Oh look, there's the herbwoman's gate. I hope she's at home."

They had left the kremlin far behind and come to a neighborhood of modest cottages. Vladislava pushed open a small gate in a plain fence, and started down the narrow path in the snow that led to the herbwoman's front door. Slava followed numbly. She knew that she had just received information of great value, and that she would need to take action, probably unpleasant action, but right now she was so shocked she was not sure she could speak, let alone act.

"Slavochka!" cried the woman who opened the door, and Slava started, wondering how this stranger could have learned her name, and then realized that, of course, Vladislava was a Slava too. And also a Vladya, just like Slava's sister. She was just like both of them.

"Good day, Alina Marinovna," said Vladislava. "Look: I brought someone. Alina Marinovna, this is the Tsarinovna—I don't know her first name. Tsarinovna, this is Alina Marinovna."

"The Tsarinovna's name is Krasnoslava, child, everyone knows that," said Alina Marinovna, before freezing in the doorway and staring at Slava with her mouth open. She was dressed for indoors, and she stood there for so long that she began to shiver violently, but did not seem to notice until Slava said, "May we come in, Alina Marinovna? It is cold on the street."

"Come in," said Alina Marinovna, backing away from the door on unbending knees. She was a woman of middle years with a round kind face, which made the shock and fear on it particularly out of place.

"You have a very pleasant cottage, Alina Marinovna," Slava remarked as she stepped inside. Although she was no less shocked than Alina Marinovna, even if for different reasons, she had had a moment longer to compose herself, and a lifetime of good manners was coming to her aid. "May I hang my cloak on this hook?"

"Tsarinovna," said Alina Marinovna wonderingly. "Are you..." she turned to Vladislava, "a real Tsarinovna?" she finished. "Did you really bring a Tsarinovna into my home, Slavochka?" Slava couldn't tell how much of the question was astonishment, and how much was an awakening horror of the danger this posed.

"Oh, she's very nice, Alina Marinovna," said Vladislava carelessly. "Much nicer than most of the princesses I know. And she wants to find the sorceresses, just like I do, don't you, Tsarinovna?"

"Yes," said Slava. That much was most definitely true. "I have heard wondrous things of your Lesnograd sorceresses, Alina Marinovna," she continued, doing her best to sound innocently flattering despite the fact that her head was still whirling from surprise and, she suspected, hunger, thirst, and exhaustion. "I was most disappointed to hear that they had left the city, but Vladislava Vasilisovna assures me that we will be able to find them. I would be most grateful for any help you could offer us, Alina Marinovna."

"Really a Tsarinovna?" said Alina Marinovna, giving Slava a disbelieving look. "How?"

"I arrived in Lesnograd today with Olga Vasilisovna," Slava said, speaking more smoothly with every word.

"Olga Vasilisovna is in town?" cried Alina Marinovna. "Really? What is she doing here?"

"Oh, Aunty Olya came in today," said Vladislava. "I think she's mostly quarreling with Mother and Andrey Vladislavych and the others. So the Tsarinovna and I decided to come here instead. We don't like quarreling."

"Tea," said Alina Marinovna, in the voice of a woman clutching at anything she could to save herself from drowning. "Would you like some tea? Tsarinovna?" She started to meet Slava's eyes, but then lost her nerve and quickly looked away.

"Tea would be wonderful, if it wouldn't be too much trouble," said Slava, sincerely hoping that it wouldn't be too much trouble.

"With pleasure, Tsarinovna," said Alina Marinovna faintly, and hurried off into the other room, presumably the kitchen.

"Alina Marinovna's very nice, isn't she?" said Vladislava. "Let's sit down." She sat down in what was clearly a chair she had occupied many times before. After a moment, Slava sat down in another chair.

"Do you come here often, Vladislava Vasilisovna?" Slava asked. She found she was having a hard time looking Vladislava in the face and not screaming at her. A curse! A curse against Slava's sister! And it was all Vladislava's idea! She wanted to grab Vladislava by the shoulders and shake her until her teeth shattered against each other and came out.

As soon as the image rose in Slava's mind, though, she was repulsed and horrified, and she found herself remembering Vladislava's voice as she said, "What do dying people look like? Do they look like Grandmother? Is it scary?" and a wave of heartbroken tender protectiveness rose up and threatened to engulf the rage entirely. Slava had many times before thought her feelings would tug so hard in opposite directions that they would tear her apart, but never, she thought, so acutely.

She wished she had a moment alone to compose herself, and to... she didn't know what...pray, maybe. Not as most people did, begging for selfish favors they were too weak to win on their own, but the way priestesses were said to do when they were seeking wisdom. Right now, sitting in a strange woman's cottage in a hostile town, looking across at the innocent author of so much evil, Slava wished for the first time in her life that she had learned how to pray, that she had learned how to seek wisdom and guidance from without and within.

Please, she said to herself, *if anyone is listening,* and then she realized that it didn't matter whether or not anyone else was listening, because what mattered was her own inner voice, the one that was so often silenced by the clamoring shouts of all the other voices around her. *Let me know what to do,* she said, and then changed it to, *When the time comes, I will know what to do. When the time comes, I will know what to do.*

"Is something wrong, Tsarinovna?" asked Vladislava. "You closed your eyes for a moment."

"I am just very tired," Slava told her. "It has been a long journey."

"How many days?" asked Vladislava.

"Many weeks," said Slava.

"Weeks!" exclaimed Vladislava. "Really? Weeks? Why? Where did you go?"

"The Midnight Land," Slava told her.

"Really?" said Vladislava, her eyes growing large. "Aunty Olya talked about it, but nobody thought she'd make it. Was it nice?"

"It was dark," Slava said.

"Why did you go, then?" asked Vladislava.

"For knowledge," said Slava.

"But what could you learn, if it was dark?" asked Vladislava. "Why didn't you wait until summer? Or is it dark all the time there in summer, too?"

"No, in summer it is light all the time there, I believe," said Slava. "But the traveling is easier on snow than mud."

"That makes sense," said Vladislava, nodding wisely. "Grandmother always preferred traveling in winter to summer, too. Did you hear that, Alina Marinovna? The Tsarinovna has been traveling for weeks in the Midnight Land!"

Alina Marinovna, who was carrying a tray of tea things into the room, stopped and gave Slava a look in which appraisal was beginning to flicker amongst the fear. "Yes, one can see that," she said eventually. "Or at least, one can see that she has been consorting with the gods." She gave Slava another uncertain look, as if consorting with the gods made her both closer and farther away. "Did you have much luck with it, Tsarinovna?" she asked.

"What luck is there to be had with gods?" Slava asked.

"The luck of not dying, Tsarinovna," said Alina Marinovna, almost smiling.

"In that case, I had much luck," Slava told her, also smiling. "And now I am in Lesnograd, and eager to meet with the famed Lesnograd sorceresses, who, Vladislava Vasilisovna tells me, have fled, leaving only their curses behind."

"Well, they had their reasons, Tsarinovna," said Alina Marinovna, setting the tray down and pouring tea with hands that barely shook. Like everyone else, she was beginning to feel at ease around Slava, a gift of Slava's that, like all her other gifts, was not without its benefits, even as it brought her much inconvenience.

"I'm sure they did," Slava said sympathetically. "Vladislava Vasilisovna has told me some of the story already."

"Grandmother was very rude to them," said Vladislava, nodding in agreement. "But we have to get them back, don't we, Alina Marinovna?" She made no move to help Alina Marinovna distribute the tea, which struck Slava unpleasantly, until she realized that she was not doing anything to help Alina Marinovna, either. She stood up to assist, but Alina Marinovna gave her a look of such horror when she heard Slava's offer that she was forced to sit back down and wait while Alina Marinovna brought her tea and pastries, accompanied with many bows and apologies for the coarseness of the fare.

A few months with Olga and the others may have rendered her unfit to be a noblewoman, Slava thought, and for the first time since Krasnograd had disappeared behind her, she wondered what people would think of her there when she returned. Lesnograd might be the barbaric North, but it was still a city of sorts, and as such was a distant sister to Krasnograd, just as Vladislava was a distant sister to Slava. With the walls of Lesnograd closed around her, she could feel the walls of Krasnograd close around her too. That image was so unpleasant that Slava quickly forced her mind away from it and back to the missing sorceresses.

"We'll do our best to get them back, don't worry, little princess," said Alina Marinovna, once Slava and Vladislava had been served and she felt able to sit down herself and drink her tea, which she did with one eye cocked nervously at Slava. "The sorceresses aren't going to go far from Lesnogorod."

"Alina Marinovna thinks she knows where they went, don't you, Alina Marinovna?" said Vladislava, sitting there drinking her tea with an air that was both comically adult and endearingly childish. Slava was forcing herself to see Vladislava as a child, but she also reminded herself that children often were, after all, much cleverer and more ruthless than adults, and Vladislava was certainly no exception.

"It's no secret where they've gone," said Alina Marinovna. "They've gone to live with the priestesses, well, most of them, anyway. They're in the sanctuaries."

"Are they far from here?" Slava asked.

"Not if you know where to look," said Alina Marinovna. "But if you don't know how to find them, you can stumble around in the woods till you starve and never catch sight of them."

"I would very much like to speak with the sorceresses," said Slava "What do you think my chances are of finding them?"

"I would say none, except that you claim you have been to the Midnight Land, Tsarinovna," said Alina Marinovna. "That might weigh heavily in your favor."

"Should I go to a sanctuary?" Slava asked. "Perhaps the gods will help me; they have thus far."

"Or we could send them a message, couldn't we, Alina Marinovna?" said Vladislava. "We've tried before, but maybe they'll listen this time, won't they?"

"Maybe they will, little princess," said Alina Marinovna. "I'm going into the forest tomorrow, Tsarinovna. I'll tell them of you, and perhaps they'll listen. Wait for word from me in three days' time."

"My many thanks, Alina Marinovna," said Slava.

"It's not every day that I have the honor of serving a Tsarinovna," said Alina Marinovna. "They say"—she gave Slava an unexpectedly shrewd look—"they say that trouble comes to those who fall into the affairs of empresses."

"Oh, this Tsarinovna is very kind, aren't you, Tsarinovna?" said Vladislava confidently.

"Yes," said Slava. "I am very kind, and trouble does come to those who fall into my affairs. But perhaps there is worse trouble for those

6

who don't."

"Should I tell the sorceresses that, Tsarinovna?" asked Alina Marinovna.

"No," said Slava slowly. "Tell them...Tell them that the gods have
said I have a purpose in life, and that they have taken an interest in my
fate. Tell the sorceresses I would speak to them of this."

"That will make them come running, Tsarinovna, them and the
priestesses too, I have no doubt," said Alina Marinovna. "Or run the
other way, I don't know. But run they will."

"My many thanks," Slava repeated, standing up. "I will trespass no
longer on your time."

"You have done me great honor, Tsarinovna," said Alina Marinovna, standing up too and bowing deeply, but with evident relief at the
thought of Slava's imminent absence.

"You'll tell us as soon as you know something, won't you, Alina
Marinovna?" said Vladislava, jumping to her feet. "I'll be waiting and
waiting to hear from you."

"Of course, little princess," said Alina Marinovna. "I won't make
you wait a moment longer than I have to."

"Thanks so much, Alina Marinovna," said Vladislava. "You should
come to the kremlin more often."

"Perhaps someday, little princess," said Alina Marinovna with a
sad smile. "In the meantime, you can come visit me whenever you
wish." She led Slava and Vladislava out the front door, and bowed
them out of sight.

"Alina Marinovna is so kind, isn't she?" said Vladislava, as soon as
the wicker gate had closed behind them and they had gone around
the corner to the next street. "She's really the only person who's kind
to me. No one else lets me come sit in their sitting room and drink tea
with them. She used to live with us in the kremlin, but then she left,
I don't know why except that Mother said she was trying to steal me
away, which isn't true, so it must be something else, and then Mother
said I wasn't to come see her, so I have to sneak away when she isn't
paying attention to me, which isn't that hard, really. Mother pays a lot
more attention to the me she has in her head than to the me I have in
my head, so she's very easy to fool. I can normally manage to see Alina
Marinovna two or three times a week; isn't that nice?"

"Very nice," said Slava, pity and anger rising up and threatening
to choke her again. She felt so sorry for and so horrified by Vladislava
that for a moment she wished she could just run away from her and

pretend that she had never existed.

Some hero, she thought to herself. *If the gods could see me now...*

"Why do you look so sad and angry, Tsarinovna?" asked Vladislava. "Is it true what you said to Alina Marinovna, that the gods have taken an interest in your fate?"

"Yes," said Slava.

"Why?" asked Vladislava. "What have you got that they could want?"

"They say...They said that I was born to be a hero," said Slava.

"Really?" Vladislava gave her a considering look. "You don't look much like a hero," she said doubtfully. "A hero should look more like... more like Aunty Olya, or someone like that."

"I agree," said Slava.

"What can you do to be a hero, anyway?" asked Vladislava. "You're not very big or strong—can you heal people?"

Slava started to say "No," but then found herself saying, "Has anyone every stood up for you, Vladislava Vasilisovna? Has anyone ever treated you like they cared about you?"

"Mother says she cares about me, but she doesn't," said Vladislava. "Grandmother sometimes cared about me, but she always got bored. Sometimes Lisochka cries and talks about how we're sisters and we have no one but each other and we must take care of each other, but most of the time she's angry at me—she wishes my mother had run away instead of hers, or that I'd never been born so that she could rule Lesnograd, even though it's plain she couldn't do it and doesn't want to anyway. The sorceresses tried to teach me things, but that was because they thought I was useful. Alina Marinovna is nice to me, but she has daughters and granddaughters of her own she cares about more than she does about me." Vladislava said all of this with a brave voice, but her face grew further and further cast down as she recited the litany of people who didn't care about her.

"Well, I care about you," said Slava.

"That doesn't make you a hero," said Vladislava, her voice now tinged once again with the arrogant contempt of the very young and clever. "*Anyone* could care about me if she *wanted* to. Caring about other people is easy: all you have to do is do it. Besides, why would you care about me? What are you going to try to make me do? What do you want from me?"

"I want you to be a better person," said Slava. "I want you to be a good person rather than a bad person."

8

"I *am* a good person!"

"Of course you are," said Slava soothingly. "What I meant was that I'm going to try to help you be an even better person, and also a happier one, by getting other people to take better care of you and teach you the things you need to know."

"How are you going to do that?" asked Vladislava, doubt in Slava's abilities radiating from every feature.

"I'm going to start by speaking with Olga Vasilisovna and your mother," said Slava. As soon as she said it, she knew she had a purpose and a plan. It was a strange feeling for Slava, and to her surprise, it made her feel braver than usual. No, not just braver than usual, but truly brave. She supposed she had been what other people called "brave" before, when she had saved the snow hares or thrown herself at the leshiye, but those had been instinctive acts of desperation, and she had had no awareness of her own bravery as she had engaged in them.

Now, though, she knew what she was going to do, and she wasn't afraid to do it. In fact, she was not only not afraid, she was filled with a courage and resolve she had never suspected in herself before. It was an intoxicating feeling. This must be, she thought, the way some mothers feel as they await the birth of their child. She looked back down at Vladislava. All her earlier revulsion and anger had melted away, and now all she felt for her was a fierce protective tenderness.

"Perhaps your mother will send you to Krasnograd," she said. "You could foster with me." Despite her new-found courage, she was surprised to hear herself suggest it, but as soon as she did, she knew it was the right thing to do, and that she had found the way to approach Vasilisa Vasilisovna. She could already hear the persuasive words in her head: *So taken with Vladislava Vasilisovna...Such a clever, promising young princess...Should make friends with the other young princesses...Imperial ward...*

"Why?" asked Vladislava, interrupting Slava's visions. "Why would you take me to Krasnograd?" She was trying to be suspicious, but Slava could hear the upwelling of desire in her voice. Apparently she had found the way to approach Vladislava, too.

"You are a clever girl, and will one day rule Lesnograd," said Slava. "It is only right that you should spend time in Krasnograd. I have taken no wards as yet, which has been greatly remiss of me. It is high time that I start." As soon as she said that, another great rush of excitement poured over Slava, as she realized that she had yet another purpose. Vladislava was not the only young princess who could benefit from her care. Her sister occasionally took on wards, but never took an interest in them. Slava should take them, and any other young princess who struck her fancy and was willing, under her wing. She could make a whole school! She could invite sorceresses, scholars, priestesses, healers...

"Mother won't let me," said Vladislava, interrupting Slava's dream. Slava didn't mind, though, because she knew it was much too strong a dream to abandon her, and that something had just happened to her that would affect the whole course of her life. If she had ever had to guess when such a life-changing event would occur, she never would have said while sneaking down a back alley in Lesnograd with a truant and treasonous little princess, which was why, she told herself, you shouldn't try to second-guess the future too much.

"It won't hurt to ask her," said Slava.

"I guess," said Vladislava, not sounding very confident in either Slava or her mother.

"Why don't you take me to her as soon as we arrive at the kremlin," said Slava.

Vladislava gave her another doubtful look, but, once they had slipped unnoticed back into the kremlin—Olga really needed to know about that, Slava told herself—Vladislava led her to a private set of chambers not far from those of Princess Severnolesnaya, and when the serving girl let them in, Vasilisa Vasilisovna was standing there by the fire.

"Where have you been!" she demanded as soon as they appeared. "You've been gone for ages! I've been worried sick about you!"

"At Alina Marinovna's," said Vladislava, making sure to say it as infuriatingly as possible. She was successful, for the red spots on Vasilisa Vasilisovna's cheeks grew even redder, and for a moment Slava thought she might scream again. She managed to keep it down to a hysterical tirade, but, Slava could tell, only with extreme difficulty.

"I've told you...I specifically ordered you not to go there," she hissed, shaking. "I don't do that on a whim, you know! It's for your own good! How can you do this to me! What is wrong with you?!!"

"I like Alina Marinovna," said Vladislava, gazing at her mother with deliberately cruel indifference, that, Slava could tell, was her only shield against her mother's unintentional cruelty. "She's much nicer than anyone here at the kremlin."

"And how could you..." Vasilisa Vasilisovna wheeled around to

Slava, "how could you let her go? What's wrong with you! How could you do this to me!!" Somewhere, Slava could see, something inside her was telling her she was being supremely stupid on many levels, but that only drove her on. For a moment, Slava felt her resolve start to waver, as she had to fight the urge to reach over and shake Vasilisa Vasilisovna till her teeth rattled and scream at her, "How can you be so stupid! What's wrong with you!"

"I wished to speak with Vladislava Vasilisovna," said Slava. "I was greatly impressed with her the moment I saw her, and I wished to get to know her better. And I, too, as it turned out, had business with Alina Marinovna." She thought about adding, *And we were perfectly safe*, but decided it would only make Vasilisa Vasilisovna even angrier. "I would like to take Vladislava Vasilisovna with me when I return to Krasnograd, as my ward," she said instead.

"How...What?" Vasilisa Vasilisovna stopped in mid-tirade, and stared at Slava.

"I wish to take her on as my ward, as a ward of the Imperial family," said Slava. "She is a very clever young girl, and could have a great future ahead of her. I wish to aid her in that. She could learn from the best teachers and make friends with other highborn young women. It would be a great opportunity for her."

"I can't let her go to Krasnograd! Who would look after her!" said Vasilisa Vasilisovna, but Slava could already see the dream of seeing her daughter as an Imperial ward rise in her eyes, along with—although so hidden that Vasilisa Vasilisovna would never admit to its existence—the dream of getting Vladislava off her hands.

"She would naturally have her own guard and her own maid, and I would take a personal interest in her welfare," said Slava. "And, of course, you would be welcome to visit often. The Severnolesnaya family sends its members to Krasnograd far too rarely."

"You just want to use her! To take her away from me and use her as a hostage! Or turn her against me!"

Vladislava opened her mouth to say something cutting, but Slava forestalled her by stepping closer to Vasilisa Vasilisovna and saying, with every ounce of sincerity she could muster, "On the contrary, Vasilisa Vasilisovna! And even if I tried to turn her against you, I doubt I would succeed. I have only known her a few hours, but already she strikes me as a young girl who keeps her own counsel and knows her own mind."

"You mean stubborn as a mule, and twice as difficult," said Vasilisa Vasilisovna, giving Vladislava a look of resentful shame, through which a smile almost threatened to break through. Vladislava stared back with challenging indifference.

"Vladislava has all the fine qualities a ruler requires," Slava said hastily, before Vasilisa Vasilisovna could notice Vladislava's expression and become hysterical again. "Where better for a ruler to learn to rule than in Krasnograd? Vladislava has it in her to be great, Vasilisa Vasilisovna, and I wish to help her down that path. We have need of more great women, Vasilisa Vasilisovna."

"Great? Do you really think so, Tsarinovna?" said Vasilisa Vasilisovna. Everything about her had softened at hearing those words, and she was now gazing up at Slava—even though she was the taller of them, it still seemed somehow as if she were gazing up at her—with a look of hungry devotion in her eyes.

"I knew it from the moment I laid eyes on her," Slava said.

"And you think Krasnograd will help her? You really think she should go to Krasnograd?"

"Krasnograd is the very place for a girl like Vladislava," said Slava.

"And you will take care of her? You promise, Tsarinovna, that you will watch over her personally?"

"Of course," said Slava. "I will watch over her as I would over my own daughter."

"Then...Then...Then of course she must go! Of course! Do you hear that, Slavochka? You're going to Krasnograd!"

Vladislava continued to stare back at her mother coldly. Slava knew that she desperately wanted to go to Krasnograd, and that she desperately resented her mother making the decision for her, and the two feelings were warring within her, and that at any moment one or the other would come bursting out.

"I would be most honored if you would consent to my plan, Vladislava Vasilisovna," said Slava. "Your presence would be greatly valued in Krasnograd."

"When would I go?" asked Vladislava cautiously.

"With me, if you wish. Or you could come in the summer, if that pleases you better."

"I would like to come with you, then, Tsarinovna," said Vladislava, after careful consideration. "Unless Grandmother needs me to remain."

"Of course," said Slava.

Somehow this erased all of Vasilisa Vasilisovna's hysterics and everything else that had gone wrong that day, at least in Vasilisa Vasil-isovna's mind, and Slava soon found herself being led—finally!—to the room she had been given, where she was greeted with clean clothes and the information that the bathhouse was heated and waiting for her. She gratefully followed the serving girl to it, where she steamed in solitary peace until she was almost too light-headed to stand. She kept expecting Olga or Dunya to join her, but she saw no sign of them, either in the bathhouse or in the guest quarters.

Once she had finished her steam and returned to her room, she found herself with nothing to do and no one to talk to, something she had grown unaccustomed to in the past months. She lay on her bed and thought about what she would do about Vladislava—what she would try to show and tell her, and how she would find out about the supposed curse and lift it. She told herself that the curse could be lift-ed, with no harm done to anyone. This pleasant thought turned her mind to the sorceresses, and she began to imagine what she would say to them and ask them, once they came to her. The faces of the yet-un-known sorceresses paraded across her mind, and priestesses, too, and many others...

Chapter Two

A gentle knocking on the door let her know that she had fallen asleep, and must wake up. She got up to answer it, surprised at how sore her body was and how clear her mind was, as if all the accumulated struggles of her journey had decided to take their toll all at once, exhausting her body and emptying her mind. She moved slowly across the room and opened the door, finding a nervous maid waiting on the other side of it.

"I beg your pardon, Tsarin…" the girl gulped and trailed off, clearly unsure whether she was actually facing a Tsarinovna and if so, how to address her. "I mean…I hope I didn't wake you…" she stuttered. "Only…Supper…"

"Is it time for supper already?" asked Slava, smiling reassuringly at the frightened girl. "I'm so hungry!"

"I'm sorry, Tsarinovna…If I'd've known…" The maid was so frightened she was having trouble articulating her words.

"There was nothing to know," Slava told her kindly. "The hospitality I have received here has been excellent. I had a pleasant rest, and now it seems that supper is ready, and just when I was beginning to wish for it. Is it time to go down?"

"Y-y-yes, Tsarinovna," gulped the girl. "If…If you are ready, that is."

"As soon as I put on my boots," Slava told her. She slipped on her boots and followed the trembling maid out the door and down the corridor. She looked around, expecting to see some of her companions coming to join her, but there was no sign of them.

"Do you know where the others are?" she asked the maid.

"Others, Tsarinovna?" said the girl, staring at her in terror.

"The others of Olga Vasilisovna's party," Slava told her.

"I...I...I surely don't know, Tsarinovna," said the girl, but her face showed she was lying. Clearly something was going on with the others. Slava supposed that the issue of whom to invite to the Princess's table was being hotly contested, with Dima's name being bandied about frequently. She sighed to herself. She had to admit that the problem seemed insoluble, unless Dima took the high road and moved out of the kremlin. Which he would probably do, Slava thought, except that Olga was likely to resist that solution simply in order to annoy Andrey Vladislavovich. Who was a very annoying person, but that didn't mean Olga should be deliberately cruel to him...

"H-h-here we are, Tsarinovna," stuttered the maid.

They were in, not the Great Hall where they had been originally greeted, but a smaller room, which Slava thought was close by. It was filled by a table just large enough for the people there, and had a pleasant, cozy atmosphere. Or would have, if its occupants had not been glaring daggers at each other. A quick chair count told Slava that she was the last and final member of the party to arrive, and that Dunya, Dima, and the rest of Olga's men would not be joining them. Olga, Andrey Vladislavovich (who were foolishly seated next to each other), Lisochka, Vladislava, Vasilisa Vasilisovna, and a very strange-looking man were all seated at the table, and radiating a chill that overpowered the warmth coming from the blazing fire in the fireplace.

"If you please, Tsarinovna," said the maid, struggling to pull out a chair with trembling hands. Slava took her seat as graciously as possible.

"You can go now," Olga said to the maid, and turned away from her dismissively.

"I see you have no difficulty issuing orders in my kremlin," said Andrey Vladislavovich, burning resentment rising from every word. "I see your lack of interest in governing Lesnograd does not extend to an unwillingness to tell my people what to do!" The icy superiority Slava could see he wished to project was abandoning him with every word, so that the sentence ended not in the firm tones of a ruler, but a strangled shriek.

"I would go now if I were you," Slava whispered to the maid, giving her a conspiratorial smile. The maid almost responded with a similar smile before remembering her terror and hurrying out gratefully.

"Your kremlin! *Your* kremlin!" Olga was saying. "Of all the people at this table, you have the least right to it! What is Lesnograd to you!"

"More than it is to you, it seems," Andrey Vladislavovich replied, forgetting about icy superiority and choosing instead a nasty sneer. A sharp pain started at the base of Slava's neck and shot up to her head.

"Papa is right!" cried Lisochka. "You never gave a bent grosh for Lesnograd, and you have no right to come riding in and telling us what to do..."

"Stop whining!" Andrey Vladislavovich gave her a look of such intense loathing that for a moment Slava was afraid he was going to lunge across the table and attack Lisochka before the assembled company. "Why do you have to whine so much! You're nothing but a spoiled little girl...you see what your daughter's become, Olga, a useless hanger-on who does nothing but carp at her betters..."

"Well, you raised me, papa—it's your fault!" shrieked Lisochka. She said a number of other things as well, but her words were lost in the general noise as she, Olga, Vasilisa Vasilisovna, and Andrey Vladislavovich all started shouting at once. Vladislava stared at the scene before her with blank-faced contempt through which tears were threatening to irrupt, and the strange-looking man sitting next to her put his hands over his ears and began rocking back and forth and moaning. No one paid him any attention, and Slava saw that this was normal behavior for him. She guessed he must be Vladislava's father.

Slava looked around the room, hoping for some kind of escape. She was starting to fear that Olga and Lisochka might start hitting each other, or that Andrey Vladislavovich or Vasilisa Vasilisovna would have another attack of hysterics. The unnamed man was moaning louder and louder, unmistakably suffering unbearable distress. Vladislava seemed to be shrinking deeper and deeper into herself, as if hoping to sink into her chair and disappear altogether...

"Stop it!" The voice that shouted was Slava's own. The words rang out across the room with a tone of command that froze the quarrelers in mid-sentence, and they all stared at Slava in shock.

"What is this!" Slava heard herself saying. "Is this any way for the Severnolesnaya family to behave?!? And in front of an Imperial guest! Do you really want to be airing your dirty laundry and your succession troubles in front of the Tsarina's sister? Come to your senses! Nobility is not just a matter of fancy clothes and kremlins, it is a matter of right conduct, and right now you are conducting yourselves like market fishmongers! I am ashamed even to be in the same room with you!!"

Vasilisa Vasilisovna, Andrey Vladislavovich, and Lisochka all swelled up to shout back in indignation, but before they could, Olga burst out laughing.

"Ai-da Tsarinovna!" she cried. "Your blood runs true, I see! I knew I needed you the moment I laid eyes on you, and once again I am proven right! Sister, take Dmitry Vladislavovich away from here; the poor man has enough troubles of his own without being saddled with fools like us. Let him eat his supper in peace."

Vasilisa Vasilisovna looked for a moment as if she wished to argue, but then got up and, with much anxiously solicitous fluttering, got the moaning Dmitry Vladislavovich up from his chair and out of the room.

"I don't know why she bothers bringing him down," said Olga. "The poor man has been out of his wits for years, and being with the rest of you only makes it worse—although that's hardly a sign of being crazy. If I had to eat with you day in and day out, I'd start putting my hands over my ears and moaning, too."

"So you just ran off and left us, instead," said Andrey Vladislavovich spitefully. "You were too much of a coward to stay, so you ran off and abandoned your husband and daughter. Forgive me, Tsarinovna," he gave Slava a look that was half-fear, half-contempt, and continued, "I know we're 'airing our dirty laundry' in front of you, but the truth is the truth. Olga Vasilisovna is an irresponsible coward, you can't deny it. And as for our 'succession troubles,' judge for yourself: would you entrust the ruling of Lesnograd to someone who runs away at the first sign of trouble? Who can't even be bothered to raise her own daughter?"

His face twisted into another ugly sneer for a moment, before settling into an expression of self-righteous satisfaction. He was clever enough, Slava could see, to know that he had hurt the others in the room in a petty and cruel way, but not clever enough not to take pleasure in the fact. For a moment Slava thought she might burst out again, but then she had a better, crueler, idea.

"Vasilisa Olgovna," she said, turning away from Andrey Vladislavovich, "are you happy?"

"What?" Lisochka started and gave her a puzzled look. "Why? What business is it of yours? Tsarinovna," she added as an afterthought. Slava could tell she was already forgetting the terror and shame she had felt a moment ago, after Slava's reprimand, and that her mind was already repainting the scene into something that did not require her to make herself a better person. Slava had told her something unpleasant, and therefore, now that the initial shock was over, Slava must be seen to be wrong and be put in her place. And, as

happened so often, the significance of Slava's title was already draining out of her mind, leaving behind nothing but the insignificance of
Slava's figure, enabling Lisochka to treat her as she pleased.

"I can see that you are not happy, Vasilisa Olgovna," Slava said,
kindly but firmly. "Your words, your actions, your very tone and bearing all scream out your unhappiness."

"Well...Well...How could I be happy?" Lisochka burst out, trying
to cover up her unhappiness with self-righteousness. "My mother left
me! If I'm unhappy, it's her fault!"

"Did your mother have a great hand in your raising, Vasilisa Olgovna?" Slava asked her.

"No, of course not!" Lisochka gave her another look of puzzled
contempt. "How could she? She left me! She never did anything for
me at all!"

"Except give birth to you, and save you from that disastrous marriage my mother wanted," said Olga under her breath. "Many a mother has done worse."

"Yes," said Slava. "Many a mother has." She looked Lisochka firmly in the eye. It was not something she was accustomed to doing, but
she must have been doing it fairly well, for Lisochka quailed back under the force of her gaze. "If you wish to find a source for your unhappiness, Vasilisa Olgovna, you should look closer to home," Slava told
her. "Perhaps to those who raised you, who cared for you every day.
Had they done a better job, you might be less unhappy. The absent
parent is only partly at fault when a child sticks its hand in the fire.
The one watching over it should bear the brunt of the blame. And,
of course, the true culprit is the child itself. It decided to test the fire,
and it must suffer the burns, and no one else can do anything about
that. You are a woman grown now, Vasilisa Olgovna, and it is time to
act like one. Are you a helpless leaf in the wind, or are you mistress of
your own destiny? Do you want to be happy? Truly? Because you are
not acting like it. It seems to me that you enjoy reveling in your unhappiness and the wrongs you have suffered, and you refuse to let them
go. But this is a burden only you can lay down, Vasilisa Olgovna. And
as for you," she turned to Andrey Vladislavovich, "You were given a
charge, and you failed. Your daughter is suffering, and you do nothing
but add to her misery! If this is how you care for your child, how will
you care for your city? How can you be trusted with so many children,
if you have already failed one, and that one the most precious to you
of all? No, Andrey Vladislavovich, you are not fit to rule a city. You are

not even fit to rule yourself. A ruler must have strength, wisdom, and compassion, and you have none of those things. I fear some beggar on the street would be more fit to rule Lesnograd than you."

Slava's torrent of words suddenly dried up. There was a ringing silence. Just when Slava thought she couldn't take it anymore, it was broken by a sudden sobbing, coming from Vladislava.

"What's the matter?!" everyone demanded at once.

"Oh...Oh...Oh...I'm so happy!" she cried. "Finally...Finally! I've wanted to say all those things for so long, but I thought no one would listen, and now someone has! Someone has spoken them for me! Thank all the gods!" And, to Slava's great surprise, she got out of her chair and buried her face in Slava's shoulder.

Slava reached up hesitantly and stroked her back. It was so thin and fragile. Slava felt even more sorry for her, even as she remembered that she had, perhaps, done terrible things and brought a curse down on Slava's family.

I must fix this, Slava said to herself. *I must fix this, whatever it takes.*

"Oh yes, tell me my troubles are my own fault, and then comfort her," said Lisochka, her face screwing up as if she were preparing to scream or cry. "Shout at us, and then comfort her! It's always her, isn't it! It's always her! Always her!" And Lisochka did, in fact, start to cry too.

"Now see what you've done!" said Andrey Vladislavovich. He was groping for his former spitefulness, but he was too shaken to find it, and sounded merely hysterical instead. He made no move to get up and comfort Lisochka, but only watched her squeamishly out of the corner of his eye. Slava almost felt a little bit sorry for him again. Perhaps in some other life he would have been a good man, but the life he had been given was completely unsuited for him, and he didn't know how to escape from it. Kind of like Slava herself, she thought, only she had, at long last, perhaps found her escape, by going deeper into herself and coming right out the other side, so that she had some shield with which to face her tormenters.

"Oh, by all the gods!" cried Olga in exasperation. "Come here, girl." She gave Lisochka a good hard slap on the shoulder, which was probably her version of a motherly hug. "Cheer up and stop crying! It's not so bad, you know. You're young, you're healthy, you're free—why don't you just leave this mess behind? Leave them to stew in their own juices and come with me."

"Where to?" asked Lisochka. She was still sniffling, but it was a sniffle that almost had a hint of a laugh to it.

"Oh, I don't know," said Olga. "Wherever! We could see all of Zem', if you like.

"I don't know..." said Lisochka.

"Oh, come on, you've never even been out of Lesnograd," said Olga. "That's your problem! You need to get out more! You'd be amazed the way your troubles melt away when you're on the road."

"Maybe..." said Lisochka wistfully. "But I don't know..."

"You could come to Krasnograd," Slava suggested. "At least at first. As an escort for Vladislava Vasilisovna."

"Now there's a thought!" said Olga. "We could all make a journey to Krasnograd in order to see your sister off! It'd be both proper and jolly, and you could learn about life on the road."

"No!" cried Andrey Vladislavovich. "I forbid it! You can't just...just run away from your troubles whenever you feel like it! You have responsibilities, both of you, whether you like it or not!"

Until then Slava had felt such a strong antipathy for him that whatever empathy she could generate had been overwhelmed, but now he sounded so forlorn that she found herself rising and going to him without a conscious thought.

"Dear Andrey Vladislavovich," she said. "I know your life has been hard, very hard, and I am sorry! But try to find it in your heart to forgive and forget. I know you may have had to shoulder burdens you were not prepared to carry, but who has not? I am sure, Andrey Vladislavovich, that if you search your heart, you will find the strength to let them go, and take up the burdens that need to be borne. It is there, Andrey Vladislavovich, I am sure of it! Search within yourself, and find it!"

And to her immense surprise, Slava's words seemed to have the effect she wanted on Andrey Vladislavovich, and he gazed up at her hopefully as he started to speak, his face wearing a more human expression than it had all day. It was almost as if his soul, so long in hiding, had decided to peek out for a moment.

"Do you really think so, Tsarinovna?" he asked. "You said it yourself: my life is hard, very hard. Is there any hope for me, Tsarinovna?"

"There is always hope," Slava told him. "Especially when your troubles are in your own heart, and not elsewhere. And our troubles are always ultimately in our own hearts. Let them go, Andrey Vladislavovich! Become the man you wish you could be!"

"Oh yes, papa, yes please!" cried Lisochka, tearing herself free from Olga and throwing herself in Andrey Vladislavovich's lap. She was bigger than him, but neither of them seemed to notice. "Let us... let us put all this behind us! Let us be happy!"

And somehow they all—Olga, Andrey Vladislavovich, and Lisochka—started to laugh, and Olga poured them all wine, and they drank and laughed and talked about their plans until late into the night. Vasilisa Vasilisovna returned and joined them, and there were many toasts "To Krasnograd!" and "To the Tsarinovna!"

Vladislava sat next to Slava and they both watched in quiet fascination. Slava could sense that her part in this was over, and she had best sit silently on the side, so she did, only talking quietly with Vladislava when it became apparent that the others had forgotten them.

"I think you were right, Tsarinovna: you are a hero," said Vladislava at one point. "How did you know what to say?"

"I don't know," Slava confessed. "I just opened my mouth, and out it came. I just spoke what was in my heart. Perhaps the gods put it there; I can't say."

"Do you think it will last?" whispered Vladislava. "Even as long as tomorrow? Or do you think they'll be sorry and ashamed when they wake up in the morning, and it will all be even worse than before?" She sounded as if she had witnessed many such supposed transformations for the better, and been disappointed every time. Probably she had.

"I don't know," Slava whispered back. "Such changes seem to be more lasting in some people than in others."

"If it were you, would you change?" asked Vladislava. "Or would you go back to what you were before?"

"I would change," Slava said, surprised at how certain she was of this. "Once I change, I change forever. I will not go back to what I was before I came here, of that I am sure."

"And you won't forget me, once we're in Krasnograd?" asked Vladislava anxiously.

"No, under no circumstance," Slava assured her.

"I'm glad," said Vladislava. She yawned. "I'm very tired. It's very late."

"Perhaps you should go to bed," suggested Slava. She was a little afraid to break into the happy circle that the others had formed, but when Vladislava went up and told Vasilisa Vasilisovna that she was going to bed, Vasilisa Vasilisovna only laughed and kissed her good night. Slava and Vladislava slipped out of the room.

"I'll lead you to your room," said Vladislava. "Otherwise you might never find it." Many of the torches in the corridors were unlit, due to the lateness of the hour, but Vladislava made her way surely through the dark passages, and left Slava at her door with a cheerful "Good night! Until morning, then!" before disappearing into the darkness around the corner.

The frightened maid was waiting up for Slava in her room, much to Slava's mortification. She dismissed the girl with many thanks and apologies, which only seemed to frighten her even more, and undressed herself and put on a—oh, luxury of luxuries!—clean nightgown before sliding into the warm bed.

Despite the very long and eventful day, or rather, because of it, Slava was unable to fall asleep for a long time. She kept going over and over in her mind what had happened with the others downstairs. How had she done that? Normally, in such situations, which were all too frequent in families, she either retreated in revulsion, able to see the others' stupidity but unable to reach out and help them, or found herself drawn helplessly into the argument, only to lose as she lost all control of her thoughts and feelings and was unable to do anything other than hit back with surprisingly stinging but ultimately useless blows.

Perhaps the gods spoke through me, she thought. But then she thought about it some more, and decided that that was not true. No, this time, the part of her that needed to withdraw had withdrawn to some safe place from which she could watch and decide impartially, and the part that needed to reach out had reached out. It was not "magic," as it had been when she had struck back at the bandits. There was nothing of the gods or their powers in it. It had been Slava's own heart that had found the strength and wisdom to do what needed to be done, and had found the way to do what she had always wished she could do—give people the gift of choosing the good in themselves, while rejecting the evil. At least for the moment.

The same frightened maid came and woke Slava up the next morning, her voice trembling as she did so.

"What is your name?" Slava asked her sleepily.

"Wh-wh-why, Ts-ts-tsarinovna?" quavered the girl.

"So that I know who you are, of course," Slava said. Unfortunately, this only provoked more terror in the girl, so that she stared at Slava in frozen horror.

"You take such good care of me," said Slava, smiling as reassuringly as possible. "I would like to know the name of such a conscientious servant."

"D-d-d-dasha, Tsarinovna," the girl said. She made some indecisive fluttering movements in the direction of Slava's clothes, which were lying on a chair next to the bed, but couldn't actually summon up the courage to pick them up.

"Are you from Lesnograd, Dasha?" Slava asked. She concentrated as hard as possible on appearing reassuring and non-threatening, and was delighted to see Dasha grow more and more relaxed with every word.

"Yes, Tsarinovna," said Dasha. "My whole life."

"It is a very beautiful city, although I have seen only a small portion of it," said Slava.

"Yes, Tsarinovna," said Dasha, and then, gathering up her nerve, added, gulping and stuttering a bit, but managing to get the words out reasonably coherently, "It's a bit run down from what it used to be, Tsarinovna, but it's still a fine city. You should ride around it while you're here, though like I said, it's a bit run down."

"That's too bad," said Slava with all the sympathy she could muster, and then, concentrating firmly on being as innocent and noncommittal as possible, asked, "Has it been that way long?"

"Oh, only the past couple of years, Tsarinovna, but it's been getting worse and worse, especially these past few months. And now that the Princess is ill, everything's going to wrack and ruin, you wouldn't believe how. The streets are in shambles, the guards do nothing but lounge around playing cards and running after anyone who will have them, and it's not safe to walk alone at night."

"That's too bad," said Slava. This time she didn't even have to concentrate on being sympathetic, as it really *was* too bad.

"Yes, and they say...Pardon me for saying this, Tsarinovna, maybe I shouldn't, but maybe you can do something about it, the maids are sick of it...They say that Vasilisa Vasilisovna does nothing but cry,

wring her hands, and quarrel with Andrey Vladislavovich and Vasilisa Olgovna; they all think they want to rule but none of them has
the stomach for it. We all thought Andrey Vladislavovich had gone
crazy, Tsarinovna, when he run off, we don't know why, but he was crazy with rage when he come back, and he hasn't been the same since,
and nothing's being done except the guards got even more arrogant
than they was before, and they haven't been fit to talk to since Andrey
Vladislavovich started running around town with them and that for-
eigner that was with them before he run off too, do you think Olga
Vasilisovna will step in and rule now, Tsarinovna?"

"I don't know," said Slava.

"And now the sorceresses is gone off, and everything's fallen apart,
and we don't know what will happen to us, Tsarinovna! Tell me true,
Tsarinovna: are you here because of treason? Are you here to bring
down the family?" And the maid wrung her hands and stared down at
Slava desperately.

"You have no reason to fear, I promise you that," Slava told her.
"Whatever happens, the servants are certainly in no danger."

"Really, Tsarinovna?" The girl blushed with relief. "Really? Everyone in the kitchen's so afraid! We talk of nothing else! We drew lots
over who had to serve you, and I lost, and now the other girls are all
saying I won't last the day! They're teasing, of course, but we're all so
afraid! When we heard from one of the sorceresses the Princess was
plotting treason, we all got so afraid, and we've been afraid ever since!"

"You have no reason to fear," Slava repeated. "What did the sorceress tell you? Perhaps you misunderstood."

"Oh no, Tsarinovna, she said straight out it was treason," said Dasha. "She came down right after the Princess had her attack, she was
second-sister to one of the under-cooks, and she said this was what
you got when you tried to plot treason, and they were going to declare
a curse on the Princess but we should all be afraid, if the Empress sent
someone it would be the end of us all, and now here you are!"

"Oh, certainly not," said Slava. "I have no intention of punishing
anyone, let alone servants. But you would be doing me a great favor by
introducing me to the under-cook who is second-sister to the sorceress. You see, Dasha, I came here in search of sorceresses, not traitors. I
mean no one any harm; I only want knowledge."

Slava's powers of persuasion were evidently growing by the hour,
for Dasha promptly helped her into her clothes and led her down to
the kitchen, where, even though breakfast preparations were in full

The Gift

swing, one of the under-cooks broke away from her duties and went with Slava into a quiet storeroom.

"You're really a Tsarinovna?" she asked Slava, staring at her in fascination. She was a short, round, lively woman of about Slava's age, although her curiosity and energy gave her a much younger appearance.

"Really a Tsarinovna," said Slava, smiling brightly. "They say you can tell by my eyes."

The under-cook smiled brightly back. "And they're fine eyes, Tsarinovna, fine and sharp, slanted like a wolf's, but forgive me—you don't have the manner I'd have expected. Not so high and mighty. And you just came down to the kitchen to talk to me, no guards or nothing! Most noblewomen can't take two steps without a whole herd of guards and maids following them around and fussing over them."

"In Krasnograd they dog my every step, but up here I've finally managed to shake them off," said Slava.

The under-cook laughed heartily over that, and said with great alacrity that her name was Sonya, although what her mother had been thinking she didn't know, as a name meaning "sleepy" certainly didn't suit her, since she had always been lively as a young horse, and twice as disobedient, which was why she was an under-cook—none of the noblewomen could stand her sass, so she had been hidden away in the kitchen, where she got to run things as she pleased.

"Dasha said you were second-sister to a sorceress," said Slava. "She said that after the Princess's attack, this sorceress came down and told you of it, and warned you to watch out."

"That's true enough, Tsarinovna," agreed Sonya readily.

"Do you think you could arrange a meeting for me?" asked Slava.

This, unlike anything else, stilled the flow of Sonya's words for a moment, as she drew back and cocked her head to the side, considering Slava as a bird might consider something that might be dangerous, or might be tasty.

"Why do you want to meet my sister, Tsarinovna?" she asked finally.

"I have questions," Slava told her. "Questions about my gifts, and I thought perhaps a sorceress could answer them." When Olga had first proposed it, Slava had not given her plan to talk to the Lesnograd sorceresses much importance, but now that she was in Lesnograd and there were no sorceresses to be found, Slava was, somewhat to her own amusement, determined to flush them out no matter how much trouble it took.

"Surely you have sorceresses in Krasnogorod, Tsarinovna," said Sonya.

"But right now I am in Lesnograd," Slava pointed out.

This made Sonya laugh quite a lot, which seemed to be what tipped the scales and caused her to tell Slava that she would attempt to send her second-sister word and see if she would meet with Slava. Slava thanked her as profusely as she knew how for this, which sent Sonya off into another peal of laughter at the experience of being thanked by a real live Tsarinovna.

"And they say you made Vasilisa Vasilisovna, Olga Vasilisovna, and Andrey Vladislavovich all act like friends last night, Tsarinovna," she said when she had finished laughing. "You must really have gifts then, I suppose."

"Or perhaps I am merely a smooth talker," suggested Slava.

"You must be as smooth as silk then, Tsarinovna," said Sonya cheerfully. "Those three have been squabbling for half their lives, and don't seem like to stop as long as they have the breath to quarrel. Do you think Olga Vasilisovna will stay?"

"I can't say," Slava answered.

"Probably not, now that I think about it," said Sonya, "and maybe she shouldn't. I can't see Olga Vasilisovna staying in one place for long, can you? Or making a good ruler. I mean, she'll get things done, but then she'll get bored and go running off on another adventure. We're probably better off with what we already have."

"Probably," said Slava. She thanked Sonya again, and, disentangling herself from her chattiness as gracefully as she could, she let Dasha lead her off to where the others were already breakfasting.

Once again, it was only Olga, Vasilisa Vasilisovna, Andrey Vladislavovich, and Vladislava at the table when she arrived. Slava was about to ask where Oleg Svetoslavovich was, at least, but some inner voice told her that would be a bad idea to remind the others of Olga's party, so she only wished them a good morning, and allowed the maid to serve her porridge as she examined the party for signs that the reconciliation was going to be permanent, or, on the other hand, that it was already over and everything had gone to being even more bitter than before.

Olga looked as hale and hearty as ever. When she asked where Slava had been, and heard that she had been down in the kitchens, speaking with an under-cook, she burst into a laughter that made Sonya's seem small by comparison, and said that perhaps the thing she loved most about Slava was that she never failed to surprise. Vasilisa Vasilisovna and Andrey Vladislavovich both smiled in a strained way at this. As far as Slava could tell, neither of them knew what to do, now that they weren't quarreling, but were too afraid to break their fragile peace to say anything. She could also tell that they were dying to ask her why she had been down in the kitchen, talking to an under-cook, but they didn't know how to ask it. Vladislava, though, straightened up from the tense pose she had been hunched in over her breakfast, and said, "The kitchen is very nice, isn't it, Tsarinovna?"

"Very nice," said Slava.

"And all the maids and the cooks are very nice, aren't they, Tsarinovna?" She sounded even more like a child than she had the day before, and Slava could see how she really was still just a little girl, with no training in how to be a woman, let alone a princess. Someone needed to do something about that, thought Slava, and that someone should be her.

"Very nice," she agreed. Out of the corner of her eye she saw Vasilisa Vasilisovna open her mouth to reprimand Vladislava for going down into the kitchen and befriending the servants, but then, after a tense internal struggle, she closed it. Slava wished she could pat Vasilisa Vasilisovna's shoulder without appearing patronizing.

"Sonya's my favorite," said Vladislava. "Did you meet her?"

"I did," said Slava. "She was very kind to me."

"I'll have to meet her, then," Olga interjected affably. "But do tell me, Tsarinovna, since I'm dying of curiosity: what were you doing in the kitchens?"

"Looking for sorceresses," Slava told her.

"In the kitchen?" asked Olga, grinning. "Surely a library would be better?"

"I thought I needed to search farther afield, seeing as how they've all run off," Slava told her, smiling back.

"So you went to Sonya, didn't you, Tsarinovna!" cried Vladislava, excited. "Because her sister is a sorceress! I went to her a few days ago, but she couldn't promise me anything. Did she tell you she would try to find her?"

"She did," said Slava.

"Oh good!" Vladislava actually clapped her hands in delight.

"I thought my first order of business today would be to start the search for the sorceresses, but I see you've cut ahead of me, and rightly so," said Olga. "Let's move on to my next order of business, then. My mother's condition: who's responsible? I mean, what healer is in charge of her care? Since as usual she had no one to blame but herself for the mess she's ended up in."

Andrey Vladislavovich and Vasilisa Vasilisovna, after both giving Olga a look of reproach for speaking ill of her mother, both answered at once. Unfortunately, they both answered with different names. A tense silence reigned over the breakfast-table for several breaths, broken only when Olga said, with forced calm, "Good: I can see that she is being well cared for. Now, the state of the kremlin guard and the public square..."

Slava watched sadly as Vasilisa Vasilisovna and Andrey Vladisla-vovich both stared at Olga's brisk manner with silent resentment. She wanted to say something to stop what was unfolding, but she must have spent all her strength the night before, for at the moment she seemed even more paralyzed than the others. Her state of chained immobility was broken only when Vladislava slipped her hand in Slava's and whispered, "Let's go."

They both rose and bowed, but the others were too caught up in trying not to shout at each other to pay attention to them, and so they left the room unnoticed.

"There's nothing you could have done, Tsarinovna," said Vladisla-va, once they were out of earshot of the others.

"How did you...?" asked Slava, surprised that Vladislava had guessed her thoughts.

"You looked so sad and guilty, and I would have felt the same way," said Vladislava. "But there's nothing of use anyone could do. They just can't stop quarreling. Would you like to go see Oleg Svetoslavovich and the others? We'll have to sneak out."

"Where are they?" asked Slava. "And I don't think we should sneak out."

"Oh, no one will care," said Vladislava. "The only person who cares where I am is Mother, and she's too busy right now to notice what I'm up to—as usual. We'll be back before they know we're gone. They're all in an inn near the kremlin. Oleg Svetoslavovich decided they need-ed to leave the kremlin in order to keep the peace, even though Aunty Olya said she wouldn't hear of it. But he convinced her—well, there was a big fight, only with more laughing than usual—and so they're staying there. I think it would be nice to visit them, don't you? It must be very lonely and boring for them, stuck in an inn in a strange town.

Do you know Oleg Svetoslavovich very well? He seems nice, doesn't he? And so does Dunya. And so does Dima. I want to meet him. My mother hates him, but I think he sounds very nice."

"They're all very nice," Slava told her.

"Oh good, let's go then," said Vladislava, and somehow Slava found herself being led by a girl of ten off on yet another illicit venture out of the kremlin. If she thought it really was dangerous, she would have stopped them, Slava told herself, and followed Vladislava willingly enough.

Chapter Three

This time Vladislava went straight out the front entrance and across the square. The few guards that Slava saw paid them absolutely no attention. Although this was presently convenient, it still made Slava uneasy, and she hoped Olga would be able to get the guards into shape quite soon.

Vladislava led her confidently out of the square and down a side street. "How do you know where to find them?" Slava asked her. "How do you know where the inn is?"

"Oh, I've been to it before," Vladislava told her. "It's not hard to find."

"Does the family visit it often?" Slava asked, picturing something rich and lavish, with, perhaps, private rooms for the ruling family.

"Oh no, just me," said Vladislava cheerfully. "I used to be friends with the innkeeper's daughter, and I would sneak out and play with her. We had a disagreement." She stopped and stared sadly down at the street, lost in thoughts that seemed much too serious for such a small face.

"That's too bad," said Slava, once it became clear that Vladislava wasn't going to say anything more. "It's always sad to fall out with a friend. Perhaps you'll be friends again someday."

"I don't think so," said Vladislava. "She said she didn't want to have anything to do with any princesses, that princesses were all bad and dangerous, and that I was going to be a princess someday and I'd be bad too, and the Empress would find out about what we'd done and we'd get in trouble, and she wanted me to stay as far away from her as possible." Slava could hear the tears creeping into Vladislava's voice.

"That was unkind of her," she said. "Probably she was upset about something else, and didn't mean it."

"But princesses *are* bad," objected Vladislava. "At least, all the ones I know."

"They don't have to be," Slava told her. "Just because you're a princess doesn't mean that you *have* to be bad."

"I suppose," said Vladislava doubtfully. "I wish I were an innkeeper anyway, though. I still go to visit Aunty Shurya sometimes, since she's so much nicer than anyone else I know. Well, except for Alina Marinovna. My mother hates that I go there because she thinks it's too poor and run-down and I shouldn't be associating with people like that. Masha—my friend—well, she used to be my friend—she's kind of silly, but I still think it's silly that my mother doesn't want me associating with people like that, don't you? After all, I'll have to rule them someday, won't I? I should know who they are. I said this to my mother, but she got upset. She doesn't like to think of me ruling someday. Do you think that's because she doesn't like the thought of me being grown up some day, or the fact that that means she'll be dead?"

"Probably both," said Slava.

"But they're both *true*," said Vladislava. "There's nothing I can do to stop either of them from happening. I wish I could make her understand that."

"Yes," said Slava. "Sometimes it's difficult. Some people have a harder time facing the truth than others. Sometimes truths are very painful. Sometimes all you can do is tell it to them as kindly as possible, and hope that they'll listen."

"But what if they *don't*?" asked Vladislava, her small face suddenly twisting up in childish anguish, so that she looked much younger than ten. "What if they *don't*, and I have to suffer because of it?"

"Yes, it's very bad," said Slava. "I wish I could tell you something better, but all I can say is: you won't be a little girl forever. Someday you'll be grown up, as you said, and—I won't say that you won't suffer because of it, but the suffering will be less. Someday you'll be a woman grown, and—just remember what it was like to be a little girl, and to suffer because others wouldn't listen to what you had to say, and be sure to listen when others have something to say to you. Even if they're wrong, listen to them anyway, and think about what you can do to help them be right."

Vladislava nodded thoughtfully and slipped her hand into Slava's. "I wish you were my mother, Tsarinovna," she said. "Oh look! There's the inn! Isn't it pretty?"

"Very pretty," said Slava. Vladislava's words, and the feel of her hand in Slava's, made tears prickle in Slava's eyes, and she had to shake her head to pull herself back together.

"Is something the matter, Tsarinovna?" asked Vladislava.

"You're very nice, did you know that?" Slava told her. "Who carved the decorations?" As they drew near the inn, she could see that the door and window frames were all fancifully decorated with elaborate carvings of people and animals from fairy tales.

"Uncle Misha, the innkeeper's husband," said Vladislava. "Aren't they pretty? He told me all the stories once. It's a shame about the rest of it, isn't it?"

"Yes," agreed Slava. The frames were the only part of the inn that was in good repair. Everything else was shabby and faded, and when they came to the entrance, she had to open the warped door with a wrench. Slava couldn't help but wonder what kind of a person put so much effort into the window frames, and so little effort into keeping up the rest of the inn, and if she were also that kind of person. As they stepped into the shabby interior, she had to admit to herself that, as much as she would like to spend all her time on fairy tales, her dislike of drafts would have forced her to fix the door. Probably that meant she was a very worldly person, despite all appearances to the contrary.

"Little princess!" cried a friendly-faced woman when they came in. She rushed over and folded Vladislava into her arms. "What are you doing here? Naughty girl: you've been sneaking off unescorted again, haven't you?" She drew back in order to shake her finger in Vladislava's face, but she didn't sound very angry about it. She was a plump, medium-sized woman with lots of hair that kept slipping out of the lazy braid she had put it in, and Slava could already guess that everything about her inn was warm and homey and not very neat.

"I brought her," said Vladislava, pointing to Slava as her escort. "I didn't come alone."

"So you did, little princess, so you did," said the innkeeper. She bowed with more good humor than respect, which was very pleasant. "So pleased, noblewoman! Would you do me the honor of telling me your name?" She smiled a broad smile. "Have you traveled far? You don't have the look of our Severnolesnoye nobility."

"Krasnoslava," said Slava. "From Krasnograd."

"From Krasnogorod!" exclaimed the innkeeper. "Now there's a long journey! Have you been here long?"

"Since yesterday," Slava told her. "I am part of the party..."

"Who got kicked out of the kremlin last night and had to come stay with us," the innkeeper finished for her, smiling even more broadly. "Tell me, Krasnoslava Noblewoman: how did you avoid getting kicked out too? They say Vasilisa Vasilisovna and Andrey Vladislavovich were both in a rare mood when they saw who'd arrived on their doorstep, and," she winked cheerfully, "we all know why! And serve them right, too! Olga Vasilisovna's always been my favorite, I'm not afraid to say so, and anything she does counts as right as far as I'm concerned. I hope you don't mind me saying all this, Krasnoslava Noblewoman, but I doubt you will, seeing as you're part of Olga Vasilisovna's party yourself. Misha? Misha! Look who's here! Go call the big group: someone's come to see them!"

A dreamy-faced man, who looked like exactly the type of person to carve fairy-tale window frames but not replace a warped door, appeared from a back room and cried, although in softer tones than his wife, "Little princess! And a guest!"

"Uncle Misha!" Vladislava threw herself into his arms. "I'm sorry I haven't come to see you for so long: we've had so many troubles! But I wanted to come see the people who came with Aunty Olya, and I brought you someone, look!" She pointed at Slava.

"All the way from Krasnogorod!" added the innkeeper.

"She's a Tsarinovna!" said Vladislava proudly, sounding for the first time as if Slava's title actually meant something to her.

The effect, however, was not what she had been hoping for. Instead of being pleased, the innkeeper and her husband both gasped and drew back sharply, as if Vladislava had suddenly poured a viper out of a sack.

"Ts-ts-tsarinovna?" the innkeeper finally managed to choke out. It was hard to tell under her natural ruddiness, but her lips looked rather ashen to Slava.

"Oh, there's no need to be afraid of her," said Vladislava. "She's very nice, aren't you, Tsarinovna?"

"I sincerely apologize for any inconvenience my arrival may have caused you," said Slava. "Believe me: there is no need to put yourself out. I merely wish to speak with my traveling companions."

Misha beat a hasty retreat at these words. Slava could hear him calling for the others, telling them that she had arrived and was waiting for them. He made it sound very threatening.

"You have a very pleasant inn," Slava said. "I can see why Vladislava Vasilisovna is so fond of it. And the window- and doorframes are exquisite. Vladislava Vasilisovna tells me your husband made them; you must be glad to have such a master craftsman in your household."

"Y-y-y-yes, Ts-ts-tsarinovna," said the innkeeper faintly. Slava could tell that she was only listening with half an ear: the rest of her was concentrated on her own terror.

"I spent so long on the road on the way here that I have grown quite unused to civilized lodgings!" Slava carried on. "Lesnograd has been a very welcome relief, I assure you!"

The innkeeper only nodded distractedly. To Slava's immense relief, the horrid pause that was looming in front of them was broken by the sound of Oleg Svetoslavovich and the others bursting out of their rooms and hurrying in their direction.

"Krasna Tsarina!" several of the men cried at once. "You came to see us!"

"Couldn't escape fast enough, I'll bet," said Oleg Svetoslavovich. "I certainly couldn't. Tell me: have the sounds of their quarreling filled the entire kremlin, or is there still the occasional quiet corner?"

"They stopped quarreling for a little while last night because the Tsarinovna made them make up, I don't know how, except that she shouted at them," Vladislava told him, staring at him in open fascination. "But I think they were about to start quarreling again when we left. We didn't stay to find out."

"And right you were, little princess!" said Oleg Svetoslavovich. "I've never seen such a family for quarreling. As I lay there dying, or so I thought, my last thoughts were: 'I'm sorry to be leaving my Olya, but by all the gods, at least I'll be free of their bickering and bother. It's more than an ordinary man can stand.'"

"Are you going to stay in Lesnograd, Oleg Svetoslavovich?" Vladislava asked hopefully.

"No, I'm only here for...for a bit. I'll have to go back into the woods soon enough, little princess. But you're welcome to come visit me there," Oleg Svetoslavovich told her, patting her arm kindly.

"Yes! Except," Vladislava suddenly remembered, "I'm going to Krasnograd, aren't I, Tsarinovna?"

"Yes," Slava told her. "But perhaps we will find the time to visit Oleg Svetoslavovich too. And he could always come visit us if he wanted to."

"Krasnograd!" said Oleg Svetoslavovich. "That's a big journey! What takes you to Krasnograd, little princess?"

"The Tsarinovna invited me," Vladislava told him proudly. "To be

34

her ward."

Oleg Svetoslavovich gave Slava an interested look. "You're taking her on as your ward, are you, Tsarinovna?"

"Taking on Imperial wards is a duty I have neglected for far too long," said Slava. "I realized this when I first met Vladislava Vasilisovna, and vowed that she would be the first of many. I may have no children of my own, but that does not mean I cannot care for the children of others. I think I will find great pleasure in it." For a moment she felt almost as excited as Vladislava, and wanted to pour out all her plans to Oleg Svetoslavovich, but stopped herself.

"That is very good of you, Tsarinovna," said Oleg Svetoslavovich, giving her another interested look. He really was, Slava thought to herself, a good man, as well as being quite handsome. Now that he had bathed and shaved, she could see even more clearly why he turned so many women's heads. She wondered what Olga would think if she could hear Slava's thoughts.

"Is something amusing, Tsarinovna?" asked Oleg Svetoslavovich, smiling at her smile as if he, at least, could hear her thoughts.

"Oh, nothing," said Slava, now struggling hard not to laugh.

"The Tsarinovna's probably laughing at your temerity for praising her," said Dima, stepping forward to join them. He gave Slava a welcoming smile. He looked more at ease than he had for a long time, maybe since Slava had first met him. Life in the inn seemed to be agreeing with everyone. Slava wished *she* could be at the inn, too. All her companions looked to be having a fine time, coming up with jokes instead of listening to the Severnolesniye's whining and complaining. "Isn't that a breach of Krasnograd protocol, or something?" Dima continued. "Isn't it forbidden to praise the Tsarina?"

"The Tsarina, yes, but anyone can praise a lowly Tsarinovna," Slava told him. "It is assumed that we have no pride. But enough about that. I came here—we came here—to see you. This looks to be a very comfortable inn."

"Very, and its mistress is very hospitable," said Dima. "Although I fear you've frightened her out of her wits, Tsarinovna! Shurya! Aunty Shurya!" he called.

The innkeeper came sidling over, bowing so deeply she almost fell down.

"Aunty Shurya, the Tsarinovna," said Dima. "Don't worry: she won't bite. She's very friendly, for a Tsarinovna."

"Y-y-y-yes, Dmitry Marusyevich," said the innkeeper.

"Aunty Shurya, the little princess and some of the boys are looking hungry," said Oleg Svetoslavovich. "You wouldn't happen to have a few more of those delicious pies you served us earlier, would you?"

"Lots, Oleg Svetoslavovich," said Aunty Shurya, cheering up slightly, but still watching Slava with a frightened expression on her face.

"Perhaps you could take them all into the kitchen," suggested Oleg Svetoslavovich. "The boys are all still feeding up after their long journey, and the little princess is a growing girl. And who knows what they give her at the kremlin…"

"Everyone was quarreling so much, I didn't even want to eat breakfast or supper," put in Vladislava. "I haven't eaten much in two days, I think."

"Two days!!" cried Aunty Shurya, a look of horror chasing away the terror. She took Vladislava by the arm with the air of a woman who knew her duty and would let no one keep her from it. Tsarinovnas might come and go as they pleased, but no growing girl was going to go hungry in her household, not if she could help it, not while she still had the strength to put together a pie. "You must be starving! This way, little princess! Boys! Boys! Who wants pies?"

There was a hearty cheer from the "boys," and, after receiving a look of permission from Dima and bowing to Slava, they all filed after Aunty Shurya and Vladislava, already speculating eagerly about the pies that awaited them. Soon only Slava, Oleg Svetoslavovich, Dima, and Dunya were left in the room.

"That should keep them busy for some time, and I doubt they'll be able to hear us from in there," said Oleg Svetoslavovich. "Let's sit in the far corner, if that suits you, Tsarinovna."

"Of course," said Slava. She followed him to the table at the far corner of the room.

When they all took their places, she couldn't help but notice that the others had all arranged themselves so that they each had a view of one of the doors—Dunya of the door to the bedrooms, Dima to the kitchen, and Oleg Svetoslavovich to the main entrance. When he caught her inquiring gaze, Oleg Svetoslavovich nodded and said, "Yes, we don't want to be overheard, Tsarinovna."

Slava sighed.

"I would have thought you'd be used to intrigue, Tsarinovna," said Oleg Svetoslavovich with a grin. For some reason, Slava blushed.

"That doesn't mean I have to like it," she said, firmly arranging her face into the appropriate expression of seriousness. "Don't people have anything better to do?"

"Indeed!" echoed Dunya, with uncharacteristic warmth.

"Oh, I'm sure they have something—many things—better to do, but that doesn't mean they'll do them, Tsarinovna," said Oleg Svetoslavovich, still grinning. "Not when they could be sticking their noses in other people's business. I'm afraid we'll have to reconcile ourselves to that, Tsarinovna."

"You're probably right," said Slava, smiling up at Oleg Svetoslavovich through her lashes. As soon as she realized what she was doing, she stopped herself, hoping that no one else had noticed. From their faces, the only one who had noticed was Oleg Svetoslavovich, who looked to be laughing to himself. Dunya was frowning down at the table, and Dima was still watching the kitchen door intently, apparently oblivious to what was going on closer at hand.

"So, what intrigue faces us now?" Slava asked. "Plots against Olga Vasilisovna? Against myself? Against Krasnograd?"

"Yes, Tsarinovna," said Oleg Svetoslavovich, no longer grinning. "Did you already know, or was that a lucky guess?"

"Both," said Slava. "What have you learned?"

"First of all, Tsarinovna, there's some talk that someone might try something against our Olya," said Oleg Svetoslavovich.

"When our hostess heard that Olga Vasilisovna had returned, she didn't know whether to rejoice or lament, Tsarinovna," said Dima, still watching the kitchen. "When pressed—not that it took much pressing to get more words out of her than you'd ever be able to sort through— she told us the old Princess had threatened to disinherit her, and had told the kremlin guards not to admit her. She was astonished that Olga Vasilisovna had even been allowed in the city, but told us that perhaps it was just a plot to lure her in and then dispose of her in some way."

"That seems unlikely," Slava interjected. "As far as I can tell, the old Princess is barely even alive, and the others couldn't organize a supper between them, let alone a real plot. Everyone other than Andrey Vladislavovich seemed desperately grateful to put everything in Olga's hands the moment she arrived—although now that she's taking control, I'm not sure how much they're enjoying it. But I can't see them joining forces to plot against her, and the guards don't know whose orders to follow—Olga's, Andrey Vladislavovich's, or maybe Vasilisa Vasilisovna's. It seems that Olga's main enemy is the rampant confusion flourishing in every corner of the kremlin, not plotters planning to take her out."

"I am glad to hear it, Tsarinovna," said Dima, sounding relieved. "When they threatened to turn us out of the kremlin...And then we actually did leave..."

"Andreyushka's a milk-sucker, but you have to feel for him, Dimochka," put in Oleg Svetoslavovich. "Hosting the man who took his place in his wife's bed...If I were him..."

"If you were him, it wouldn't be a problem," said Dima sharply, causing Oleg Svetoslavovich to laugh out loud. Even Dunya broke into a faint smile, and Slava found herself blushing hotly. Luckily their table was situated in the shadows.

"I don't think either Andrey Vladislavovich or Vasilisa Vasilisovna—or even Lisochka—have much fondness for Olga, but none of them seem capable of doing anything about it," said Slava. "I think the old Princess was the real danger." *And Vladislava*, she almost said, but decided not to. Vladislava's secret was so dangerous that it could be shared with no one, not even the people sitting before her, in case it should somehow make its way back to Krasnograd and the Empress.

Slava had a brief vision of the mangled remnants that would be left of Vladislava's slender, childish body if her sister ever found out what she had done, and her gorge rose. For a moment she wondered if inviting Vladislava to Krasnograd had been the right thing to do. But leaving her here was equally impossible...She must be saved in some way before she consciously carried on down the path she had unwittingly started...

"Is something the matter, Tsarinovna?" asked Oleg Svetoslavovich. Slava could feel his eyes following her every expression closely, and weighing every flicker of her face.

"I think Olga has nothing to fear from her family but added burdens," she said. "But you spoke of intrigue against Krasnograd. This, naturally, concerns me greatly. Please, tell me all that you know. And fear not," she added. "In this matter, telling me is *not* the same as telling my sister. If this can be resolved without bringing harm to the plotters, then I will be glad of it. I have no wish to spread about anyone's secrets, if I can avoid it."

"I am sure of it, Tsarinovna," said Oleg Svetoslavovich. "Dunya was the one who first heard of it."

"Yes," said Dunya. Although occasionally glancing up at the door to the bedrooms, she for the most part kept her gaze fixed on the table, and seemed unusually depressed and hesitant. Slava remembered her sudden fear of Lesnograd on the road here, and felt sorry for her. Dunya's adventure was turning out to be rather less of an adventure, and more of a trial, than she had probably hoped for.

"I was in the bathhouse with Aunty Shurya and Masha—her daughter—yesterday," continued Dunya slowly. "They asked me of my family and my home, and I of theirs, and soon they began to tell me many things, and suddenly Masha—who must not be more than ten—blurted out that they were planning to take down the evil Empress in Krasnograd."

"Who are 'they'?" cried Slava, rather more loudly than she should have.

"I tried to ask her, Tsarinovna, but if she did know—and it seems her knowledge is hazy—her mother frightened it out of her with her hushing and her insisting that it was all just a joke and a misunderstanding. I was unable to get anything more out of either of them. But Masha seemed convinced of it, which makes me think she must have heard something."

"Misha—the innkeeper's husband—also knows something, although he's not saying anything," said Dima. "He started to tell me something yesterday, then changed his mind. But you saw how he and Aunty Shurya were terrified of you, Tsarinovna."

"I have also gotten that impression from servants in the kremlin," said Slava. "It seems that the sorceresses might be involved, somehow." That seemed safe enough to reveal.

"The sorceresses who all left?" asked Oleg Svetoslavovich.

"Those sorceresses, yes," said Slava. "I'm trying to track some of them down in order to speak with them. I had originally started on this endeavor in order to ask them about...about myself, but now that more and more rumors are arising about this treason, well..."

"You should be very careful, Tsarinovna," said Dima. "Treason is the business of desperate people, and desperate people are dangerous. And since we have no idea who the traitor is..."

"The old Princess, of course," whispered Dunya to the table.

"You think?" asked Dima.

"Who else could it be?" demanded Oleg Svetoslavovich. "Ultimately, everything in Lesnograd begins and ends with her. I know my wife."

Everyone stared at him for a moment in astonishment, before realizing that of course, the old Princess *was* his wife, strange a thought as that was. Slava found herself blushing again.

"You think she is might be disloyal to Krasnograd, then, Oleg Svetoslavovich?" she asked, to cover up her confusion.

"Vasilisa Lyudmilovna?" He laughed. "The only person she was ever loyal to was herself, and even in that she couldn't be trusted completely. The only question is: was she working alone, or did she have an accomplice, someone to do her bidding?"

"I see," said Slava. She didn't know whether to laugh or despair at the thought of Vladislava as the accomplice.

"You may see that, Tsarinovna, but what I don't see is who this accomplice is," said Oleg Svetoslavovich. "I might guess Princess Primorskaya, except that even she has more sense than that, and I doubt she has forgiven Vasilisa Lyudmilovna for marrying me yet. I can't see them working together, especially on something so delicate."

"Princess Primorskaya warned me about her," Slava suddenly remembered. "About Vasilisa Lyudmilovna. She said she was up to something. I just...With everything that's happened, it flew out of my mind, but whatever Vasilisa Lyudmilovna was 'up to,' rumors of it had reached all the way to Vostochnoye Selo."

"And even Malaya Gora," said Dima. "Princess Malogornaya's... shack was rife with rumors about it."

"True," said Slava. "She even said something to Olga about it, but none of us knew what she meant at the time. But even she knew that Princess Severnolesnaya was involved in something shady."

"I wonder what she could have been 'up to' with all those sorceresses," said Dima.

Slava was about to open her mouth and tell him about the curse, but stopped herself. That could so easily lead back to Vladislava. She decided she would need to come up with a story that kept Vladislava's part in everything a secret. She would also have to be sure to be the first, and preferably only, person to talk to any sorceresses they managed to find about the curse. And how could she convince the sorceresses to talk to her truthfully, while concealing everything, especially everything about Vladislava, from everyone else? For a moment Slava's heart sank at the prospect.

"What's the matter, Tsarinovna?" asked Oleg Svetoslavovich, who was still watching her closely, for, she suspected, many reasons.

"What isn't the matter?" she replied rather tartly, but as she spoke she had the sudden thought that the sorceresses would hardly want to implicate themselves any more than they had to, and might be quite amenable to threats and promises, and she found herself smiling at the end of her sentence. Oleg Svetoslavovich smiled back in response, for, she still suspected, many reasons.

"Well, it's hardly the first trouble we've faced," he said encouragingly. "No doubt we'll clear matters up in two or three days, and you can be on your way back to Krasnograd. Or you could stay here in the North if you wished, you know. You might prefer that to Krasnograd—I know I would." He smiled at her very directly.

"I, unfortunately, can't always do what I want," Slava told him. "Although I have no doubt my absence from Krasnograd would be very welcome. There was even talk of getting rid of me entirely." As soon as she said that, she knew she had made a mistake, but it was too late to take back. Dunya sat bolt upright and stared at her in shock and horror, while Dima and Oleg Svetoslavovich nodded grimly.

"Talk—of getting rid of you—*in Krasnograd?*" asked Dunya incredulously.

"Just rumors," said Slava quickly. "Third-hand. There were suggestions...For example, Dima suggested to me that our expedition could be a good way for...for the Empress to rid herself of a troubling relation and a troubling Princess all in one fell swoop. If something were to happen to me 'accidentally,' that would provide a good excuse to get rid of the Severnolesnaya family as well, and then Krasnograd could claim Severnolesnoye as its own. So it was suggested."

"That sounds very much like treason to me, Tsarinovna," said Oleg Svetoslavovich, while Dima stared at his fingernails. "Anything threatening the life of the Tsarinovna..."

"Unless it comes from the Tsarina," said Slava. "Obviously, nothing she does can be treasonous, even if it involves removing her own sisters. Although...even for an Empress, killing a sister is a black day's work, and Vladya always did like to fancy that she had clean hands... But on the other hand, if she could use me to get rid of the Severnolesniye...I doubt she'd cry too hard over my loss..." Slava trailed off. Dunya was still staring at her in shock and horror, but she couldn't pay attention to that, because she could feel that there was something there, something she needed to understand, something that would explain it all...

"The curse," she murmured, realizing that she was going to have to mention it, and she would just have to be very, very careful not to mention Vladislava's name in connection with it.

"Curse? What curse?" demanded Oleg Svetoslavovich.

"I heard...Part of the rumor was that maybe, perhaps what the sorceresses were doing, what the treason was..."

"Was a curse," finished Oleg Svetoslavovich. "A curse on the Imperial family. Why else would you need so many sorceresses?"

"Yes, and somehow I feel...I just have this feeling that this plot against me, if it exists..."

"Is part of the curse?" asked Oleg Svetoslavovich.

"I am a member of the Imperial family," said Slava. "The Empress's only sister, in fact...and a curse could so easily go astray...Princess Severnolesnaya and her sorceresses only finished the spell recently, but they must have been working on it all fall, and things could have already been set in motion..." *Dark fingers reaching out to Krasnograd,* she finished in her mind, and thought of the murdered little girls that had been turning up there for months. Part of the curse? Or part of the curse that was Krasnograd? How could she tell? But it had led to her coming here, and arriving at what would have been just the right moment, if the princess's spell had not gone awry...Perhaps the whole thing was aimed at her...

"Perhaps it didn't go astray," said Oleg Svetoslavovich, mirroring her own thoughts. "Who's to say that getting rid of you and taking out the Severnolesniye wouldn't come back to haunt the Empress? Curses are funny things. Who's to say it wouldn't bring her down as well? Such things have happened before."

"Yes, who's to say..." echoed Slava, thinking of Vladislava's description of the curse. *Her own blood would turn against her...*So could that mean Slava? Or was Vladya going to turn against Slava? The gods alone knew on which of them the shattered remnants of the broken spell had fastened.

"At the moment, though, this is all just rumors and guesses, thank the gods," interjected Dima. "We have not a shred of proof to stand on."

"Yes," agreed Slava, shaking off her reverie, but not too hard. She wanted to be sure that she would be able to call back the feeling she had had, the feeling of being just on the edge of a tremendous discovery, when she had the time and space to think it over thoroughly. Dima was right, they had nothing to stand on, but she still couldn't help feeling that she was *right*, that all the half-told rumors that had been coming her way for months now were coalescing into something solid, that something was happening...And the hatred of sister for sister was certainly curse enough to strike down both her and the Empress, leaving the Wooden Throne open for anyone who could gain control of her sister's heir...Who knew how many would fall under this curse…

"We must gather more information," she said. "Try to find out what you can from the innkeeper and her family—give her whatever bribes or assurances are necessary to loosen her tongue, tell her she has no need to fear me, unless she remains silent—and I will see what I can discover from the sorceresses and whatever other sources I can find at the kremlin. You know, it is turning out to be quite fortunate that, ah, that you had to move out of the kremlin and into this inn. Now, instead of being trapped in there all day, you can move about the city, meet people, hear the news of the street…"

"Fret ourselves sick over what's happening to the rest of you," put in Oleg Svetoslavovich. He said it with a grin that belied his words, but Slava could see that it was true enough for Dima and Dunya. She was about to say something comforting, when a sudden commotion arose in the kitchen, and all the others came bursting back into the front room, and her words were lost in the noise.

For a moment everyone was distracted by the incomers, who were describing in loud voices the wonders of Aunty Shurya's kitchen, and the results of the pie-eating contest they had held in there. Dunya took advantage of this to tug on Slava's sleeve.

"Can I show you something in my room, Tsarinovna?" she asked. "I have something to give you."

"Of course," Slava said, and followed her back to the bedrooms. Several people asked Dunya where she was taking the Tsarinovna, and she smiled and said that some of their things had gotten mixed up in her pack, and she wanted to return them before the Tsarinovna thought she had taken to stealing.

"I didn't notice any of my things being missing," Slava said, once they were in Dunya's cramped but comfortable room.

"Oh, it's just some trifles," said Dunya, wringing her hands in a manner much more reminiscent of Vasilisa Vasilisovna than herself. "I just needed an excuse to…to talk to you alone."

"About what?" asked Slava. When Dunya, instead of telling her, continued to wring her hands and pace the three paces back and forth that her room allowed, Slava sat down on the soft but lumpy and narrow bed, and repeated her question, this time smiling up at Dunya in as reassuring a way as she knew how. It seemed to work, for Dunya joined her on the bed and started talking.

"Do you remember when I told you I had a bad feeling, Tsarinovna?" she began.

43

"Of course," said Slava.

"Well, it's worse now."

"How so?" asked Slava. She could tell that Dunya was afraid Slava wouldn't believe her, so she made sure to look Dunya in the eyes with every sign of sincere interest.

"I don't know, just stronger," said Dunya. "Do you remember, Tsarinovna, after...when I told you that it didn't bother me that you had seen into all our souls, because I had nothing to hide or be ashamed of?"

"Of course," said Slava.

"Well, you see, that wasn't exactly true. Or rather...You see, Tsarinovna, I think that I might...You see, Tsarinovna, some in our family have a gift. I always said I didn't have it, but that was a lie, I said that because I didn't want to have it, I scorned it and those who had it, I didn't want to be anything like them, so I became myself instead, only now I think the gift is making its way to the outside anyway."

"What sort of gift?" asked Slava, careful not to show any surprise.

"Oh, the gift of foreseeing," said Dunya, sounding very dismissive. "You know: visions of the future, premonitions, hysteria, bad dreams, self-importance...that sort of thing."

"I am, alas, all too familiar with that sort of thing," said Slava with a smile. "There are many in my family who could be accused of all those things, including sometimes myself."

"Oh no, Tsarinovna, you couldn't possibly be that bad," said Dunya quickly. "I have an aunt...in fact, my father's whole family...I simply couldn't bear it, so I said I was going to be like my mother, and I am. I'm very good at what I do, and I don't want to do or be anything else. Only, this bad feeling now..."

"You think it might be a premonition," said Slava.

"Yes, the Black God take it," said Dunya with deep disgust.

"Premonitions can be very useful," Slava pointed out.

"Yes, but...And what if it *is* very useful, Tsarinovna, or it would be, only I can't hear it properly because I've been ignoring it all my life? What if I've endangered us all through my selfishness?" Dunya sounded much more desperate and doubting than Slava could have ever imagined her to be.

"What if you'd spent all your life cultivating your self-importance and hysteria instead of your woodscraft?" Slava countered. "What use to us would you have been in that case? We can't all do everything we think we should, you know."

"True enough, Tsarinovna," said Dunya, brightening visibly.

"That being said, about this bad feeling of yours..." continued Slava.

"Well, yes," said Dunya, smiling a smile that was full of both embarrassment and relief. "It grows stronger by the hour, especially ever since Masha told me what she told me. I think there *is* treason afoot, Tsarinovna, and I think we all, and you especially, are in grave danger. I do not like the sound of this curse at all. As soon as you mentioned it, my heart went cold. I think there most certainly is a curse, and we must guard ourselves against it."

"I don't like the sound of it either," said Slava. "That's why I want to find out more about it. If I could contact the sorceresses...Surely one of them will come forward..."

"Hunters and trackers!" cried Dunya, hope suddenly dawning on her face.

"You think they could help us?" asked Slava.

"Why not, Tsarinovna? They at least might be able to help us find the sorceresses, if they won't come forward on their own. And who knows what else they might know—you hear a lot, you know, if you know how to stay silent, and we certainly know how to stay silent."

"It's worth a try, for sure," said Slava.

"I'll start this afternoon, Tsarinovna!" promised Dunya. "No doubt Aunty Shurya knows someone who knows someone..."

"No doubt," agreed Slava.

"Oh, and you did leave something of yours in with my things, Tsarinovna," said Dunya. "Some footcloths. Here." She handed Slava a pair of what had once been warm comfortable footcloths, but were now just two dirty pieces of felt.

"Thank you," said Slava, shoving the old footcloths into her dress pocket, where they made an unattractive bulge.

"I should get started right away," said Dunya. "Every moment is precious."

"Of course," said Slava, rising from the bed. She could see that fresh life had been poured into Dunya, making her into the confident Dunya of before, and that for Dunya, the crisis of a moment ago was nothing more than a moment in her past, not to be forgotten, but not to be dwelt upon either. Slava wished she could stop dwelling on things so easily, too. It could be a new skill she could work on acquiring when she made it back to Krasnograd, she told herself. She followed Dunya out of the bedroom and back to the others.

45

Slava stood by the wall and watched as Dunya went over to Aunty Shurya and began a conversation with her. It was remarkable, Slava reflected, what a few words could do: every movement of Dunya's body showed that she was a Tracker again, not a Doubter. Even from across the room, Slava could sense the calm confidence flowing from her.

"What did you do to our Dunya, Tsarinovna?" asked Oleg Svetoslavovich, sliding over beside her.

"I just talked with her," said Slava.

"No magic?" asked Oleg Svetoslavovich.

"Not as such," said Slava with a shrug. "Only words."

"Words are a kind of magic too, Tsarinovna," said Oleg Svetoslavovich.

"Yes," agreed Slava. "I am discovering that to be the case."

"It was a good thing, what you did, Tsarinovna," said Oleg Svetoslavovich, looking at her intently. "For Dunya, and for all the others you've used your words on."

"Yes," agreed Slava. "It seems so."

"Are you going to take them back to Krasnograd?" asked Oleg Svetoslavovich.

"Who, Dunya and the others?" Slava asked.

"No, Tsarinovna, your words."

"I don't see how I can avoid it," said Slava, with a lightness she didn't feel. She knew that Oleg Svetoslavovich was asking her about something more frightening than she cared to think about right now.

"No, Tsarinovna, you most likely can't," said Oleg Svetoslavovich very seriously, making Slava's heart sink even more, because she knew he was right. The Slava who returned to Krasnograd would be a frighteningly different person from the one who had left, and even though that was what Slava had wanted when she had set off, the vision of what that would mean was not an altogether pleasant one. There would be no more hiding behind her soft, shrinking heart and retreating into her daydreams, no matter how much she might want to. She had turned down the offered armor, but that did not mean she wouldn't be called onto the field of battle all the same.

"It's probably time for me to bring Vladislava back," she said, in order to change the subject. "They might be looking for her."

"I'll come with you, Tsarinovna," said Oleg Svetoslavovich. "I'd like to see what they've been up to in my absence."

"Why are you calling me Tsarinovna?" Slava asked suddenly. "I just realized...you didn't when we first met."

46

Oleg Svetoslavovich grinned. "Now that I've gotten to know you better, Tsarinovna, it seems more appropriate," he said.

Slava wanted to ask him what he meant by that, but for some reason she found herself blushing too much, so instead she went and collected Vladislava, with profuse thanks to Aunty Shurya, who still seemed too frightened to speak in her presence. She was moving towards the door, with both Vladislava and Oleg Svetoslavovich in tow, when Mirik came up to her and stopped her.

"I had a question, Krasna Tsa...Tsarinovna," he said, shuffling his feet and looking embarrassed but determined.

"Of course," said Slava kindly. "What did you want to know?"

"Have you seen...him?"

"He means Andrey Vladislavovich," Oleg Svetoslavovich put in. "He can't stop thinking about him, even though I keep telling him he's not worth it. Milochka's story has a happy ending."

"Yes," said Slava.

"And is he...Do you know, Tsarinovna, if he's suffered for what he's done? For what he did to our village? Not that it would ever be enough...But I wanted to know if he was suffering, even just a little bit. I couldn't catch more than a glimpse of him while I was in the kremlin, and now I've no chance of seeing him, let alone avenging her..."

"There is no need," Slava told him comfortingly. "Andrey Vladislavovich is a very unhappy man, Mirik. There is nothing you could do to him that would equal the suffering he has already inflicted on himself. And besides, you heard what was said: your sister's story has had a happy ending. You should forget your dreams of vengeance, and turn to better things. You could come to Krasnograd, you know, and seek her out."

"I can't just let it go like that!"

"Oh, grow up and be a man, Mirik," said Oleg Svetoslavovich. "Do what the Tsarinovna says and go to Krasnograd, or go back home, or do something other than hanging around here and wasting your time. You're not helping anyone."

"But..." began Mirik, but Oleg Svetoslavovich had hurried them out the door before he could finish his sentence.

"You'll be bringing all of the North with you back to Krasnograd if you keep this up, Tsarinovna," said Oleg Svetoslavovich, once they were out on the street. "Picking up strays like that."

"I feel so sorry for him, though," said Slava.

"You'd feel less sorry for him if you'd had to spend the past few days listening to his whining and complaining, Tsarinovna," said Oleg Svetoslavovich. "You're right, you know: Andrey Vladislavovich has already made himself so unhappy that Mirik would have quite a job to make it worse, anyway."

"Do you think he'll try something?" asked Slava. "I'd hate for him to get into trouble..."

"He's certainly silly enough for it," said Oleg Svetoslavovich.

"He's still very young, and very unhappy," Slava pointed out. "We can hardly blame him..."

"He'll soon be seventeen, Tsarinovna! Were you like that at seventeen? Or were you already a woman grown?"

"Women grow wise much sooner than men," said Slava, and then realized she'd just repeated the kind of stupid saying that poured unceasingly from the mouths of her sister's vapider princesses. Not only that, but she'd said she was less foolish than Mirik, which was unkind. Although it could be argued that it was true.

"But I was a very silly young woman," she said with a smile, in order to cover up her unkind thoughts. "Living only in my head, full of foolish hopes and dreams and fantasies, that seemed much stronger to me than anything the waking world had to offer. I was a dreamer, Oleg Svetoslavovich. I suppose I still am, at heart. I love to think on things, and dwell on the pictures in my mind."

"Is that so, Tsarinovna," said Oleg Svetoslavovich, giving her a look that was almost a smile, but much more dangerous than that.

"What are you two talking about? Why are you smiling so much? What's so funny?" demanded Vladislava, who was clearly tired of being excluded from the grown-up's conversation.

"Oh, nothing," said Slava, smiling up at the eaves of a house they happened to be passing by.

"It's not nothing!" insisted Vladislava indignantly. "I can tell by your faces that it's not!"

"You'll understand when you're seventeen," said Slava.

"Or maybe thirty-seven," said Oleg Svetoslavovich. "Some of us are not so quick on the uptake as our Tsarinovna here."

A sullen expression crossed Vladislava's face, and very properly so. Slava didn't know whether to laugh or slap herself. Surely she should have known better by now than to tell someone like Vladislava, "You'll understand when you're older." It was unforgivable stupidity, nothing better. Her only excuse was that Oleg Svetoslavovich had flustered her. "Think of it as something to look forward to," she told Vladislava soothingly. "We can't all understand everything at once, after all." Seeing that Vladislava was, and most rightly, not to be appeased by this, Slava quickly started asking her about other friends or acquaintances she might have who could prove useful in their search for the sorceresses, which distracted her enough that she was able to forget her hurt, at least for the moment.

Chapter Four

They arrived back at the kremlin without incident and were making their way as stealthily as possible to Slava's quarters—they had agreed that that would be the best staging-ground for their assault on the hotbed of kremlin intrigue that awaited them—when a serving woman cried out at the sight of them and snatched Vladislava by the arm, saying, "Where have you been, little princess! Your mother has been going frantic with worry! How can you keep tormenting her like this..."

She tried to drag Vladislava along after her, and when Vladislava resisted, the serving woman shook her hard and began scolding her in ever more heated tones, causing Vladislava first to shrink back, and then to gather herself together as if preparing for a vicious spring, possibly aimed right at the serving woman's throat.

"Come, Vladislava," Slava said, taking Vladislava by the same arm the serving woman was shaking, and gently disengaging her. "We should go speak to your mother."

"She's in the breakfast chamber, noblewoman," said the serving woman. Her face was red with rage, and she was so focused on glaring at Vladislava with malevolent loathing that she seemed barely aware of either Slava or Oleg Svetoslavovich. "She's been in a state ever since she discovered the little princess was missing, shouting at everyone, sending us out in the cold to search for her, imagining she's hurt or dead, driving everyone crazy...and it seems she's just gone off wandering again, as usual, without a thought for anyone else...if she were my daughter, I'd whip her till she couldn't walk, every day I'd do it till she learned her lesson and gave up that nonsense...causing trouble for all of us..."

"I'll be sure to mention that to Vasilisa Vasilisovna," Slava said. The sudden flare of hatred she felt for the serving woman was so strong that she felt as though her head might crack from the pain, and she could feel her hands shaking. Unfortunately, the serving woman was either too dull or too caught up in her own unhappiness to understand the threat behind Slava's words, and she carried on ranting.

"Someone should do something...running around causing trouble...Someone should teach her better...I used to whip my own daughters every day, for a whole year I did, and they never got up to this kind of nonsense..."

"Good, then they're used to it," said Oleg Svetoslavovich. "That will make it much easier for them."

"What?" The serving woman stopped and stared at Oleg Svetoslavovich in bewildered rage.

"It will make it much easier for them when Vasilisa Vasilisovna has them whipped in the little princess's stead," said Oleg Svetoslavovich. "Don't you know? All this talk of beating the little princess that everyone is bandying about is just so much weak-headed nonsense. The Severnolesniye are blood kin to the Imperial line, and so laying a hand on them is death. Substitutes will have to be found for the whipping. I'll be sure to mention your idea to Vasilisa Vasilisovna, and suggest that she use your daughters. And as you already said, it will be good for them—teach them better. They say the kremlin headswoman has a heavy hand—two men died last year from her floggings—they're still talking about it in all the inns of Lesnograd."

He grinned at the serving woman's appalled face, which was rapidly changing from scarlet to ashen (although, Slava couldn't help but think, it was very unreasonable of her to be upset at the thought of her daughters being flogged, since she had just been bragging of flogging them), and walked jauntily down the hallway.

Slava tried to say something to comfort the serving woman, but her hatred was still too strong for her to come up with any kind words, and so, after a brief moment of wavering, she hurried after Oleg Svetoslavovich.

"That was cruel," she said as soon as she had caught up with him. "She didn't know what she was saying. She was just...upset."

"I don't care," said Vladislava, who was shaking even more than Slava. "I hate her! She's always mean to me, if she thinks she can get away with it, and I can always feel her eyes following me, hating me, and I know she beats her children, and she likes to kick dogs and step on cats' tails whenever she can, and anything else she can get away with. Her husband was a terrible drunk and knocked out half her teeth before she smashed in his head and made him a halfwit. He just sits at home and cries now, so she has to work all the jobs she can to feed them, and so my mother always uses her to do the most tiresome tasks, because she knows she can't say no."

"That's awful!" cried Slava. "Every bit of it! Poor woman—she has no idea of what she's doing."

"Yes, and she would have cheered for joy if she could have seen the little princess whipped till she fainted, and not known what she was doing then, either. Probably she was at the front of the crowd, cheering for all she was worth, when those two men were flogged to death last year. Besides, it's no more than you thought, Tsarinovna—and knew needed to be said. In fact, you tried to say it yourself, only you made a mistake."

"Which I'm *sure* you're going to explain to me now," said Slava. With another man she would not have dared to say such a thing, or smile such a mocking smile, for fear of hurting his feelings, but Oleg Svetoslavovich seemed to have that rare and precious trait in a man, a sense of humor.

"Oh, of course, Tsarinovna, of course," said Oleg Svetoslavovich, with a smile to show he found himself just as funny as she did. "You see, Tsarinovna, your kind nature always assumes that everyone is as quick and sharp as you are, but that's not true, not true at all. Some people will only hear you if you hit them with a hammer—and if you don't, they'll go right on and beat children and torture dumb animals and every other helpless creature they can get their hands on, and it's all precisely because they don't know what they're doing—and maybe they're not capable of knowing." Oleg Svetoslavovich was no longer smiling now, and Slava could see that he was thinking of something sad, some sad personal story, and so she stifled her arguments, which she knew were wrong anyway, and only said, "I'm sorry."

"About what, Tsarinovna?" asked Oleg Svetoslavovich, flashing his eyes up at her and pretending he had not just fallen into melancholy.

"About the fact that sometimes people do bad things, and the rest of us have to suffer," she said.

"It's sad, but it's certainly not your fault, Tsarinovna," said Oleg Svetoslavovich, who had gone back to grinning. "That would be a little too much guilt even for you to bear. But speaking of such things, I believe I hear the angry roar of an enraged mother in the next room."

And indeed, Vasilisa Vasilisovna's hysterical voice was spreading out from the breakfast chamber to the hallway. Vladislava shrank against Slava, who was forced to repress a sigh. She also noted, with what at a less unpleasant moment would have been amusement, that, although she felt slightly bad about causing Vasilisa Vasilisovna so much unhappiness, everything about Vasilisa Vasilisovna caused Slava's natural urge to sympathize and comply to transform into an overwhelming need to antagonize and rebel.

"Where is she! Where is she! Have her brought to me at once! I must put a stop to this!!" Vasilisa Vasilisovna was screaming, with, it sounded, tears in her voice.

"Calm down, Vasya," Slava could hear Olga saying impatiently. "She probably just went to play somewhere when she saw we were about to start quarreling again, and who can blame her? I would have done the same."

"Yes, because we all know how much you care about your nearest and dearest," Andrey Vladislavovich's voice said spitefully. "Don't flatter yourself that you have any inkling of what it means to feel a mother's love."

"And thank all the gods for that!" said Olga. "If it means making a fool out of yourself morning, noon, and night, then I'm better off without it."

Vasilisa Vasilisovna emitted a sharp scream at those words, and then carried on hysterically, "I don't know where I went wrong, I don't know what I did wrong, I did everything right, I did my best, it's not my fault, it's not my fault, it must be some flaw in her blood..."

"Which she got from you," said Olga.

"No no no, from Dima, from Dima..."

It took Slava a moment to remember that Vasilisa Vasilisovna's husband was also called Dima, which again, at another moment would have made her laugh.

"The line is flawed, it's flawed, she's flawed, she's going to be a half-wit like her father, I just know it, I know it, gods, why have you laid this burden upon me..." And Vasilisa Vasilisovna trailed off into tears.

"I feel sick," murmured Vladislava, huddling up even closer to Slava. "My tummy hurts. I think I'm taking ill."

"You're probably just upset," said Slava, stroking her hair, something she was sure Vladislava would never permit under normal circumstances. Vladislava buried her face in Slava's side.

"By all the gods, how do we stop them?" Slava asked, looking up at

Oleg Svetoslavovich. "They'll drive her mad if they carry on like this. I'm afraid to take her into the room."

"Then don't, Tsarinovna," said Oleg Svetoslavovich. "Take the little princess to your quarters, and let me deal with them."

"They're very crazy right now..." Slava said doubtfully. "Who knows what they'll do."

"All the more reason for the two of you to leave. I'll knock some sense into them, while you take care of the little princess."

"I can't leave you to do my dirty work!"

Oleg Svetoslavovich laughed. "If ever there were a person ill-suited to do dirty work, Tsarinovna, that person is you. Besides, some of that screaming in there is my fault. No reason for your kind heart to have to suffer through all that. Take the little princess and go do...whatever it is little princesses do, when they're not being persecuted by their nearest and dearest."

Much as it pained Slava to leave Oleg Svetoslavovich to deal with the others on his own, especially as it felt like cowardice to retreat from something she so strongly wanted to avoid, she had to admit that bringing Vladislava into the room just then was probably unwise, and so she only nodded gratefully and set off in the direction of her quarters, the sound of Vasilisa Vasilisovna's hysterical crying, Andrey Vladislavovich's spiteful comments, and Olga's scornful rejoinders following her down the hall. Even so, her heart felt strangely warm as she walked away. Having another person—and a man!—voluntarily take on an unpleasant task so that Slava wouldn't have to was so shocking, such a pleasant surprise, that Slava was a little afraid she might cry with gratitude.

"Do you think he'll really knock some sense into them?" Vladislava asked hopefully, once they were out of earshot of the others. "They need to be threatened properly! Your shouting didn't work on them for very long, Tsarinovna."

"Then threats probably won't either," said Slava. "Some people you just can't teach." As soon as she said it, she was sorry for saying something so unkind, especially about Vladislava's own family, but Vladislava only nodded and said, "My mother won't be coming with us to Krasnograd, will she, Tsarinovna?" Her tone made it very clear that she hoped not.

"If she wants to, I don't see how we can stop her," said Slava. "You may have to...you may have to learn to manage her."

"I'm not giving in to her! I'm not becoming her little doll! And it would make me a bad ruler, anyway," said Vladislava with considerable heat. Slava could feel her start to tremble again at the very thought of dealing with her mother.

"I didn't say give in, I said manage," said Slava. "Perhaps if you learn to control yourself...If you have control of yourself, it can be surprisingly easy to control others."

"Like you do, Tsarinovna? Did it take much practice?"

"Apparently not, since I just started," confessed Slava with a laugh. "But just because this is slow-won wisdom for me, doesn't mean it has to be for you. You can learn from my mistakes, and perhaps have an easier time than I did."

"It's so hard, though," Vladislava objected. "People make me so angry, especially my family! And they don't *deserve* my kindness! It's not fair that I should have to change myself, just because they're selfish and stupid! They don't deserve it!"

"The gods forbid that we should ever get what we deserve," said Slava. "And I think...I am coming to the realization that...that change is power. That if you can change yourself, you can change others, and even, perhaps, have great power over people and events. I think this was what they were trying to tell me all along this journey.

"My whole life I thought I was helpless, Vladislava, but now I see that that is not true. Perhaps I am not so strong, or so brave, or do not possess great magic or grand armies, but I do have one thing that no one else has, and that is myself. My whole life I've felt that I am at the mercy of everyone else's passing emotions, that I was nothing more than a rag for sopping up other people's pain, but I am beginning to see that that is not true. Because, you see, I can see them, but all too often, they can't see me. Not on the inside, that is, and the inside belongs to me alone. If I am strong and brave, that is, strong and brave on the inside. Perhaps you, too, Vladislava, can learn to be strong and brave on the inside. We can learn it together, because I dare say it won't be easy."

"Like a kind of magic," said Vladislava. "Like what sorceresses and priestesses do."

"Something like that, I think, yes," said Slava.

"We should ask the sorceresses, when they come to us," said Vladislava. "And we should call some priestesses as well. I would like to speak to a priestess, and find out what she thinks. Grandmother didn't like priestesses, so she would never let me talk to them. She said they were always poking their noses in things no normal woman would want to know, and she didn't even want them in the kremlin. I think the priestesses are very angry with Grandmother."

"Oh," said Slava. "Yes, perhaps we should talk to some priestesses." An angry priestess, she thought to herself, might be an excellent ally against whatever it was that they were facing in the way of treason and curses.

"Didn't your mother become a priestess, Tsarinovna?" asked Vladislava. "Didn't she leave the throne for a sanctuary? I thought I heard Grandmother say so."

"Yes, she did," said Slava.

"Do you ever see her?"

"No more than once every other year, or maybe even less," said Slava. "The point of a sanctuary is to be safe from the world. Even daughters are not welcome there, and she rarely returns to visit us."

"Were you sad when she left you? Were you angry?"

"Yes," said Slava. "But it was still the right thing for her to do. She had done all she could in this world, and it was time, as she said, for her to journey on to others. And it was also time for my sister to assume the throne. My mother said—and rightly so—that the responsible ruler trains her successor, and then hands her her power when she is ready to take it, not when the giver is ready to let it go."

"Maybe *my* mother will go join a sanctuary," said Vladislava. "It would be very good for her, don't you think, Tsarinovna? They say that at some you're not allowed to talk for days on end."

"I'm afraid the shock would be rather cruel," said Slava, and then wished she hadn't when Vladislava laughed spitefully at that thought all the rest of the way to her bedchamber.

She was finally able to distract Vladislava from her vengefulness by asking her about her favorite dolls. Vladislava promptly stopped her evil chortling and showed Slava a collection of dolls, dresses, and even that most precious commodity in the provinces, books.

"I would like to be a scribe and make illuminated books, wouldn't you, Tsarinovna?" Vladislava asked, turning the pages of a very fine book with an eager familiarity that made Slava, who, while having no real concept of money if it was not piled in her sister's treasury, at least knew the value of a good book, wince. "Perhaps *I* should go join a sanctuary. They say that some sisters spend all day every day doing nothing but copy and illustrate books."

"Their hands must get very tired," said Slava. "I don't think it would really be as much fun as it sounds."

"I suppose," said Vladislava. She looked crestfallen for a moment, but then brightened up and said, "I know! Let's make a book while we wait for Oleg Svetoslavovich to finish knocking some sense into them!"

"Do you have the things for a book?" asked Slava.

"Of course I do! Look, paper! And I have ink here too!" And Vladislava pulled out a crumpled wad of paper and a rather bedraggled-looking quill from under an ink-stained desk, whose untidiness was a surprising contrast to Vladislava's normally neat appearance. She made some vague smoothing motions over the paper, while totally failing to smooth it in any significant fashion, and then sat there, looking at Slava expectantly.

"What are you going to make your book about?" Slava asked. "A genealogy? A map of Lesnograd?"

"Don't be so boring, Tsarinovna!" cried Vladislava. "Who would waste paper on something like that?"

"Oh, lots of people," said Slava. "So what *will* your book be about, then?"

Vladislava stared out her snowy window for a moment, and then said decisively, "Stories. Let's make a book of stories, like what grandmothers tell, only we'll make them ourselves. You can start, Tsarinovna, since you're the guest."

"Stories about what?" asked Slava.

"*I* don't know. It's *your* story." When Slava continued to sit there silently, Vladislava said, rather contemptuously, "Don't you know how to make stories, Tsarinovna? After all, you were just talking to Oleg Svetoslavovich about how you liked to make things up in your head."

"I did when I was your age," said Slava.

"So why did you stop?" demanded Vladislava.

"I don't know...I suppose I just got out of the habit...lost the ability..."

"You lost the ability to tell *stories*?" demanded Vladislava, horror-stricken. "It that *possible*? How did it happen?"

"I had more important things to occupy my time," said Slava.

"That's stupid!" declared Vladislava. "Like what?"

"Oh...You know..." said Slava, feeling rather foolish. "My duties..."

"What duties?"

"I have to be present at all the meetings of the Princess Council, and whenever the Empress receives petitioners..." Saying it out loud made Slava realize what a feeble excuse it was, and how much she should be ashamed of telling Vladislava such nonsense.

"Why?" demanded Vladislava. "What do you do there?"

"I give council," said Slava, trying, but, she could see, failing, to salvage the situation.

"That's no excuse to give up more important things," said Vladislava severely. "I bet it doesn't even take up all your time. I bet you could even make up stories while you were sitting there at council meetings—they couldn't possibly be very interesting, and no doubt most of the people there are too stupid to say anything worth listening to anyway."

Although Slava did in fact while away the tedious hours of most council meetings thinking about other things in order to distract herself from the stupidity of what was being said, long years of training had taught her not to say that kind of thing out loud, and she was also afraid it might be a bad influence on Vladislava, so she only smiled in a vague way that probably did more harm than good.

"I'll tell you what," said Vladislava commandingly, giving Slava a look of pronounced disdain, "I'll start the story, and then you can finish it once you've remembered how. I think I'm going to write a story about priestesses. Do you think that's a good idea?"

"Certainly," said Slava.

"And leshiye!" said Vladislava, inspired. "I love stories about leshiye, don't you? I want to meet one someday, don't you?"

"I have," said Slava.

"Have what?" asked Vladislava.

"Met leshiye."

"Tsarinovna!!" Vladislava actually dropped her quill and shrieked in delight. "You *met* leshiye?! Lots of them?! Tell me about it!! No, wait—we'll make our story about it! That will be the best thing ever! A story that's also a real story about leshiye! Start at the beginning! Why did you meet leshiye?"

"First I thought I saw things in the woods, but only out of the corner of my eye, and then I had a dream about them, only it turned out it wasn't just a dream..." Slava began.

"What kind of a story is that! Tsarinovna! What *really* happened?"

"Well..." Slava was so unused to people being anything but bored by the details of what she had done, she had to stop to think about how to organize her thoughts. Before she could pull them together, there was a loud knock at the door.

"I bet that's Oleg Svetoslavovich! You can tell him too!" cried Vladislava, scrambling up and running to the door.

It was, in fact, Oleg Svetoslavovich, who looked distinctly hulking and out of place in Vladislava's bedchamber. He took a cautious seat on a free chair that had been made for a small girl, and raised his eyebrows at Slava when she suppressed a smile at the sight.

"Did you knock some sense in them?" asked Vladislava, rather more eagerly than Slava would have liked. "Are they scared now? Do you think they'll behave?"

"Probably not," said Olga, coming in the door without knocking.

"Oh, Aunty Olga, I didn't mean you, of course," said Vladislava, with rather questionable sincerity.

"Oh, I'm sure," said Olga, grinning.

"I threatened them," said Oleg Svetoslavovich, interlacing his fingers and stretching his arms out in front of him ostentatiously, like a man warming up for swordplay under the admiring gaze of his sweetheart.

"And? Did you shout at them?" demanded Vladislava, her eyes gleaming.

"Quite loudly," said Oleg Svetoslavovich with a grin.

"And? Did it make them shut up?"

"For the moment," said Oleg Svetoslavovich, still grinning. "But only for the moment, I fear," he added more seriously. "Andrey Vladislavovich was quelled, and Vasilisa Vasilisovna was forced to see sense, but only for the moment. No doubt by tomorrow they'll have forgotten all about it, just as they've already forgotten the Tsarinovna's attempts to make them behave. Even Lisochka—I'm sorry, Olga, but I'm afraid she's got too much of Andrey Vladislavovich in her. Why didn't you take a lover and pass off his child as your husband's? I'm sure we'd all have been grateful."

"I'm afraid it didn't occur to me at the time," said Olga. "I had no father to guide me, you see, so I foolishly remained faithful to my husband until the damage had been done."

"True enough," said Oleg Svetoslavovich. "Well, there's nothing to be done about it now. Lisochka is what she is, and my sole consolation is that only a quarter of her blood is mine. The quarter that seems to be asleep, alas. Do you think there's any hope for her? The way she whined and then backed down, like a beaten dog..."

"It was a disgusting sight," agreed Olga. "My own flesh and blood..."

"I can't believe she's my sister," put in Vladislava. "Even my second-sister. She's pathetic!"

"Well, maybe she has reason to be!" interjected Slava hotly. "Raised as she's been...Maybe I should invite her to Krasnograd, not just as a visitor, but as my ward," she added. "She's old for it, but...or I could take her on as a highborn maid, like those who serve my sister. It is a position of great honor—she might agree."

"No!" cried Vladislava. "Just when I'm about to escape!"

"It's only right. Olga is my ally, and I've already invited you," said Slava. "And Krasnograd is very big, after all. You wouldn't have to see each other very often, if you didn't want to."

"She might not go, even if you asked her, Tsarinovna," pointed out Olga. "She can be stupidly difficult like that."

"Perhaps," said Slava, and decided to stop talking about it. Although it was true that Lisochka had not made a very favorable impression on her so far, the obvious antagonism of her own mother and second-sister, and the clear neglect of her father and aunt, made her feel terribly sorry for her. Slava wanted to think that all Lisochka really needed was a chance to learn how to behave properly. She had to admit to herself that that might not be enough, but, she told herself, there was no harm in trying.

She returned her attention to Olga and Oleg Svetoslavovich, who were commiserating with each other over the scene they had just witnessed. They both were aware that Olga had been an important part of that scene, but neither of them seemed bothered by that now, and in fact they both laughed heartily when Olga repeated some of the unkind things she had said to Andrey Vladislavovich. Vladislava, to Slava's sorrow but not surprise, laughed heartily too, and with a good deal more cruelty in her eyes.

From what was said, Slava gathered that Oleg Svetoslavovich had gone into the room and shouted harsh words at everyone until he caught Olga's attention by saying he was ashamed to have her as a daughter, if this was the kind of petty squabbling she was constantly stooping to. This had made Olga stop quarreling with Andrey Vladislavovich and, after laughing for some time, turn on the others and join Oleg Svetoslavovich in his shouting. He had said every shocking and unpleasant truth he could come up with, until Vasilisa Vasilisovna, Andrey Vladislavovich, and Lisochka had all been reduced to quivering wrecks, unable to speak a word in their defense. Slava didn't know whether to be terribly guilty that she had let such a thing happen, or terribly glad that she hadn't been in the room when it had, and so settled for a general state of unhappiness.

"It won't last, though," said Olga with a sigh. "It never does. You'd think people with no spines would be easier to beat down, but on the contrary..."

"Well, at least we've gotten ourselves some peace for a few hours," said Oleg Svetoslavovich. "Let's use it to go see the city, shall we? You should survey your domain."

"I thought we were going to plan..." said Slava, but was interrupted by Vladislava jumping up eagerly and crying, "I'll show you!"

"No, little princess, you've already been out once today already, and without permission at that," said Oleg Svetoslavovich. "Don't you have...lessons and things? Instruction on how to be a princess?"

"Grandmother was overseeing all that, but she dismissed everyone shortly before...and no one's done anything about it since then..."

"And I'm sure you made sure not to remind them of it," said Oleg Svetoslavovich with a laugh.

"No! I asked them and asked them!" said Vladislava, looking highly offended, with a suddenness that made even Oleg Svetoslavovich pause. "I asked every day until they told me to shut up and stop bothering them, they had more important things to worry about!"

"What kind of lessons did you have?" Slava asked, before Vladislava could start crying or screaming, as, judging by the look on her face, she was threatening to do. "Perhaps I could help you—be your tutor. It would be fun."

"What do you know about being a princess?" Vladislava demanded.

"Oh, this and that," said Slava. "And I also know much of law, ancient lore, courtly etiquette, the histories of the great families, the founding of Krasnograd, the unification of Zem'...not to mention dancing, and dressing, and riding, and embroidery—including magical symbols—and music, and the languages of the lands along the Middle Sea, and even a little of battle strategy and the stewardship of great estates. And of course I can do sums and write with quite a fair hand. What would you like to learn?"

Olga and Oleg Svetoslavovich, Slava noticed out of the corner of her eye, both looked quite impressed at her list of accomplishments, which made her sorry she had listed them off like that. Oleg was, after all, of peasant stock, even if he had been rubbing shoulders—and rather more than just shoulders—with princesses for years, and Olga was, for all her Severnolesnaya name, hardly much better. Both of them could read, after a fashion, but neither of them could do much more than that, Slava was sure. Sometimes she forgot that other people tended to think she was bragging when she told them of her store of knowledge, and that they could get very sulky about it.

"Battle strategy!" cried Vladislava, her eyes gleaming again. She, at least, did not seem to think that Slava was bragging. "No, the embroidery of magical symbols...no, battle strategy..."

"Does the kremlin have a library?" asked Slava. It seemed likely that their earlier plans to plan their strategy to deal with the Lesnograd intrigue had gone out the window anyway, so if she could find the kremlin's library, the day would not be a total loss.

"Oh yes! Why didn't I show it to you earlier!"

"Then let us go to it now, and we can see what books you have. Perhaps you even have Miroslava Praskovyevna's treatise on war—she gave a copy to all the great families before her death, and the Severnolesniye are descended from some of her closest allies when she was conquering the North, as well as being blood kin in their own right from later marriages."

"Wouldn't it be very old, though? Wasn't that centuries ago?"

"Well, at least two," Slava agreed. "I wouldn't dare touch the original, in case it fell apart. But your scribes might have made copies."

"What if they didn't?" asked Vladislava, suddenly crestfallen at the thought. "What if it's not there at all?"

"Then we'll just have to settle for the embroidery of magical symbols," Slava told her.

"That would also be useful," said Vladislava thoughtfully. "Can you use them to curse your enemies?"

"Yes, but only if you can trick them into putting on the clothes you made for them..."

"Even so! Let's go, Tsarinovna!" And, with the briefest of nods to Olga and Oleg Svetoslavovich, Vladislava took Slava by the hand and led her out of the bedchamber at a very brisk walk that in anyone other than a princess would have been a skipping run. Olga and Oleg Svetoslavovich let them go with no talk of planning at all. It seemed Slava was the only one who remembered, but, she suddenly wondered, perhaps Oleg Svetoslavovich didn't want to speak of it in front of Olga, who was, it seemed, about to come into the rule of Lesnograd...Surely this was all just nonsense, Slava told herself. Probably a visit to the library would be the most fruitful way for her to spend her time anyway.

The Lesnograd library was at the other end of the kremlin, and separated from Vladislava's bedchamber by so many twisting corridors that Slava began to worry she would never be able to make it back to the habitable parts of the fortress, should Vladislava take it into her head to abandon her.

At the moment, though, Vladislava showed no such inclination, and instead quizzed Slava closely about battle strategy all the way down, until Slava began to regret having brought it up at all. She had, of course, studied battle strategy in her youth, as any good Tsarinovna should, but as it had held absolutely no fascination for her whatsoever, much of what she had learned had leaked out of her head or been buried under more interesting information since then. Even when she had been studying it actively, she had shown an unusual lack of ability in it, confounding her tutors, who had, despite the rumors that were already circulating about the younger Tsarinovna's tendency to hysteria, come to expect nothing but the most remarkable quickness of understanding from her. In fact, it was the only thing she had ever quarreled with them about: when they had demanded to know what she would do, should she suddenly find herself commanding armies against hostile forces, she had said, "Find someone competent to do it for me."

Her tutors had been highly offended and reported the incident to her mother, but her mother had only laughed and said that those were the words of a true strategist. Then she had pulled Slava aside and whispered to her that a true strategist also knew how to escape from a disadvantageous situation as quickly as possible, and if that meant deception or trickery, such as feigning an interest or competence one did not feel, so be it. Slava wondered if perhaps she should share that thought with Vladislava.

The library was a large room, but so stuffed with books and scrolls, and so lacking in lamps, as to appear rather cramped.

"How do you find things here?" asked Slava, looking around at the jumble of old papers.

"Oh, there's a system," said Vladislava. "Kseniya Marusyevna knows where everything is."

"Where is Kseniya Marusyevna?" asked Slava.

"Visiting her second-sister in the country," said Vladislava. "Grandmother sent her away after they quarreled."

"Oh," said Slava.

"Grandmother quarreled with a lot of people before her attack, didn't she?" said Vladislava. "Do you think there was a reason?"

"Probably," said Slava.

"I mean, do you think she was ill? Before her attack, that is? Do you think all the quarreling was a sign?"

"Possibly," said Slava.

"Although she did quarrel a lot in general," said Vladislava thoughtfully. "Like everyone else in our family. Oh well"—she shook off that melancholy thought—"let's look over here."

A closer examination of the shelves showed that what Slava had originally taken to be complete disorder did, in fact, have its own kind of order, and the shelf that Vladislava had indicated was devoted to books of wisdom and instruction. There were books and scrolls on treating diseases, recognizing edible mushrooms, running a household, training horses, recognizing magical gifts...

"Is this it?" asked Vladislava, holding up a dusty scroll cover. "It says," she squinted at the faded letters, "The Art of Conquest. Miroslava Praskovyevna."

"That should be it," Slava told her. "Is there anything inside?"

Vladislava opened the case and peered inside. "Yes, and it's quite new, too," she said. "They must have put the new copy in the old case." She shook out the scroll, and held it up. On the top was written, in fresh ink and a clear modern hand, *The Art of Conquest.*

"That's it," said Slava.

"Let's take it back to my room! It's too dark and dusty in here," said Vladislava.

"Can I take some other books?" asked Slava. "There might be useful things in them..."

"Sure," said Vladislava carelessly. Slava took the book on how to recognize magical gifts off the shelf, and then, impelled by some mysterious need for secrecy, took a book on horse training and one on plants of the Far North, and put the one on magical gifts between them, so that no one could see what she was carrying. She thought Vladislava might notice and ask her what she was doing, but Vladislava was already too engrossed in *The Art of Conquest* to pay attention to what Slava was doing. They left the library, carrying their spoils and sneezing violently from the dust all the way back to Vladislava's room.

When they arrived, Olga and Oleg Svetoslavovich were already long gone, and food was waiting for them. Vladislava attacked the food and the lesson with equal enthusiasm, and spent the rest of the day reading through "The Art of Conquest" and quizzing Slava about battle strategy with slightly worrisome intensity, alternating with a disconcerting playfulness. Slava could not help but recognize something of herself in Vladislava's unpredictable behavior, and wasn't sure what to think of that. Once again she was assaulted with equal parts fearful revulsion and fierce protectiveness.

"Will you be my tutor when we're in Krasnograd?" Vladislava asked at the end of the day. "You're very good, even though you don't know much about battle strategy. Was Miroslava Praskovyevna really your many-times great-grandmother? Because you don't seem much alike."

"We are not always like our foremothers," said Slava, reminding herself that it was foolish to be offended by the words of a girl of ten, especially when she was saying exactly what Slava also thought. "You, for example, are not very much like your own mother."

"That was very clever of you, Tsarinovna!" exclaimed Vladislava, impressed. "So will you be my tutor?"

"I might be your tutor about some things," said Slava. "But I think you'll need real tutors as well."

"They might be stupid, though," Vladislava pointed out. "Lots of tutors are."

"True," agreed Slava. "But the Krasnograd kremlin does have a few good ones. I'll make sure you only get the best."

"What will I learn there?" Vladislava asked. "More battle strategy, I hope. What about fighting? Will I be trained how to fight?"

"Perhaps," said Slava. "Some noblewomen are, if they think they will have to lead their men into battle." She didn't say that, given the complicated relations between Krasnograd and the Severnolesniye, it seemed unlikely that her sister would ever give permission for the Severnolesnaya heir to be trained in battle strategy and fighting. Maybe Vladislava could be distracted or bought off with other subjects. Slava looked at Vladislava's determined young face. It was not the face of someone who could be distracted or bought off, even at the tender age of ten.

"There is also history, genealogies, natural lore, the tongues and customs of other lands, riding, dancing..." she said.

"I only want to know *useful* things," Vladislava interrupted, frowning intensely.

"All those things are useful," Slava told her.

"Dancing isn't useful!"

"Oh no, dancing is perhaps the most useful of all," said Slava. "If you cannot carry yourself like a princess on the dance floor, how can you carry yourself like a princess on the throne? If you cannot lead a man on the dance floor, how can you lead many men into battle? Do not underestimate the value of dancing, Vladislava." As she was talking, Slava had to suppress a grin: she, too, had at one time protested the value of dancing, which she had loathed—and still did not care for to this day. In fact, the usefulness of dancing had not crossed her mind until this very moment. Truly, the wise were right, Slava said to herself, fighting harder and harder not to laugh at her own pompous seriousness: in order to know something, one must try to teach it to others.

"Well, if you put it like that..." said Vladislava, without much conviction. But just then a serving woman came in and said it was time for supper, and they went down to rejoin the others.

Chapter Five

Supper was a very subdued affair. Olga had sent word that she had gone back with Oleg Svetoslavovich to spend the evening with her people, and Vladislava's father had had another fit and was unable to leave his rooms, so it was just Slava, Vladislava, Lisochka, Vasilisa Vasilisovna, and Andrey Vladislavovich at the table.

Vladislava's face pinched down into an expression of sullen suffering as soon as she entered the room, Slava made a solemn oath to herself to remain silent as much as was humanly possible, Lisochka picked at her food in ashamed depression, Vasilisa Vasilisovna sat there twitching nervously, and Andrey Vladislavovich seemed sunk into a state of impotent rage. It appeared that Oleg Svetoslavovich's shouting had, in fact, had some small effect, although Slava was not optimistic about its long-term effectiveness, given her own previous failure and the current sulkiness of everyone else at the table. No one ate very much, and Slava and Vladislava both excused themselves as soon as possible.

Once back in her room, and having dismissed her maid for the night, Slava pulled out and dusted off the book on magical gifts. There was no reason, she told herself sternly, for this fluttering she felt in the pit of her stomach. It was just a book, and it was perfectly logical for her to read it. She had come to Lesnograd to consult with its sorceresses, and since the sorceresses were absent, she would consult with its library instead. And it was unlikely that there was much of use in such a book anyway. What was it likely to have that the books she had read from the Krasnograd library didn't have already, and in much more detail?

Nonetheless, and to her embarrassed amusement, she found herself opening the book with the same awkward gentle care and breathless excitement she would have felt at undoing the shirt of a lover for the first time, when she was still wondering about the exact color and texture of the hair on his chest...She wrenched her mind away from such thoughts and back to the matter at hand, although not without smiling her way through the first few sentences in a way that made it very hard to concentrate on the words on the page.

And in fact, the words on the first few pages were not very interesting at all, and certainly much less entertaining than a lover, even—or maybe especially—an imaginary one. There were the same usual platitudes about farseeing, and foreseeing, and beastspeaking, and the efficacy of prayers to the gods, without anything that Slava had not read a dozen times already. But then, just as Slava's eyelids were starting to droop, and she was beginning to think she should just put down the book and go to bed, she read:

> *Our great foremother Miroslava Praskovyevna was known for her ability to farsee, and her prowess in battle, but on her deathbed she said that her greatest victories came from her ability to read the hearts of others. It is this gift that gave her line its name, "Mirrorface," and it is this fickle gift that has flared in and out of the Zerkalitsa line ever since. Its singular nature has led some sorceresses and learned women to speculate that it is not a true "gift" at all, as it has little to do with magic, and the gods and magical creatures do not, to the best of our knowledge, possess it. Neither magic nor prayers can control it, and it seems remarkably impervious to every attempt to influence it, despite its seemingly soft nature. Miroslava Praskovyevna herself called it her double-edged sword, one that cuts the bearer as much as those on whom she wields it. Images, she said, leave their traces on the mirror that reflects them, long after the original has walked away and forgotten what she has seen. Our first Empress gave a special blessing to all her descendants who inherited this most painful of gifts, along with the secrets to harnessing its power and turning it on others.*

Slava turned the page with bated breath.

> The magical properties of certain herbs have long been
> known...

"What!" cried Slava. Luckily, it seemed that all the servants had long gone to bed, and no one came running to investigate her shout. She paged through the rest of the book hastily, but saw nothing more of interest.

Annoyed, she put the book down (hidden under the book on horse training and the one on plants of the Far North, just in case the serving girl who came in in the morning knew how to read and took it into her head to spread it all over the kremlin that the Tsarinovna was reading about magical gifts and the news somehow reached someone who wished Slava ill and would be able to use this information against her, although how that would be possible Slava didn't know, but she hid the book anyway), blew out her candle, and crawled into bed, but her head was whirling too much to allow her to sleep.

She had known that her family name was supposed to mean that they were the mirror that reflected only reality, of course, but she had never heard that that had been explicitly tied to her own unwelcome gifts, or that Miroslava Praskovyevna had shown any sign of them. From what everyone around her had always said of the first Empress, she had been hard as horseshoes, wholly without feeling—the exact opposite of Slava's shrinking nature. She was supposed to have had an unerring sense for the truth, it was true, but it had always been described as something cold, unfeeling, like the sense of a snake for striking...Slava had always resented that her cold rough blood flowed through her, Slava's, tender veins. She could not possibly have been anything like Slava, not possibly...but it seemed that she was. Which, Slava reflected, should be a good lesson to her not to jump to conclusions.

Sleep, unsurprisingly, was a long time coming. Slava kept imagining what she would say if she could speak to Miroslava Praskovyevna, and how Miroslava Praskovyevna would respond. Most of the time, she imagined Miroslava Praskovyevna telling her she needed to toughen up and stop whining so much, in a voice that sounded very much like her sister's.

But she was also my mother's foremother, she reminded herself. *My mother, who is so kind—well, sometimes, except when she's not—also has Miroslava Praskovyevna's harsh blood running through her gentle heart— or was it Miroslava Praskovyevna's blood coming out when she was being unkind?*

And Slava remembered dozens of incidents in which her mother had demonstrated an unsuspected, although understated, strength of character, putting her foot down and making sure that things went the way she wanted them to. How many times had she made her uncooperative councilors and princesses stop their infighting and toe her line? How many times had she quelled obstreperous foreign dignitaries with a single look? How many times had she checked Slava's sister in her arrogant excesses? Not to mention her occasional cruelties to Slava herself...although those seemed to be due more to weakness rather than strength of character.

But in any case, in the end, had she not refused the pleas of her princesses, councilors, and her own daughters, and retired to a sanctuary to contemplate the will of the gods and the patterns of the world in peace? Slava's sister had always counted their mother weak because she gave so much, to those who asked and those who didn't, but really, Slava saw, their mother had been strong, often much stronger than either of them, and her failures, while spectacular (at least in the case of her care of Slava), had been fewer than those of many mothers...Miroslava Praskovyevna would not look down upon her too much, Slava thought...Perhaps her mother had received Miroslava Praskovyevna's special blessing...Armor against the double-edged sword...

WE would have given you armor, said the golden-eyed leshaya. *Armor of ice, against which all weapons would freeze and shatter.*

Armor is heavy, Slava said, more to herself than the leshaya. *Heavy and clumsy. The steppe warriors and those from the Hordes rarely wear more than a chainmail shirt, and some of them go into battle in nothing more than flowing silk, in order to confuse and evade their enemy.*

What happens if they are struck? asked the leshaya.

They rarely are, Slava told her. *They are so strong and quick. And if they are struck, often as not the weapon becomes tangled in the folds of their clothing, or if it does pierce them, often as not it draws the silk in with it, and can be pulled back out again with ease. Or so they say. I do not know: I am not a warrior.*

We are all warriors, said the leshaya, and fixed its golden eyes upon her. *You made a promise,* it continued after a moment.

Yes, said Slava.

You promised you would give us everything, everything we needed, everything we asked for, it said.

Yes, said Slava.

Do you still hold to your promise?

Yes, said Slava.

And will you deliver?

Slava reached out and took its rough-barked hand. *What do you need?* she asked.

Oh, many things, it said. Its slender branches curled around her even slenderer fingers, so that she saw how soft her skin was, and how softly the leshaya held her. *But now,* it said, gazing into her gray eyes with its golden ones—*to see. To see as you see. The world of women is pressing closer and closer about us, and we must learn to read them as you do. We must see what you see.*

Then look, said Slava.

Slava was awakened the next morning by a serving woman shaking her shoulder with the fearful, squeamish expression of someone handling a lizard. Even in her half-asleep state, Slava couldn't help but be both offended and amused.

"Wake up, Tsarinovna, wake up," the serving woman was whispering. "It's late, Tsarinovna, wake up."

"What time is it?" asked Slava groggily. Pre-dawn light was already filtering through the windows.

"Time for breakfast, Tsarinovna," said the serving woman, retreating with grateful relief. "The others are already gathering at the table."

"Oh..." Slava sat up, and discovered that the room was spinning.

"I don't think I want any breakfast," she said weakly, and lay back down.

"No, no, Tsarinovna, get up, the others are waiting..." cried the serving woman in despair.

"I think I'm ill," said Slava. She looked up, and saw that the ceiling was swinging back and forth. "No, I *know* I'm ill," she continued, and closed her eyes to try to regain the strength that speaking had cost her.

"No, Tsarinovna, no, you can't be ill..." said the serving woman desperately. Through her fever-sharpened ears, Slava heard her rush out of the room.

I can't believe I'm ill, Slava said to herself, annoyed. Even the voice in her head sounded weak. Then, thinking back on the past few months, she corrected that to *I can't believe I'm ill NOW. Well, better here than the tundra.*

After an indeterminate amount of time, the serving woman returned, with another woman whose clothes smelled of herbs.

"Feeling poorly, are we?" she asked, staring down at Slava with good-natured interest.

"I hope I'm the only one feeling poorly," Slava said. She started to laugh at her own feeble joke, but had to stop when everything started to spin again.

"They say you're a Tsarinovna. Is that true?" asked the herbwoman, putting her hand on Slava's forehead. She had very kind, motherly hands, which made Slava feel better just by their touch. Unlike the serving woman, she did not appear to be frightened by Slava's title at all.

"Yes," said Slava.

"Are you often ill, Tsarinovna?" asked the herbwoman, peeling back one of Slava's eyelids.

"No," said Slava.

"How do you feel, Tsarinovna?" continued the herbwoman, feeling Slava's chin and throat.

"Dizzy and tired," Slava told her. "Everything's spinning, and my head hurts." She was going to say that she hardly had the strength to talk, but she thought the herbwoman might be able to guess that by the sound of her voice.

"Did you drink much last night, Tsarinovna?" asked the herbwoman, leaning over and pressing her ear into Slava's chest.

"No," said Slava.

"Did she?" the herbwoman asked the serving woman sharply.

"N-n-no," said the serving woman. "No one brought her anything."

"Could you be with child, Tsarinovna?" asked the herbwoman, feeling Slava's stomach.

"Alas, no," said Slava, and tried to smile to show it was a joke.

"You're sure, Tsarinovna?" asked the herbwoman.

"Alas, yes," said Slava. "I lead a quiet life."

"And all those handsome men around you, too, Tsarinovna," said the herbwoman, feeling Slava's pulse. "When did you begin to feel ill?"

"Just now...when I woke up...I must have slept late, and then when I tried to get up, I felt so weak and dizzy..."

"But you felt fine last night, Tsarinovna? Did you sleep well?"

"I couldn't sleep at first, but then I fell asleep, and I had the dream…" Slava's mouth felt so weak it had trouble forming the words, and she couldn't blame the herbwoman for suspecting her of drinking.

"Dream, Tsarinovna? What dream?" asked the herbwoman, with more interest than Slava would have expected.

"I dreamed about the leshaya…the one with golden eyes… she came to me and asked if I was ready to hold to my promise…I said yes…and she wanted to look through my eyes."

"And did she, Tsarinovna?"

"Yes."

"And what did she see?"

"The hearts of others," said Slava.

"And was she happy, Tsarinovna?"

"So much evil…and so much goodness hidden out of fear…How could she be happy?"

"And will she come back, Tsarinovna?" asked the herbwoman.

"Probably," said Slava. "She fled after only a little while…but she said she needed to know more…"

"I'm going to give you a tisane, Tsarinovna," said the herbwoman. "A tisane to help you regain your strength. And I will consult with my sisters on this matter. Meanwhile, you should rest."

"What's wrong with me?" asked Slava. "Why am I ill?"

"You have given so much of yourself, Tsarinovna," said the herbwoman, giving her another kind pat, which made Slava feel better for an instant. "It's no wonder you need rest. And of course, it's not uncommon to catch chills in winter. So stay here, rest, drink the tisane, and wait for my return."

"Does the illness seem dangerous?" asked Slava.

"I have every hope you will recover, Tsarinovna," said the herbwoman.

"No, I mean…can my friends visit me?"

"Right now you should rest, Tsarinovna," repeated the herbwoman firmly. "Drink all the tisane, and rest. But try not to dream."

"If I could learn to control my dreams…" said Slava, annoyed once more.

"Well, think on pleasant things, then, Tsarinovna," said the herbwoman. "I will return later in the day, with someone who knows more of these things than I do. Come." She beckoned to the serving woman, and they both went out the door, leaving Slava to her feverish reveries.

She dozed until the serving woman returned with the tisane. It was mild and slightly sweet, but Slava could still only manage a mouthful at a time. After she had downed an entire cup's worth, at the serving woman's insistence, she went back to dozing.

It seems I took too much from you, Tsarinovna, said two golden eyes. *I am sorry, but my need was great.*

It always is, said Slava. *Everyone's is.*

Your strength will return, I promise, said the golden eyes. *Here, have some of mine.* It reached out a barky hand and laid it on Slava's forehead. Although it was not so soft and kind as the herbwoman's, its healing powers were even greater. Slava slipped into a true sleep.

When she awoke, it was late afternoon, and the room was no longer spinning around and around. The herbwoman was standing over her, flanked by the serving woman and a third woman Slava didn't recognize.

"Do you feel better now, Tsarinovna?" asked the herbwoman.

"Yes," said Slava. Her voice was still weak, but not so pathetically shaky as it had been in the morning.

"Did you sleep long, Tsarinovna?" asked the herbwoman. She handed Slava another cup of the tisane, now cold. Slava drank it down thirstily, and held out the cup for more. "Yes," she said.

"Did you dream, Tsarinovna?" asked the herbwoman, refilling the cup. "Of the leshaya?"

"Yes," said Slava.

"And what did she say, Tsarinovna?" asked the third woman, stepping forward. She was in her middle years, with a wise, proud face, and she was, Slava realized, in the robes of a priestess.

"She said she had taken too much, but her need was great," said Slava, drinking down another cup of the tisane.

"Ah," said the priestess and the herbwoman together. "You must tell me more, Tsarinovna," added the priestess.

"About what?" asked Slava.

"The leshaya, of course, Tsarinovna, and your dreams, and anything else that comes into your head."

"That could take a while," said Slava.

"I have the time, Tsarinovna," said the priestess. "See: I am pulling up a chair and sitting down."

"Why do you want to know?" asked Slava. "Do you think I was ill because of the leshaya?"

"That's why I asked Vlastomila Serafimiyevna to come speak to you, Tsarinovna," said the herbwoman. "You never know with these sorts of things."

"You never do," agreed Vlastomila Serafimiyevna. Even sitting down, she still seemed taller and statelier than anyone else in the room. If a stranger came in and was told to pick out the Tsarinovna in the room, Slava thought, she would surely choose Vlastomila Serafimiyevna and not her.

"As soon as you told me about your dream, Tsarinovna," continued the herbwoman, "I said to myself: 'This sounds like priestess business.' Well, or sorceress business, but sorceresses are hard to scare up these days. So are priestesses, but Vlastomila Serafimiyevna is my near-sister's second-sister, so I went to my brother and asked him to ask his wife, my near-sister, that is, if Vlastomila Serafimiyevna might be visiting, and he said—"

"That I was," interjected Vlastomila Serafimiyevna. "I happened to be in Lesnograd for a few days, gathering provisions for my sisterhood."

"Which sisterhood?" asked Slava.

"Of the forest, Tsarinovna. And so I await your tale with keen anticipation." Vlastomila Serafimiyevna gave Slava a firm look, but, seeing Slava's eyes wander over to the herbwoman, said, "Is there anything else you need with our patient, Yevpraksiya Yarmilovna?"

"Ah, no, Vlastomila Serafimiyevna, I don't think so..."

"Then do not let me keep you from your other charges."

"Oh, of course, Vlastomila Serafimiyevna, you are too kind..." And Yevpraksiya Yarmilovna backed out of the room, followed by the serving woman.

"Yevpraksiya Yarmilovna is a good woman, but these things are out of her ken," said Vlastomila Serafimiyevna. "Now, your story, Tsarinovna, if you please."

Slava started by recounting her dream, but that led back to their last encounter with the leshiye, which led back to her other visions, which led all the way back to their journey from Krasnograd, which took them until suppertime. She thought she would soon lose her strength, but instead she seemed to regain more and more of it as she spoke, and when servants came in to light candles and bring food, she got out of bed and ate at the table with Vlastomila Serafimiyevna.

"And then yesterday, when I was in the library with Vladislava Vasilisovna, I found this book," Slava said, after they had finished eating. "It seemed important, I don't know why, so I took it and read it, or at least part of it, and then I had the dream."

"You were in the library with Vladislava Vasilisovna, Tsarinovna?" asked Vlastomila Serafimiyevna, with more interest than Slava would have expected.

"Yes, we were looking for *The Art of Conquest...*"

"And did you find it, Tsarinovna?" asked Vlastomila Serafimiyevna, with a faint smile. Slava couldn't tell if it was condescending or not.

"Yes, and we brought the books back here and Vladislava spent the afternoon studying battle strategy, and then..."

"Did she seem to show much aptitude for it, Tsarinovna?" asked Vlastomila Serafimiyevna, now with a look that was definitely not condescending at all.

"Yes, I suppose, not that I'm much of a judge, it was never an interest of mine, but she's a very good pupil and a quick study..."

"You think so, Tsarinovna?"

"Of course," said Slava, surprised. "I don't see how anyone who has spent even half a morning in her company could think otherwise."

"What would you say if I told you that she has a reputation all over Severnolesnoye as a hopeless pupil?"

"I'd say Severnolesnoye was wrong," said Slava hotly. "Who could think such a thing? Only a fool could fail to see the brightness inside of her. She will be a great woman someday, I am sure of it."

"So am I, Tsarinovna," said Vlastomila Serafimiyevna. "And so, it seems, are the gods. Lesnograd, however, is of a different opinion."

"Then Lesnograd is a fool!"

"That, I fear, Tsarinovna, is all too true. They say you will be taking Vladislava Vasilisovna back with you to Krasnograd, to live there as your ward?"

"Yes," said Slava. "Someone needs to take care of her."

"You consider her neglected, Tsarinovna?"

"Yes! And your words make me even more sure of it!"

"I am glad, Tsarinovna. Glad that she will be going to someone who will train her to be what she is meant to be. But let us return to your book."

"No, first let us go back to Vladislava," said Slava. "What do you mean, the gods think she will be a great woman someday?"

"Just what I said, Tsarinovna." Vlastomila Serafimiyevna smiled. "I am a priestess, you know. Not only a priestess, but the mother of the Sisterhood of the Forest. The gods' will is clear to no woman, but it is, I hope, a little less dark to me than to others. When news of Vladislava's birth arrived, I went out into the woods and prayed for my beloved Severnolesnoye, and the gods told me that my prayer had been heard, and that finally, a ruler worthy of my native land had been born."

"They did?" said Slava.

"They did, Tsarinovna," said Vlastomila Serafimiyevna. "And now, back to your book, if you please. Do you have it here?"

"What else did they say of Vladislava Vasilisovna?" asked Slava, ignoring Vlastomila Serafimiyevna's question.

"You truly care for her, Tsarinovna," said Vlastomila Serafimiyevna, giving her a measuring look. "You have truly taken a heartfelt interest in the little heir to Severnolesnoye."

"Well, of course," said Slava, now very annoyed. "I asked her to be my ward, did I not?"

"One can have a ward without taking an interest in her, Tsarinovna," pointed out Vlastomila Serafimiyevna.

"Well...true enough," said Slava. "But I can't. I'm not going to waste my time taking in wards I don't care for. Especially since they would be living in Krasnograd, cheek-by-jowl with me and my family, not to mention the entire kremlin. So what did the gods say of Vladislava?"

"They said she had a dark and dangerous path ahead of her, Tsarinovna," said Vlastomila Serafimiyevna. "But what woman of greatness does not? Her fate is her fate, and for the moment we must leave her to it. Do you still have your book?"

"Yes..." Slava tried to stop worrying about Vladislava, and got out her book. Now that Vlastomila Serafimiyevna was asking for it, for some reason Slava was embarrassed to show it to her, impelled by the same inexplicable desire for secrecy of the night before. She had so few things she was allowed to keep secret—despite most people's complete indifference to her actual wellbeing—that she was loath to share something this important with anyone else. But Vlastomila Serafimiyevna looked at her expectantly until Slava handed it over, and showed her the exact passage she had read, just before her dream.

"Ah..." said Vlastomila Serafimiyevna, once she had read the passage on Miroslava Praskovyevna's special gift.

"What do you mean?" demanded Slava. "Do the gods have something to say about this, too? I'm sorry," she added quickly. "I didn't mean to be rude. But, you see, my gift...And to know that it was passed down to me from Miroslava Praskovyevna, that most unlikely of foremothers—for me, I mean—and to read those words and nothing more..."

"You find your gift a burden, then, Tsarinovna?" asked Vlastomila Serafimiyevna.

"Yes," Slava began, and then changed it, she didn't know why, to "No. Not a burden. A source of pain."

"Pain is a burden too, Tsarinovna. How many have prayed to the gods for relief from a life of pain?"

"I know, I know, and I have too, but...I have wished so many times I could lay my gift down, but now that I truly think on it, I think that I would not do it, given the chance. I don't know why. It truly is very painful, Vlastomila Serafimiyevna."

"Why is that so, Tsarinovna?" asked Vlastomila Serafimiyevna, with more sympathy than Slava would have expected her capable of exhibiting.

"How can it not be! To know what is in the hearts of others...I suppose if I just knew, and nothing more, it would not be so bad, but you see, I do not just know, I feel it too."

"All the time, Tsarinovna?"

"No, not all the time, or rather, yes, all the time, but sometimes more clearly than others, and I don't always know why. I mean, I may know that someone is sad, or angry, or happy, or frightened, but not why. So I feel their sadness, or anger, or happiness, or fear, but I don't know *why* I'm feeling what I feel, and my head whirls with all kinds of wild suppositions, and long after they have gone away or changed their mood, I am still going over it again and again..."

"Yes, that does sound very painful, Tsarinovna," interjected Vlastomila Serafimiyevna, who seemed to be already losing patience with Slava's problems. "The gods often ask great things of those to whom they give great things. Will you come to my sanctuary?"

"What, now?" asked Slava.

"Well, probably tomorrow."

"For how long?" asked Slava.

"A few days, most likely. It seems you are running around in circles here, looking for sorceresses, quarreling with the locals..."

"Alas, yes," said Slava. "There has been a lot of quarreling."

"There often is in Lesnograd," said Vlastomila Serafimiyevna, with another slight smile. "But not in my sanctuary. We may, however, have answers to your questions, or at least that which you are seeking."

"You do?" cried Slava. "You have sorceresses? I thought they had gone into hiding!"

"There are people other than sorceresses who have wisdom, Tsarinovna. Although we do have sorceresses as well. Come with me tomorrow. By the evening you will already be among people who may have answers to your questions."

"What if I'm too weak?" objected Slava. "I was just ill…"

"We will be traveling by sleigh," said Vlastomila Serafimiyevna. "It is an easy ride."

"I will have to ask Olga," said Slava.

"If I were you, Tsarinovna, I would *tell* Olga," said Vlastomila Serafimiyevna. "You are a Tsarinovna, not some half-grown girl seeking her mother's permission."

"It is the nature of a Tsarinovna to be a half-grown girl seeking her mother's permission," said Slava. "That is the difference between a Tsarinovna and a Tsarina."

Vlastomila Serafimiyevna's mouth twitched.

"But I see what you mean," said Slava. "I'll send for Olga right now."

"In that case, Tsarinovna," said Vlastomila Serafimiyevna, rising, "I'll come for you in the morning, before first light. Dress warmly."

"What else should I bring?" asked Slava.

"An open mind, open ears, and open heart, Tsarinovna," said Vlastomila Serafimiyevna. She bowed. "Until the morning."

"Yes, until the morning," said Slava.

Once Vlastomila Serafimiyevna had left, Slava went out into the corridor—she was still, she noted, weak enough that a simple trip out of her room left her slightly dizzy, but at least she was able to do it—and hunted down her serving woman, whom she then dispatched to find Olga. She had hardly had the time to catch her breath after her exertions when Olga came striding into her room, followed by Vladislava and Oleg Svetoslavovich.

"Are you better?" demanded Vladislava, as soon as she saw Slava. "I asked and asked them to let me come visit you, but they said I couldn't."

"I'm better, or I soon will be," Slava assured her. "It was nothing serious."

"A chill?" asked Vladislava. "Those can be dangerous, you know."

"Perhaps a very slight one," Slava told her. She turned to Olga, and said, "Vlastomila Serafimiyevna has invited me to her sanctuary, and I have accepted."

"She has?" cried Olga. "I've been begging to go for years, and she always tells me I'm not ready!" She grinned. "Perhaps I should fall ill, too?"

"Perhaps," said Slava. "We will be leaving in the morning. I'm sorry to be leaving you, but it will most likely be only for a few days, and she said I may be able to gain valuable information, and..."

"Say no more," Olga cut her off. "Of course you have to go, although I'm envious as a poor girl at a dance that it's you and not me. We'll muddle on as best we can, won't we, Vladenka?"

"You're *going?!*" said Vladislava. "You're *leaving?* Without me?"

"Only for a few days," Slava told her. "Then I'll come back, and we'll set off for Krasnograd together."

"You promise?" Vladislava's lip was actually trembling in her fierce little face.

"Of course," said Slava. "While I'm gone, you can pack your things in preparation for our journey. Olga Vasilisovna can help you choose what's important and what's not."

"An excellent idea!" said Olga, cheering visibly at, Slava guessed, the thought of a task that could fill the long empty hours in the Lesnograd kremlin.

"Mother will probably have strong opinions on that," said Vladislava. "She'll want me to take all my finest gowns."

"True," said Olga, a lot of the cheer draining out of her face.

"Fine gowns are essential in Krasnograd," Slava said. "But we may not be able to carry very many with us on our journey there. You can tell Vasilisa Vasilisovna that I will have many fine gowns made for you once we are there. And that way we can be sure you are dressed the same as the other little princesses, too."

"I don't *want* to be dressed the same as the other little princesses," said Vladislava scornfully.

"Yes, but this way you won't have to haul lots of gowns all the way down to Krasnograd," Slava explained to her.

"I knew you were a sharp one the moment I met you, Tsarinovna," said Olga, cheering back up.

"I will accompany you to the sanctuary, Tsarinovna," Oleg Svetoslavovich put in suddenly.

"Oh, Vlastomila Serafimiyevna will never accept that," said Olga. "I told you: she's very strict about whom she lets there. An unmarried man and a stranger will never have a chance."

"I have to go," said Oleg Svetoslavovich, and his face and his voice were much more intent than usual. "And she and I are not strangers."

"Still, I doubt she'll agree. She's very strict," said Olga, apparently oblivious to the sudden urgency in Oleg Svetoslavovich's voice.

"There's no harm in asking, I suppose," said Slava, before Oleg Svetoslavovich and Olga could start arguing over the matter.

"I knew you were a sharp one from the moment I met you, Tsarinovna," said Oleg Svetoslavovich, provoking a loud laugh from Olga. The three of them soon left, although not before Vladislava had extracted a promise from the others that they would make absolutely sure she got to say goodbye to Slava before she set off.

Despite having slept for a good part of the day, Slava was still weak enough that as soon as her visitors had left, she collapsed back into sleep, awakening only the next morning, when servants came for her and told her it was time to ready herself to leave. Deciding to take Vlastomila Serafimiyevna's words on faith, Slava went down to the front hall with nothing more than some warm clothes, all borrowed from the kremlin household, since her own clothes were such disreputable rags by this time that the servants had taken them away and never brought them back, probably because they were now being used to clean the floor.

Olga, Oleg Svetoslavovich, and Vladislava were all waiting for her. Vasilisa Vasilisovna, Andrey Vladislavovich, and Lisochka were also hovering unhappily in a corner. Slava went over and thanked them for their hospitality and promised to return in a few days' time, which elicited a faint murmur from Vasilisa Vasilisovna and nothing more than fearful, suspicious looks from the other two. Slava gave up on them as a bad job and returned to Olga.

"It's a snowy day for travel," Olga told her. "Are you sure you're strong enough after your illness?"

"I feel stronger than before," Slava said, and it was true. New strength was pouring back into her, as often happened after an illness, and she was looking forward to the journey with keen excitement.

Vladislava was extracting another promise from her to return as soon as possible, when Vlastomila Serafimiyevna arrived. Oleg Svetoslavovich promptly went over to her and spoke to her privately, and to the great astonishment of the others, she agreed that he could ride with them as far as the sacred woods surrounding the sanctuary.

"There is a cabin there on the edge of our territory for seekers," said Vlastomila. "You will be very welcome there, Oleg Svetoslavovich."

Oleg Svetoslavovich bowed, Olga hugged both him and Slava, Vladislava made them promise one more time they'd be back soon, and then the sleigh was carrying them swiftly through the snowy streets.

Chapter Six

The snow was falling so fast that Slava soon found she couldn't look around without it filling her eyes, and she couldn't talk without it filling her mouth, so, despite her desire to see more of Lesnograd and to question Vlastomila Serafimiyevna and even the sister driving the sleigh, she passed the first several versts of their journey in squint-eyed silence. It was only around midday, when they had left the city long behind and were traveling through a dense fir wood which offered them a little shelter from the snow, that she was able to come out from her cocoon of clothing and orient herself.

"Late winter snows are often the heaviest," observed Vlastomila Serafimiyevna, on seeing her try to shake some of the snow off her hat. "We were lucky to be able to travel at all."

"How far have we gone?" asked Slava.

"Perhaps twenty-five versts. We have not made very good time, but, as I said, we were lucky to able to travel at all."

"And how much farther?" asked Slava.

"Another twenty-five versts or so. We should be there just after sunset."

"Will it be fir woods all the way?" Slava asked, trying not to stare too obviously at the darkness that filled the narrow spaces between the trees.

"There will be a small village, and some other woods as well," said Vlastomila Serafimiyevna.

"And you have nothing to fear here, anyway, Tsarinovna," said Oleg Svetoslavovich. "This is the prayer wood, after all."

"All the more reason to be afraid," said Vlastomila Serafimiyevna calmly. "I should think that you of all people would realize that, Oleg

Svetoslavovich."

"Well, the Tsarinovna still has no reason to be afraid," said Oleg Svetoslavovich, grinning. Vlastomila Serafimiyevna, in striking contrast to every other woman Slava had seen, showed no inclination to grin back.

"I am glad you think so," she said, and went back to gazing at the trees, evidently uninterested in any further conversation.

"What are you doing—praying?" asked Oleg Svetoslavovich, after another verst or so of silence that was obviously weighing heavily on his spirits.

"Yes," said Vlastomila Serafimiyevna. After a little while, she added, "Should you not be doing the same, Oleg Svetoslavovich?"

"Well..." said Oleg Svetoslavovich, and it was clear from his voice that Vlastomila Serafimiyevna was absolutely right, and he knew it, but for some reason did not want to admit it.

"A great duty may lie before you, Oleg Svetoslavovich," continued Vlastomila Serafimiyevna, still staring serenely at the snow in front of them. "Is that not why you begged me to let you accompany us? I would spend every moment of this journey in prayer, if I were you. And fear not: you will not go down your father's path. You have other things to fear, but not that."

Slava desperately wanted to know what great duty could be lying in front of Oleg Svetoslavovich such that he would do something that could even remotely resemble begging, not to mention what his father's path was, and why he wouldn't want to go down it, but when she glanced his way, she saw that he was uncharacteristically uncertain and embarrassed, and so she quickly looked the other way, and kept her questions to herself. It wouldn't hurt her to engage in a little praying too, she told herself. By the very next tree, though, she was sunk deep into daydreams and had forgotten all about any thought of prayer.

They passed the village Vlastomila Serafimiyevna had mentioned. Its inhabitants bowed silently as they went by, in a show of respect that was much quieter but somehow even more frightened than anything Slava had ever seen for the Imperial sleigh.

"Is there much traffic between the village and the sanctuary?" she asked.

"No," said Vlastomila Serafimiyevna. "Our gods are very strong, and they fear them." And that was that.

Slava made another feeble attempt at prayer. It was not something she was very good at, or cared much for—which was probably, she told herself, why she wasn't very good at it. She knew that some people—such as Vlastomila Serafimiyevna, for example, and even, to her surprise, Oleg Svetoslavovich, it seemed—could spend hours engaged in prayer, but she always got bored and went for a walk instead.

"Do you not care for prayer, Tsarinovna?" Vlastomila Serafimiyevna asked suddenly.

"How did you...?"

"You're fidgeting, Tsarinovna," Vlastomila Serafimiyevna pointed out. "Do you not pray regularly?"

"No, I always get bored and go for a walk," Slava admitted.

"How wise of you, Tsarinovna," said Vlastomila Serafimiyevna. "The gods are so much more likely to speak to us when we go to them, rather than demanding that they come to us, in our stuffy houses and crowded cities. But since you are trapped in this sleigh, simply pretend that you are walking, and see what falls into your mind."

By now they were back in the woods. Slava stared out at the snowy trees. *I wonder who lives here*, she thought. *What creatures are watching us go past? I wonder what they think of us? I wonder...*She drifted off into fantasies of what they must look like in the eyes of the woodland creatures watching them from behind the trees...The forest was so vast, and she was so small...Some strange monster with a strange, mingled smell went sliding by with a strange noise...She bounded off deeper into the woods...And then she could see herself from above...She was so vast...Full of living creatures...A strange monster with a strange, mingled smell went sliding through her with a strange noise...She was so vast...Spring was coming soon...Things were waking up inside of her...Some deep evil was stirring...It had hidden away inside of the strange sliding thing with the mingled smell...Aimed far to the South, at that proud woman in the great city...A curse...Even though it was not meant for her, it was poisoning her...A curse...For the proud woman in the South...

"The curse!" cried Slava, making everyone jump. Everything whirled around her for a moment, and then it all snapped into place, and she was riding in a sleigh through the woods once again.

"What about the curse, Tsarinovna?" asked Vlastomila Serafimiyevna.

"The curse...It's in me! I mean...Not in me, in the sleigh...I sensed it when I was the forest..." Slava trailed off, aware of how peculiar that sounded, even to her own ears, but it seemed to make sense to Vlastomila Serafimiyevna.

"You were the forest, Tsarinovna?" she asked. "A vision?"

"I suppose...I just drifted off...and at first I was a snow hare, and I sort of spread out, and I was the whole forest, and I could see and feel everything inside of me, I could see us driving through the middle of me, and then I felt the curse, poisoning me..."

"You knew of this curse already, Tsarinovna?" asked Vlastomila Serafimiyevna.

"Oh, well..." Slava and Oleg Svetoslavovich glanced back and forth, and then Slava plunged in and told Vlastomila Serafimiyevna everything she knew or guessed about the curse, except Vladislava's involvement in it.

"I see," said Vlastomila Serafimiyevna when she was done. "I see. A curse in the prayer wood. That is serious indeed, especially as we are the ones to bring it here."

"Can you do anything about it?" asked Oleg Svetoslavovich. "You and the sisters?"

"I do not know," said Vlastomila Serafimiyevna. "But it seems that the Tsarinovna can. A rare gift indeed, Tsarinovna."

"What? Why?"

"You just read the heart of the entire forest, Tsarinovna, did you not realize that?"

"I did?" exclaimed Slava. "Why? How?"

"If I could answer those questions easily, Tsarinovna, I would be a much better priestess than I am," replied Vlastomila Serafimiyevna. "And I suspect this is a matter outside of even the gods' ken, anyway. But we are almost to the sanctuary, and there we may find answers."

"If we are going to find them, we will find them there," said Oleg Svetoslavovich, with more seriousness than Slava would have expected. She had—not forgotten—but somehow not really given much thought of late to the fact that he was, after all, the gods' chosen. But of course, he would be much more knowledgeable, and more devout, than she could ever be.

The sanctuary, when they arrived, looked more like an ordinary waystation than Slava had expected, although why she would have expected it to be anything other than what it was, she didn't know. She had never been to a sanctuary before, and had always vaguely imagined that one would have more obvious signs of the gods' presence than this rather homey-looking wooden building with a large porch in front and a barn in the back.

"Come and have supper with us, and then you will be escorted to our cabin," Vlastomila Serafimiyevna told Oleg Svetoslavovich. "The sisters will give you provisions."

Oleg Svetoslavovich thanked her, and they climbed out of the sleigh and went up onto the porch, while their silent driver drove the sleigh around to the barn. Sisters in plain brown robes came out to meet them, and if they were surprised by the presence of Slava and Oleg Svetoslavovich, they gave no sign of it, merely welcoming them to the sanctuary, giving them slippers, and leading them to a large table in a central room, where supper was already waiting for them. Even Vlastomila Serafimiyevna's announcement that Slava was the Tsarinovna was greeted with nothing more than polite bows, which was very pleasant.

There was a long prayer before the meal, of course, which gave their driver time to slip speechlessly into the room. Even after all the words of the prayer had been said, the sisters sat for a long time in silent contemplation, their heads bowed and eyes closed. Slava felt very shallow and worldly in comparison, and had to make a strong effort, only partially successful, not to fidget, since no one else seemed to be fidgeting, not even Oleg Svetoslavovich.

The problem with prayer, she thought, as the silent prayer dragged interminably on, was that, despite Vlastomila Serafimiyevna's words earlier, everyone seemed to expect you to pray to something, about something, and in general put in a lot of concentrated effort in a way Slava found completely mystifying and incomprehensible, instead of just letting the mind wander, something Slava was so naturally good at...she wondered how many of the sisters there were just letting their minds wander, as she was...she wondered, not for the first time, but more seriously than she had in a while, what other people thought when they let their minds wander...were their heads filled with strange and wonderful visions, more real than real, as hers was...she wondered how Vladislava was doing, and whether or not Vasilisa Vasilisovna was being kind to her...she wondered what kind of thoughts went through Vladislava's father's head, locked as he was in his witlessness...she wondered what Oleg Svetoslavovich was thinking right now, and if he bothered to pray over his dinner when no one else was looking...she wondered what kind of thoughts went through the gods' heads, if they could be said to have either heads or thoughts...and what did trees think, or birds or bears or any of the other creatures of the forest...she could see the little building in the middle of her, full of strange creatures who sat and stared at their food before eating it, and amongst them was someone who had been given a duty, a heavy duty, and not even the gods know how that would turn out…

"May the gods bless our food and our union here tonight at this table," said Vlastomila Serafimiyevna. Slava hoped no one had noticed her start as she was jerked out of her thoughts and back to the table.

Although there did not seem to be any particular prohibition against talking at the table, conversation was sparse. Vlastomila Serafimiyevna informed everyone that she had acquired the necessary provisions, "and also two guests," and the other sisters made comments meant to express their gladness, and then everyone went back to eating.

From what little discussion took place, Slava gathered that some of the sisters at the table were actually sorceresses in hiding, but they wore the same plain brown robes as the others, and by the end of the supper she still couldn't tell for certain which of the women were sorceresses and which were sisters of the sanctuary.

Anxious as she was to speak to the sorceresses, the urgency of her task had diminished in her mind since her arrival at the sanctuary, and she did not even attempt to seek out any of the sorceresses and ask them to speak with her privately. Her lack of interest in pursuing them surprised her, but she decided it must be on account of her recent illness. Surely the sorceresses wouldn't be going anywhere, she told herself, and so tomorrow would do just as well. Perhaps by then she would be able to tell who was who, and could draw aside a sorceress without also drawing attention to herself. The sisters were no doubt as trustworthy as any woman in Zem', but that, alas, was not very trustworthy. Better to wait until the right moment presented itself, Slava told herself, and finished her meal in silence.

When they were done, Oleg Svetoslavovich was led in one direction, and Slava was led in another.

"Where are you taking him?" Slava asked the brown-clad sister who was directing her.

"The kitchens, sister, and then the cabin for guests. He will be happy there. You can retrieve him when you leave. Many women choose to bring their husbands with them when they come to us seeking aid, and if we deem them deserving of our help, we are happy to provide a place for their husbands as well."

"He's not my husband," Slava said. She was about to say something about how surely the whole country knew the Tsarina's sister was unmarried, but fortunately she heard the words in her head before they were able to reach her mouth, and she was able to stop them in time. Even the thought of saying something so self-important made her squirm. "He is a traveling companion," she said instead. "Kin to Olga Vasilisovna, and so Vlastomila Serafimiyevna gave him leave to come pray in the prayer wood." Slava realized she was in danger of being suspiciously chatty, and stopped herself from giving more misleading details about Oleg Svetoslavovich. "But do you not allow men to stay in the sanctuary, then?" she asked instead. "Do the gods forbid it?"

"The gods most likely look upon such matters with indifference, sister," the sister told her. "It is we women who are easily distracted. Some priestesses, like those of the wolf, may allow and even encourage such...liaisons, but we are a very strict sisterhood."

"Is it hard?" Slava asked. "Hard to make the choice?"

"Oh no, sister, not at all. Or rather, some of us may have spent much time in thought beforehand, but when the time comes, it is never hard."

"And is it hard to keep to...to live in such a strict sisterhood?"

"Oh no, sister, not at all. It is easy. Because it is so strict, you see. It is easy. It is living in the world that is hard."

"True," said Slava. The idea of joining a sanctuary was starting to glimmer in her thoughts as a happy possibility. Then she remembered how bad she was at praying, and told herself not to be foolish.

The room her guide showed her to was just big enough for the bed and a small desk, neither of which were very fine, but everything seemed comfortable enough. The sister gave her a brown robe like the ones everyone else had on, and told her she should wear it for the duration of her stay. Slava feared it would be scratchy, but it, too, seemed comfortable enough when she put it on.

"As it is still winter, we will hold our evening prayer in the common room, sister," she was told. "It will begin soon." Her guide's voice held no note of command, but she also made it clear that *of course* Slava would want to attend the evening prayer, and so Slava said she would be delighted to join them. Which is why she soon found herself making her cautious way back to the common room without a candle, as there were none in her room.

The evening prayer lasted for a very long time, and seemed to consist of endless silent kneeling. Slava tried to fix her thoughts on the will of the gods, and when that failed her, on her vision of earlier in the day, but instead her mind wandered terribly. She was afraid she

was going to jump up with too much alacrity when the end was finally announced, but by that time the pain in her knees made any sort
of jumping, especially jumping with alacrity, entirely out of the question. She hobbled stiffly back to her room, where, despite being in a
sanctuary in the heart of the prayer wood, she slept deeply and with
only the most faint and ordinary sort of dreams all night.

The next morning there was another prayer—of course—followed
by breakfast, which was also started by a prayer. When Vlastomila
Serafimiyevna came over to Slava after breakfast was finished, Slava
braced herself for more praying, but instead, to her grateful if surprised relief, Vlastomila Serafimiyevna suggested that she go to the
library.

"You have a library here?" Slava asked.

"A library of sacred scrolls, yes," Vlastomila Serafimiyevna told
her. "Where better to start in your search for knowledge? The thought
came to me during our morning prayers. I often find my best thoughts
strike me at that time—the reward of years of prayer, I suppose. I will
call the sister who keeps it, and tell her to find you everything she can
on unusual gifts, and unusual interventions by the gods, and...unusu-
al things."

Slava was about to say that what she really wished to do was speak
with the sorceresses who had taken shelter at the sanctuary, but when
she thought about it, she realized that what she really wanted to do
was go to the library, and so she agreed, still surprised at how easily
she had decided to postpone her mission to speak with sorceresses,
but sensing nonetheless that she was making the right choice.

The library-keeper was a kind-faced woman of at least Slava's
mother's age, who was delighted to engage in a project of this sort.

"All most of the sisters want from the library is prayers," she confided to Slava as they went into the library. It was a room no bigger
than Slava's bedroom, but full of shelves of scrolls. "Prayers and more
prayers. Vlastomila Serafimiyevna always tells them that true prayers
have to come from the heart, not dusty scrolls on a shelf, but these

new priestesses never listen, do they? They have to find things out for themselves, the same as everyone else. But...Oh, here we go. This might be of interest." The library-keeper pulled out a scroll, and blew the dust off of it before handing it to Slava. "Oh, and this one, and this one. Call me when you've finished, and I'll find more for you. Oh, and take care with the lamp, won't you? We wouldn't want to start a fire."

Slava promised to be very careful with the lamp, and the chatty library-keeper bustled off. Slava heard her hail someone as soon as she stepped out into the corridor. Slava wondered how she was able to stand the life of the sanctuary, determined as most of her sister priest-esses were to remain silent except when at prayer, but she certainly seemed happy enough. Slava decided to stop thinking about other women's non-existent troubles, and turn her attention to the scrolls.

The first two were accounts of unexpected appearances of the gods to unsuspecting peasants, and as such, were not very interesting. The third scroll was entitled *The Story of Our Sister, Lyubov the Nobly-Born, As Told by Our Mother, Yevpraksiya Lyudmilovna.*

Slava unrolled it without much hope, wondering why the library-keeper had given it to her, other than the fact that she, like Lyubov, was nobly born. She spent a moment speculating how long this search could take her, and whether it was even worth beginning this scroll, and then decided that it least as long as she was reading, she was not engaged in more endless prayer, and started to read:

> *The story of Sister Lyubov is so strange that I felt called to write a separate account of it. Sister Lyubov came to us one night in midwinter. She was of very high birth, it was written plain on her face and everything else about her, but when asked, she wouldn't name her family. "You are all sisters here, are you not?" she asked. "I wish to become your sister too, and leave my old life behind." Since many sisters say that when they come, we welcomed her to our sanctuary, and asked no more questions.*

> *Sister Lyubov obeyed all the sanctuary prescripts without complaint, but she was hopeless at any task other than embroidery. We knew from this that she was a very fine lady, but she continued to say nothing of her past.*

Sister Lyubov was a very shy girl. She never looked anyone in the eye, and if someone else tried to look her in the eye, she would like as not flinch away. She cried over the slightest thing, too. It seemed as if she had been born with a much more sensitive spirit than ordinary women. One day I asked her if this was true, and she said, "Yes." I asked her if she was gifted, and she said, "No, cursed." I asked her what the curse was, and she said, "To be born with a more sensitive spirit than ordinary women."

Soon afterwards, I found out that Sister Lyubov could read minds. Two sisters got in a quarrel over a pair of scissors, and Sister Lyubov knew right away which had stolen them. Then we had a guest, and Sister Lyubov warned us she was up to no good, and that night she tried to rob us. Then Sister Lyubov said that Sister Mariya was ill, and a few hours later, Sister Mariya had a fit. Then many more things happened, which I do not have the time to list here, but Sister Lyubov could read minds, that was soon plain enough. I asked her if she had some magical gift, like a sorceress, and she said no, so I asked her how she could read minds, and she said, "Because I was born with a more sensitive spirit than ordinary women."

Sister Lyubov was often troubled by strange dreams where she would become the forest. The more she prayed for deliverance, the more she had the dreams. Then she took to walking out in the prayer wood, but the dreams got even worse, and she started having waking visions too, and hearing voices in her head, and soon she would scream if you even looked at her sideways. Then one day she came to me, and said that the gods had called her. She was shaking all over and crying. I asked her if she was sure, and she said she was, and I could see she was, so I let her go.

We never saw her again, except sometimes maybe out of the corner of our eyes when we were walking in the prayer wood, although maybe it was an elk or a bear, we could not be sure. Then many fine women and soldiers came looking for the Tsarinovna, and it turned out Sister Lyubov was the

Empress's daughter, the great-granddaughter of Miroslava Praskovyevna. They said Miroslava Praskovyevna's blood ran too strong in her, and she was crazy and had run away. They went out into the woods and searched for her, but they never found her, and eventually they went away.

One day I had a dream, and the gods came and spoke to me in it. They told me that Sister Lyubov was safe in their care, but that someday she must return to the world of women, for her gift was of and for people, not gods. They knew nothing of it. Then one day I heard news that Sister Lyubov had made her way back to Krasnogorod, and her mother had died, and she was now Empress.

"Lyubov the Kind!" cried Slava in surprise. She had heard the story, of course, many times, but never in that form. As it had been told to her, Lyubov had had a great yearning for a life of contemplation and prayer, and so, with her mother's blessing, she had dwelt in a sanctuary in the Far North for many years, before returning to assume the Wooden Throne after she had had a vision of her mother's death.

As her name would suggest, she was famed for being kind, not something for which Slava's foremothers were greatly renowned. It was her kindness, so it was said, that led her to end the practice of slavery in Zem'. But she had also been, Slava remembered, wise. It was said she could always tell truth from lies, no matter how skilled the liar...Perhaps she, too, was an inheritor of Miroslava Praskovyevna's double-edged sword...Funny to think of her, Slava, and Miroslava Praskovyevna all linked together by the same gift, if it could be called that...Funny to think...

"Sister!" Slava called out the corridor. "Sister! Are there more scrolls on Lyubov the Kind?"

The library-keeper came bustling back from the other end of the corridor, where she had evidently been chatting with someone trying to sweep the floors. "Lyubov the Kind, sister?" she said, puzzled. "Why would we have scrolls on an Empress? Surely Krasnogorod is the place for that."

"Yes, but she was here!" Slava cried. "She was a sister in this sanctuary! Look!" She shoved the scroll under the library-keeper's nose, making her jerk her head back and give Slava a stern look.

"Oh, that," she said, once she had glanced over the scroll. "Vlastomila Serafimiyevna did you say you wanted to look at anything un-usual, so I got that out, since Sister Lyubov was so strange—imagine reading other people's minds! And they say she was a strange woman altogether. It's just a story."

"Written by the mother of this sanctuary!"

"Yes, of course, sister, I meant to say, it's true, of course, but Sister Lyubov was just a sister, you see. Nobly born, of course."

"She became Empress!" Slava cried. "It says so right here!"

"Yes, but you see, while she was here, she was just a sister, just the same as anyone else, sister," the library-keeper explained with the thoughtless condescension of a dull-witted person speaking to a small but very intelligent child. "It matters not who her mother was. And it says right here that our mother had a dream telling her that her gift—the gift of Sister Lyubov, that is—was not of the gods, anyway. So not of interest to us, you see."

"Yes, but of interest to me! Do you not have anything else about her?"

"I can look, of course, sister," said the library-keeper, with the air of someone who has decided to humor the fancies of others, no matter how unreasonable. She went back to the shelf where she had found the original scroll, and started poking around, raising clouds of dust and making both of them sneeze violently.

"Sorry about that, sister," said the library-keeper. "Ah, here we go. *The Writings of Yevpraksiya Lyudmilovna.* Scrolls 1, 2, 3, and 4. Mother Yevpraksiya liked to write a lot. It's a shame she wasn't a more lettered woman. These are all fair copies of her writings done by sisters who had clearer hands—and heads too, like as not. They say they tried to set her style straight in places, but when someone as untutored as Mother Yevpraksiya sets to writing, it takes more than a simple sister to clean up the mess."

"Maybe that's why she liked to write so much," said Slava, feeling suddenly defensive of Mother Yevpraksiya. "Because it was a wonder-ful skill to her. Perhaps she felt touched by the gods every time she set quill to paper."

"You're too kind, sister," said the library-keeper, giving Slava a pat on the hand. "And Mother Yevpraksiya was certainly touched. It's a shame she wasn't touched with a little more sense. Here you are. I'll be in the kitchen if you need me, but those scrolls should keep you busy until dinner."

The scrolls were, in fact, very long and tightly rolled, and also very old, which meant that they cracked as Slava tried to unfurl them, much to her distress. However, they were still mostly intact and legible, and it did, in fact, take Slava until dinnertime to read them. Mother Yevpraksiya had written extensively on the daily doings of the sanctuary, the lives of all the sisters in her care, the doings of the nearby village, and, every now and then, the visions she experienced from the gods.

These she recorded in the same matter-of-fact manner as she did an early snowfall or a purchase of barley. Judging from them, though, Mother Yevpraksiya was, despite the untutored nature of her writing, highly skilled in reading the will of the gods. In fact, she seemed to consider their frequent visitations to be ordinary events, something any woman could experience, should she choose to do so. She described in detail all her conversations with them, and the nature of the powers they had given her and the other chosen sisters. There was nothing there that sounded remotely like anything Slava could do.

Towards the end of the fourth scroll, Slava read:

> *Today I got a letter from Sister Lyubov, calling me to Krasnogorod. I shall set out as soon as the rivers thaw enough to sail on.*

Slava ran her eyes impatiently over musings on spring planting until she came to the words:

> *I am come to the great city of Krasnogorod. Sister Lyubov received me in her private chambers with much kindness. There is little trace of the tearful girl who showed up at our sanctuary in the middle of winter all those years ago. There were even a husband and a little Tsarinovna there, who greeted me as kindly as Sister Lyubov before leaving us to speak. When I asked her about the change in her, she said, "Some gifts are harder to accept than others, mother. It took me many years to accept mine. Only when I became convinced that the gods could not help me was I able to face it on my own." When I chided her for her lack of faith, she said she meant no disrespect to the gods, but her gift was of the world of women, not spirits. She was neither a priestess nor a sorceress, she said, even if sometimes it seemed otherwise.*

"I realized that when I took up my duties, my husband, my child," she said. "When I came to you, I was lacking in courage. What I had to find was courage. You and the gods gave me that. The rest had to come from me. All my life I was being torn apart. I had to learn how to keep myself together before I could go back into the world. Other women are born with skin and bones already formed, but I had to grow them on my own. And once I had grown them, I was able, however painfully, to take up the life of ordinary women."

When I asked her what she meant, she said exactly that. I questioned her no more, but wished her happiness and success in her reign. She thanked me and saw me with great politeness to the door of her chambers. When I said my farewells it seemed to me that she truly was more fragile than other women, although I cannot say why. It was as if a great light was shining out of her.

I pray for her every day. They say she has become famed all over our great land for her kindness. We spoke of her desire to end slavery. She wanted to know my will, and the will of the gods. I approve, and so do they, and so I told her. Buying and selling our own kindred hardens the heart and closes the ears to the will of the gods. And kindness is certainly what we lack the most, and have the greatest need for. I pray that she will have enough, for I fear we take more than she can give.

The scroll ended there, just as the library-keeper returned to summon Slava to dinner. She joined the others with her head in a whirl. The interminable pre-dinner prayer passed before she could begin to feel bored, as images of her many-times great-grandmother swirled through her head. She ate without noticing what was being served, and Vlastomila Serafimiyevna had to call on her several times before she realized she was being asked a question.

"Did you find anything of interest, sister?" Vlastomila Serafimiyevna asked, once she had gained Slava's attention.

"Oh yes," said Slava.

"And what will you do now, sister?" Vlastomila Serafimiyevna asked.

"I think I must...I think I must go out..." Slava had an intense desire to tell someone of all she had discovered, but when she looked at Vlastomila Serafimiyevna and the other sisters, she saw that her story would have no meaning to them.

"Oleg Svetoslavovich," she said suddenly. "Can I go see Oleg Svetoslavovich? I have a great desire to go out in the fresh air, after my day in the library, and I must confide—I must consult..."

"Of course, sister, if he is willing to be disturbed," said Vlastomila Serafimiyevna. "Do you wish to go tonight?"

"Is it so late already?" asked Slava, crestfallen at the thought of putting off her outing until tomorrow. After spending so many hours with the scrolls, she was tired but also restless, and the thought of returning to her room for the night was unwelcome.

"No, not so late at all, sister," said Vlastomila Serafimiyevna. "We eat dinner at sunset, but sunset is still early this time of year. The path to the cabin is not hard to follow, even in the dark, and we will send a sister to guide you."

"Thank you," said Slava, relieved. "When can we set out?"

"Immediately, if you wish, sister."

"If it's not too much trouble..."

"Of course not, sister," said Vlastomila Serafimiyevna. "Sister Alyona! Are you ready to guide our sister to the cabin? She must consult with our guest."

The same woman who had driven them silently the day before nodded speechlessly and rose, evidently prepared to leave at once. Slava jumped up too.

"Sister Alyona will escort you there and then come back," Vlastomila Serafimiyevna told her. "Oleg Svetoslavovich can escort you back, whenever you are ready to return." She gave Slava a calm look that nonetheless seemed to contain some meaning Slava was embarrassed to read into it.

An icy snow was falling as Slava and Sister Alyona set off, making sleety, silvery sounds through the fir needles on its way to the ground.

"Spring snow," said Sister Alyona, and then returned to her habitual silence for the rest of the walk.

Warm candlelanterns were glowing from inside the cabin when they arrived, and smoke was coming from the chimney, but no one answered when they climbed up onto the tiny porch and knocked at the door. Slava called for Oleg Svetoslavovich, but her voice disappeared into the snowy woods.

"Do you want to go back, sister?" asked Sister Alyona.

"No...No, I think I'll stay here," Slava decided. "He must be back soon, if the candles are burning."

"Just don't go out into the woods, sister," said Sister Alyona. "Stay in the cabin."

"Why?" asked Slava. "What dangers are out in the woods?"

"What dangers aren't out in the woods, sister?" said Sister Alyona, giving her a funny look. "Wolves, snow, bears, cold...and other things, too, of course. This is the prayer wood. There is a reason why we pray here. Stay in the cabin."

"I will," promised Slava. To show her good faith, she went inside and latched the door behind her.

"What about you, sister?" she called through the door. "Will you be safe to walk back alone?"

"Safe enough, sister," Sister Alyona called back. "I am a sister of the sanctuary. Don't worry about me. Just stay in the cabin."

"I will," Slava promised again. This seemed to satisfy Sister Alyona, for she stepped off the porch and disappeared into the darkness.

The cabin was only one room, with a bed against one wall and a stove against the other, and a crude table and two chairs in the middle. Slava first sat at the table, but that was both uncomfortable and boring, so when Oleg Svetoslavovich didn't appear by the time the candles had burned down another half an inch, Slava lay down on the bed and soon fell asleep.

She was awakened by the sound of something tapping at the single window.

"Oleg?" Slava cried, remembering that she had latched the door, which meant he couldn't come in unless she let him.

There was no answer. Still half-asleep, Slava rose stiffly from the bed and went over to the window, but there was no one there.

"Oleg Svetoslavovich?" she called again. Instead of a reply, though, all she heard was a faint cry from the door.

"Are you hurt?" she called, running to unlatch the door. Somehow

97

it was harder to open then she had expected, as if her hands weren't quite working properly. When she finally fumbled the latch free and wrenched the door open, there was no one there.

"Oleg Svetoslavovich?" she shouted into the darkness. There was no answer. The snow had stopped and the sky had cleared, and she thought she saw a flash of red hair in the trees.

"Are you hurt?" she asked again.

Something cried at her feet. She looked down, and saw a baby in a basket.

"By all the gods!" She snatched up the baby without even pausing to think. "The cold! You! You out in the trees! There's no need to be afraid! Is this your child? There's no need to be afraid! I'll help you! I'll help you take care of it!"

"You will?" said Vladislava. "What about me? You promised to take care of me."

"Yes, of course, but I can do both," said Slava. "I can't leave her!"

"I thought I was going to be your daughter," said Vladislava tearfully.

"You will, you will," Slava assured her. "And she will be your sister."

"Really?" said Vladislava, cheering up. "A sister? Better than Lisochka?"

"Yes," promised Slava. "The best sister ever. You can help raise her."

Vladislava gave the baby a kiss on the cheek, and then disappeared into the darkness.

"Do you really mean to take her?" asked the leshaya with the golden eyes.

"Yes, of course," said Slava. "How could I not?"

"It's not too late," said the leshaya. "You could refuse, and she would disappear as if she had never been—which would be true. She would have never been. Do you really want to bring her into this world?"

This was a powerful argument, and Slava even tried to put the baby back in the basket, but her arms wouldn't open.

"I can't let go of her," said Slava eventually. "I think I have to have her."

"Is that a promise, little woman?" said the cold wind.

"Yes," said Slava.

"You are sure, little woman?" said the cold wind.

"Yes," said Slava.

"No matter what?" asked the cold wind.

"Yes!" said Slava.

"You will not rethink your sacrifice, as you did the last time we offered it to you?"

"I offered my own blood then," said Slava. "It was you who refused to take it. I will always be able to sacrifice my own blood. It is the blood of others I will not spill."

"Then so be it," said the cold wind. "Let it be your own blood. Those are the terms."

"Let me take you inside," Slava said to the baby. She carried her back into the cabin. When she started to fuss, Slava put her to her breast, which was overflowing with milk. The baby gazed up at her adoringly, and her eyes glowed gold.

Chapter Seven

"Hey! Who's in there!"

Slava jerked awake. She was in the cabin, lying on the bed on top of the bedclothes. A cold wind was wafting in through a crack in the wall, and someone was pounding on the door.

"Oleg Svetoslavovich?" she called, rising stiffly.

"Tsarinovna? Is that you?"

"Yes. I'm sorry—I wanted to come speak with you, and Sister Alyona told me to keep the door latched..."

"And she was right. But are you going to let me in?"

"Oh! Of course!" Slava hurried over to the door and opened it. The sky had cleared, she noted as she looked outside, and a cold wind was whistling through the firs. She told herself that it didn't sound like the voices who had spoken in her dream at all.

"I'm sorry if I'm disturbing you, and that I locked you out," she apologized again, once she had let Oleg Svetoslavovich in and latched the door firmly behind him. "But I was reading today..."

"Reading what, Tsarinovna?" asked Oleg Svetoslavovich. "Tea?"

"No, scrolls," Slava answered, and then realized that he was asking her if she wanted tea. They both laughed at the same time. "Yes, please," she said.

"Tell me about the scrolls, Tsarinovna," said Oleg Svetoslavovich. "What was so important that you had to come out to my cabin in the dark to speak to me about?"

So Slava told him about everything she had read in the scrolls that day, and also about what she had read in the book in Lesnograd, and several surmises she had made about her foremothers and their gifts. The pleasure of sharing her thoughts with another person, instead of merely listening to what others had to say, was so great that she talked and talked and talked, until she was embarrassed at taking up so much of Oleg's time, but she couldn't seem to stop herself, and he didn't seem bored at all.

In fact, he listened to her with flattering interest, nodding appreciatively and making sensible comments whenever she said something particularly exciting, as if he were actually listening to her and hearing what she was saying. In the back of her mind, Slava was aware that this was one of the most pleasant evenings she had ever spent, and she didn't know whether to laugh at herself or feel sorry for herself for being so easily pleased.

"It's very strange to think of being so closely connected to Miroslava Praskovyevna," she finished. "I always thought that she and I were completely different. But it seems that she, Lyubov the Kind, and I all shared the same gift, but it is not a gift of the gods. They say that over and over again...And of course, the leshiye couldn't take my gift, they couldn't use it, I had to do it for them...And my strange dream just now..."

"What strange dream, Tsarinovna?" asked Oleg Svetoslavovich.

"I dreamed...I dreamed that someone was tapping at the window, and when I opened the door, there was..."

"Yes?" asked Oleg Svetoslavovich, when Slava trailed off.

"There was a baby in a basket, and when I picked her up, her eyes glowed gold."

"So what did you do then?" asked Oleg Svetoslavovich intently.

"I took her in, of course," said Slava.

"Of course you did," said Oleg Svetoslavovich, and Slava couldn't tell what he meant by that. "You didn't think of refusing her?"

"Of course not! It was cold! Vladislava—Vladislava started speaking to me in the dream—Vladislava complained about it at first, but I explained to her that she would have a sister."

"And then what?"

"And then she was happy, of course. She said she would help take care of her. And the gods asked me if I were sure, and I said I was."

"And are you sure, Slava?" asked Oleg Svetoslavovich.

"Sure about what?" asked Slava.

"That you would take her in?"

"Of course I am! If I found a baby by the door, *of course* I would take her in! I wouldn't even stop to think about it!"

"Even if her eyes glowed gold?"

"That's not her fault!"

"No, but she could be troublesome. She could be dangerous."

"Lots of people are troublesome and dangerous! *You're* trouble-some and dangerous!"

That made Oleg Svetoslavovich laugh for a moment. "So my fa-ther always told me," he said. "He kept trying to beat it out of me, but I guess he failed." He became serious again. "Are you sure, Slava?" he asked again. "Sure that you want to take her in?"

"Why?" asked Slava, and then, struck by a sudden thought, jumped up and cried out, "By all the gods! Is she really out there somewhere? Is that why you were out there so long? Because of her? Is she yours? Where is she?"

"She's not out there, Slava," said Oleg Svetoslavovich. "She doesn't need immediate rescue, don't worry. But she *could* be out there, if you wanted her to be. And yes, that was why I was out there so long."

"What do you mean?" asked Slava, sitting back down. The back of her mind was telling her that she knew exactly what he meant, but she ignored it. It seemed so unlikely, and the back of her mind had been wrong before. "I thought you came out here to learn the will of the gods," she said instead.

"So I did. I have spent the day in the most serious prayer, and the gods called on me to come out to them, and when I did, they told me of their will. Not that I hadn't known it for some already, but they re-peated their command yet again, in case I was wavering in my pur-pose. Slava...Do you not think that your dream might...might have some special significance? That it wasn't just a dream?"

"Like a vision of some kind? A message?"

"Exactly like that. A message. From the gods."

"A message about what?"

"Slava! What do you think?!"

"A baby?" said Slava. Even though she was growing more and more certain that the back of her mind had been right, her disbelief in what the dream and Oleg's words meant made her blurt out, "Where would I get one of those?"

This made Oleg Svetoslavovich laugh a good deal more.

"Oh," said Slava. "Really? But why...I mean, a message from the gods...that's a bit extreme...I don't think that's the normal way..."

"Do you remember what you have been asked, Slava, over and over again? First by the leshiye, and then by the gods themselves?"

"If I would give them what they needed," said Slava. "And I said I would, of course."

"And what if this is what they need?" said Oleg Svetoslavovich.

"A baby? Surely there are lots of those around already."

"Not whose eyes glow gold," said Oleg Svetoslavovich. "Those are much rarer. And that, Slava is what they need. They need a way into the world of women, Slava! At first they thought you were that way, but it turns out your gifts are...not accessible to them. Gifts often come in unwelcome packages, even for the gods themselves. But your daughter, Slava, your daughter! Given to you by the gods themselves! She would be a force to be reckoned with, both in the world of women and the world of spirits! And she would be the sacrifice that would seal the deal—the sacrifice of your own blood, just as you offered."

"They wouldn't kill her!"

"No. Of course not. She would be precious to them. But like any child, she would be a blood sacrifice. Your own blood. So you have to be sure, Slava."

"In that case," said Slava. She raised her eyes up to meet his. "I'm sure."

"I never noticed the color of your eyes before," said Oleg sometime much later, possibly the next morning. "They're golden."

"No they're not," said Slava. "They're gray. Zerkalitsa gray."

"In this light they're golden," said Oleg. "At least when the lantern flame catches them. Who knows what color they are in the darkness."

"Probably black," said Slava. After a moment she added, "What color do you think her eyes will be? Blue like yours, or gray like mine?"

"Oh, probably green, then," said Oleg, laughing. But then he suddenly turned serious and asked, "Can I come see her sometime?"

"Of course, said Slava. "Anytime. As often as you want. And she might be a boy, you know—half of babies born are."

"Not mine," said Oleg. "I seem to be able only to father daughters. A valuable gift."

"Well, if for some reason she *is* your first son, you can still come visit her," said Slava.

"My word isn't good enough for you?" asked Oleg with a laugh. "You don't believe me when I say all my children are daughters? I see you are more hard-headed than meets the eye."

"Perhaps all your children *thus far* have been daughters, but I must consider all eventualities," said Slava, running her fingers through his hair.

"Of course you must," said Oleg, and she could feel him laughing into her breasts. "Well, if it is a son, I'll come visit him too. But no doubt she'll be a daughter."

"Let us hope," said Slava, although privately she thought that a little son might be very sweet, too, and might cause fewer problems with her sister. Which probably meant she was destined to have a daughter, then.

"I've never been to Krasnograd before," said Oleg. "Do you think it will be a good place for her to grow up?"

"Not at all," said Slava with a smile. "But better than many other places, I'm sure."

"I'm afraid she'll have a hard life," said Oleg. "The gods' chosen normally do."

"I'll take care of her," said Slava. "And when she's grown, she'll be able to take care of herself. And Olga and Vladislava will watch over her too, I'm sure of it. And...would you think it strange if I find her sister, the one who ran away to Krasnograd? She could watch over her as well. I want to watch over Milochka myself, and make sure she wants for nothing."

"Of course you do," said Oleg. He moved so that his head was resting on Slava's stomach. After months of traveling, it was hollow when she lay on her back, and her breasts almost disappeared into her ribs. It was strange to think that in a few months, her body could be firm and swollen with new life.

"Do you think she's in there already?" asked Slava.

"We certainly tried our best," said Oleg.

"Lots of times, too," said Slava.

"Yes, I can feel it," said Oleg. "I think I might be bleeding."

"Oh!" Even in the flickering lantern light, Slava could see that he right. "I scratched you," she said, mortified. "Your shoulders..." There were other scratches there too, she could see, old scars that looked more like the marks of a lash, like what criminals who had been flogged had, or children who had been beaten by their parents...she bent down to kiss the marks, both the ones she had left, that would heal, and the older ones, that wouldn't. There was large scar below his shoulder blades that looked as if someone had pressed a hot pan against his back and held it there until the skin burned away...

"And not just my shoulders," said Oleg, laughing. "Who knew you would be so fierce? A real wolf! Until now I wasn't sure you had it in you. You warned me not to challenge your bloodlust, but I admit, I didn't think you were serious. More fool me, eh? Well, no matter. After all, you seem to be getting on just fine." He patted her scarred arm affectionately. "Now we'll have matching scars from our encounters with the gods."

"I'm so sorry," said Slava. She reached out to touch the burn scar, but Oleg shifted out from under her hand, as if by accident, and turned to examine his shoulders, and she knew that that was the only injury he cared to speak of. "I didn't mean to," she said, pretending that she had only seen the fresh scratches, not the old scars. "Not that that's any excuse..."

"Oh, I wasn't complaining," said Oleg. "The spoils of war, ah? Or possibly battle scars. I'll wear these with pride for a long time to come."

"It seems I can't stop hurting people," said Slava. "Even when I don't mean to...This is terrible. I shouldn't...Even with a lover...This is terrible...I can't seem to stop myself." The thought that Oleg had suffered in the past, and she had only added to it, even if by accident, made her feel almost ill.

"So I take it this isn't the first time," said Oleg, laughing even more.

"Oh..." said Slava. "I'm really, really sorry."

"Well *I'm* not," said Oleg. "Some of us like that kind of thing, you know."

Slava stared at him in shock, and then saw that he only meant what had happened that night, that he had deliberately forgotten all about the other scars, the ones that she could see and he couldn't. She tried to smile at him, and he grinned brightly in response.

"You're just saying that to...you're just trying to make me feel better," said Slava. "It's inexcusable, and I know it."

"Oh no," said Oleg. "I think you should do it more. More, and more often. Preferably with me."

"You're just..." said Slava again, and then stopped. "You mean it," she said. "You really mean it."

"Oh yes," said Oleg. "I really mean it."

"You don't mind? You really don't?"

"Oh no. Quite, quite the contrary, don't you worry about that. They say babies born of pleasure are blessed: well, our little girl is going to be blessed twice over."

"Lucky Darya, then," said Slava, starting to smile. She bent over and kissed one of the worst scratches on his arm.

"Darya?" said Oleg, moving his shoulders in a way that suggested he did not, in fact, mind at all.

"Because she's a gift, and because she will be gifted," explained Slava. "Do you like it?"

"Darya Krasnoslavovna," said Oleg dreamily. Slava couldn't help but wonder if he was like this with all his women.

"With red hair and golden eyes," she said, looking up at the ceiling to hide her smile at the thought of how not-special she was to Oleg. She knew that under other circumstances she would have been very hurt and angry, but right now she felt nothing but a great sense of joy. For once the act of love had left her feeling uplifted and cleansed, as it was supposed to, and not soiled and ashamed, as it so often did.

For once she had felt that it really was the life-giving union of the earth and the sky, the expression of the purest love...and all because, Slava suspected, the two of them had been the only beings present in that bed that night. Slava was used to sharing her lover's bed with her lover's vanity, who tended to be a selfish and frigid party to their actions. But not this time. This time, unlike all the other times, it had just been the two of them. And, of course, he did have the benefit of experience...lots of experience. Probably best not to mention any of that to Oleg, though.

"She will be beautiful—and very special," she said instead. "I'm sure of it."

"But just to be even more sure..." said Oleg, kissing her navel. "And because we're getting cold without our clothes..."

"Smart, too, I can see, and very observant," said Slava, laughing.

Sometime that was definitely the next morning, Slava was awakened by the sound of something heavy walking around the cabin.

"What's that walking around the cabin?" she asked. "It sounds heavy."

"Gray Wolf," said Oleg, lying there with his eyes closed. "Come to get me."

"Why?" asked Slava.

"To take me back," said Oleg, still not opening his eyes. Slava suddenly realized that he was anticipating a scene with her, and was afraid to open his eyes and look at her.

"Then you should go," she said, as kindly as possible.

"I don't..." he began, and Slava could see that he didn't know what to say, or even what he wanted to say, or even what he wanted in general, but it didn't matter, because he thought he had to leave.

"If the gods are calling, then you should go," she repeated more firmly. "And I must return to the sanctuary, anyway." She got out of bed and began dressing herself.

"You're very calm," said Oleg. "Aren't you..."

"What?" asked Slava.

"Afraid? Worried? Concerned?"

"No," said Slava.

"I never can understand how women can be so calm about this," said Oleg, finally opening his eyes and looking at her. "You're going to have a child! Alone!"

"*I* won't be alone," Slava pointed out. "I will have all of Krasnograd at my disposal, and probably most of Severnolesnoye as well, once Olga finds out. If ever a woman was going to be well cared for, that woman would be me."

"Yes, but..." said Oleg, looking uncharacteristically lost and unhappy.

"And I expect you to watch over her—over both of us—as well," Slava said. "I'm sure you will do your best. Our daughter will be lucky, having you as her father."

Oleg laughed disbelievingly at the idea of anyone being lucky to have him as a father.

"And you can come see her whenever you want, you know," Slava pressed on, annoyed by his disbelieving laughter and determined to prove him wrong. "It would be nice if she were able to know her father. My own father died when I was so young I scarcely remember him. Sometimes I think it would have been nice to have a father around. When she's older she will probably need to spend time with you, too. You can teach her about service to the gods."

Oleg's face cleared. Once again, Slava was amazed at how easy it was to make people feel better with just a few well-chosen words.

"I wish you could come with me," he said. As far as Slava could tell, he meant it, at least for the moment. She wondered how often he sincerely meant what he said at the moment he said it. Probably most of the time. Just like he had sincerely meant what he had said last night, but it had been last night when he had said it, and now it was this morning.

"And live in the woods?" Slava asked, with a smile to show that it was meant to be a joke.

"It's not so bad," said Oleg. "I have a house. Well, more of a cabin. Well, actually, more of a...Well, anyway, it's not so bad. Better than the hovel my father...Better than those tents you lived in for weeks and weeks. It's very quiet. Peaceful. You'd probably like it."

"I probably would," agreed Slava, keeping her doubts to herself. Oleg's house was probably a horrible shack. Although right now even a horrible shack didn't sound so bad, if they could stay in it and be alone together, away from the rest of the world. For a moment Slava was distracted by that happy fantasy.

But then something twinged inside of her, and she knew that that was not an option. Running away was not an option. Krasnograd was at the end of her journey, whether she wanted it or not. She thought of Vladislava's dark path, and suspected that hers was darker still. She remembered how she had seen herself sliding through the forest the day before, bearing some black evil, and she knew without a doubt that, were she to run away to Oleg's cabin to live with him, she would bring that evil with her, probably in the form of a vengeful Empress seeking her lost sister as well as every opportunity to wreak death and destruction on these dangerous Northerners.

Now there was a curse indeed, Slava thought, and one that required no sorceresses to wield it: her sister could easily bring about her own destruction with only the slightest nudge from outside forces, or maybe not even that. And Slava's place was, inescapably, by her side. At least perhaps that way the damage could be controlled somewhat. Probably by making it even worse than it was to begin with. Slava would have cursed her fate, except that she knew that cursing her fate was the surest way of having fate curse her in return. Too many curses, she thought with chagrin, and probably some of them centered around this daughter who was not even in existence yet.

"But I have to go back," she said. "I cannot just disappear, much as I might like to."

Oleg raised his head and gave her a surprised look, and she knew she had hurt him without even meaning to. He, she remembered, had just disappeared, and they had both gotten caught on the other edge of the double-edged sword of words. She said quickly, "And when our daughter is of age, I promise you, she can come and see your house for herself. Any time you want to visit her, or she wants to visit you, I promise you, I will make sure it happens."

"You're very kind," said Oleg.

Slava shrugged.

"And you feel sorry for me, don't you?"

"Of course," said Slava.

"Of course you do," said Oleg, shaking his head. "I'm leaving you to fend for yourself, and you feel sorry for me. I'd laugh if I weren't angry about it."

"It is my nature," said Slava. "No need to get angry about it. It won't help, anyway."

"Are you *ever* going to come out?" someone called. It took a moment for Slava to realize that it must be Gray Wolf, and he was speaking inside their heads. "Surely you've done the deed by now."

"Patience is the crown of princes," Slava said back to him.

"Lucky for me I'm not a prince, princess," said Gray Wolf.

"That's Tsarinovna to you, my fine fellow," said Oleg, getting up and beginning to dress himself. "And I don't see what you're in such a rush about, anyway. We have all the time in the world, you and I."

"Send her out here," said Gray Wolf. "We want to see her."

"Who's 'we'?" asked Slava.

"We," said Gray Wolf. "Come out and see."

Slava left Oleg to finish putting his clothes on, and went outside. Gray light was already filtering through the trees. Gray Wolf was standing by the front steps. He was even more monstrous than she remembered.

"You're so *huge*," she told him.

"Save it for the men, Slava," said Gray Wolf. "That kind of flattery doesn't work on me."

"Who said it was flattery?" said Slava. "I was just thinking how monstrous you are."

"That *is* flattery for a monster like me," said Gray Wolf. "Can I come closer? Can I rest my head on your shoulder?"

"Of course," said Slava.

"Of course," said Gray Wolf. He stepped closer and rested his very heavy head on her shoulder. "You aren't afraid?" he asked.

"No," said Slava.

"You carry a very heavy burden, you know," he said.

"Yes, my shoulder can tell."

Gray Wolf laughed in her ear. "Our hopes are high for you, Tsarinovna," he said softly. "That is the burden I meant."

"I can carry it," Slava told him.

"The leshiye are here for you," he said. "To escort you back to the sanctuary."

"Won't that draw attention?" Slava asked with a smile.

"Only the good kind," said Gray Wolf. "The sisters are used to that kind of thing. This is a prayer wood, you know." He lifted his head from her shoulder, which really was growing tired, and pressed it against her belly. "What better place to conceive a child of the gods."

"Yes," said Slava, stroking his neck. "She will be blessed, I can feel it. I felt their spirits settle inside of me last night. Or something, anyway—happiness, perhaps." She thought of the curses swirling around them, and took heart from that germ of happiness currently lying in her heart. A little counter-curse, as it were.

There was a rustling noise, making Slava look up. Leshiye were coming out from the trees. The one closest to Slava had golden eyes.

"Are you ready, Krasnoslava?" she asked.

"Yes," said Slava.

The candles went out in the cabin. After a moment, Oleg stepped out onto the porch.

"Well, let's go, brother," said Gray Wolf, moving away from Slava. "Enough mooning around here! This is women's business. We have no place here!" He said it boldly because, Slava could see, he knew that Oleg did not want to go, and did not know what to do, and was generally sad and at a loss.

"I will come to Krasnograd next year," said Oleg, looking at Slava and then looking away.

"That will be good," said Slava. "You will be welcome. Come to Krasnograd any time."

"I wish I didn't have to go," said Oleg, and once again he really meant it, at least for the moment. "I wish I were going back to Krasnograd with you."

"Then come," said Slava. A wave of tenderness rose up inside her in response to his own momentary tenderness. "Come back to Krasnograd with me. You can be my consort, if you wish. I'll even marry you, if you wish."

"My wife might have something to say about that," said Oleg, with a painful smile that told Slava her proposal had been rejected. "Last I heard, she wasn't dead yet."

"She can set you aside," said Slava, unable to stop herself even though some part of her knew it was already hopeless. Now that she had thought about it, *of course* Oleg should marry her and come back to Krasnograd. It was such a blindingly obvious solution to so many of their problems that she was ashamed neither of them had thought of it earlier. Their child would have a father, Slava would have a husband and be free of her sister's attempts to satisfy both her greed and her hatred of Slava by marrying her off to rich but spoiled princes, Oleg would be able to return to human society, and they would—if they came up with a clever enough story—have a marriage alliance with Severnolesnoye. It was too perfect for Slava to give up on just because of Oleg's fearfulness and Princess Severnolesnaya's general obstreperousness

"And you really think she'd do that? You must not know her bad temper like I do." Oleg gave her another painful smile, one that showed he had been thrown into a panic by her offer and was blurting out any excuse he could come up with to avoid accepting it.

"She will if the Tsarinovna asks," said Slava. "If that is what you wish, then I will ask it, and she will agree. Come back to Krasnograd with me and help me raise our daughter. Because, while I may be the most well-cared for woman in all of Zem', I will also be surrounded by enemies, ill-wishers, and, it seems, imported as well as home-grown curses, and Darya will be doubly so. We could use your strong right arm at our sides."

For a moment Slava could see desire rush to Oleg's face, as he pictured the life she had offered him. But then, with bitter clarity, she could see him crush it.

"I can't," he said, looking at the ground to avoid looking at Slava, but she could still see by the set of his shoulders that what he meant was *I'm afraid to*. If he had really wanted to, Slava was certain that all the leshiye in the world wouldn't have stopped him from coming to Krasnograd, and—judging by the eyes of the leshiye standing around them—they might not even have tried.

But there was no need to put that to the test, because she could read in his eyes, his shoulders, his whole body, that Oleg was terrified of coming to Krasnograd and being mixed up in this "women's business," at least not until next year, and not until he was sure he could leave again a free man. Slava had never thought to see him afraid, but she could see that, now that the prospect was facing him squarely, he feared Krasnograd and the bondage of being "her man" and possibly even being happy more than any pangs of separation and remorse. Because his idea of happiness was, just as it was for so many others, nothing more than the slender branch of his own satisfied desires, and that branch was already breaking.

She remembered what the cold wind had said, how others would use her and then turn away from her in dislike after they were done with her, and she wondered how much of that weakness was guiding Oleg right now. She would have liked to say none at all, but just then she couldn't be sure of that. She wondered what he would have done if Slava had been facing, not comfort and safety upon her return to Krasnograd, but cruelty and danger, and she couldn't help but suspect that he would have run just the same—after all, he had not offered to come with her when he had thought she might be leaving him to go to a dark fate, only expressed regret at the necessity for his absence.

For a moment she thought she might choke on her own indignation at this revelation of faint-heartedness, but then she swallowed it down. After all, what else could she have possibly expected from him? His courage was the courage of fearlessness, not conviction. He too, just like everyone else around her, was mired in the way things seemed to be, and was too afraid to change them. He might have taken on a few unpleasant tasks for her sake, but only a few. The heaviest burdens she would have to carry by herself, and no amount of word-magic could induce him to shoulder so much as an extra ounce of her troubles.

"I know you can't come," she said. For a moment it looked as if he were about to say something, to offer some sort of excuse or justification, but she cut him off by saying, "Then there is nothing more to be said."

For a moment she felt another twinge of unease, and she wondered if she should put her foot down and insist. If she really did bear a child, then—despite all that she had just said to allay Oleg's and her own fears—she really would be surrounded by enemies and ill-wishers, not to mention curses, and she really would need, or at least like to have, someone's strong right arm at her side, and Oleg's was probably better than most.

She looked at his hunched shoulders, and saw that he was still poised for flight, and flight in the opposite direction of both Krasno-grad and her. She could also see that he was already rewriting their whole conversation in his head into something that made it impos-sible for him to have accepted her offer. She could see that he had already formed his opinion of his options, and, ill-founded as it was, she would have a great deal of difficulty in disabusing him of his con-fused and frightened notions, if she could have any success at all. She thought again of putting her foot down and insisting, but an even stronger twinge told her that the only thing worse than letting him go would be to make him come with her.

"Enough standing around in the cold: we should leave," she said.

"I really will come next year," he said, looking up her as if he re-ally meant it. She wondered how many different moods a man could go through in a single morning. Surely Oleg had already managed to go through them all. She had to suppress a sigh, or perhaps tears, or perhaps the desire to shout at him to make up his mind. None of that would do any good anyway. Either he would come next year, or he wouldn't, and in any case, he wasn't coming now. It occurred to her that right now he was the one in need of her mercy, and that she must give it to him, but not too much, because what he needed right now was a gentle guiding hand, not the turned back or the firm shove she longed to give him. If she hadn't been standing where she was just then, she would have shaken her fists at the sky, or perhaps laughed heartily, over the quandary she had been placed in. How could she help them both without crushing him in the process? She wondered if taking his hand and stroking it gently would be the right thing to do. It was what she wanted to do.

"Come, Krasnoslava," said the leshaya with the golden eyes, stretching out its branches at her. Slava climbed down from the porch before she could do anything very wise or very foolish.

"I will be waiting," she said, looking back up at Oleg. Now his hand was too far away to take, and she wished it were in her own, but she could see that throwing herself at him right now would frighten him away, as if he were a beaten dog who didn't know whom he could trust. Even so, she still, selfishly, wished she had taken his hand, even if only for a moment. It might be the last moment she had with him. She squelched that thought firmly. "But not for too long," she added. "I do not have all the time in the world, as you do." The leshaya swept her up in its branches, and within a few breaths she was carried out of sight of the cabin and everything else.

Chapter Eight

"**W**omen are strange," said the leshaya after a little while. "And so are men. How long would you have stood there, if we had not taken you?"

"A long time, probably," said Slava.

The leshaya, flanked by many more of its kind, strode along in silence for a little while longer, and then said, "Yes, Gray Wolf said it would be best to take you away as quickly as possible. The world of women is strange. Let us hope our plan works. Let us hope enough of the power of the gods has passed into you."

"I felt it," Slava repeated.

"Let us hope it was enough. The ways of women are strange. The gods' youngest daughters are also the most difficult to manage. Let us hope it was enough."

Privately Slava thought that any child of hers—and, judging by Olga, any child of Oleg's—would be difficult to manage indeed, and that the gods were going to be sorely disappointed if they were hoping to plant a puppet in the world of women, but she said nothing of this to the leshaya.

The leshiye moved very fast, and they reached the sanctuary even sooner than Slava had expected. The golden-eyed leshaya set her down by the front gate, which was open.

"We will be watching over you, Krasnoslava," it said. By the time Slava had made it to the sanctuary porch and looked back, the leshiye had disappeared into the trees.

Sister Alyona let her into the sanctuary silently, but with a curious look on her normally impassive face. Vlastomila Serafimiyevna, who must have somehow been alerted to her arrival, came hurrying up while Slava was still taking off her outer clothes.

"Were you...successful?" asked Vlastomila Serafimiyevna, with more animation and less calm than Slava had seen in her before.

"Yes," said Slava, hanging up her coat.

"Here...let me..." Vlastomila Serafimiyevna helped Slava out of her shawl and hung it up for her. "Let me look at you." She took Slava's face in her hands and turned it this way and that. "Yes...I think I can see the signs..."

Slava blushed hotly, thinking that Oleg must have left marks from his kisses on her.

"I can see the inner glow..." continued Vlastomila Serafimiyevna. "The mark of the gods..."

"Oh," said Slava, relieved.

"Come, Slava, you must be hungry." Vlastomila Serafimiyevna took her by the arm and led her, not in the direction of the main room, but to a small chamber that must have been her private room. She sat Slava down at the small table and started fussing over her about drafts until Sister Alyona appeared with tea and jam and set it down in front of Slava.

"There were leshiye," said Sister Alyona suddenly. "With her." She nodded at Slava.

"Yes...I know, sister...We must pray on this..."

"The others are already talking about it," Sister Alyona told her.

"Then tell them to gather in prayer," said Vlastomila Serafimiyevna with some of her old firmness. "But first bring us food."

Once Sister Alyona had returned bearing bread, and been dismissed to go join the others in prayer, and Slava, who really was very hungry, had started eating, Vlastomila Serafimiyevna sat down across from her and took her free hand. This made it more difficult for Slava to eat, but she could see that Vlastomila Serafimiyevna had a strong need to hold Slava's hand, and so she let her.

"You are sure you were...successful, Slava?" she asked.

"Very," said Slava. She smiled for a moment, provoking an unexpected smile out of Vlastomila Serafimiyevna as well.

"I am glad for you, Slava," she said. "Forgive me...you must think it strange that I presume to know so much about your private business..."

"I assume the gods told you, and probably Oleg Svetoslavovich as well," said Slava, who had been doing a lot of thinking on the walk home in the leshaya's branches, and had put together a number of things that had happened ever since she had first set off from Lesnograd. "He was supposed to...The gods made a plan, didn't they, when the leshiye were unsuccessful in their attempts to take me as their own? They made a plan, and he was the instrument. And they told you about it as well."

"Yes...They spoke to me earlier this winter, when I was at prayer. They spoke to me and said that I would be called upon to render a service to someone who would be called upon to render an even greater service to them, and I would know her when I saw their servant beside her. As I was walking into the kremlin in Lesnograd I caught sight of Oleg Svetoslavovich, and I knew that he was the servant. I know Oleg Svetoslavovich of old, you know. Our families are from the same village, not that my family would be very proud to claim any connection to his. But I know him, and I know what...what was done to him, and I knew he was the servant I was waiting for.

"When I was brought to you, I guessed you might be that person I was supposed to serve...And then Oleg Svetoslavovich told me, on the morning we set off, that the gods had called him to go with us, they had laid a heavy duty on him, and he begged me to take him with you, so I did. And then, the first night you were here, I had a dream...I saw what the nature of the service you would be called upon to perform was. I knew it was a true dream, and when you came to me and said that you must go to him, I knew that the time had come, and I sent you. You are not angry? Many find service to the gods onerous, and rebel against it. And your service will be heavy indeed."

"No, it will be a gift," said Slava firmly.

"The gods have chosen well, I see," said Vlastomila Serafimiyevna, cocking her head and looking at Slava curiously. "Truly, your mind is strong as well as your gift."

"The gods had no choice, as I understand it," said Slava. "Is that not what is said about my gift? It is of the world of women. Neither magic nor prayer can control it. Which means that it is to the world of women that I must return, Vlastomila Serafimiyevna. I thank you for your hospitality and help, but I must return to Lesnograd, where I am needed."

"Tomorrow," said Vlastomila Serafimiyevna. "Return tomorrow, when you are rested. And it is already too late for any of the sisters to set out and return in a single day, anyway."

"Very well," said Slava. "Tomorrow."

"And in the meantime we will pray for guidance," said Vlastomila Serafimiyevna. "Perhaps the gods will speak to us, and if they do, we will share with you the wisdom that we gain."

"That would be welcome," said Slava.

"I am glad," said Vlastomila Serafimiyevna. She released Slava's hand and stood. "Once you are finished eating, you should return to your chamber and rest."

"No doubt you are right," said Slava politely, hiding her smile at the way Vlastomila Serafimiyevna was mothering her. She suddenly thought of how everyone fussed over women with child, and realized with horror that this was the fate awaiting her, only more so. She probably wouldn't be able to stir a step for the next nine months without someone hovering anxiously over her, demanding to know how she felt...she'd be lucky if she were allowed to feed herself.

That, Slava thought to herself, would be very unpleasant, but it also solved the problem of when to tell Olga, which she had been worrying over all morning. Clearly no one could know until she was on her way back in Krasnograd, or they'd never let her leave Lesnograd. For a moment Slava worried that she was being much too lightminded about this. After all, people fussed over women with child for a reason. She *should* be taking care of herself, she knew. And she *would*, she told herself, and she would start by not allowing anyone to bully or harass her into agreeing to anything she didn't want to.

"Actually, I am not tired at all right now," she said, also rising. "And so with your permission, I would like to copy out those scrolls I looked at yesterday. They might still be of use to me."

"The scrolls?" repeated Vlastomila Serafimiyevna. "You think so?"

"I do," said Slava. "That was why I came here, after all."

"The will of the gods called you here, Slava," said Vlastomila Serafimiyevna. She smiled slightly. "Although I believe their pretext was for you to consult with the sorceresses."

"Yes..." said Slava. "I suppose I should at least try to speak with them..."

"Unfortunately, they all left during the night," said Vlastomila Serafimiyevna. "You were not the only one who heard the will of the gods. The sorceresses were tainted by their association with Princess Severnolesnaya and the curse; they could not have remained here once you returned without endangering you and your...task. I did not even have to ask them to leave: they took off of their own free will, as soon as it became clear that you would not be returning last night. So you will have to go seeking your magical answers elsewhere. If you still have questions, that is."

"I think most of my questions have been answered," said Slava. "Which is why I want copies of those scrolls."

"Well, in that case, very well. Sister Marfa will assist you."

Sister Marfa turned out to be the library-keeper. She showed up shortly afterwards and led Slava off to the library, clearly delighted with her task.

"They say you've been called to render a great service to the gods, sister," she said as they walked along.

"So it seems," said Slava.

"Well, may they watch over you, sister, may they watch over you. Serving the gods is a blessing, but it's also a curse, if you know what I mean. Sometimes they lay a heavy burden on you, and you must carry it and carry it, you can't put it down. I hope I'm not frightening you, sister."

"Not at all," said Slava. "No doubt you are correct."

"Do you think your service will be a burden, sister?" asked Sister Marfa, looking up at Slava with suddenly sharp eyes. Slava could see that Sister Marfa was dying to know the exact nature of her service—although she seemed by the look in her eyes to have a pretty shrewd guess—as well as trying to read Slava's nature in the bargain, and that she was much quicker than someone might think on first glance.

"I think it will be a gift," said Slava. "Although some gifts can be very heavy to carry, it is true. But I am not afraid."

"And rightly so, sister, rightly so. There's no use in fearing anything the gods give us, for it won't do any good—we'll get it just the same. Ah, here we are. The copying materials are in this desk. I kept the scrolls set aside, in case you wanted to see them again. Do you think you'll need any help, sister?"

"I think I will be able to manage on my own," Slava assured her. "Do not let me keep you from your prayers."

"Ah, thank you, sister, you're so thoughtful..." and Sister Marfa scurried off, apparently eager to return to the others, probably in hopes that more would be revealed about Slava's service. Slava supposed it was no secret where she had been last night, and that even if the gods remained stubbornly silent on the subject, soon enough every sister in the sanctuary would be able to figure out on her own what Slava had been up to and exactly what service she was rendering the gods. That was, Slava had to admit to herself, mortifying, but as there was nothing she could do about it, she decided to put it out of her mind as much as possible.

Despite her desire—both professed and actual—to copy the scrolls, she spent a little while wandering around the room restlessly, wondering where Oleg was and what he was thinking. Such a pointless subject for her thoughts, she knew, but she couldn't help it. She wondered what the sorceresses who had left in the night thought of her, whether they resented the trouble she had unwittingly caused them...She wondered how much danger they really posed her...It rather seemed that her family had no need of outside curses when they were so efficient at bringing down harm on their own...She had slid so smoothly through the forest, bearing the evil within her even before she had come here...Slava's sister's face was both angry and delighted as she heard the news, and Slava couldn't tell what her true feelings would be...She jerked back awake from where she had dozed off.

Somehow she had ended up sitting at the copying table, and was in danger of falling asleep with her face in the scrolls. Her breasts itched from Oleg's beard. She wished she could take a steam, but even if the sisters would agree to heat their bathhouse for her, she didn't want to take the trouble of seeking them out and asking them. She pictured the looks on their faces if she said she needed to bathe...much too knowing...Intolerable, and it would probably only get worse...She sighed and decided to focus on the matter at hand. There was nothing she could do about the rest of it anyway.

She spent much of the day copying out the scrolls, including portions that were not directly of interest, as a way of avoiding the sisters as much as possible. By evening, though, there was no escaping the supper table. Slava toyed with the idea of making use of her privileged status and asking to be served in her room, but quickly rejected it and made herself go to the common room instead. There was the lengthy period of prayer—Slava would have thought they would have long grown tired of praying, and would want to cut this prayer short, but no such luck—and then Vlastomila Serafimiyevna made a short speech about how grateful they were to have Slava as their guest, much to her embarrassment.

All the sisters stared at her in rapt fascination as she ate, which quite put her off her appetite. By the looks on their faces, she would bet that they had already guessed everything, and their devout admiration was mixed with the much more human curiosity about all matters pertaining to love. Slava wished she weren't so shy, especially about such matters. She supposed she would have to get over that in the coming months, as the court at Krasnograd would be even more curious, and much less reserved in asking about it, than the sisters. No doubt she would be pressed for a detailed description of Oleg, as well as the precise configuration of their bodies at the moment of conception...At which point she would have to admit she couldn't be sure, they had tried so many...Suppressed laughter made her choke on her bread, provoking a stir of consternation at the table.

"It's nothing," Slava assured them once she had recovered. "Nothing to worry about."

"You don't think you are taking ill, I hope?" Vlastomila Serafimiyevna asked anxiously.

"No, I was just laughing," Slava told her.

"Laughing?"

"At the thought of my sister's face when I tell her the news," said Slava.

"Ah." Vlastomila Serafimiyevna nodded understandingly, and her mouth twitched in a smile. "It will be unexpected, I take it?"

"Very unexpected, although she's been urging me for years to... Well, you know."

"No doubt she will be pleased, then."

"Let us hope so," said Slava, who was privately full of doubts. Despite all her urging of Slava to take a lover and get a child off of him, Slava wasn't sure how pleased her sister would actually be when she discovered that Slava had followed her advice, especially when she discovered just what kind of child Slava had gotten off of just what kind of lover.

Vladya's desire for Slava to bear a child had always struck Slava as yet another aspect of her desire to make Slava her miserable slave, thereby preserving Vladya from any contemplation of her own enslavement to misery. She remembered her half-dozing dream of earlier in the day. Although she was no foreseer, Slava suspected the dream meant that there would be scenes in her future, once her sister found out what she had been up to. Well, Slava said to herself, her sister would just have to learn to be happy about it. It would be good for her.

Unsurprisingly, Slava found herself growing extremely tired after supper, and immediately after lying down, fell into a deep dreamless sleep in which she was bathed in a golden glow.

She awoke the next morning feeling rested and...she couldn't find the words for it at first...happy. Yes, happy, even content, and, what was even more surprising, brave. Or rather, unafraid. She had no fear of whatever stood before her. She spent a moment imagining her return to Lesnograd, what everyone would say, the journey back to Krasnograd, what everyone would say, the birth of the baby—that was always said to be bad—what everyone would say, the growth of the child with golden eyes, what everyone would say...

"Well, they'll just have to stop saying it," Slava said to herself, and got up.

The morning prayers seemed less lengthy than before, and Slava really did try to pray in them, too. For a moment it even seemed as if she had been heard. Then she said goodbye to Vlastomila Serafimiyevna, who told her the sanctuary would always be open to her, whenever she found herself in the North, passed on her thanks to all the sisters, and climbed into the waiting sleigh, driven once again by Sister Alyona.

A clear blue sky was already shining through the trees as they set off.

"Spring will be here soon," said Sister Alyona. "It grows light so early now."

"Yes," said Slava, and that was the extent of their conversation, all the way back to the gates of the Lesnograd kremlin. Slava tried to give Sister Alyona some money for her troubles, but Sister Alyona refused.

"For the sanctuary, then," said Slava, thrusting the coins into Sister Alyona's hand once again.

"We take nothing from the world, sister," said Sister Alyona.

"But the world takes from you, sister," Slava said back. "Do you not sometimes have people come to you for sanctuary?"

"All the time, sister," said Sister Alyona, this time with a faint smile. "We are a sanctuary, after all."

"Then this is for them. I am sure that many of them cannot contribute much—after all, I didn't."

"True enough, sister," said Sister Alyona, still with a faint smile on her thin lips. "At least for the moment. Thank you. May the gods watch over you."

"And over you, sister," said Slava, not bothering to say that the gods seemed unable to let her out of their sight. Sister Alyona must have guessed her thoughts, though, or been thinking along the same lines, for she added, "Their reach is short in Krasnograd, sister. Take care."

"I will," Slava promised, not sure whether to feel relieved or worried that the gods' reach was apparently so short in Krasnograd. She was about to say more, to thank Sister Alyona again, when guards came out of the gatehouse and demanded to know who they were and what they were doing, loitering in front of the kremlin gates.

Unfortunately for them, they said all that and only then saw Sister Alyona's sanctuary robes, which threw them into such confusion and embarrassment that they didn't know what to say when Slava asked to be taken directly to Olga. Slava could see that they wanted to say something impudent to her, in order to make themselves forget their own confusion and embarrassment, but were afraid to in case she turned out to be another priestess, or worse yet, a person of importance. They settled for telling her that they would have to announce her arrival to the kremlin stewardess, who would decide whether or not to pass on her name to Olga Vasilisovna, who would decide whether or not to speak with her.

"I am glad to see you take your duties so seriously," said Slava, with an encouraging smile. "It must be a great responsibility, being a gate guard."

"Oh it is, girl...aunty..." the guard stumbled a bit over what to call Slava, who was of an awkward, indeterminate age for that sort of thing, but when she continued to smile at him encouragingly, he regained his courage and boasted all the way from the gate to the front hall about his duties. By the time he left Slava in the hands of the kremlin servants, he was clearly feeling much better about himself and had forgotten all about his earlier embarrassment. Slava made sure not to smile at him until he was out of sight.

When the serving girl whose duty it was to wait in the front hall and greet visitors demanded to know who Slava was and what she wanted, Slava told her, "Please tell Olga Vasilisovna that Slava has returned," which first brought nothing but disdain, until the girl remembered that Olga Vasilisovna had arrived with an important guest, who had left a few days ago, but was now back, and that the important guest was said to be the Tsarinovna herself, unlikely as such a wild rumor seemed. Nonetheless, the mere possibility caused the serving girl to jump out of her seat and bow down to her boot tops, just in case, before scurrying off to announce Slava's arrival to someone else, in order to get rid of the responsibility as soon as possible.

It took a surprisingly long time for someone to come fetch Slava and bring her to Olga. Her escort was an older, steadier serving woman, but despite her age and experience, she appeared to be quite shaken. At first Slava thought she herself must be the cause of the other woman's unease, but by the time they had started up the stairs towards the bedchambers, the other woman had begun unburdening herself to Slava, as people were so in the habit of doing. And a good thing, too, for by the time they reached Olga's bedchamber, Slava had discovered what she would be walking into.

It seemed that while she had been gone, Mirik had come to the kremlin demanding to see Andrey Vladislavovich. The latter had, of course, refused to see him, but before being dragged away by Dima, Mirik had managed to let the whole kremlin know that Andrey Vladislavovich had caused terrible trouble by chasing after Mirik's sister last spring, and he had finished by insisting that Olga do something about her husband. This had provoked a terrible scene between Olga and Andrey Vladislavovich, which had thrown the whole kremlin into the greatest of confusion.

"I see," said Slava, when the serving woman had finished telling her tale. "And what does Olga Vasilisovna intend to do about it?"

"I don't know, noblewoman—Tsarinovna, but they say she's threatening to send him back to his mother. The merchants are calling for his exile—they say he'll be a bad influence on their own sons, especially as he's been trying to rule the city in Vasilisa Vasilisovna's stead, which they say now—even though they weren't raising a peep about it a week ago—that they won't hold for at all, they say no good will come of having a man in charge, and rightly so. Andrey Vladislavovich has been screaming and shouting all day—Olga Vasilisovna locked him in his room for his own good—and Vasilisa Vasilisovna fell into such a fit of hysterics that they had to call a healer for her, and Olga Vasilisovna's been going around with a face like thunder, and the merchants and noblewomen have been besieging her night and day—well, it's only been a night and a day, but you know what I mean, Tsarinovna, and in general it's been such an uproar, you can't imagine."

"I am sorry to hear that," said Slava.

"Where is Oleg Svetoslavovich, Tsarinovna? Olga Vasilisovna has been asking for him."

"He did not return with me," said Slava.

"Olga Vasilisovna won't like that one bit," said the serving woman, shaking her head darkly. Fortunately, just then they arrived at Olga's bedchamber, and her shouted "Come in!" to the serving woman's knock spared Slava the need to respond.

Olga did look to be in a thunderous mood, just as the serving woman had said, and her first words on seeing Slava were, "Where's Oleg Svetoslavovich?"

"He did not return with me," Slava repeated.

"The Black God take him! When will he be here?"

"I don't know," said Slava, and then, realizing that was not a very honest answer, amended it to, "He's not coming back. He's gone back into the woods. The gods called him."

"Curse the gods! Cut off their nipples with a rusty spoon! May they wither and die childless! Why did they call him now?"

"He had done what they required of him," said Slava guardedly. Luckily, Olga was too consumed with her own problems to worry about anyone else's, and she only cursed the gods in the most colorful terms before pouring out all her troubles to Slava. It seemed that Mirik had not only spread his story all over the kremlin, but he had gotten his companions—that is, the rest of Olga's men—to spread the story all over Lesnograd, and now half the town was up in arms against Andrey Vladislavovich and demanding his punishment or at least removal.

"It's not that he doesn't deserve it, or that I don't enjoy locking him in his room and listening to his screams of rage," said Olga. "But now is not the time! My mother still lies in her unwaking sleep, Vasya is in no state to assume control, Lisochka is no use, and Vladya is too young. Besides, there's been so much bungling since I was last here, I'm surprised the kremlin doesn't fall down around our ears, and now these rumors of curses and treason...Our rule—our family—is in a delicate state right now, and the last thing I need is more trouble, since it seems that I will have to rule for the moment, whether I want it or no.

"The noblewomen and merchants are on the verge of mutiny, they say that lawlessness and licentiousness are on the rise and this is simply the most flagrant example, soon the peasants will be infected, especially if they don't feel safe in their own villages, and then what will we do...There are bandits in the woods, as we know to our cost—curse Mirik!—the harvest was poor this year, and many other troubles as well. The streets are practically impassable, for example. And as much as I would love to send Andrey back to his mother where he belongs, our relations with Vostochnoye Selo have been strained for a long time, and I fear that this could break our fragile peace, and as much as I would love to give my mother-in-law a good slap, metaphorically speaking, well, and literally too, now is not the time, now is not the time..."

"Let us sit down and plan, then," said Slava, interrupting Olga's breathless tirade before she could become truly hysterical. "Let us put our heads together and plan. Where is Dima?"

"You're right!" cried Olga, seizing on Slava's words gratefully. "He should be planning with us! He has the coolest head of all of us! I was afraid to inflame things more by sending for him, but you're right!" She ran over to the door and called for a servant to send for Dima immediately, and then ran back to where Slava was now sitting at her table.

"When did you last eat?" asked Slava.

"Eat?" repeated Olga. "I don't know. I've been too busy. So much trouble! I'm not cut out to be a ruler."

Privately, Slava agreed, if this was how Olga was going to react to every minor crisis. Olga, who had always been so calm and cheerful in the face of physical danger, seemed to have lost her head completely over this one small affair. Of course, anything involving Andrey Vladislavovich or the rest of her family did seem to make her lose her head, but still...

"You should eat," Slava said firmly. "You're not going to do anyone any good if you faint from hunger. You need a clear head."

"You're right!" And Olga ran back to the door and called another servant—the first had gone off in search of Dima—and sent her down to the kitchens for food.

It took a large supper and many soothing words, as well as the stalwart presence of Dima, before Olga was calm enough to make any kind of a reasonable plan. It seemed that the matter was not actually so black as it had originally been painted to Slava, and that the noble-women and merchants, while unhappy, were not on the verge of mutiny, and that, if they could be appeased over the matter with Andrey Vladislavovich, they could prove to be valuable supporters, and that everything could be brought back to normal with very little trouble on Olga's part. If, that is, Andrey Vladislavovich could be brought back under control.

"You have the perfect pretext to send him back to his mother now..." Slava began, but then, struck by a sudden idea, finished, "But what if we could do something else with him?"

"What, take him back to Krasnograd?" asked Olga sarcastically. "Are you going to take him in like you have all the other strays you've picked up along the way? Let me guess: you feel sorry for him, don't you?"

"Of course I do, but that's not the point," Slava told her. "I mean: what if we could find some better use for him? Something more diplomatic."

"The noblewomen and merchants—and Mirik—are not wrong about one thing, though, Tsarinovna," Dima interjected. "He is a bad influence on others. And what he did was wrong—unkind, surely you can see that—and he deserves to be punished."

"The gods forbid that we should get what we deserve," Slava said. "I do not deny that what he did was wrong, or that he caused harm, but this is still an opportunity we could take advantage of. Is there anything he's good at? Any skill that he possesses?"

"Quarreling, and chasing women, apparently," said Olga angrily.

"I would speak to him," said Slava.

"Why?" demanded Olga. "Why would you subject yourself to that?"

"Why not?" asked Slava. "Perhaps I will learn something of value."

"What could you possibly learn of value from *him*?" cried Olga.

"I won't know until I ask," Slava told her, rising. "It is still early; I will go to him now."

Olga tried to talk her out of it some more, and when she refused to change her mind, turned to Dima for support, but Dima, his head bowed, said that in matters involving Andrey Vladislavovich his heart was too divided to give good counsel, and so Olga let her go, although with many imprecations against Andrey Vladislavovich's character and intelligence.

"If only Oleg Svetoslavovich had come back, instead of running off again!" were Olga's final words. "Why'd you let him go? Couldn't you have influenced him somehow? I know you haven't had a chance to grow truly close to him, not as I'd hoped you would, but you could've if you'd tried! Couldn't you have kept him?"

"No," Slava told her. "It was the will of the gods."

"Well, what do they know! I don't see what task they could possibly have set him, if he ran off without accomplishing anything, and just when we need him the most! No, I suspect he was just leaving us again, just as he always does, he never could be relied upon, he never cared about anyone else, especially the women in his life, no, it was always him, he never could be relied upon for anything..."

Slava left before Olga could finish, sensing that there was nothing she could say to calm Olga down, now that she was dwelling on Oleg's abandonment of her. Slava hoped that Dima would be able to soothe her, although at the moment Olga appeared to be beyond any soothing...Perhaps sleep would overcome her, and she would awake the next morning more refreshed...Slava had to hope so.

And in the meantime she would speak with Andrey Vladislavovich, in the hopes that she could find some tiny shred of sense, of decency, somewhere inside of him, and rescue him from his own stupidity. Slava was aware that she had set herself a hard task, but somehow she had been unable to sit there in silence as Olga criticized him, just as her criticisms had been. Slava had to admit to herself that her previous attempts to bring out Andrey Vladislavovich's better side had met with very limited success, but she still couldn't stop herself from trying.

From Olga's account of his behavior, Slava half-expected to find Andrey Vladislavovich banging on his door and screaming, but when she arrived at his chamber, all was quiet. Two bored guards were sitting outside his door and playing cards. They rose reluctantly when they saw Slava, and at first refused to let her in or even believe who she was. It was only when Andrey Vladislavovich called through the door, "Tsarinovna? Is that you?" that the guards agreed to unlock the door and allow Slava to enter, although it was plain that they still didn't believe in her identity.

"What brings you here, Tsarinovna?" asked Andrey Vladislavovich as soon as she came through the door. "Come to gloat? Or to lecture me some more? They say you are a good person; are you come to remind me of my own lack of goodness?"

Despite his angry words, Slava could see that behind them, he was shaking, and that in another moment he might burst into tears. She also noticed for the first time that his hair had a reddish tint that made it seem like a thin, lank shadow of Oleg's, and that his face, while thin and weak, also bore a resemblance to Oleg's, as if they were many-times-distant brothers—which they probably were, Slava thought. The population was sparse up here in the North, and everyone was probably everyone else's fourth-sister, so to speak.

Part of Slava felt more kindly disposed towards Andrey because of this, but part of her recoiled back for the same reason, and she guessed that perhaps one of the causes of Olga's intense antipathy towards him was that he was a rather sad and pathetic reflection of her own father, something any woman would have a hard time stomaching in a husband, Slava thought. But of course, none of that was Andrey's fault. He stood there by the table, glaring at Slava with sullen resentment and wringing his hands just like Vasilisa Vasilisovna.

"A good person would not come to gloat," said Slava.

"So I bet you're not coming to gloat because you're too good for that! I bet you think such base passions are the lot of us ordinary folk, especially us poor, pathetic, foolish men." His voice rose to a hysterical shriek. "Well, you know what, Tsarinovna, it's true! I'm not above base passions, and I proclaim it proudly! I…I am learning to…to understand the true nature of manhood! To get closer to the earth and the gods—some of us have been talking of that here, did you know that? The sanctuary brothers have been spreading word of such things from Krasnograd and the West all the way even to our barbaric North! We have been talking of freedom!"

For a moment Slava was distracted from Andrey's words by her need to repress the urge to roll her eyes and sigh. It seemed that this nonsense had, just as he had said, spread all the way to Lesnograd. Slava couldn't help but spend a few breaths considering the foolishness of the sanctuary brothers, who, despite their supposedly lofty aims of retirement from the world and contemplation of the will of the gods, for the most part seemed to her to be the same squeamish boys that one encountered every day in Krasnograd.

Probably there were some noble ones mixed in with the others, but so pervasive was the disease of human folly that even a sanctuary provided no safety from it. In fact, anywhere where men were jammed together with no leavening of the good sense provided by their mothers and sisters was no doubt one of the most concentrated sites of human folly in the land…

"We men have feelings too!" Andrey Vladislavovich was saying, trembling slightly with the overflow of his own emotions.

"I can see that," said Slava. "Most men of my acquaintance seem to have feelings in abundance." She thought of adding, *in excess, even*, but refrained for fear of hurting Andrey Vladislavovich's vaunted tender feelings. It was probably a needless precaution, though, as he carried on, his voice rising and rising and his eyes fixed on Slava with a fierce hatred, without actually, as far as she could tell, seeing her at all.

"Tell me," she said, trying to bring his attention back to her, rather than his ugly inner vision of her, "these sanctuary brothers: they wouldn't happen to be hosting foreigners, would they?"

"And what of it!" demanded Andrey Vladislavovich. "Foreigners are people too! From foreigners comes wisdom!"

"No doubt, no doubt," said Slava. "The wisdom of freedom, for example?"

"Yes! And putting aside our backwards ways that are holding us back! We could be...did you know that we could be, we could be living like they do in the West, on the Middle Sea, if only...did you know how wealthy they are? They eat off plates of gold down there!"

"Some of them do," said Slava. "But others..."

"And they don't slave away like we do!" Andrey Vladislavovich interrupted her. "They have slaves to do that sort of thing! That's how they get their wealth, that's how they get their freedom, and we could to! That's what lets them...instead of making men serve in their guards and armies, they have slaves to do that sort of thing! So that men like me can, can live as equals, can be free!"

"Yes, well..." said Slava, who had spotted a rather large flaw in that argument, but Andrey Vladislavovich barreled on, not hearing her at all.

"And after all, if my wife could run off with a lover, why shouldn't I?" he was ranting. "Why should she have all the happiness? Why should I have to be locked up here, wasting away my life with crazy people, with no hope of ever doing anything, of ever seeing anything, of ever having anything worth having, just because my wife couldn't be bothered to do her duty and stay with me? Why? It's not fair! It's not just! I won't even have the honor of fathering an heir, because my daughter, my poor, pathetic, foolish daughter, is not even going to rule Lesnograd! No, Vasilisa took care of that, didn't she? After all those years of not being able to bear the touch of her husband or any other man, of being a dried-up, self-satisfied old stick whose every attempt to bear fruit ended in miscarriage, she suddenly realized that Lisochka was going to inherit the rule of Lesnograd, and so what did she do? She got a child!

"I even think she did as she claimed and got it off her half-wit of a husband. No doubt she was hoping the child would turn out to be a half-wit as well, so she could run its life just as she does her husband's, but as the gods would have it, she got Vladislava instead! Much as I hate Vladislava and everything about her existence, I have to admit, it gives me pleasure to see her set her mother down the way she does all the time! A just punishment, don't you think, Tsarinovna? That Vasilisa, who will never set the world on fire, let's be frank, and her half-wit husband got Vladislava, whom even I have to admit is the cleverest girl this side of the Krasna, even though we all like to pretend that isn't so, that there's something wrong with her…But there's not! A just punishment for all of us, wouldn't you agree, Tsarinovna?"

"A child should not be a punishment," Slava said, once it appeared that Andrey had finished his rant. The sight of so much sorrow mingled with so much stupidity was almost unbearable. She wondered what Andrey Vladislavovich would have been like had he been born a woman. Perhaps even almost tolerable. Sometimes life was such a tragic waste. Sometimes people were born in punishment, even though they shouldn't be…

"But so often they are, Tsarinovna!" Apparently Andrey Vladislavovich had not finished his rant after all, probably driven on by the horrifying knowledge of his own guilt in the production of a punishment-child. "How many parents do you know who wish they'd never had their children, or how many children do you know who wish they'd never been born? I certainly wish Olga and I had never had Lisochka"—Slava didn't know whether it was good or bad that he was admitting it, but she nodded sympathetically nonetheless—"just between you and me, not that it's any great secret, I suppose, and I've no doubt she feels the same way—both Olga and Lisochka, that is, they both feel the same way, I'm sure of it. You have no children, do you, Tsarinovna?"

"Not as of yet," said Slava.

"And you're right to do so! None of us should have been born, Tsarinovna! Look at what trouble we get into, look at what misery our lives bring us! By all the gods, I wish I'd never married!"

"Your mother arranged the marriage, did she not?" asked Slava softly.

"She did, the Black God take her! I hear they're planning to send me back to her, as if I were a...a bolt of cloth that turned out to have a tear in it. Is it true?"

"Nothing has been decided yet," Slava told him gently. "That is why I came to talk to you, Andrey Vladislavovich. I wanted to find out..."

"Why I did it?" Andrey interrupted her. "You wanted to know what I could have possibly been thinking, to go chasing after that girl, with no thought to my own or anybody else's honor or convenience?"

"I think I know why you went chasing after her," said Slava softly. "I know a thing or two about mad passion myself."

"You! Mad passion! What do you know about anything! And women...They talk and talk about love, about passion, but what do they know about it? No, it's all business to them! Women don't care about *people*, they don't care about *happiness*, they don't care about *passion*, they just care about continuing the family line! We—we men, we children—we're just grist to their mill! Just breeding animals on their farms! What do you know about passion?"

"A little while ago—not as far back as I would like it to be, not so far back that I can blame it on my giddy youth—I went chasing after someone too," said Slava.

"You did, Tsarinovna?" Andrey stopped staring inwards at his own unhappiness, and stared at Slava for a moment instead. "Why?"

"Because I thought I couldn't live without him, and I thought he felt the same, or at least, I could make him feel the same," said Slava. Somehow, the fact that she was confessing this to Andrey Vladislavovich, whom she didn't know very well and didn't like at all, made it easier to tell this story, which still made her feel sick with shame and sorrow every time she awoke in the middle of the night and remembered it.

"And, Tsarinovna?"

"I was wrong," said Slava. "I wanted to give him everything I had in my power to give, and all he wanted was...I don't know. I don't think he knew either. He just let me turn his head, but it turned out there wasn't much more to him than his head. No heart, or rather, his heart was small, and it was all filled up with him, there wasn't any room in there for me, I guess. He was...He wasn't a nobleman, he was a bard, wintering in Krasnograd, and he liked the idea of having the Tsarinovna's heart in his hands, but the reality was much less pleasant. It turned out my heart was both heavy and fragile, and the burden was too much for him.

"When he was with me, he was intoxicated by the vision and I became the most wonderful woman in the world to him—I could see it in his eyes—but as soon as I was out of his sight, he began to think of all the reasons why he didn't want to have anything to do with me. He had—I only see this now, or rather, I only let myself see this now, before I always turned a blind eye to it—along with all the good things about him, he had a weakness to his character, so that other people only existed for him if they were in front of him. If they were out of his sight, or if they needed more from him than he was willing to give, they were not people for him at all. So he spun me some pretty tale—he was good at that!—and then disappeared, saying he would be back soon."

"And!?" cried Andrey.

"And he wasn't. So I became worried—because how could he lie to me? I was the most wonderful woman in the world to him, I could see it in his eyes! Something must have happened to him!—and I set off in search for him. I spun my sister some pretty tale too—I am not normally good at that, but that day I was the most silver-tongued bard in all of Zem'—and I set off in search all over Krasnograd after him, and then I found him."

"And!?" cried Andrey.

"In the arms of another woman," said Slava. "He had sung for his supper at a small tavern where I was searching late one night, and the tavern-mistress's daughter had invited him out to the stable afterwards. You can guess why. Only I arrived very late and disturbed them."

"And!?" cried Andrey.

"He told me he was no good for a fine lady like me, a Tsarinovna, that I needed a great prince, and he was destined for nothing more than giving himself to every girl who needed a man and couldn't find a better one, and that I should leave and forget about him." Slava smiled painfully. "I argued, of course. I told him he *was* destined for better things, if only he'd let himself take them, instead of rolling around in the filth like that, and that I'd help if he'd let me, because I saw something great in him, and not only that, I saw that he loved me, and it must be true because my eyes were the mirror that reflected only reality."

"Sometimes our eyes deceive us in matters of love," said Andrey softly.

"Sometimes, yes, but not this time—for if he hadn't loved me, at least a little, he wouldn't have run so far so fast, or thrown himself so hard into the arms of another woman. But even in my madness I had the sense not to say that to him. Instead I begged him to return with me, I told him I would forgive everything, because I couldn't live without him. But he refused, of course."

"Of course," said Andrey. His face was drawn with pain, and just then he looked less like a sulky child and more like a man. "Of course he did."

"Yes," said Slava. "The reality that my eyes reflected was, for once, the better part of his soul, not the baseness I normally see. I wanted him to be a man worth loving, you know, and so I searched out the parts of him that deserved my love. Underneath, you know, he was a good man. I really do still believe it—or rather, I believe that there were good things in him. I still believe in what I saw in there, in his soul, just as I know that some tiny part of him really did love me.

"But it was buried too deep under fear and all the other things that people wrap themselves in, and he couldn't unwrap himself from that cloak. He didn't even want to try, and I didn't want to see that. I was so used to seeing the evil in people that I had almost learned to overlook it. I had grown accustomed to telling myself not to take so much heed of their bad points, their dark sides, because I was tired of seeing it and I was afraid that I would never see anything else.

"So this one time I overlooked all that. I begged and begged him to let me help him, but in the end I saw that he didn't want my help. I may have been the most wonderful woman in the world to him, but he didn't want the most wonderful woman in the world, he wanted to think about how he had let the most wonderful woman in the world slip through his fingers. And of course he didn't think about my pain at all. Even the most wonderful woman in the world was still just a hollow doll to him, something to admire and then discard with no regret except for the effort he had expended on her. I...I could look at him and see a kindred soul, but when he looked at me, he saw...nothing but a receptacle for his own desires. As he made abundantly clear that fateful night."

She shuddered and fought back the bile that threatened to rise in her throat at the memory, even now. "So I ran home and fell ill," she continued, pushing the unhappy words, the hateful, hateful words he had said, the words that still made her want to die, out of her mind. "No, that's not quite right. I ran home and I waited and waited for him to come back to me. I told him I would wait before I left, and I thought—I was so foolish—I thought that he would come to his senses and realize I was right. Then I fell ill. Then, a year later, I heard he was married. He had married some tavern-mistress's daughter—not the one I had found him with, a different one—who, they said, sold herself to travelers looking to buy their men some quick and shameful pleasure...they say it helps keep them under control...to think that a mother would do that to her own daughter!...The West is not the only place where people sell their daughters into slavery! But no matter. That is not the point. The point is that he had sunk so low he would even consider such a thing...Then I fell ill again.

"I thought I had known before everything there was to know about the depravities of the human heart, but I was wrong. So many times I had seen people pretend to be good, when they were rotten on the inside, but this was the first time I had seen someone throw away and trample on their goodness like that, even when I begged them not to. Well, the first time it had touched me so directly. It's a common-enough sight, if you pay attention. I would have helped him, if he'd let me! I would have made him happy, if he'd let me! They say he's lost his talent and taken to drink, that he's crushed everything good he had in him, crushed it and thrown it away! And worst of all—no, I'm afraid I'm not that selfish, the taking to drink is worst of all, but—almost as bad! I was so foolish! I was tired of believing what I saw all the time, for what I saw all the time was so grim, and so I decided to try to see as others did, and I was sorely punished for it—just as they so often are. And every time I think of it, I feel so ill I wish I could just lie down and never get up again."

"So you were right, Tsarinovna," said Andrey. "You couldn't live without him."

"Well, I didn't die, in the end," said Slava. "It turns out it's much harder to die of love than we would like. I did think about it a lot, though." She felt lighter, having told someone all this, after carrying it around in silence for such a long time, but then she remembered that she had come to listen to Andrey's problems, not burden him with her own, and felt ashamed for her outburst. But then she looked at Andrey's face, and saw that she had done the right thing, because by telling him her story she had stopped being a hollow doll for him, and become a person.

"The Black God take singers, eh, Tsarinovna?" said Andrey with a painful smile that matched Slava's. "Why did the gods make them so beautiful? Milochka was the most beautiful girl I'd ever laid eyes on. And she sang so sweetly, too. And she always looked up at me and smiled when she sang. And...well, it was just as you described it, Tsarinovna. Or at least, it felt like that to me. Almost mad with loneliness here, with no one but my vapid, foolish daughter to give me company, I had befriended some of the guards and grooms, and we had taken to going out into the town together. Most of them were coarse and foolish, of course, but I...I had never had any brothers, or any real friends, either, and they were so easy to win over! For the price of a glass of vodka and a word in the princess's ear, they would say they loved me like blood kin. I guess that should have been a warning to me, but I was too infatuated, and so were they.

"And then...a sanctuary brother came, and introduced us to his friend, his new friend from the West, from the Middle Sea...he was the handsomest man any of us had ever seen, and he made us feel... as we'd never felt before. Special and important and powerful, like we could snap our fingers and others would—should!—jump to obey us, and if they didn't, we could—should!—crush them beneath our boots. We roamed all over town together, in larger and larger groups, and soon I could tell that I had...a following, followers loyal to me and not to my mother or my mother-in-law. It was when we were out together that I first saw her in the market, and I was so enchanted I asked her to come and sing in the kremlin, and she did. And I asked her to come again, and she did, and again, and she did. She came and sang for me, just for me, all winter. Whenever she was with me, I felt like I was the most wonderful man in the world to her. For once in my life, it seemed like a woman loved me. I felt like a starving man who'd suddenly had a feast set before him. Do you know what that's like, Tsarinovna?"

"All too well," said Slava softly.

"I was starving, Tsarinovna, starving! Anyone could have had me for a kind word, Tsarinovna, and she gave it to me! But then she snatched it back. She told me there was no point, a prince like me, and married to boot, and a simple village girl like her, and besides, she'd met a man who was closer to her station, who could make her happy, and she wanted nothing more to do with me. I begged her to reconsider, I gave her all the same reasons you did, Tsarinovna, but she refused to listen! She snatched the food out of my hands, Tsarinovna, and left me to starve again! She ran off and left me, and I thought I would die, Tsarinovna, I thought I would die without her! So I ran after her! I couldn't stop myself, Tsarinovna! I couldn't stop myself!"

"And then?" asked Slava softly.

"And nothing! Some of my new friends, one of whom is now guarding my door, helped me go to her village, but she refused me yet again, and then she ran off with her other lover. Well, her only lover. I would be flattering myself grossly if I counted myself as one of her lovers. I was never her lover at all, except in my own mind."

"And?" asked Slava.

"And I fell ill, Tsarinovna, just as you did, ill from a broken heart, and my men brought me back to Lesnograd more dead than alive. I, too, thought a lot about dying, life seemed so joyless without her, but I didn't, alas, I didn't!"

"And the village?" asked Slava. "The villagers? What about them?"

"What about them?" asked Andrey, puzzled. "No doubt they had a good laugh at my expense, that's what."

"But the village! It was burnt to the ground!"

"What!" cried Andrey. "When! By whom?"

"By you!"

"What! Says who!"

"Andrey!" cried Slava. "Why do you think all this trouble has arisen? Not merely because of some singer from some gods-forsaken village! The village was burnt to the ground and all its inhabitants lost their homes and their livelihoods, and they claim it is because of you! Lyudmila's brother has accused you directly—that's why he came to Lesnograd, that's why he came to the kremlin! Not just his sister, Andrey, but the entire village!"

"Burnt to the ground!" repeated Andrey, shocked. "Burnt to the ground! This is the first I've heard of it! I knew that Lyudmila's brother had come and accused me, but I thought...All I heard was that it was about Lyudmila, and I thought it was because I'd gone after her, and she'd run away. I never raised a hand against the village or anyone in it, Tsarinovna, my head for beheading, such a thought never even crossed my mind."

Slava stared at him, also shocked. She examined his face, his shoulders, his whole body for signs of a lie, but found none. Either he was telling the truth, or he believed he was telling the truth. Could he have done it and then, overcome with guilt and remorse, convinced himself that he hadn't? Slava had heard of such cases before, and Andrey Vladislavovich did not possess the strongest of characters. If there was ever a man who could face the truth unflinchingly, he was not that man. But still, that seemed mad even for him.

"Nothing?" she repeated. "You know nothing of this?"

"Nothing!" he insisted. "It's a lie, I swear, Tsarinovna! The villagers...Someone is setting me up, Tsarinovna, someone is plotting against me! As usual! I have enemies everywhere, Tsarinovna! They won't let me have a moment's peace or a morsel of happiness!" His face had gone back to looking like a sulky child's, and the brief moment of communion between him and Slava, which had arisen over their mutual broken hearts, was ended. Once again Slava found herself feeling genuinely sorry for his genuinely sorry situation, while also feeling repulsed and annoyed.

"I will get to the bottom of this mystery," she told him. "I will make sure the truth comes out. And now...Wait!" Slava suddenly remembered her original reason for coming to see him. "However it ends, whatever truth comes out, you may not want to stay here in Lesnograd, Andrey Vladislavovich. You may not even be able to stay here in Lesnograd. You have said you do not wish to return to your home in Vostochnoye Selo, is that right?"

"Right," said Andrey, now looking distinctly sullen again. "Return to my mother's apron strings, a man of forty! Anything is better than that!"

"So where *would* you like to go, then?" Slava asked. "What *would* you like to do, Andrey Vladislavovich?"

"Come to invite me to Krasnograd, like you have everyone else, Tsarinovna?" asked Andrey, and now there was a hint of a sneer on his face. Whatever brief moment of kinship they had shared had been well and truly crushed and disposed of before it could trouble him anymore, and he was once again looking at her as if she were nothing more than a hollow doll, nothing more than a thing whose only worth was in how well it made him feel good about himself at this very moment. Slava told herself she should not be so surprised and disappointed at how quickly he was able to shake off his previous, better feelings, but somehow she was anyway.

"Only if you think you would be of use there, Andrey Vladislavovich," she said. "If Olga Vasilisovna and Vasilisa Vasilisovna consented, you could represent Lesnograd's interests there, especially since Lesnograd is currently experiencing so many...complications."

"Of use! What use is anyone in Krasnograd?"

Although Slava was privately in agreement with him, she was now too annoyed to let him see this, so she asked, "Or perhaps you would prefer to go to a sanctuary?" instead.

"A sanctuary!" he cried in horror.

"They are not so bad," she told him with a smile. "I was just at one myself."

"A sanctuary!" he repeated. "I might as well be buried alive!"

"Well, what do you want, Andrey Vladislavovich?" she asked. "What do you think is your best way out of this situation?"

"It's not my fault!" he said, instead of answering, and Slava could see that he didn't know, because he didn't want to think about it, because he didn't want to be in the situation he was in, and was therefore not going to try to find a way out of it. And some, even a lot, of it was not, as he said, his fault, and Slava did feel very sorry for him when she thought about that, especially the part about him being starving, and how the food had been snatched out his hands before he had had a chance to do more than sample it, but unfortunately that changed nothing.

"That is true," she said. "And I'm sorry you were married off so unfortunately, while you were too young to know any better, and I'm sorry that your wife left you for another man, and I'm sorry you found love with someone who wasn't able to love you back, and I'm sorry that you've been led into this sad state, but I can't change any of that. You can, though. You can change that by doing something about it. Think on it," she said, rising from the table. "Because like as not, you will have to do something, and sooner rather than later. I will attempt to find out the truth of this story about the village being burnt to the ground, but still, you will have to do something. So think on it hard."

He bowed in a way that suggested that everything she had said was too terrifying for him to even contemplate, and therefore he was going to pretend that he had heard nothing of it, and showed her to the door, which the guards opened at her call. She left, still feeling terribly sorry for him, and terribly annoyed.

She returned to Olga's chamber and knocked softly, in case Olga had gone to bed, but Olga was still up and still pacing around the room unhappily, while Dima tried to comfort her and calm her down. Ruling, Slava reflected, did not sit well on Olga's shoulders. Princess Severnolesnaya had been very unfortunate in her daughters in that respect, for neither of them had been born to sit a throne. But there was nothing Slava could do about that.

She told Olga and Dima about Andrey's denial that he had burnt down the village, although she left out the part about him being starving, on the assumption that Olga didn't need to know that and would only react unkindly if she did.

"He's lying!" insisted Olga. "He always was a liar, and he's lying again! He wouldn't know the truth if it hit him between the eyes."

"I think he believes to be telling the truth, at least," Slava said.

"How would you know?" demanded Olga. "He could have worked on your sympathies...that's easy enough to do..."

"Yes," said Slava. "It is very easy to enlist my sympathies. But it is rather more difficult to cloud my vision. And Andrey sincerely believes that he did not have that village burnt down. He insists that he gave up and rode back as soon as he discovered the girl to have left."

"That does seem more in his character..." agreed Olga. "Giving up like that...I'm astonished he managed to make it that far, to be honest. I never suspected him of being capable of doing something so bold."

"Desperation will make anyone bold," said Slava.

"Desperation! What does he know about desperation!"

"Quite a lot, apparently," said Slava. She tried not to look in Dima's direction, but found herself glancing his way despite herself, and promptly wished she hadn't, since he was hunched up with guilt and misery. She felt almost as sorry for him as she did for Andrey Vladislavovich, but once again, there was nothing she could do about that. Nothing, except try to find a solution to their problems. She quickly turned back to Olga, and changed the subject. "But that is not the point. The point is that there is more to this story than meets the eye. We should try to find out what is behind all this."

"We know what's behind all this! My stupid husband's stupid foolishness!"

"There is more," Slava repeated tiredly. "I'm sure of it." But she could see that Olga had no desire to hear anything that didn't confirm Andrey's guilt in her eyes, and arguing with her about it right now would be pointless.

"It has been a long day, and morning is wiser than evening," she said instead. "I think I'll go to bed now. We can return to this with fresh heads tomorrow."

"A wise thought, Tsarinovna," said Dima, straightening up and looking more hopeful.

"Yes, I suppose so," said Olga, still pacing distractedly. "Oh, and what did you learn at the sanctuary? What did you do there?"

"Many things," said Slava. "Too many to tell right now."

"Some other time, then. But it was a fruitful journey?"

"Very," said Slava. She was unable to stop herself from smiling as she answered, but Olga was so preoccupied with her own cares that she didn't notice. Slava left them to go sink into her bed, which rose up around her and refused to let her go until dawn.

Chapter Nine

In fact, she awoke only because one of the nervous serving women whose unenviable duty it was to wake her, woke her up with the news that she was needed.

"What is it? Is Olga Vasilisovna calling for me?" she asked, wishing her head were clearer. She would have thought that the return to civilization would have caused her to be more rested than camping out in the tundra, but instead it seemed to be an excuse for everyone to stay up late and sleep at odd hours, with the result that Slava found herself staggering out of bed at mid-morning.

"Not Olga Vasilisovna, noblewoman..." said the serving woman hesitantly.

"Then who?" asked Slava. But it came out much too sharply, driving the serving woman into such a state that it took some time for her to work up the courage to tell Slava that it was Vladislava who wanted to see her.

"Well, take me to her, then," said Slava, who was dressed by this time. The serving woman cringed back at Slava's tone. Slava suppressed a sigh and forced herself to smile kindly and say a few soothing words, for which she was amply rewarded. The serving woman cheered up immensely and told Slava all kinds of things as she led her to Vladislava's chambers. Most of the gossip was of little interest, but she also let slip that Sonya's second-sister had arrived before first light that morning. At first Slava paid no attention to that particular piece of news, but then she remembered that Sonya's second-sister was a sorceress, and that she and Vladislava had gone to Sonya to find her. So that must be why Vladislava wanted to see her.

And in fact, as soon as Vladislava had finished throwing her arms around Slava and squealing with joy over her return, she cried out, "Guess what! Sonya's second-sister has come! She arrived before first light this morning! Let's go see her!"

"Let's," said Slava. "Is she in the kitchens?"

"Probably. Sonya will be, anyway, and she'll know where to find her."

"Good. Maybe we can have some breakfast as well."

"Have you not eaten yet? Why haven't you eaten yet? Here, take this," and Vladislava thrust a roll left over from her own breakfast into Slava's hand, before rushing off without bothering to see if Slava was following her.

Slava jogged briskly down the corridors after her, attempting to eat the roll at the same time, but with only moderate success. Every now and then Vladislava would glance over her shoulder to tell Slava something and to cry, "Let's go! Let's go!" before dashing off even more quickly than before. She was, Slava could see, desperately keen to see Sonya's second-sister.

The kitchen was full of what seemed to Slava to be chaos, as all the cooks and servants were cleaning up after breakfast and starting on dinner, and it took them a while to find Sonya, who was mixing dough with an air of steely determination and muttering something under her breath about people who ordered pies as if they just appeared out of the clear blue sky. On catching sight of Slava and Vladislava, she nodded in the direction of a corner, before returning to her dough and her muttering.

In the corner sat a short, round woman with a strong resemblance to Sonya, except that Slava couldn't see her muttering to herself about people who ordered pies as if they just appeared out of the clear blue sky. She seemed more like someone who would make pies appear out of the clear blue sky, probably raining them down on the other person's head. She was sitting and watching the commotion with a look of amused indifference, and drinking tea with an expression that showed she knew the tea had caused someone trouble to prepare, and she didn't care.

"You're Sonya's second-sister!" said Vladislava.

"Anastasiya," said Sonya's second-sister, bowing without rising from her seat.

"I'm Vladislava, and this is Slava. She's a Tsarinovna," said Vladislava.

"Yes, Sonya told me about you," said Anastasiya, this time getting up to bow, although without too much concern about appearing respectful. "She said you were looking for sorceresses. It seems like everyone is looking for sorceresses these days. Every herbwoman, every priestess, every hunter and tracker, and now my very own second-sister—they're all looking for sorceresses, and all for the little princess here and, they say, the Tsarinovna herself. Well, one of them. The one who counts. So tell me, little princess—oh, and Tsarinovna—" she raised her eyebrows at Slava—"why are you looking for sorceresses?"

"Why does everyone call me 'little princess'?" complained Vladislava. "I wish they wouldn't! At least not strangers."

"Because you are little and a princess?" suggested Anastasiya, smiling a smile that was almost kindly and amusing but also, Slava couldn't help but note, a trifle mocking and arrogant.

"Do they call you 'little sorceress'?" asked Vladislava, giving Anastasiya a look that showed the arrogance had not passed her by unnoticed. "Because you're little and a sorceress, you know."

"No, they don't," said Anastasiya calmly. "They call me Anastasiya, because that is my name."

"Well, in that case, call me Vladislava! That's my name, you know!"

"Not Vladislava Vasilisovna?" asked Anastasiya, still with that annoying smile on her face.

"Only if you want to," said Vladislava, annoyed.

"I like to see a girl with spirit," said Anastasiya. "They're so rare. Most of the girls who come to me are nothing but sheep."

"Yes, I'm sure they are, but *I'm* not a sheep," said Vladislava, still annoyed. "So don't treat me like one! We have questions for you, and we want answers!"

"And you don't think you need to be more polite to me?" asked Anastasiya, raising her eyebrows again.

"Would it help?" demanded Vladislava.

"Flattery and smooth talking often do."

"I don't want answers from someone who needs flattery and smooth talking! They'd just give me flattery and smooth talking in return!"

"True enough—Vladislava. Don't you agree—Tsarinovna?" Anastasiya nodded in Slava's direction.

Slava did her best to smile at Anastasiya enigmatically, which seemed to work, for a little of Anastasiya's arrogance slipped off her face. Slava waited for a moment, and then said, "Perhaps we should go somewhere more...quiet?"

"More private, you mean?" said Anastasiya, some of the arrogance returning to her face.

"If you wish." Slava was about to ask if that would inconvenience Anastasiya, and apologize for even suggesting something that might inconvenience her, but stopped herself. Anastasiya looked like the kind of person who would take that to be weakness. Anastasiya, Slava reflected, looked like someone who would be trouble to deal with.

"I haven't finished my tea yet," said Anastasiya.

Slava smiled to herself.

"You find that amusing?" demanded Anastasiya.

"I find it amusing that half the people in Lesnograd are so afraid of me they can hardly speak in my presence, and half the people forget who I am," said Slava.

"And that isn't to your taste, is it—Tsarinovna?" demanded Anastasiya.

"Just amusing," said Slava. "I'm sure we can have tea for all of us sent up to my chambers. Shall we go?"

And, somewhat to her surprise, Vladislava and Anastasiya both followed her meekly out of the kitchen and back to her rooms.

Anastasiya was querulous and uncooperative until the tea arrived, accompanied by rolls. Then she was still querulous and uncooperative, but her mouth was occupied with other things. She must, Slava thought, be a trial to the other sorceresses.

"You're smiling again—Tsarinovna," said Anastasiya, with the voice of someone who is very certain and very satisfied with her own cleverness.

"I was just wondering why you came," said Slava. "Why you came back, that is. To Lesnograd. Since they say that all the sorceresses have placed a curse on the old princess."

"I don't do what I'm told," said Anastasiya.

"Yes," said Slava. "But..."

"But what? You want to say that you told me to come back?"

"Well, we did ask," said Slava. "Although 'tell' might be too strong a word."

"I couldn't stand it there anymore," said Anastasiya. "Too boring, too many sheep."

"Really?" said Slava, looking interested. This was all it took for Anastasiya to pour out a lengthy complaint about the Sisters of the Wolf, in whose sanctuary some of the Lesnograd sorceresses had taken refuge upon fleeing the city. Anastasiya then followed it up with a lengthy speech on their mistreatment by the old princess, and how delighted they all were at the misfortune that had befallen her, which allowed Slava to look even more interested, in a harmless sort of way—while thanking the gods that Vladislava had the sense to be quiet during this outpouring—which prompted Anastasiya to spill out everything about her involvement in the old princess's scheme.

Anastasiya was, Slava quickly realized, almost as clever as she thought she was, and a great deal lonelier than she would like to admit, and like most such clever and lonely people that Slava knew, found the force of Slava's sympathy to be irresistible, and told her all kinds of things that she probably never would have breathed to another soul.

"The old princess has been scheming for years, but this past year it's gone to her head, she started demanding more and more from us, as if we were her servants, as if magic were her servant, she had all sorts of plans and schemes, some of them that any other woman would have been ashamed of if she'd thought about it for half a breath," said Anastasiya hotly. "She's been hiring every sorceress she can get her hands on, and then driving them away with her demands and her schemes, as if we wouldn't talk about it! As if we didn't know she was up to something! But every time someone displeased her, she'd send them away, and hire someone else, and...I'm surprised the Tsarina hasn't come for her already! Gossip must have spread all over Zem' by now, with all the sorceresses she's taken in and sent away in the past year!"

"Really?" said Slava, leaning forward just enough to show Anastasiya her interest without frightening her. So this must have been how Princess Primorskaya and Princess Malogornaya had gotten their suspicions...

"Yes, and you know what she did? You know what her first trial was? She wanted to try cursing people, and you know whom she cursed first?"

Slava merely widened her eyes and smiled, which was all Anastasiya needed.

"Her own son-in-law! Andrey Vladislavovich! He used to be her pet, but of late she'd turned against him, he started getting too hard to manage, he was taking more and more over the running of Lesnograd as she spent more and more time on the magic, which was making her mad, she didn't want him running things even though she wasn't doing it herself, and so she decided to see if cursing would work by trying it out on him!"

"Oh!" said Slava. "How terrible!"

"Yes! I didn't cast the curse—I refused to have anything to do with anything of that nature, but I heard from the one who did that he was supposed to suffer from his greatest desire. The old princess wasn't sure if it would work—she said she didn't think he had any desires, he was too much of a weak character for that—but they talked her into it, they told her that everyone has desires, even if they aren't very strong, and she agreed, and apparently it worked, although I didn't see any sign of it, but they say he ran off last spring, and now they say he's locked up, he's in terrible disgrace, so it must have worked."

"Yes, it must have," Slava agreed. "I wonder how it worked? I mean, did it work directly on him, or did it work on others?"

"Curses work the easiest way, like water running downhill," said Anastasiya. "And they take the form their victims give them. They get their power from the evil already within their targets. They love fear and jealousy and envy and vanity—especially vanity. It could have worked directly on him and on everyone around him, too, at the same time. I don't know. What happened to him?"

Slava debated for a breath whether telling or not telling Anastasiya the story would be more distracting, but decided that not telling her would be worse, and so gave her a brief outline of Andrey Vladislavovich's story, including his denial of having brought any harm to the villagers, in case Anastasiya could bring any enlightenment to that part of the tale.

"You see!" said Anastasiya triumphantly. "Vanity! Vanity made the girl go after him, and vanity made the other man go after her, and vanity made her leave him, and vanity made him go after her, and probably vanity made one of his men burn down the village when they failed."

"Yes," said Slava. She thought that was probably too simple an explanation, but instead of arguing, said, "Vanity is a terrible vice."

"Yes, and the old princess had more than her share of it!" said Anastasiya, which was just what Slava had hoped she would say, because it launched Anastasiya into more stories about the old princess.

"But she got her comeuppance in the end, didn't she?" said Anastasiya. "Stricken down just as she was trying to cast her biggest curse. Of course she couldn't wield any magic on her own, but she liked to think she could, or that she was helping just by being there, anyway, so she always insisted on being in the room whenever any of us were doing anything, troublesome as that was, she wouldn't take no for an answer, and so of course she was there when they were trying to cast a tricky and dangerous spell, and we see how that turned out, don't we? I wasn't there, of course, I wouldn't have anything to do with it, the others knew better than to ask me to take part in something like that, they know I won't soil my hands with that kind of thing, but they've talked of nothing else since then, and of course I knew more or less what they were doing at the time, too. They were trying to curse Krasnograd—the Imperial family, that is—but that's a dangerous business, Krasnograd and its family are protected by powerful spells of their own, even if it's down in the South, but they were trying to curse Krasnograd, only they say that instead a cold wind rose up and spoke to them, and the old princess collapsed in a fit, and that was the end of that spell, wasn't it, and good riddance! They still don't know whether the curse worked, though—maybe it took effect anyway, they can't tell yet."

"How will they know?" asked Slava.

"Well, they say the Empress was supposed to be betrayed by the person closest to her, so I suppose if we hear of any betrayals, we'll know."

"Did they say how this betrayal would manifest itself?" asked Slava.

"That's the thing with curses, you can't know beforehand. They run downhill, just like water. Who knows what the Empress would consider betrayal? It wouldn't have to be something so simple as selling secrets to an enemy, you know, it could be something else—something someone in her family or her guard did, for example, or betrayal by a lover—who knows? But I heard that it was supposed to be more dangerous than betrayal by a lover. Something that would strike at the very foundations of her rule, that's what the old princess wanted. She never was very fond of the old Empress, the old princess wasn't, but at least she thought she could rule, which was more than she would say for the new Empress, although I don't know—maybe she just doesn't like her because the new Empress refused to grant her more land. The old princess wanted to extend her territories up into the Midnight Land, claim everything up in the tundra, but the Empress said no, and the old princess's taken a terrible dislike to her ever since."

"I see," said Slava.

"Yes, and then there was the terrible fight with Olga Vasilisovna, because she was determined to go, wasn't she? She said she had to go to the Midnight Land, didn't she, and nothing would stop her, and she didn't care whom she claimed it for, her mother or her Empress, so when the Empress said the old princess couldn't have the land, the old princess said Olga Vasilisovna couldn't go, and so what did Olga Vasilisovna do? She went straight to the Empress, didn't she? She went straight to the Empress and she got permission to go and map out the territory for the Empress and not her mother, and you can imagine how that news was received here.

"And then the old princess got the idea of cursing the Empress, she was so angry, she wanted the Empress to suffer like she had, only it didn't work for her, did it? She was struck down instead. Magic isn't a well, you know. You can't just draw from it whenever you want, however much you want to. Magic is a mighty torrent, a raging river, and you step in at your peril. But the old princess didn't want to hear that. She didn't believe there was anything she couldn't control, and magic was just another lapdog for her. Only even lapdogs can bite, if you step on them."

"Yes," agreed Slava. "I wonder..."

"Yes?" said Anastasiya eagerly. She had clearly forgotten her earlier antagonism, and, now that she had poured out everything that was pent up inside of her into Slava, she was feeling kindly disposed to her, almost tender, even. Like a lover, Slava thought to herself, and suppressed a grin.

"I wonder...has anything been done to...to reverse the curse? Is that even possible? I know so little about magic, you see."

"Oh, that's a dangerous business, reversing curses. Well, of course, you wouldn't want to reverse it, because then it would just come rushing back onto you—like damming a flood and having it flood you instead—you'd want to stop it, only it's difficult. Difficult and dangerous. You'd want to dissipate it, you see, spread it out so that it became too weak to have any effect, but like as not you *would* reverse it, you would make it pour right back onto you, which is what must have happened to the old princess, only the question is, did she get all of it, I mean, did the whole force of the curse come back on her, or was there still enough left over to affect the Empress. I guess we'll find out."

"I suppose so," said Slava.

"And now I don't know what I'm going to do," continued Anastasiya. "I can't stay here, none of us can, not till we know what's going to happen to the old princess and what the new princess will be like. Everyone's afraid that the curse will come back on them, you see, and they think that leaving Lesnograd will help protect them.

"Even I—I only gathered some herbs for it, you know, I didn't have anything to do with it at all, not really, but I've only been here a few hours and I'm already thinking that I should leave, I can feel the curse hovering over me, I shouldn't be here. The curse doesn't know that I didn't have anything to do with it, all it knows is the touch of my hand on those herbs, and it's marked me, not as much as those who cast it, of course, but it's still marked me.

"And I can't go to Krasnograd, none of us can, because the curse will be waiting for us there, too. And I can't stay with the others, I can't stand it, we've done nothing but quarrel since we arrived, quarrel and point fingers, and I don't want to have anything to do with that anymore, especially since I didn't have anything to do with the problem, I don't want to be punished for something I didn't do, so I have to leave, and the others don't want me there anyway, I make them feel bad, I'm always reminding them of what they did wrong—and someone should! They should feel bad, and I'm not afraid to tell them that! But I can't stay with them anymore, and I can't stay here in Lesnograd, and I can't go to Krasnograd..."

"Perhaps Pristanograd or Vostochnoye Selo?" suggested Slava.

"You think so? Do you think they'd take me in there? Those Western barbarians—what do they know about magic?"

"Very little, it seems, which means you would be all the more valuable," said Slava. "And Princess Primorskaya would love to take in someone who had been cast off by Princess Severnolesnaya, I'm sure of it. Only I would be careful around her, if I were you. She strikes me as a formidable woman."

"Oh, after Princess Severnolesnaya, I'm not afraid of anyone else, I can assure you," said Anastasiya, cheering up. "Do you really think... Vostochnoye Selo...I suppose I don't have any place better to go." She stood up. "You're right, you know! I should go there. I should leave right away."

"No doubt you are right," said Slava. "I won't keep you, then. Thank you for speaking with me."

"Oh...Of course..." said Anastasiya, obviously already thinking about Vostochnoye Selo. She gave Slava a sketchy bow and left without bothering to thank her for the tea.

"She was very odd, wasn't she?" said Vladislava, as soon as Anastasiya was gone. "She wasn't very polite, was she?"

"No, but she gave us a good deal of useful information," said Slava. "Much more than she would have had she been polite."

"And she was very arrogant, wasn't she? But not very happy."

"Yes," said Slava. "The danger of being very clever, but not quite as clever as you think you are."

"Really?" asked Vladislava, looking impressed. "I never thought about that before. What useful information did she give you?"

"Oh...This and that..." said Slava, unwilling to discuss the curse in front of Vladislava.

"It was about the curse, wasn't it?" said Vladislava, with the look of someone who had been struck with a sudden realization. "But you don't want to talk about it in front of me."

"Well..." began Slava.

"Why don't you want to talk about it in front of me? You'd be much better off talking about it to me than you would to mother, you know, or even Aunty Olya—she doesn't care much for that kind of thing, and she wasn't there, you know, and I was."

"Yes..." said Slava.

"It was even my idea, you know!"

"Yes..." said Slava again.

"Is that why you don't want to talk about it with me? Because it was my idea?" demanded Vladislava.

"Well..." said Slava, wondering how Vladislava could be so quick and so slow at the same time. Although, she reminded herself, the same could be said about her much of the time too. "It is a very delicate business," she said instead. "The fewer people who know about it, the better. And you...you really shouldn't tell people it was your idea. That would be a bad thing for others to know."

"Because it would be dangerous?" said Vladislava, once again with the look of someone who had been struck with a sudden realization.

"Very dangerous," Slava told her. "Especially if it became known in Krasnograd. That would be very dangerous indeed."

"Really?"

"Really," Slava told her. "Although after what Anastasiya said, I'm beginning to wonder how safe Lesnograd is as well."

"Because you think the curse might have come back here, like Anastasiya said? You think...You think it might come back on me, don't you?"

"Possibly," Slava admitted.

"After all, Anastasiya was afraid of it, and she only gathered herbs for it! But it was my idea."

"Yes," said Slava. "I don't know what that means, for curses."

"But Krasnograd might be dangerous for me too, then."

"Yes," said Slava. "I don't know."

"Well, why didn't you ask Anastasiya about it?" demanded Vladislava. "We could go ask her right now, you know—she can't have left yet. She's probably still in the kremlin. She's probably gone back to the kitchens."

"The fewer people who know about it, the better," said Slava. "If she doesn't know about it, we shouldn't tell her. We shouldn't even talk about it. The less said about it, the less likely it will be to come back on us, I would think."

"But she might know something!"

"Vladislava." Slava sat down in front of her and looked at her seriously. "I'm not angry at you—but do you know what you've done? Many would consider it treason, do you know that? So it must be a secret, do you understand? A secret that no one can ever know. Just you and me."

"And grandmother," put in Vladislava.

"Well, let us hope she won't say anything about it either," said Slava. "But, Vladislava, this is very, very important. *No one can ever know*. I don't know if you are in any danger from it returning on you now, but if anyone ever found out about it, you would be cursed for sure, a more terrible curse than you could possibly imagine. Do you understand?"

"I suppose," said Vladislava, squirming slightly in her seat.

"And do you promise never to tell anyone? Do you promise to keep it a secret?"

"I suppose," said Vladislava again, squirming even more.

"I need you to do more than suppose," said Slava. "I need you to *promise*. Do you promise?"

"Yes! I promise!" Vladislava burst out, and then screwed up her face and turned away from Slava.

"Oh..." said Slava, and tried to put her arms around Vladislava, but Vladislava pushed her away.

"I'm not angry with you, you know," Slava told her.

"Yes you are! You hate me, just like everyone else does!"

"No, no, I just need you to promise, that's all. I don't hate you. I'm not angry with you, either. I just needed you to promise, that was all."

"But you were angry with me!" sobbed Vladislava. "I could tell!"

"I'm sorry," Slava told her. "I just needed you to promise, in order to protect you, do you understand, Vladislava? I needed to protect you. And I *will* protect you, just like I promised, only I needed you to promise to help me, that was all."

"Really?" said Vladislava, raising her face and giving Slava a suspicious look.

"Really," said Slava.

"What if you need to protect someone else?" asked Vladislava.

"Like whom?" Slava asked.

"Like...I don't know...What if Lisochka comes with us, and you need to protect her?"

"I can do both," said Slava.

"But what if you *can't*? Or what if...What if you have your own daughters? What will happen to me then?"

"Nothing," Slava promised, trying not to squirm herself.

"I don't believe you," said Vladislava.

Slava considered several possible responses to that, all of them, she could tell, much too angry, before finally saying, "Well, you'll just have to watch me and see. You can remind me if I start to fail."

"That sounds fair," said Vladislava, after thinking it over. "When are we leaving for Krasnograd? Don't we need to go soon?"

"Are you so eager to leave Lesnograd?" asked Slava, smiling.

"Of course I am, but that's not why I asked," said Vladislava, rolling her eyes at Slava's stupidity. "Anastasiya said that the curse could have made its way to Krasnograd by now! Don't we need to be there, in case we can stop it?"

"True enough," agreed Slava. "And there is little holding us here now. I will speak with Olga about this."

"Oh good! I'm going to start packing right away!" And Vladislava, apparently forgetting—although Slava was sure she had not actually forgotten—all about her momentary mistrust of Slava, got up, threw her arms around her, and then left the room, skipping slightly.

Slava also got up and set off in search of Olga. She found her in the Great Hall, with Vasilisa Vasilisovna. Vasilisa Vasilisovna was sitting on the throne, rather uncomfortably, and Olga was sitting beside and slightly behind her in a somewhat menacing fashion. Dima stood in the back of the hall, looking as if he wished he were somewhere else, the tundra for example. He brightened at the sight of Slava, and slipped away from his position in the corner, leaving Olga and Vasilisa Vasilisovna to give contradictory and confusing orders to the poor expedition they seemed to be sending off to investigate Andrey Vladislavovich's and Mirik's opposing claims.

"How goes it?" Slava whispered to Dima.

"Poorly, Tsarinovna," he whispered back. "Olga has many virtues, but patience for the tedium of rule is not one of them, much less patience for the tedium of counseling the ruler. She and her sister have done nothing but quarrel all morning, and in front of their subjects, too. I fear that something bad will happen soon."

"Yes," said Slava. "One reason among many I wish to leave Lesnograd as soon as possible. Which is why I came to speak to Olga, in fact."

"Leave Lesnograd?" Dima brightened up even more. "And do you think Olga will come with you? Do you think she *can* come with you? With the old princess still hovering between life and death, there is no one to rule but Vasilisa Vasilisovna, and it becomes ever more apparent that she is not fit to run a waystation, let alone a vast territory."

"Is Olga any more fit?" asked Slava.

"No," admitted Dima. "But she gives the appearance of being more fit, which is all many people need. At least she *acts* like a ruler, even if her actions are often unwise."

"True," said Slava. "But Vladislava and I need someone to escort us back to Krasnograd. Someone who is not only capable, but of noble birth. We couldn't possibly be entrusted to a party of soldiers—my sister would take it as a terrible insult, and it would be just the excuse she needed to wreak some kind of revenge against the Severnolesniye. Olga may have to take on the duty herself, as there is no one else in Lesnograd capable of doing it."

"True, Tsarinovna, true," said Dima, grinning. The sound of raised voices from the raised dais caused the grin to slide off his face. Both he and Slava looked over, to see that Olga and Vasilisa Vasilisovna had risen from their seats and were arguing vehemently, with no thought of the party of soldiers fidgeting uncomfortably in front of them.

"We should leave soon," said Slava.

"Very soon," agreed Dima.

"I would leave tomorrow, if I could," said Slava.

"As would I, Tsarinovna," said Dima. "But I fear we may be stuck here until they get to the bottom of this mess with Andrey Vladislavovich. If only Oleg Svetoslavovich were still here! He told me before he left only that he had a duty to perform, one that he couldn't put off any longer, and that he had to go. He seemed to be dreading it, as much as a man like him can dread anything. Do you know what that duty was, Tsarinovna?"

"You'll have to ask Oleg Svetoslavovich," said Slava, trying to pretend that she hadn't heard what Dima had said. For a moment she couldn't stop herself from imagining being Oleg Svetoslavovich, and dreading his duty of providing her with a child...Stop, stop, stop, she told herself. He seemed eager enough at the time, however he may have felt about it beforehand. She remembered the look on his face as they had separated, and wondered if perhaps he had dreaded his duty because it would then mean leaving...Best not to think too much about it, she told herself. It was unlikely that Oleg was suffering any particular pangs of longing over her. Probably he was already with Svyatoslav, helping him become accustomed to his new role as the gods' servant, and wasn't thinking of her at all...

"What is it, Tsarinovna?" asked Dima.

"I'm sorry?" said Slava.

"You seemed to be thinking of something very important, Tsarinovna."

"Oh, nothing," said Slava. "I was thinking about how best to leave, that was all. I'll return and speak with Olga about it when she is less...occupied."

"I think that would be best, Tsarinovna," said Dima. "Meanwhile, I will return to my post." He wrinkled his nose in distaste.

"Good luck," Slava told him.

"Thank you, Tsarinovna—I'll need it." He walked reluctantly back to his position behind the raised dais where Olga and Vasilisa Vasilisovna were still arguing—over some incredibly meaningless triviality involving whether the party of soldiers should spend two nights or three in the burnt-down village, as far as Slava could tell—and Slava, thanking the gods that she could slip out of there unnoticed, slipped out of there unnoticed.

Slava did manage to find Olga in a slightly better frame of mind later that day, and broach the subject of leaving, which Olga leapt upon joyously.

"Let's leave tomorrow!" she cried, as soon as Slava mentioned it.

"Will we be ready in time?" Slava asked.

"Well, we don't really have any possessions that would require packing, and the road is comparatively easy from here back to Krasnograd, so we would need few provisions," said Olga.

"It may take slightly longer than that for Vladislava to prepare, and we will have to travel more slowly and carefully because of her... And Vasilisa Vasilisovna may not be ready for us to leave quite yet..." said Slava, trying to think of how to ask Olga if she really thought she should abandon her responsibilities in Lesnograd so soon.

"Who cares about them?" demanded Olga. "It will be good for them not to lean so much on us!"

"And your mother...Still between life and death...She has not woken up for days, has she?"

"Oh, knowing her, she'll probably stay like that for months, and then suddenly get well just when it's most inconvenient," said Olga dismissively.

"And the situation with Andrey Vladislavovich...Is this something we should really leave in Vasilisa Vasilisovna's hands?"

This argument did give Olga pause, and after a moment she conceded, although not with very good grace, that they should wait at least until the party who had been dispatched to the village could return and report.

"Which means we won't be able to leave for another four days at the earliest," she groaned. "Well, perhaps my boys would like to do some training! They've had more than enough time sitting around in inns, flirting with innkeepers' daughters! They're long overdue for a good beating!" And she strode off energetically, leaving Slava to hope that she meant "a good beating" to be a vigorous session of swordplay, and not anything more sinister.

While waiting for the party to return from the village was not to Olga's taste, Slava found it very relaxing. She spent the next few days re-reading the book she had found and the scrolls she had copied, and contemplating what Miroslava Praskovyevna and Lyubov the Kind had meant. She also went with Vladislava to visit Alina Marinovna, who treated them both with kindness, greeted the news of Vladislava's impending departure for Krasnograd with appropriate sorrow and delight, and informed them that she had heard nothing from any sorceresses, except that they all seemed to be fleeing farther from Lesnograd, for "A terrible fear had overcome them," according to her sources.

"I've never heard of the like," she told them. "Sorceresses are many things, but cowards they are not. Normally they go running right towards the things that ordinary women run away from—that's why they're sorceresses. For them to be running away when the rest of us are sitting here drinking tea and waiting for spring is a new thing, I must say. Makes you worry, though. What do you say, Tsarinovna: should we all be fleeing along with the sorceresses? Is some threat heading our way?"

"I think most likely only the sorceresses are in danger," said Slava. "Let us hope the rest of Lesnograd will be passed by."

"True enough, and I can't flee anyway, and neither can the rest of us. It's only sorceresses that travel so light they can drop everything and run whenever they want. Of course, it's only sorceresses that need to drop everything and run all the time. The rest of us know better than to go meddling in things that don't concern us." And with that, Alina Marinovna turned the conversation back to the doings of a niece of hers who was, in her words, "trying to lure in some young man who couldn't make up his mind whether he wanted to be lured or not." This furnished them with an afternoon's worth of conversation, and the terrible fear that had overcome the sorceresses seemed to be completely forgotten.

The next day, when Olga was already fidgeting around the kremlin demanding to know where her scouting party was, even though they were not due back for at least another day, maybe more, their dinner was interrupted with the news that a group of ragged men were asking for Olga Vasilisovna at the city gates. Seizing this gods-given opportunity to get outside, Olga rushed off to interrogate them personally, and returned with the welcome news that the ragged men were, in fact, her own men that she had left behind in Khladniye Vody. Although not completely recovered, they had left as soon as they had found the strength to walk.

"They say there were all sorts of uncanny doings there," she reported. "There was something strange about that girl caring for them, and especially the old herbwoman, and at night, they said, leshiye would walk right by the bathhouse door, they were sure of it, leshiye and maybe other things, as well, even stranger and more frightening. They were starting to think they'd never make it out of there alive, and their healing was going so slow, too, but then a few days ago they woke up one morning full of new strength, and the old herbwoman came to them and said a bargain had been honored and they could leave, so they did. The villagers drove them to the nearest waystation, and then they caught a ride with some merchants, and here they are. I wonder what that bargain was, don't you? Oh, and they asked for their 'Krasna Tsarina.' They said they needed to thank you."

"I'll go now," said Slava.

Misha, Vova, Volodya, Vladik, and Zhenya were all lying in a large room full of small beds when Slava went to them. Although they looked better than the last time she had seen them, they were very thin and weak, and when they rose at her arrival, they did so slowly and stiffly.

"Krasna Tsarina!" cried Misha, but in a voice so weak it made Slava wince.

"Please, sit," she told them. "You have still not regained your full strength yet, I can tell."

"Ah, well, you may be right, Krasna Tsarina, but if you'd seen us a week ago, you'd be singing a different tune," said Misha, attempting to grin as he collapsed back onto his bed.

"Yes, I thought we'd never get out of there, Krasna Tsarina," put in Zhenya. "The healing went so slow, it's hardly worth calling it healing at all."

"But then five days ago we all woke up cured," said Misha. "Well, not cured, Krasna Tsarina, but we could stand. And then Baba Anya came to us and told us we should go, and that we should thank you for holding up your end of the bargain. So thank you, Krasna Tsarina, for holding up your end of the bargain."

"It was my pleasure," said Slava, rapidly calculating. Five days ago...Five days ago she had parted from Oleg. She had to suppress a smile.

"What did you do, Krasna Tsarina, if you don't mind my asking?" said Vladik. "It must have been some powerful magic. Baba Anya seemed to think it was something marvelous."

"It was nothing," said Slava.

"Yes, but..."

"Be quiet, silly, can't you see that's between our Krasna Tsarina and the gods?" said Misha, reaching out and giving Vladik a very feeble swat on the back of his head.

"Really, Krasna Tsarina?" asked Vladik, gazing at her wide-eyed and not even bothering to respond to Misha's assault.

"Misha is right," said Slava. "But I am very glad that you were able to leave Khladniye Vody and return to Lesnograd. I hope your recovery continues to be as speedy as it has been of late."

"Oh, I'm sure it will, Krasna Tsarina, now you're looking out for us," said Misha. "But is it true what Olga Vasilisovna says? You're planning to return to Krasnogorod soon?"

"Yes," said Slava.

"We won't be fit to accompany you, no doubt," said Vladik sadly. "We'll be left behind again, like useless invalids."

"The services you have already rendered have proven your worth many times over," Slava assured them. "We will all be eternally grateful."

This cheered them up considerably, and Slava was able to leave them in high spirits. She returned to her own rooms thinking over what they had told her. It seemed that the gods, or the leshiye, or someone, had been holding them as hostages of sorts, waiting to see if Slava would fulfill her part of the bargain she had made for their healing. Although she had not been informed of that. She had thought that the leshiye, or whomever she had made her bargain with, had already done all the healing they were going to do when the bargain was first struck.

To be honest, she hadn't given the men left behind in Khladniye Vody much thought of late. She felt ashamed of her callousness, but there was nothing she could do about that, other than not tell them. And, she reminded herself, she *had* carried out her part of the bargain, and they *had* been healed, at least enough to leave Khladniye Vody, so she *had* rescued them, even if that had not been her intent. Truly, the ways of the gods are strange, she said to herself. If they had even had a plan, that is. Perhaps they had had no more of a plan than she had, and they were all merely reacting to events, instead of acting upon them. Well, there was nothing she could do about it either way, except hope for the best, she told herself.

It took another two days, by which time Olga was practically beside herself with boredom, for the party dispatched to Mirik's village to return. They sent word from the city gates that they needed to speak with Olga and Vasilisa Vasilisovna directly.

"At last!" cried Olga on receiving the message. They were all sitting at the breakfast table, and Olga and Vasilisa Vasilisovna were arguing over yet another triviality. "Let's go hear what they have to say! Tsarinovna, you should be there too, you know." Which was how Slava found herself sitting on a small stool in the corner of the Great Hall, closer to the blazing fire than she would have liked, and waiting to hear the news from Mirik's village.

The party had returned with an extra member, a stocky, red-faced man with lank hair and an expression of angry defiance. It was quickly discovered that when the party had arrived at the village, they had found the villagers attempting to rebuild it and casting curses against "That nobleman from Lesnogorod" who had done this to them. The red-faced man, whose name was Innokenty, had been casting curses the loudest. When they had questioned him about what had happened, he complained loudly and at length about the death of his wife, which had left him widowed, bereft, and destitute.

"I am the real victim of that nobleman," he had said several times. "I'm the one who lost the most from his cruel, shameless behavior. Where is he? I'd like to tell him what I think of him!"

On further questioning, though, it turned out that his wife had told him the very day of the fire that she was setting him aside for another, and much younger and handsomer, man. Not only that, but Innokenty's wife and new lover were the only people to have died in the fire. The search party had thought this warranted further investigation, and had brought Innokenty back to Lesnograd.

"Oh...What do we do now..." said Vasilisa Vasilisovna at this news, wringing her hands.

"Did you kill your wife and her lover in the fire and blame it on the nobleman from Lesnograd?" asked Olga.

"No!" said Innokenty, drawing himself up proudly. Too proudly, Slava thought. He was lying. She thought about telling Olga of her guess, but couldn't decide if that would be a good idea. What would Olga do...and it was only a guess...and she already disliked him, she could tell, she hated the waves of vindictive selfishness brought on by suffering rising off of him, and she could already see that this story would have no good ending...he was guilty (and how wrong was it that a guilty man should have the name Innokenty?), and they would all be touched by his guilt in their judgment of him...he was cursed, she could feel it, and now they would all be cursed in turn...if, that is, his curse could even get a foothold in amongst all the other curses teaming around them...

"How do I know you're not lying?" Olga asked, interrupting Slava from her thoughts by echoing them disconcertingly. "I don't, of course. Probably you are lying. What do you think we should do with him, Vasya?"

"Oh...I don't know...If he didn't set the fire, then who did?"

"Not I!" cried Innokenty proudly. "And you'd best set your own house in order before accusing innocent men! They say the nobleman who came chasing after one of our girls is husband to the old princess's daughter! I see the kind of morals that hold sway in Lesnogorod! And then you blame it on us simple folk! Probably you drove him to it, you know—they say his wife—is that you, you with the red hair?—took up with another man—well, no wonder he went mad, any man would..." Innokenty was so beside himself with rage that he had, it seemed, completely forgotten where he was and whom he was addressing, or at least the consequences of shouting at the people he was addressing, and fell silent only when his anger choked him completely.

"We'll get nothing of use out him now," said Olga, looking at Innokenty and his accusations with extreme distaste. "Perhaps we should put his feet to the fire...See what he says then..."

"WHAT!" screamed Slava before she could stop herself.

"What?" said Olga, looking at Slava with surprise.

"Torture!" cried Slava in horror. "You would torture him?!"

"How else are we to get the truth?" asked Olga. "And I want to get to the bottom of this." She gave Innokenty another look of intense dislike. Slava couldn't tell if it was because he was proving Andrey's innocence, or because he was reminding Olga of her own guilt. Probably both.

"So you would torture him?" demanded Slava, her voice cracking with revulsion. She could see by Olga's face as soon as she had said it that it had been the wrong thing to do. Now Olga had become so determined to hide her own guilt that she would do anything to prove her innocence, and if that meant torturing Innokenty, so much the better. At least it would break up the tedium.

"Wait," said Slava, as Olga opened her mouth to utter some angry and self-serving explanations. *Don't be angry*, Slava reminded herself.

Don't think about how much she disgusts you right now, about how much she makes you want to hurt her. Just think about how to stop this as quickly as possible. "Wait," she repeated. "There is no need to put his feet to the fire to get to the truth. The feet bear no truth, as you well know. The feet bear no truth, but I do. I can see my way to the truth much better than any torture."

"So what!" demanded Olga. "If he's guilty, your squeamishness won't let you allow him to be punished—you might even lie on his behalf, if you thought you needed to save him! I know your weaknesses, Tsarinovna! You should leave the room and leave this business to the real rulers!"

For a moment Slava was afraid she was going to shout at Olga that she was no ruler, that neither she nor Vasilisa Vasilisovna were fit to rule a rose-patch, let alone a province, but she clamped her mouth shut just in time. "Call Vladislava Vasilisovna," she said instead.

"What?" asked Olga, startled.

"Call Vladislava Vasilisovna to the Great Hall," she repeated. "Let her see how real rulers rule, since she is fated to follow in their footsteps."

"This is no place for a child, Tsarinovna, even you should be able to see that," said Olga, trying as hard as possible to assume a superior expression as she looked at Slava. For a moment it almost worked, and Slava began to doubt herself, but then her own rightness rose up in her like a wave and drowned any residue of Olga's self-righteousness that had contaminated her.

"Vladislava Vasilisovna is not a child, she is the heir to Lesnograd and the Severnolesnoye province," said Slava, impressed at how strong her voice sounded. "All judgments should be made in front of her."

"No!" cried Vasilisa Vasilisovna, now horrified in turn. "I won't let her witness something like this!"

"Why not?" asked Slava.

"It's horrible...Dirty..."

"And yet you have said nothing against it, even though it is taking place right in your own Great Hall! And it will most certainly not remain a secret. You must send a report of it to Krasnograd, you know, so that all of Zem' can look upon your judgments and cast their own judgments of your judging—is that not our law? And I, the Tsarina's sister, am here witnessing it, so you can be sure I will spread the news of what takes place in this hall today far and wide."

Both Olga and Vasilisa Vasilisovna stared at Slava with the aghast expressions of people who have just been bitten by their own bed-clothes, but appeared too shocked to summon up a suitable reply.

"Call Vladislava Vasilisovna to the Great Hall," Slava ordered one of the soldiers who was standing with Innokenty. He bowed, also looking shocked, and hurried off.

"Innokenty," said Slava, rising and going over to him. "You did it, did you not? You set the fire that killed your wife and her lover, and it spread to the rest of the village."

"No!" cried Innokenty, but his voice was not the voice of someone telling the truth, but of someone desperately trying to conceal it, from himself as much as from his judges.

"Yes," said Slava, lowering her voice. "Your wife was always unkind, was she not?" A vision of Innokenty's wife rose up in Slava's mind, and she found herself describing it. "She was always loud and bullying, was she not? And when you dared to stand up for yourself, she beat you down twice as hard, did she not? Told you you weren't fit to be a man, especially her man, did she not?"

"Yes!" cried Innokenty, staring at her. "How did you know?"

"I have seen it," said Slava, somewhat honestly. She supposed her vision, which was little more than a guess, was sort of like seeing. Vague memories of Mirik's words about those who had been killed in the fire came back to her, and she used them to build on her guesses. "She made your life one long torment, did she not, until you were finally forced to seek comfort with another, and when she discovered it, she decided to toss you aside for someone else…Some other young victim…"

"Yes!" cried Innokenty.

Out of the corner of her eye Slava saw Vladislava slip into the room, her face both puzzled and eager.

"And when the woman to whom you had entrusted yourself, with whom you had sought comfort, found out that you were being set aside, she turned away from you, abandoning you to a fate she had helped create."

"Yes!" cried Innokenty.

"And so you were left with no choice," said Slava. "No choice but to strike back, to protect yourself…"

"Yes!" cried Innokenty, now looking at Slava with an expression of dawning hope that she couldn't bear to think about.

"The rest was an accident," she said, trying to think only about what she should say, not what it would mean for Innokenty. "You seized the opportunity caused by the nobleman's arrival, and you decided to strike back, to protect yourself, only it got out of hand..."

"The guards!" Innokenty cried. "The nobleman left behind some guards, in case our Milochka—that heartless bitch!—came back! When they saw the fire, instead of putting it out, they ran to loot our homes! And everyone ran to fight them, to protect their own homes from looters, and no one would protect her neighbor from fire, and soon the whole village was caught! And when they saw what had happened, the guards took off without doing anything to help. It was all their fault...And Milochka's...If she hadn't lured that nobleman to our village, none of this would have happened...But that's women, those wolves—never satisfied unless the whole pack is snarling over them, ripping each other apart for the pleasure of serving her..." Innokenty trailed off in tears.

"Vasilisa Vasilisovna," said Slava sharply. "Do you not have road crews in Severnolesnoye?"

"Yes," said Vasilisa Vasilisovna faintly.

"Let Innokenty serve on a road crew," said Slava. "Let him make restitution in that way."

"Very well," said Vasilisa Vasilisovna, still looking as if she wished she could just faint away instead of sitting there and thinking whatever it was she was thinking.

"Take him away," Slava told the soldiers surrounding Innokenty, when it became apparent that no one else would give the order. The soldiers, looking somewhat lost, led Innokenty, who looked even more lost, stumblingly out of the hall.

"I assume you feel you've been very lenient," said Olga.

Slava gave her a look.

"Life is not so sweet on those road crews, you know," Olga continued maliciously. "They work them into the ground, you know, and beat them when they fall. And the newcomers are used for pleasure by the 'granddads,' the old hands. Often they cut off their balls their first day there, just to teach them a lesson." Olga gave Slava a look of spiteful triumph.

"Yes," said Slava. She had a vision of proud, stocky, red-faced Innokenty being beaten and gelded and raped by the "granddads," the men who had been there longer, and wished she hadn't. There was nothing, other than torture, that could be worse than the evil the prisoners made of their lot. Everyone said life on the road crews was little better than death, perhaps worse, and said that it was the prisoners themselves who made it that way. Slava tried to push that vision out of her head. Then she had a vision of his wife and her lover dying in the fire. *The forest was filled that night with the screams of dying animals caught in the flames*, Mirik had said, and Slava could see and hear it so clearly she thought for a moment she might be sick. Unfortunately, the one vision did not cancel the other out; instead they hung there in her mind, poisoning her. "And it is all in your family's name," she said.

"And so, what, we should just let them go free?" cried Vasilisa Vasilisovna, shedding her faintness and showing a rare flash of spine. "Let murderers like Innokenty go free to kill again?"

"No," said Slava. "But perhaps we should try to be better than they are."

"And what, stop them from...from what they do there on the road crews?" said Vasilisa Vasilisovna. For a moment Slava could see, just as she had on their first meeting, that she was Princess Severnolesnaya's daughter, and Olga's sister, not the rag she usually appeared to be. Slava wished she could have chosen a more opportune time to develop a backbone.

"Insist that they behave like, like civilized people?" Vasilisa Vasilisovna continued. "Hah! You know how men are! Weak-minded idiots, unable to perform when called upon, but secretly dreaming of rape if the opportunity should present itself! If they're not worse, that is! Better that they should be amongst their own kind than causing us trouble! Well, well, well...if it makes you feel better, Tsarinovna, perhaps he's better off where he'll be going. Perhaps he'll learn to like...what will happen to him there. They say that many men do. They finally get to be women of a sort, just like they've always wanted—except for all the ways that matter, that is. Never in all the ways that matter. But where else should we send him? After all, you wouldn't take Innokenty into your house, would you? Who would!"

"No one," said Slava. "No one has ever wanted Innokenty in her house, and now he is unfit for anyone. One might say that he has been cursed, and now he has become a curse to the rest of us. Perhaps you are right, and where he is going is the only place he should be. I hope he does become reconciled to his lot quickly there, that he does 'learn to like it,' as you say, because he will have no other choice. I hope he does not make his sufferings any greater than they are destined to be.

"But that does not mean that we should sink to his level, because the Innokenties of this world will always manage to sink even lower, and then where will we end up? Even lower than we are now, no doubt. Good day to you all. I am glad to see that the truth has been revealed, and justice has been done. Let us all feel proud of the part we have played in this day's doings." She walked out of the hall back to her own chamber. Halfway there her hands started shaking, and by the time she had come to her door, her heart was beating so fast that spots were floating before her eyes. Courage, she could see, did not come naturally for her, and its price was always going to be very high.

She tried to calm herself by re-reading her copies of the scrolls from the sanctuary, since that was the only thing she had to read, but that was only somewhat effective. She told herself she had to be calm, since her health now was not just her own—presumably she was also responsible for a child. That, alas, did not have an especially calming effect. When there was a knock at the door, she twitched all over and then ran to open it, hoping that her visitor would bring distractions, and not more problems.

The visitor was Vladislava. Slava let her in, waiting to see what she would say. Vladislava could be a distraction, but she was also a problem.

"You made them come and get me and witness the judgment today, didn't you?" said Vladislava as soon as she had stepped into the room.

"Yes," said Slava.

"That was good of you. They never let me witness that kind of thing. And now I know why. They're not very good judges, are they? All they could think about was themselves, and not the person they were judging, couldn't they?"

"Yes," said Slava.

"It's very sad, isn't it? When I'm ruling Lesnograd, I'm going to do a much better job. Did you have them send Innokenty to the road crews so that he wouldn't be killed?"

"Yes," said Slava.

"I'm glad. I don't like executions one bit, even when they deserve to die. Mother used to never let me go, she said it wasn't something

I should see—like the sight of her sitting in judgment, that was horrible, I wish I hadn't seen that, no wonder she never wanted me to see that—but Grandmother talked her into it after a while. I wish she hadn't, though. I always feel like it's me being killed, don't you?"

"Yes," said Slava. "Although I dare say it would be much worse if we were actually the people on the block."

"Oh yes, but it's still so horrible, and you can feel how much the crowd likes to watch other people being killed, and I just feel disgusted with them, it makes me want to kill people, don't you? I mean, when I see people who want to kill other people, I want to kill the people who want to kill people, don't you? Isn't that strange?"

"Yes," said Slava. "And you can see how it would never end."

"Oh yes," said Vladislava. "Because then someone would want to kill me for killing someone for killing someone, wouldn't she? Not if she were like the crowd that likes to watch, of course, but if she were like me. I suppose there must be a few more people like me out there somewhere, although there don't seem to be very many of them. Is it true what Aunty Olga said about the road crews? That life is still very bad for them there?"

"No doubt," said Slava.

"When I rule Lesnograd, I'm going to make things better for the road crews," said Vladislava decisively. "And I'm not going to kill people!"

"That sounds wise," said Slava.

"But that's not why I came. I wanted to talk to you. Do you think that it was the curse? The curse that Grandmother put on Andrey Vladislavovich? Is that what made Innokenty do what he did?"

"Perhaps," said Slava.

"But then he's innocent! It wasn't his fault at all! It was the curse!"

"No," said Slava. "Or rather, perhaps the curse found him and worked through him, I don't know, but he wanted to kill his wife before the curse was ever dreamed of. He probably would have done it anyway. Do you remember what Anastasiya said? A curse takes the form its victims give it, and it goes where it can, like water running downhill. Innokenty was just the lowest point in that village, because he already wanted to kill his wife. And do you remember what he said about the guards from Lesnograd? The curse, if that's what it was, worked through them too. But they were still guilty, all of them, even if the curse was working through them. Even Innokenty's wife—she was cruel, and her cruelty came back on her."

"You mean she deserved to die? He was right to kill her?"

"No, I mean that all of them already carried evil inside of them, and did evil things to other people, and so it was easy for the curse to find them. And now Innokenty has killed his wife and faces a life—probably a short one—of even more suffering than he had before, and the rest of the village had to suffer as well, and so did Andrey Vladisla-vovich...So many people were touched by that evil." Slava realized that she was speaking much more heatedly than she intended, and fell silent.

"Yes, it's very sad," said Vladislava, not sounding particularly sad about it. "When are we leaving for Krasnograd?"

"Soon, I hope," said Slava. "We must speak with Olga about it."

"Oh, that's also why I came to see you—supper will be soon, and I wanted to come talk to you beforehand, and then we could walk down together, because I didn't want to go in there alone, do you? Mother and Aunty Olga are probably in terrible moods right now, don't you think? I wish Oleg Svetoslavovich were still here, don't you?"

"Yes," said Slava.

"Why did he have to leave? I wish he hadn't left. Surely he could have asked the gods to let him stay a little longer, at least until we left for Krasnograd," said Vladislava, with the voice of someone who still felt that her own wishes outweighed those of the gods.

"He had a duty," said Slava. "And life is hard sometimes for those who serve the gods."

"Well, let's go down to supper now! I'm starving, aren't you?"

Slava was not, in fact, starving, but she was, she realized as they set off, lightheaded, and eating would probably be wise, as much as she was dreading being in the company of Olga and Vasilisa Vasilisovna.

When she arrived at the table she discovered that things were even worse than she had envisioned, since Andrey Vladislavovich had apparently been allowed to leave his room and was there too. Glad as she was to see he had been released, she had no desire to share a meal with him. Everyone took their seats in strained silence. Vasilisa Vasilisovna looked distraught, Olga looked angry, and Andrey Vladisla-vovich looked like he didn't know what to think. Lisochka, who was also there, looked like she couldn't decide whether she wanted to bite somebody's head off or sink through the floor. Probably both.

Vladislava picked at her food for a few bites, and then demanded, "When are we leaving for Krasnograd?"

This set off loud lamentations from Vasilisa Vasilisovna about how her only daughter was so eager to abandon her. As this provided an acceptable subject for Vasilisa Vasilisovna to complain about, the lamentations went on for some time. Vladislava sat there stony-faced until they dried up, and then repeated, this time much more rudely, "When are we leaving for Krasnograd?"

Vasilisa Vasilisovna opened her mouth to emit more complaints, but before she could get any out, Olga said crossly, "The sooner we get out of this thrice-cursed city the better, as far as I'm concerned. Let's leave tomorrow."

"Really!" cried Vladislava, straightening up in her chair. "Tomorrow! Let's!"

Vasilisa Vasilisovna gave up on complaining and started sniffling to herself about her abandonment by her hard-hearted and thoughtless relations instead.

"Will we be ready by tomorrow?" asked Slava.

"We will if I have to steal our provisions from the gods themselves," said Olga, without actually looking in Slava's direction.

"And will Lesnograd be ready for us to leave?" Slava pressed.

"Well, it's not like we're doing it much good by staying," said Olga. "Although you can stay and rule it if you want, Tsarinovna, since you seem to like it so much. But I'm through with it. Any beggar on the street can have my claim to it, as far as I'm concerned."

"Oh, Olya..." said Vasilisa Vasilisovna, breaking off from her sniffling.

This started another terrible but trivial quarrel that provoked a strong desire in Slava to break her plate over their heads. Instead, she turned to Lisochka and asked, "And what of you, Vasilisa Olgovna? Will you be joining us on our journey? My offer stands, you know, and you will be welcome in Krasnograd whenever you are able to grace us with your presence. Our ties with the Severnolesnaya family," for a moment Slava realized she was babbling in the face of all this bad temper and had no idea what she was going to say next, but having talked herself into this uncomfortable position, she had no choice but to continue, and so plunged on, "have been far too distant of late, and I would welcome any member of your family who could join me there. Indeed, dear Vasilisa Olgovna, I am sure you would be an ornament to Krasnograd's kremlin, and I hope to see you there before too long."

For a moment hope at the thought of escaping Lesnograd and her miserable life there, as well as pleasure at the unaccustomed phrase "dear Vasilisa Olgovna," flooded Lisochka's face, but then she shook her head. "My place is here," she said. "Especially now, with Grandmother so ill, and, well..."

Slava could see that Lisochka had no good motives for her words, that she was acting entirely out of sullen anger and fear, but she decided to pretend otherwise, and said, with all the sympathy and encouragement she could muster, "Yes, I'm sure your strength and your counsel must be of great use to your father and Vasilisa Vasilisovna at this trying time."

Lisochka gave Slava a look that wavered between shock and contempt. Slava decided to press on even so.

"Trying times such as these can bring out the best in people, Vasilisa Olgovna," she continued, leaning forward slightly and looking Lisochka directly in the eyes. "And I am sure they will bring out the best in you! Andrey Vladislavovich and Vasilisa Vasilisovna are counting on you, I am sure of it! You must be their unwavering support and the wise word in their ear, not only for them but for Lesnograd and all of Severnolesnoye!"

Lisochka shook her head dismissively, but Slava could see the look in the back of her eyes, and it was the look of a starving person, the same look she had seen in Andrey Vladislavovich's eyes when he had talked about his mad affair, the same look she had seen in her own eyes so many times. Encouraged, she looked even more deeply into Lisochka's hungry eyes and told her how much her father, her aunt, and her grandmother needed her, how she was an essential member of their family and had an important duty to fulfill, and so on and so forth, and within a very few sentences Lisochka was almost smiling. It was not much, Slava knew, but she had made Lisochka happier for the moment, and perhaps she would take some of Slava's words to heart and act as if they were true, and then perhaps they would become true, and then she really would be happy. It was, Slava knew, unlikely, but perhaps it would happen.

By then the quarrel between Olga and Vasilisa Vasilisovna had died down, and Slava was able to turn away from Lisochka, which she did with a guilty sense of relief. She had meant everything she had said to Lisochka, and she was glad she had said it, but pouring all of her own hope and energy into Lisochka was exhausting.

She was just thinking that she might be able to slip away from the table and return to her room, which would be boring but at least would get her away from the endless arguing that surrounded Olga's family, when a serving woman sidled hesitantly into the room and, after several bows and apologies for disturbing them while they were at the table, said that the old princess was calling for her daughters.

"She's awake?" cried Olga. "I thought she was headed straight for the grave!"

"Oh, Olya, how can you say such things..." said Vasilisa Vasilisovna.

"Because I prefer the truth to honey-covered lies, and it would be no great loss for her to go, anyway," said Olga, giving her sister a contemptuous look. Slava was afraid she was going to have to intervene, but luckily the serving woman mumbled something about "very urgent," and Olga and Vasilisa Vasilisovna were able to come to their senses long enough to agree that they needed to go to their mother's room immediately.

"Do you think she'll want to see me?" Vladislava whispered to Slava uncertainly. "I want to go see her, but I don't know..."

"Perhaps we should go there, just in case," Slava suggested. "She might be very weak, you know, but if she's strong enough, I'm sure she'll want to see you." She glanced over in Lisochka's direction, and saw how she was hunched up again in sullen misery. "She will want to see both her granddaughters, if she is strong enough, I am sure," said Slava more loudly. "Let us all go up together."

"Father too!" said Lisochka, trying to leap out of her seat in order not to be left behind while not appearing too eager to join the others.

"Of course," said Slava. "I'm sure you will be of great solace to each other in these trying times." She gave Andrey Vladislavovich a firm look, and was pleased to see that he rose with alacrity. They all set off together towards the old princess's chambers.

Chapter Ten

The princess's healer was sitting in the sitting room outside the bedchamber. Vladislava rushed over to her and threw her arms around her as soon as she entered the room.

"Is she really awake, Baba Vlastya?" she cried. "Really? She woke up?"

"Shhh, little princess," said Baba Vlastya. "Yes, she woke up."

"For good?" demanded Vladislava.

"Who can tell, little princess? Perhaps. Sometimes the gods are kind."

"I'm sure they'll be kind to her!" said Vladislava. Slava could see from the way Baba Vlastya's face twisted at those words that she did not share Vladislava's certainty, but couldn't find the words to say so.

"Do you think she'll let me see her?" continued Vladislava. "And Lisochka," she added as an afterthought. "She should see both of us."

"Perhaps, little princess," said Baba Vlastya. "But now we must wait and see what the gods send. Let Vasilisa Vasilisovna and Olga Vasilisovna go first."

Vasilisa Vasilisovna and Olga disappeared into the old princess's bedchamber while the rest of them sat in the dark and stuffy outer room, today lit only by a single candle and a fire that threw off too much heat and not enough light, for what seemed like a very long time, although when Slava watched the progress of the single candle, she saw that time was merely moving very slowly in her mind.

Eventually, though, their patience was rewarded, for Vasilisa Vasilisovna came out of the bedchamber and said, "She wants to see you. All of you. You especially, Tsarinovna."

Vasilisa Vasilisovna didn't look very happy about that, and neither,

Slava saw when she glanced at the faces of her companions, did Andrey Vladislavovich or Lisochka, but she went in the room with them anyway. Olga and Vasilisa Vasilisovna, after seeing them in, left the room, both with drawn faces.

It was also dark and close in the bedchamber, and smelled horribly of a sick body, but when Slava saw that Princess Severnolesnaya was sitting propped up on pillows and watching her intently with her dark, glittering eyes, she forced herself not to wrinkle her nose or purse her lips—as much as she could control such things—as she made her way to the bedside.

"Andrey," said Princess Severnolesnaya hoarsely, as soon as they had arranged themselves around her bed. "I hear you've been making trouble over that red-headed singer girl."

Andrey Vladislavovich shuffled his feet and looked foolish, but before he could summon up a response to that, Princess Severnolesnaya smiled and said, "Good for you. You should cause more trouble in your life, Andryusha. It will make a man of you."

"But she left!" he burst out. "She ran away!"

"Plenty more where she came from," said Princess Severnolesnaya. She closed her eyes for a moment, and then, opening them, said, "And your home is always here, you know."

Andrey Vladislavovich bowed.

"Now go," Princess Severnolesnaya told him. "Make trouble." She tried to smile and wave him off with her hand, but she was too weak. Andrey Vladislavovich stood there for a moment in indecision, but then she glared at him and he, bowing again, beat a hasty retreat.

"I always wanted a son," said Princess Severnolesnaya when he was gone. "Someone to coddle and fuss over. I got my wish. A fine son I have now. Needs lots of coddling. And fussing. But no matter. Lisochka." Princess Severnolesnaya closed her eyes again and took several deep breaths before continuing. "Still sulking, girl?" she asked.

"I don't sulk!" cried Lisochka.

"You're sulking now," Princess Severnolesnaya observed, correctly. "Stop it. You'd be a pretty girl if you didn't sulk so much. You might even be a clever one. But not if you sulk. Some advice from your grandmother. Your mother is never going to love you, you know, and your father is never going to be more than half a man. Best if you just stop worrying about it. Take a lover or something. Take several. It will be good for you. Make you stop thinking about your troubles so much. Lesnograd may need you, Lisochka, even if your parents don't.

Because your parents don't. So stop sulking."

This only made Lisochka sulk more. Slava couldn't help but notice that when someone else was advised to take a lover in order to take her mind off her troubles, she instantly saw the sense in it, while when she herself was given that advice, she always saw all the flaws in that plan and argued against it. Even in such serious circumstances, standing at the bedside of a dying woman, she had to fight to suppress her smile at that thought, but not, apparently, with complete success, because it seemed to her that the old princess gave her a measuring glance before dismissing Lisochka just as she had Andrey Vladislavovich.

"My first-born granddaughter," she said, once Lisochka was out of the room. "A treasure, is she not? She never should have been born." Princess Severnolesnaya stopped and breathed heavily for a moment, her eyes closed. When she began speaking again, the words seemed to pour out of her as if she had long kept them pent up inside, until they were determined to find release, even if it meant taking the last of her strength with them.

"The greatest mistake of my life was in forcing Olga to have her," she said, staring up at the ceiling. "She fought the marriage, and afterwards fought having a child, so I gave her a potion. I told her it would stop the child from taking root inside her, but instead it did just the opposite. By the time she discovered my lie, it was too late to do anything about it. So she ran and jumped out of the hayloft, but the only thing she broke was her arm. The baby inside her remained intact.

"At the time I was so relieved. I was a fool. I locked her in her room and kept her under guard until the child was born. I was so desperate for a granddaughter, you see. But what I got was Lisochka. Sometimes we cast curses on ourselves, without even realizing it. She never should have been born, I see that now. I cast a curse on my daughter through my own good intentions, and doomed my granddaughter to a life of suffering. I am so sorry."

"Did you tell her that?" Slava asked. "Did you tell that to Olga?"

"Just now," said Princess Severnolesnaya. Now that her confession had wrenched itself free of her, she was visibly weaker. "Just now I told her that she had been right and I had been wrong, and that I was sorry. But I fear it has only given her more reason to loathe her daughter. Lisochka was a terrible mistake on all our parts, and now we must all suffer for it. Olga ran away as soon as she could rise from childbed, and she's been running ever since. She'll never stop, and she'll never forgive me. Nor should she. A mistake I can never undo."

Vladislava opened her mouth, probably to argue against such a harsh judgment, and then closed it without speaking, both because Princess Severnolesnaya was too feeble to argue, and because, Slava was afraid, she was probably right. Slava, however, found herself saying, "Oh no, surely not…" before she could stop herself.

"Don't be a fool, Tsarinovna," said Princess Severnolesnaya. "Lisochka was cursed before she took her first breath, and none of us will ever be able to save her."

"But…" said Slava, knowing that arguing was futile, but unable to condemn Lisochka nonetheless.

"But nothing. The only thing you can do, Tsarinovna," said Princess Severnolesnaya, giving Slava a long measuring glance, "is to ensure that your own daughter has a better fate."

Slava opened her mouth to exclaim something, realized that she had nothing to say, and shut her mouth without speaking. Princess Severnolesnaya gave Slava another measuring glance, as if she wanted to add something, but then turned away from her to Vladislava.

"Vladislava," she said instead, and for the first time there was a note of tenderness in her voice. "My little princess. Are you being brave?"

"I'm trying, grandmother," said Vladislava, her voice wavering. "But it's very hard. I wish you'd stay awake all the time, so you could make them behave."

"I wish so too, little princess," said Princess Severnolesnaya. She reached out and stroked Vladislava's hair with a frail claw that had once been a large strong hand. "And I wish I could stand by you, to prevent you from making mistakes that will haunt you on your deathbed. But the gods have other plans for me."

"They're mean gods!" cried Vladislava angrily. "Their plans are bad!"

"Well," said Princess Severnolesnaya. "There's nothing we can do about that. Most of us, anyway." She gave Slava another sidelong glance, and then turned back to Vladislava. After gathering her strength for a moment, she said, "I hear you're leaving for Krasnograd soon."

"Yes!"

"Are you happy about that?"

"Yes! Only…I wish I didn't have to leave you, now that you've woken up."

"I doubt I will be awake for long, little princess. I, too, you see, am

174

setting off on a great journey. The sleigh is already loaded and waiting for me, my little princess, and the driver is calling. I will be stepping into that sleigh and taking off very soon, my little princess, and I won't be coming back."

"You can't go off on a journey now!" cried Vladislava. "You're much too ill! You have to get your strength back first."

Princess Severnolesnaya closed her eyes again, and this time it seemed to Slava it was to suppress tears. When she opened them, her eyes were even brighter than before.

"Are you ready to rule, my little princess?" she asked.

"Yes!" said Vladislava fiercely.

"Well then. I can be proud of that, at least. Can I be proud of you, little princess?"

"Yes!" said Vladislava, even more fiercely.

"My life has not been in vain, then," said Princess Severnolesnaya, gazing up at the ceiling for a moment. "One granddaughter to take pride in, amongst all my failures...Many women can boast of less... Kiss my cheek, little princess."

Vladislava bent over and pressed a kiss on the old princess's sunken cheek. She tried to throw her arms around her shoulders as well, but the old princess stopped her.

"I'm too weak for that," she said. "And you're much too strong for me now. Now go, little princess. Go to Krasnograd and show all those Southern princesses what it means to be a Severnolesnaya. And come back and rule Lesnograd. It will need you." She tried to wave Vladislava away, and after much hesitation and many backward glances, Vladislava left the room.

After she was gone, Princess Severnolesnaya lay there for some time with her eyes closed. Slava was about to leave herself, when the old princess suddenly opened her eyes and stared directly into Slava's own.

"Tsarinovna," she said. "Still here?"

"Yes," said Slava.

"I have been asleep for some time, you know."

"Yes," said Slava.

"Do you know what sleepers do, Tsarinovna?"

"What, Princess?"

"Dream."

"True," said Slava.

"Do you know what I dreamed, Tsarinovna?"

"What?" asked Slava.

"I dreamed of you." Princess Severnolesnaya closed her eyes again and said, "Not of my troublesome daughters, so ill-suited for the burden I will lay upon them. My poor daughters. Sometimes the gods are very cruel indeed. I thought when I gave birth I would be giving birth to something in my own image, only more perfect. I was wrong. Perhaps they would have done well in some other life, but in the life that I gave them, they have done very poorly. Olga at least is good for a laugh, if I could have allowed it of her, but Vasilisa...My poor Vasilisa, my namesake. Good for nothing."

"That's not true!" cried Slava.

"Is it not?" Princess Severnolesnaya opened her eyes again and fixed Slava with an even more piercing gaze than before. "Is it not, Tsarinovna? Tell me, Tsarinovna, what *is* Vasilisa good for?"

Slava cast her mind back on all her interactions with Vasilisa Vasilisovna, and, as she had known she would, she had to admit that she could not come up with a single example of her being of any use... Princess Severnolesnaya was, bitter as it was to think that of someone, right...right except for...

"She has always stood by your side," said Slava. "Even when others would not. And she gave you Vladislava."

"True enough, Tsarinovna, true enough. And I suppose I should be grateful that she could give me even that much. Many other daughters have given less. And so, Tsarinovna, my dreams. When I lay sleeping, I dreamed not of my all my plans and schemes, not even of my dear granddaughter, the brightest flame of my life. No, Tsarinovna, my last days have been spent dreaming of you. Unjust, is it not?"

"The gods care little for the justice of women," said Slava. "I am sorry, but it is so. You yourself have just admitted to that fact."

"True." Princess Severnolesnaya opened her eyes and looked at Slava again. "For now, that is. You may change that, you know."

"I?" said Slava.

"Yes, Tsarinovna, you. I saw you, you know, in my dreams. You and my dear husband."

"Oh," said Slava, blushing hotly.

"Are you blushing?" asked Princess Severnolesnaya, trying to smile through her weakness. "I am glad. Glad because I am jealous, and because I envy you, and because it is good to know that I may pass, but love remains."

"I don't know if it could be called love..." Slava began.

"Many things can be called love," Princess Severnolesnaya interrupted her. "Believe me, Tsarinovna, I have sampled most of them." This time something that was almost a smile flitted across her ruined face, and Slava could see the ghost of a tall proud woman who had had two husbands and more lovers than she could count kneel at her feet. "And I am glad that you have sampled some of them, too," Princess Severnolesnaya continued. "And you may have more such delights in your future, you know."

"Oh," said Slava, not sure what to say to that. For a moment she could feel how she and this dying wreck of what once had been a woman were linked like sisters through having taken Oleg as a lover and—if the gods willed it so for her—getting a child off him. His blood and theirs had been joined, and thus their blood had been joined after a fashion as well. It was a very queer thought, and not a very comfortable one.

"You may smile, you know," said Princess Severnolesnaya, trying to smile herself again. "There's nothing wrong with that. And it will be good for your daughter to see her mother smile from time to time. The gods know my daughters could have used a few more of my smiles."

"True," said Slava. Suddenly she felt very tender towards this woman with whom she had shared a lover. There were worse ways of getting a sister, after all.

"I saw her too, you know. Your possible daughter-to-be. I hope you like fiery children, Tsarinovna, for your daughter will have plenty of fire, should she have the good fortune to be born."

"Good," said Slava.

"Good," echoed Princess Severnolesnaya. "Plenty of fire, just like her father. My dear, long-lost, unloved husband. Do you know Oleg's story, Tsarinovna?"

"Only what happened...after."

"After." Princess Severnolesnaya closed her eyes and rested for a little while. "After. But not before. He was just a peasant lad, you know, before he married me. I hope you don't mind a little peasant blood."

"My family rarely does," said Slava.

"True. You have a taste for it, don't you? And who doesn't? Well. He was just a peasant lad who came and begged for a place in my guard. A runaway, you know, who was making his way in the world, if such a wretched existence could be called that, as a hunter. He was handy enough in the woods, of course, but he was still only a boy, and the winters up here are cruel, and so one snowy night he came stumbling into Lesnograd and begged to serve till spring. Anyone could see that he was too young, and that even when he reached the age of manhood he wouldn't make much of a guard. Guards have to stick to their posts, and that was something our Oleg never was much good at. But no one had the heart to cast him back out into the snow with the animals he was stalking, much less send him home. He was so charming, you know, and his home was so bad. Did you see the scars on his back?"

"Yes," said Slava.

"Some of them are from fire," said Princess Severnolesnaya.

"Yes," said Slava. "I saw."

"Some fathers don't deserve their sons," said Princess Severnolesnaya. "Or their daughters, or their wives, or the dogs who follow in their footsteps and won't even hide from the kicks aimed their way. The gods only know what Oleg would have been with a different father." She stopped to catch her breath and smile. "Well, he wouldn't have been Oleg, for a start. But you know what I mean. He was trained to grovel and beg, Tsarinovna, from an early age that was what he was trained to do. And even though that's not his nature, that's what makes him happy now. Why do you think he married me, after all? And now this...thing with you. He feels safest with people who can pull his strings so hard his arms snap. Which is why he has to run away all the time. Because half of him knows that he doesn't need any more scars, and half of him wants to add to the collection. So he's always running away from someone who can give him scars, straight into the arms of someone who can scar him even more. I take it he ran away from you?"

"Yes," said Slava.

"I wonder when he'll run away from the gods who think he serves them? Maybe someday he'll realize he needs someone to protect him." She stopped to catch her breath and smile again, this time painfully. "Someone better at it than I was. Oleg doesn't know this, but after I saw those scars, I sent soldiers to his home. I wanted to send his father to the road crews. I wanted him to learn what it was like to grovel and beg and like it. But when they got there, the villagers had already driven him away. He had picked a fight with someone's husband, you know, and half-killed him, so they drove him out. He could half-kill his own little boy all he wanted, and everyone knew it had been no accident when his wife had gone out into the woods one fall and come back the next spring as nothing but bare bones, but when he raised his hand against a grown man, that was too much. Then they decided he was a danger, and drove him away. Only then."

"I'm sorry," said Slava. She thought tears might be leaking out from under Princess Severnolesnaya's closed eyes. She thought tears might be about to start leaking out from her eyes, too.

"Well, he got away in the end," said Princess Severnolesnaya. "He had enough fire in him that even his father couldn't beat it out of him. And your daughter will no doubt be much the same."

"If she's going to set the world on fire, she'll have to have a fair amount of inner flame," said Slava.

"And do you think the world needs to be set on fire, Tsarinovna?" asked Princess Severnolesnaya.

"Sometimes I think it needs to be burnt down to the ground," said Slava. "Only I worry about the little animals and children that could get caught in the conflagration."

"Of course you do," said Princess Severnolesnaya. "Well, your daughter will most likely have inner flame and to spare."

"I'm glad," said Slava.

"You'll be less glad once you get to know her," said Princess Severnolesnaya, opening an eye to give her a stern look. "I learned that from experience, with Olga. If Oleg was anything like she was, I half-pity his poor father. Oleg always feared he'd end up like him, you know. He's certainly hotheaded enough. But you seem to have a fair amount of fire yourself, Tsarinovna. You will need it, once your daughter comes, should she have the good fortune to be born. The gods have plans for her, you know."

"Yes," said Slava.

"They think to use her to gain a foothold in the world of women. But swords often have two edges, Tsarinovna."

"They do," agreed Slava.

"It could just as easily be that your daughter will be a foothold amongst the gods for the world of women."

"Have you seen it?" asked Slava.

"Perhaps." Princess Severnolesnaya closed her eyes. "I saw many things...Who knows how many of them will come true...But the curse..."

"Yes?" said Slava, drawing closer. For a moment she was afraid that she had frightened the old princess into silence, but Princess Severnolesnaya, after gathering her strength once more, continued, "The curse. Will work through you."

"No!" cried Slava.

"Yes," said Princess Severnolesnaya. She opened her eyes, and, clutching Slava's hand with surprising force, stared at her intently. "You will bear the curse back to Krasnograd, Tsarinovna."

"With the child?"

"Yes," said Princess Severnolesnaya. "You saw it before it ever happened, on your ride through the forest. You bear the evil inside of you, and you will bear it back to Krasnograd, whether you will it or no. For, you see, little Tsarinovna, you, like Lisochka, like Oleg, were cursed at birth. Cursed with your sister's hatred. A daughter will only compound the problem."

"It's not too late!" cried Slava. "I can still stop it!"

"You can stop it this time, Tsarinovna," said Princess Severnolesnaya. "But it will stop nothing. If you do not have *this* daughter, that only means that it was not fated to happen *this* time. But it will still happen. And you will still bear the curse back to Krasnograd, whether you will it or no, because the very breath in your body is a curse in your sister's eyes. You may think that we started the curse this fall, and it is true, we did, but it truly started many years before that, at your birth, or even earlier. Who can say how much of what happened this fall in Krasnograd was our doing, and how much was yours—yours and your family's. As soon as we started, my sorceresses said that Krasnograd was already so cursed, anything we did was likely to prove superfluous, or to snap back in our faces like a rope cut under strain. As it did, and as it will continue to do. I saw much in my dreaming, little Tsarinovna. From now on until it runs its course, every move you make will work to bring the curse about. Cast the child from your body before it takes root inside of you, and you will undo your bargain with the gods. Bring it back to Krasnograd, and your sister will turn against you even more than before. All acts are for evil where there is evil, and what is more evil than the hatred of sister for sister? Or more common."

"Stop it!" begged Slava. "Stop the curse!"

"I cannot, no more than I can regather spilled water from an overturned bucket."

"But what can I do?" cried Slava.

"Nothing."

"No! I cannot do nothing!"

"Sometimes nothing is what we must do. Tsarinovna." Princess Severnolesnaya paused to swallow and regain her strength. "There is more to curses than evil, you know. Good comes of them as well. Sometimes you must just plunge into them and swim through the evil, until you come out to the good on the other side."

"But…"

"No," said Princess Severnolesnaya. "There is nothing either of us can do. The more you try to stop it, the faster you will bring it down upon you. Now…" But her strength failed her, and her eyes closed. Slava waited for some time, but they did not reopen.

Baba Vlastya came up to her. "Best leave now, Tsarinovna," she said. "There's no point in staying. She won't be saying anything more."

"I am sorry," said Slava.

"It is not your doing, Tsarinovna. The gods are unkind to us all."

"I'm still sorry," said Slava.

"You have a kind heart, Tsarinovna," said Baba Vlastya. "Even the gods can't take that away." She bowed, and Slava, feeling there really was nothing more she could do there, left.

She returned to her room and sat there for some time in a daze. Was Princess Severnolesnaya telling the truth? Was Slava bearing the curse back to Krasnograd, as she had said and as Slava had seen on her ride through the forest? Was the daughter she had supposedly conceived harboring the seeds of evil within her?

It was not too late, Slava reminded herself. She could go to an herb-woman and ask for something to stop the child from taking root inside her. Moldy rye was painful, Slava knew all too well…but not as painful as the alternative…How many women died in agony, trying to bring a child into the world…She thought of Lisochka, who never should have been born, and all the suffering that had been caused and would continue to be caused because Olga had been forced to bear her…But Princess Severnolesnaya had also said that that would not help anything…Slava found herself burying her face in her hands…Every way forward seemed bad…The gods wanted to use her…The curse wanted to use her…She was helpless once again…She felt as if a sword were hanging over her head…A double-edged sword, one that would cut her no matter what she did…

Pick up the sword, then, you fool, said a voice in her head. *Your enemy's weapon is only your own weapon, you just haven't taken it from her yet. And a double-edged sword cuts both ways.*

"Yes!" cried Slava, jumping to her feet. "A double-edged sword cuts both ways!"

You just have to grab it by the hilt, you fool, instead of constantly trying to pick it up by the blade, and then crying when you cut your hand, continued the voice in her head.

"Yes!" said Slava again. Her whole body was tingling with excitement...She could see herself taking the sword by the hilt...She remembered how many times she had been asked if she had wanted to take up this burden, and every time she had said "yes," and most emphatically...So many times before she had had the possibility of having a child, and every time she had refused, and known that she had done right, because...because it had all been leading up to *this* moment, *this* child, should she have the good fortune to be born...Now was the time, the culmination of everything she had been waiting for, all the misery and suffering she had undergone, now was the time for her to say "yes," just as she had to Oleg back in the cabin.

Now was finally the time. She was not Olga, a helpless little girl being used against her will, she was a grown woman who had chosen to fulfill her destiny of her own free will. She was running towards this, not away from it, which is why she had nothing to fear from any curse...

Just then there was a knock on her bedroom door, followed closely by Olga, who came bursting in uninvited.

"We're leaving," she announced abruptly. "Tomorrow."

"What about the others?" asked Slava. She was still tingling all over, and the words she had heard in her head were still standing before her as if hanging in the air, but somehow she still had so much strength left over that she found it easy to turn her attention to Olga, even as she continued to make plans for her own future.

"Well, my father has run off and left us already, hasn't he? Mirik is going home, he says, and good riddance—he's been nothing but trouble from the moment we first met. Misha, Vova, Volodya, Vladik, and Zhenya will all have to spend the spring here in any case. And Dunya says she wants to accompany us, at least for a little ways. She wants to see more of the South, she says."

"Will we be ready?" asked Slava. "Will Lesnograd be ready for you to go?"

"Staying won't do us any good," said Olga. "Lesnograd is better off without me."

Slava tried to come up with a response that would soothe Olga's wounded feelings but also encourage her to leave soon, but just then she was distracted by a vision of what she could say to her sister on her return to Krasnograd, and before she could find the necessary words to comfort her, Olga went on, "I'm not suited for rule, it's painfully clear. I've never been able to stand Lesnograd and I still can't. And I'm afraid I'm going to jump up and strangle both my husband and my sister if I have to spend one more day in their company. The only thing I'm good for is journeying, so let's set off on a journey. Maybe it will be more successful than our last one. I can at least get you and Vladislava to Krasnograd safely, I hope, although frankly, this expedition has been such a disaster from start to finish that I'm beginning to doubt I could make it across the street without stumbling."

"Our journey hasn't been a disaster," said Slava. "Far from it."

"We accomplished nothing," said Olga firmly.

"That's not true," said Slava. "We accomplished many things."

"Yes, we got lost lots of times," said Olga. "We were very successful at not finding our way or doing what we had set out to do."

"But we did lots of other things," Slava pointed out to her.

"My head for beheading, you're sorry now you agreed to come with us, aren't you?" said Olga. "Your time would have been much better spent back in Krasnograd."

"Quite the contrary," said Slava. "Thus far, this journey has been the best thing that has ever happened to me. I think my life will be forever better because of it."

Olga gave Slava a doubtful look, but instead of questioning her further, only said that she had already ordered the maids serving her to pack up everything she would need for the return to Krasnograd, and to be ready to set out directly after breakfast the next morning.

Chapter Eleven

Somehow it seemed odd, and much too easy, when they went out onto the square the next morning and found sleighs waiting for them, already loaded with provisions. Vasilisa Vasilisovna, who looked to have been up the entire night, packing and worrying, followed them out to the square and took a very dramatic and tearful farewell of Vladislava, much to the latter's discomfort and annoyance. She stood and watched them, her hands clenched under her chin, until they were out of sight.

"How long until we're in Krasnograd?" Vladislava demanded, as soon as they had turned the corner and the kremlin was no longer in view.

"Two weeks, maybe more," Olga told her. "It depends on the roads. Spring will be here soon, and if it starts to rain, we'll get caught in the slush and won't make much progress. And we're tied to these sleighs, I'm afraid. Well, tied to them as long as we have to haul all the clothing your mother packed for you."

"Oh, we can just leave all that behind, if we need to," said Vladislava carelessly. "Will we be staying at waystations?"

"Most of the way," Olga told her. She, like her sister, looked as if she had not slept much the night before, and was sitting slumped in her seat in a way that was most unlike her. Slava knew that she had gone to say farewell to her mother before breakfast, and that, despite their lifelong antipathy for each other, the fact that this farewell was most likely forever seemed to be weighing down on her spirits very heavily.

"I'm so looking forward to it!" cried Vladislava, who had also said farewell to her grandmother but did not appear to be particularly oppressed by it. "I've never gotten to stay at a waystation before! Will we change horses often?"

"Probably," Olga told her. "If the waystations have fresh horses for us to change."

"But what will happen to our horses, then?" asked Vladislava, this problem suddenly dawning on her. "I'd hate to lose them. Vorobey's my favorite, and all the grooms say they can't imagine the stable without Lastochka."

"They will be returned to Lesnograd by the next travelers heading that way," Olga assured her.

This satisfied Vladislava's curiosity on that score, and, having forgotten about the horses entirely, she spoke with great excitement about a number of things for several hours. It seemed as if with every verst that separated her from Lesnograd, she became more and more like the child she was, as if Lesnograd had been making her old before her time and now, in the woods and under Slava's care, she was able for the first time in her life to be a little girl, and she intended to capitalize on every moment of it.

Slava was gladdened by it, but by midday she was already finding it difficult to summon the necessary attention and enthusiasm to respond to Vladislava's words and the tumultuous flow of her thoughts. But since Vladislava was owed a whole childhood of the loving attention she had never received, Slava stifled her fatigue and spoke with her as warmly as possible about leshiye, the lives of animals and stars, the building of roads, the construction of sleighs, the geography of the Known World, the possibility that other countries lay beyond the Known World, the possibility of places that were other worlds entirely, and many other things.

Sometime in the afternoon Olga pointed out to Vladislava that they had now passed beyond the farthest extent of her previous travels, which provoked loud squeals of joy. Slava suddenly realized that one day her daughter would also go on her first real journey, and perhaps she, too, would squeal with joy in just the same way, and for a moment she felt so happy she thought tears might come to her eyes. She caught Olga staring at her in a puzzled fashion, and quickly composed her face into the appropriate expression of seriousness, because, she could tell, Olga was still in much too low a mood to tolerate very much of other people's happiness.

They arrived at the waystation just after sunset. Vladislava, who had already begun to find sleigh-riding rather tedious, leapt out from her seat as soon as they came to a halt, and ran up the steps onto the inn porch before the rest of them could even set foot upon the snowy ground. A surprised-looking serving girl came out to greet them.

"Such a large party!" she called from the porch.

"Do you have room for us?" Olga called back.

"I hope so, noblewoman," said the girl, not very encouragingly.

"Find room," Olga ordered her.

"I don't know, noblewoman..." said the girl. "I'll ask my mother... Who's here?"

"Olga Vasilisovna and her retinue," said Olga. She must have still been in a foul mood, for it was the first time Slava had seen her make use of her title outside of Lesnograd, but it had a marvelous effect. The girl bowed several times, and then stumbled over herself rushing back inside to find room for them.

The waystation mistress, accompanied by all her children and servants, came out and said, with many bows and apologies, that it would take a little time for them to shift people out of their rooms in order to make way for Olga and her party, but in the meanwhile they could be so kind as to deign to take some refreshment, for which no payment, of course, would be required. Somewhat to Slava's astonishment, Olga accepted with a curt nod of her head.

"I saved her son from the army," Olga said shortly, seeing Slava's look.

"Ah," said Slava.

"And I'm not so kind as you," continued Olga, still shortly.

Slava wanted to protest that she had implied nothing of the kind, but she knew that she had *thought* that that was no excuse for Olga to take advantage of the poor woman, and that even if she had managed to hide that thought, Olga was probably sensitive about her actions and, even if she hadn't been able to guess Slava's thought, would guess that Slava was thinking it...Slava made herself stop such circular thinking.

And, while she might not have approved of Olga being so quick to take advantage of her rank and her hostess's gratitude, she was grateful not to be spending the night in the stables, and was not about to offer to do so in lieu of one of the other guests. Although, when she thought about that thought, she realized that part of her reluctance to make the offer was the horrified protests she would receive if she made it...Luckily just then they were led by the station-mistress's nervous daughter into the front room and given beer and bread, which interrupted Slava's thoughts for good.

It turned out that no one was going to have to spend the night in the stables anyway, as the only other people at the waystation were a merchant and her daughter and servants, who had spread themselves out over all the bedrooms, but were quickly collected and arranged into two rooms, leaving two free. Vladislava was, predictably, ecstatic at the thought of sharing a room at a waystation with Olga, Slava, and Dunya.

"It's like we're real travelers, isn't it!" she cried.

"That's because we *are* real travelers," said Olga, smiling for the first time that day.

"Will we stay at waystations and inns every night?" asked Vladislava for possibly the hundredth time, writhing slightly in her seat at the excitement that thought provoked.

"Most nights," Olga told her. "Sometimes we'll stay with princesses, or in cabins in the woods."

"Cabins!" cried Vladislava rapturously. "In the woods! Are they spooky? Do you think leshiye will come up to them in the middle of the night!?"

"Perhaps," said Olga, giving Slava a sidelong glance.

"Oh, I hope so! Do you think we'll see water spirits as well? Will we be traveling on the Krasna?"

"No," Olga told her. "We'll be traveling overland the whole way, especially as the ice might start to weaken soon. Here's the Krasna"—she drew a vertical line with some spilled beer on the table—"and here's Krasnograd"—she made a dot halfway down the vertical line—"and here's Pristanograd, where the Krasna flows into the Sea of Ice"—she made a dot at the top of the vertical line—"and here's Lesnograd"—she made a dot far off to the right of the line. "So we'll be traveling like this"—she drew a diagonal line from Lesnograd down to Krasnograd—"like the long part of a triangle. If the water were open it might be quicker to take the Severnovostochnaya road to Vostochnoye Selo," she made another dot above the vertical line, and a wavy North-South line along it to represent the seashore, "and then sail across the Sea of Ice to Pristanograd and then down the Krasna to Krasnograd, but the water isn't open, so we'll be taking the Krasnogradskaya road through the forest instead."

"But then how will Dunya get home?" asked Vladislava, the thought apparently just occurring to her. "Naberezhnoye is in the opposite direction, isn't it?"

"Yes," said Olga, making another dot above the one representing Vostochnoye Selo. "But Dunya says she wants to see the South."

"When the water does open, I will in fact sail up the Krasna to Pristanograd, and then across the Sea of Ice to Naberezhnoye," Dunya put in. It was the first time, as far as Slava could recall, that she had spoken all day. Although she had not been in so foul a mood as Olga, or as nervous as she had been since they had arrived in Lesnograd, she still seemed less confident than she had when they were back in the woods and the tundra. Slava had wanted to speak with her privately, but in the sleighs there was no chance to do so.

Olga might have been in no mood for talking, and Dunya might have been even more quiet than her normal silent self, but Vladislava made up for that by talking incessantly all through supper and after they had all settled into their beds, until finally Olga told her rather sharply that true travelers sleep when they can, at which point Vladislava promptly fell silent and went to sleep.

She leapt out of bed well before dawn the next morning and fussed around the room impatiently until Olga said it was time to go to breakfast. She wanted to go say farewell to their old horses and see the new horses being harnessed, and was briefly crushed when Olga told her she'd just get in the stablehands' way, but recovered her spirits as soon as the sleighs were brought round, and she could go and introduce herself to their new horses, and learn all their names. She spent the morning telling Slava—and Olga and Dunya, although they tended not to pay the necessary attention—lengthy and intricate stories about their new horses' lives.

This activity, unfortunately, palled in the afternoon, which Vladislava spent fidgeting in her seat and asking how much longer they had to go before they reached their destination, both for the day and for the journey as a whole. Slava suggested that they continue Vladislava's lessons, but Vladislava, despite her evident boredom, put up a forceful resistance to anything resembling education, even though she had been lamenting her lack of lessons back in Lesnograd.

"You said I'd have good tutors once we got to Krasnograd," Vladislava pointed out to her. "Why would I want to waste my time taking lessons from *you* in the meantime?"

"If you're going to be my ward, you will have to know all about the other noble families before you arrive in Krasnograd," said Slava, struck by a sudden inspiration. "And the rules of courtly behavior, of course," she added.

"What do you mean?" demanded Vladislava.

"How to behave like a princess," explained Slava.

"I know how to behave like a princess! I *am* a princess!"

"Well reasoned," said Slava with a smile, which she hoped was not too condescending, "but you see, Vladislava Vasilisovna, being a princess is more than just being a princess, at least in Krasnograd. You have to let everyone know you are a princess, without telling them directly, because telling them directly would mean not acting like a princess."

"That's just stupid!"

"Oh no, it's very clever," Slava told her. "Anyone can *say* she's a princess, after all, but only someone who has practiced for years can *show* that she's a princess."

Vladislava mulled this over for a while and then agreed, although skeptically, that it might be true and that in that case, Slava should give her lessons on how to behave like a princess. This caused Olga to choke on suppressed laughter, which made Vladislava glare at her and say that maybe *she* needed lessons on how to be a princess too, at which point Dunya broke in and said that she thought the waystation lights were showing on the road up ahead, which allowed Slava to evade any need to respond to Vladislava's extremely correct but very un-princessly remark.

The lessons on princessly behavior occupied them for the next several days of uneventful travel. Slava quickly realized that Vladislava's training in this sphere had been entirely neglected, as her mother and grandmother had alternated between spoiling her dreadfully and subjecting her to cruel reproaches and humiliations, not to mention the constant hysterical scenes that filled the Lesnograd kremlin. This meant that Vladislava, while being (Slava liked to think) naturally inclined towards goodness, had no idea what constituted good behavior or even common decency, and, being much cleverer than any of her relations, tended to treat all her elders with well-deserved contempt.

Slava therefore not only had to teach her how to behave, but convince her that behaving that way was necessary, and that it was not, for instance, acceptable to interrupt people in order to point out how stupid they were, especially if the people in question were older, and most especially if they actually were stupid, which was, tragically, so often the case.

As most of Vladislava's relatives were, as far as Slava could tell, deaf to any kind of reasoned argument, and impervious to kindness, Vladislava had learned to deal with them through a combination of bullying and indifference, and retraining her would be, Slava could see, an effort of many months. Her efforts would be hindered not only by Vladislava's skepticism, but by her—entirely sensible—fear of adults, who until now had shown very few signs of trustworthiness. Vladislava seemed to trust Slava more than she did anyone else, but a lifetime—even such a short one as Vladislava's—of mistreatment and betrayal had left its mark, and Slava feared it would not be an easy one to erase.

Slava's efforts to school Vladislava in princessly behavior were also hindered by the presence of Olga in the sleigh, since Olga kept trying to alleviate her boredom by laughing at half the things Slava said. This afforded Vladislava many opportunities either to point out that Olga thought Slava's suggestions were silly, or to ignore Slava's suggestions by being rude to Olga. Slava supposed she should be grateful that this was her worst concern of the journey, but it did make maintaining her patience quite a challenge.

Was, Slava asked herself, her impending motherhood going to be nothing but years and years of this? No, she told herself, because having seen Vasilisa Vasilisovna's bad example, she would do a much better job of raising her own daughter. She was aware that those words were more in the way of self-encouragement than a statement of fact, but she repeated them to herself at least fifteen times a day anyway.

Five days out from Lesnograd they stopped for the night with Princess Malolesnaya. The Malolesniye, as their title suggested, had once ruled their own small province on the edge of the Severnolesnoye territory, but they had been swallowed up by the expanding Severnolesniye, and now the only thing left of their former glory, insignificant as it had been, was a small holding and the right to be called "princess" and sit on the Princess Council in Krasnograd. Princess Malolesnaya had not exercised that right in some years, preferring to send her eldest daughter in her stead. Slava knew that Princess Malolesnaya's daughter was ashamed of her mother's easy-going ways, and afraid that her casual generosity would leave nothing for her, the heir, to inherit.

Although Slava felt sorry for the daughter, she hoped that her assessment and Slava's own dim but fond memories of Princess Malolesnaya's character were correct, as it would make their stay much more pleasant and also provide Vladislava with a good place to practice her newly acquired skills. If she had, in fact, acquired them: Slava had some misgivings on that score.

Many of the newer princesses liked to build what they called "kremlins" on their territory, and then inhabit them with their so-called armies. Malolesnograd's kremlin, however, really was a kremlin, or had been at one point. Looking at it, Slava doubted whether the front gate had ever been closed during her lifetime, or whether it was even closable at all. If she remembered her history correctly, it was said to be the oldest kremlin still standing in the entire land, although—Slava thought as they drove past a wall leaning at a disturbing angle—"standing" was an optimistic assessment of its condition.

Princess Malolesnaya came running out to greet them herself, and was overjoyed when she discovered that Olga Vasilisovna and her retinue had arrived and that they were requesting hospitality for the night. Although the Malolesniye had no reason to love the Severnolesniye, and any other Malolesnaya would probably have taken full advantage of the opportunity to mistreat Princess Severnolesnaya's younger daughter—daughters, especially younger daughters, being such good targets for the petty rage of a mother's impotent enemies—Princess Malolesnaya showed no signs of such smallness of soul, but rather every indication of a native generosity of spirit that, Slava lamented to herself, was all too rare amongst her sister princesses. She was a large, kindly-faced woman who was passing from "motherly" to "grandmotherly," which allowed her to pat Olga—whom she remembered as a little child—on the cheek and demand a kiss from Vladislava. Vladislava, Slava was proud to see, gave the kiss with fairly good grace, despite her obvious reservations.

When Slava was introduced to her, Princess Malolesnaya stopped short for a moment in shock, bowed down to her boot tops, and then recovered herself and asked Slava if she remembered going for a ride in the park behind the kremlin with Princess Malolesnaya on her last visit to Krasnograd.

"Yes, of course," said Slava. That was not true at first, but then, as Princess Malolesnaya began reminiscing about the ride, the memories came back to her. It had been, she recalled, one of the jollier days of her childhood, made so largely by the presence of Princess Malolesnaya. Having dredged up this memory, Slava promptly shared it with the others, which touched Princess Malolesnaya so deeply that tears came to her eyes, and she begged permission to kiss Slava's hand.

Still shedding tears of joy, she then led them inside the kremlin, which was small and full of narrow dark corridors, just as an ancient kremlin should be. Apologizing for the poorness of the lodgings she had to offer them, she led them each personally to their rooms, sending whatever servants she happened to encounter in the corridors (sprinkling her words heavily with endearments, of course) to gather their things from the sleighs and carry them to their rooms.

Slava's room was small and dark, naturally, which caused Princess Malolesnaya a moment's anxiety, but Slava quickly laid her fears to rest by telling her that it was much finer than anything she would ever find in a waystation, and furthermore that she considered it an honor to spend the night in the renowned ancient kremlin of Malolesnograd, which pleased Princess Malolesnaya so much Slava thought she might burst on the spot.

Princess Malolesnaya, practically quivering with pride and joy, then left Slava to her own devices in order to show the others to their rooms, but returned shortly after that with Vladislava and a troubled look on her face. It seemed that Princess Malolesnaya had assumed that "the little princess Vladislava," who was clearly too young to be left in a strange room by herself for the night—she might have nightmares, poor thing!—would *of course* wish to stay with her dear Aunty Olga, only Aunty Olga had said, somewhat grumpily, that Vladislava should stay with the Tsarinovna instead. Princess Malolesnaya had found this lack of aunt-like feeling to be quite shocking, and also feared that the Tsarinovna would not wish to be bothered with a young girl like dear little Vladislava, which would hurt dear little Vladislava's feelings, although the gods knew that Princess Malolesnaya would consider it both an honor and a delight to have dear little Vladislava spend the night in her chambers, but...

"Vladislava Vasilisovna should of course spend the night with me," Slava managed to cut in. "She is coming to Krasnograd as my ward, and Olga Vasilisovna was right to send her to me. I was most remiss not to say something earlier."

Although this provoked a tiresome round of denials that Slava could ever do anything wrong, it did smooth over the troubling situation most satisfactorily, and Vladislava was overjoyed at the prospect of spending the whole night alone with Slava. She filled Slava's ears with everything she had observed since they had arrived at the kremlin, and was cut short only when a servant arrived to tell them that Princess Malolesnaya would be most obliged if they would deign to do her the honor of steaming in her bathhouse before supper, if they would not find it too fatiguing.

Vladislava greeted this invitation with rather more excitement than Slava would have supposed it warranted, until she discovered that Vladislava had never been in any bathhouse other than the one in the Lesnograd kremlin, and was hoping for something strange and exotic. Princess Malolesnaya's extremely ordinary bathhouse proved to be a disappointment in that respect, but Vladislava recovered her spirits by throwing water onto the rocks until the bathhouse was filled with a choking cloud of steam that forced everyone else to lie face-down on the benches and hide their heads in their towels. Vladislava took advantage of this to beat them with steaming birch branches until Slava began to worry that her skin had been steamed right off.

Vladislava then went to pour more water on the rocks, since the bathhouse atmosphere had become unacceptably breathable, but Olga stopped her with a cranky, "That's enough, Vladya!" Vladislava pouted a little, but when Olga told her it was time to go to supper, she stopped pouting in order to run out and roll in the snow and then run back in, dry off, and get dressed as if pouting were something that only happened to other people.

Servants were waiting in the dressing room with clean clothes, so they were able to dress themselves—or rather, let the servants dress them, much to the distress of Olga, who disliked that kind of thing, and Dunya, who was completely unaccustomed to it—and make their pink and glowing way to the supper table, where Princess Malolesnaya made good-natured remarks about how healthy they looked.

Although Slava had nothing but fond memories of Princess Malolesnaya from her childhood, she found as the evening wore on that dealing with her as an adult was more trying. Princess Malolesnaya was very kind, it was true, but she chattered on and on about all kinds of things, making cheerful remarks about them even when it would have been more appropriate to express sorrow or anger, or possibly say nothing at all. Although Slava envied her her sunny mood, she found Princess Malolesnaya's complete disregard for the darker reality of events to be quite grating after a few hours.

During supper she quizzed them closely, although with no apparent motive other than benevolent curiosity, about their journey. Olga, who was still in a foul mood, answered as curtly as possible, except when describing their hardship and suffering. Princess Malolesnaya would then make some kind of comforting remark, which Olga would flatly contradict, until Slava began to fear that Princess Malolesnaya's feelings would be hurt, if such a thing were possible (Slava was already harboring the uncharitable thought that Princess Malolesnaya must have no feelings at all, much as she knew that could not be the case), and took charge of the conversation herself. She asked Princess Malolesnaya if she had any news from Krasnograd, which prompted Princess Malolesnaya to send for a letter she had recently received from her daughter, which, she said, was full of interesting reports.

"Let's see..." said Princess Malolesnaya, unrolling the letter and peering at it. She brought it right up to her nose, and then, shaking her head, said, "How silly of me! I can't see anything closer than arm's length," and held the scroll out as far from her as she could. This was still not far enough for her to make out the letters, though, so she started to call for her stewardess to read it for her, but Olga jumped up and insisted on reading it herself, to which Princess Malolesnaya acquiesced with surprise but smiling good grace.

"Most honored Princess, and dearest Mother..." began Olga, only to be interrupted as Princess Malolesnaya went into a lengthy disquisition on her eldest daughter's many merits, until she was interrupted in her turn by Olga, who was still in no mood to listen to the good-natured chatter of others. Slava feared that Vladislava was being exposed to a very poor model of how to behave, but she could do nothing to check Olga without behaving poorly herself, and so resolved to suffer in silence as long as she could.

"I hope you continue in the excellent health in which I found you last...And so on and so on," continued Olga, only to be told by Princess Malolesnaya to read out the full list of compliments and courtesies, since "it would do us all such good to hear so many good sentiments."

Gritting her teeth, Olga complied in a tone of voice that belied the sugary words she was reading, but to Slava's relief, Princess Malolesnaya appeared completely oblivious to Olga's mood, and smiled and interjected multiple compliments and courtesies of her own. Slava began to wonder what land Princess Malolesnaya actually lived in, and whether or not she could join her there. But then she thought that even if she could join Princess Malolesnaya there, she shouldn't, because the inhabitants of Princess Malolesnaya's land, by failing to see evil, allowed a great deal of it to go on unchecked.

"Much of import has happened since I wrote you last—finally!" said Olga. Slava found herself closing her eyes for a moment in horror, but when she hastily reopened them, hoping that no one had noticed, Princess Malolesnaya was still smiling away.

"Marriages, births, deaths, the usual," said Olga, skimming down the letter with her eyes.

"Oh, do read them out complete, *dearest* Olga Vasilisovna," said Princess Malolesnaya. "So much good news!"

Sighing audibly, Olga read:

"Princess Malokrasnova and Princess Yuzhnokrasnova have at long last healed the enmity between their families by joining their youngest children in marriage, to the great delight of the whole kremlin. Theirs was truly a story of forbidden love that brought two warring families together, and after all the obstacles that stood in their way, it was with wholehearted joy that I witnessed their wedding. Although it took place in the midst of sad events, for Valery Annovich's sister at long last succumbed to the illness that had made her its victim since the fall, and his second-sister, it seems, will never walk again after her unlucky accident, while Serafimiya Svetlanovna's older sister is very weak and is unlikely to recover after the difficult birth of a still-born child, the wedding itself was a joyous occasion, and both princesses may take heart in the fact that they still have members of the family to carry on their line, and that these two hearts have at last been joined into what, we all pray, will be a fruitful union."

"Serafimiya Svetlanovna finally got Valery Annovich to marry her!" cried Slava in astonishment.

"You know them?" asked Olga, looking at Slava over the edge of the letter with a sour expression.

"You know them!" exclaimed Princess Malolesnaya happily. "Oh, Tsarinovna! Was there truly a great love between them?"

"Well..." said Slava. "Serafimiya Svetlanovna was certainly very much in love with Valery Annovich when I left Krasnograd, and despaired of every getting him to marry her."

"Oh, the poor young man! No doubt he suffered from the most awful longing for his beloved for so many months! Thank the gods that his mother's hard heart was finally softened enough to give him his own heart's desire!"

"Yes," said Slava, not having the heart to say that, as far as she could see, Valery Annovich was a fickle and spoiled little boy who had long grown tired of Serafimiya Svetlanovna, but had not found the strength of will to disobey his mother's command. But perhaps, she told herself comfortingly, Serafimiya Svetlanovna would become like a mother to him, and they could both learn to be happy.

"I am saddened to report that Princess Stepnaya's health continues to worsen, and she is not expected to last the winter," continued Olga.

"Oh!" cried Princess Malolesnaya, even though she must have known that was coming. "The poor thing! Her poor family! Did you know her, Tsarinovna?"

"She was my father's aunt, and my mother's most trusted ally," said Slava. "I am very sorry to hear this, although she has been in such poor health for the past two years that living has become a burden to her, I believe. But her passing will throw the entire kremlin into disarray."

"As you know, her only daughter has failed to produce an heir even after several husbands," read Olga. "However, it is said that her son's new wife has happy expectations."

"That must be a great comfort to her in her final days!" exclaimed Princess Malolesnaya.

"Her son's wife is half Tribeswoman, and it is rumored that she intends to return to her homeland beyond the mountains after the joyous event. It is also rumored that the father is not Princess Stepnaya's son, as his wife had a well-known connection with the khan of her tribe before her marriage."

"Tribeswomen," said Princess Malolesnaya, shaking her head.

"Naturally this has caused much talk about the succession of the Stepnaya family, which unfortunately of late has not been very prolific. The Tsarina has reminded everyone that her own sister, Krasnoslava Tsarinovna, is in fact next in line to inherit the Stepnaya territory after Princess Stepnaya's daughter, if her son should fail to produce a daughter or if there should be doubt about the father. Descent through the male line is such a chancy business! There is much speculation that the Tsarina intends not to permit the adoption of the prince's wife into the family, as might happen under other circumstances, but to dissolve the marriage between Princess Stepnaya's son and the Tribeswoman, in order to marry him to Krasnoslava Tsarinovna, which would cement her claim to the Stepnaya lands." Olga stopped and looked at Slava inquiringly.

"It's true that I am next in line to inherit," said Slava.

"But would you want the leavings of some Tribeswoman?" demanded Olga. "And your own, what, third-brother at that?"

"Well, no," Slava admitted. "Perhaps it won't come to that."

"Hmmm," said Olga, and went back to reading.

The rest of the letter was only meaningless gossip, leaving Slava free to think on what she had heard. As soon as Olga had spoken Princess Stepnaya's name, Slava's heart had jumped in her chest, and had gone on to pour out cold blood to the rest of her body as she had heard the rest of the story. She was not in the habit of thinking much about the Stepnaya succession issue, and tended to forget the very real possibility that she could end up inheriting the territory.

Princess Stepnaya's daughter was only a little older than she was, and Slava had always assumed that one day she would manage to produce a child, and even if she didn't, she would still be able to rule the territory for many years after her mother's death, which, despite the old princess's ill health, had always seemed such a far-off event... But now it seemed the old princess really was on her deathbed, and her heir still had not produced an heir of her own, while Slava herself might very well be expecting...Slava tried to calculate the days, to see if she really was pregnant, but decided it was too early to come to any definite conclusions...travel was so upsetting to the body...perhaps by the time they arrived in Krasnograd she would know for certain...she was going to have to break the news to her sister...she couldn't help but think (with a cold sinking sensation in the pit of her stomach) that the curse had already started working, and that the situation with the Stepnaya family was in some way connected to it, even if she couldn't quite think how...greed was a curse in and of itself, with no need for Northern sorceresses to cast it...

"What are you thinking about?" demanded Vladislava, jolting her back to the supper table.

"Krasnograd," answered Slava, fairly honestly. "I've been gone so long it's almost as if Krasnograd had stopped existing for me, and now it has stretched out its hand and is pulling me back."

"That's a horrible picture," said Olga, shuddering. "Like a nightmare."

"Yes," Slava had to agree. "Although I think I am ready to face it now." And as she said it, she realized that right at this moment, at least, she did feel ready to face Krasnograd. She had turned down the icy armor she had been offered in the Midnight Land, but right now she felt as if she had found something warmer and stronger to take its place, as if, at long last, she had finally grown the psychic skin she had been missing since birth. New skin was so fragile, though.

Princess Malolesnaya made a number of comments on the letter, all of which, fortunately, required no thought from Slava for their response, and then, showing true kindness, sent them to bed immediately after supper.

Slava awoke the next morning with a feeling of unease. At first she couldn't put her finger on what was bothering her, but then she understood: it was early, the maids had not yet come and breakfast was still being prepared in the kitchen, and yet it was already light. There was also some kind of strange sound coming from the yard...Slava got out of bed and looked out the window, but could see nothing except a clear gray sheet of water running over the glass...it was raining. There was a knock at the door.

"Did you see?" Olga demanded as soon as Slava let her in. "Rain! It will be a disgusting day for travel."

"Spring has come," said Slava.

"Yes," agreed Olga, wrinkling her nose in distaste. "Thank the gods it won't be true spring for another month at least! Let us hope this rain turns to snow before the day gets much further."

But it was still raining when they set off, despite Princess Malolesnaya's attempts to keep them until the rain stopped. Olga and Slava were both too keen to reach Krasnograd, they agreed, to be put off by a little rain.

This keenness lasted, though, only until the cold rain soaked through their clothes, which were meant to withstand nothing more substantial than snow. The rain also turned the firm snowy road into patches of treacherous ice and knee-deep slop, exhausting the horses and causing the sleighs to skid wildly on the slick patches and then jerk to a sudden stop on hitting the slush. After a few versts of this Slava would have been glad to be in the Malolesnaya kremlin, or any other shelter with four walls and a fire, but there was nothing around them but endless fir trees.

By afternoon the rain had let off, but the relief was short-lived, for it was followed closely by a rising wind that howled so eerily through the trees that Vladislava started to cry and the horses, who were little happier with the weather than they were, flicked their ears and jingled their harnesses nervously.

"How much longer till we stop for the night?" Slava asked Olga.

"I'd meant to go all the way to Sredyolochnoye, the village on the far side of this forest, but now I think we should stop sooner, if we can," Olga told her. "Sredyolochnoye's at least another fifteen versts off, but if I remember right, there's a cabin only two or three versts from here. Judging by this wind, there'll be snow during the night, so if we're lucky, we'll be able to make good time tomorrow."

"Good," said Slava, cheered considerably at the news that they only had another two or three versts to go before they reached shelter. Even Vladislava stopped crying at this, although she remained huddled up next to Slava with her face buried in Slava's chest, and shuddered every time the wind gave a particularly loud howl. It was no doubt better that she wasn't looking out into the forest, Slava thought, for the trees were moving in the wind like living things, stretching out their branches covetously towards the sleighs. Whenever she could catch a glimpse of the sky, dark gray clouds were racing across it as if fleeing the oncoming night, but the sky itself only grew darker and darker.

They had slogged through the slushy snow for what seemed like much longer than two or three versts when Olga suddenly cried out, unable to hide the relief in her voice, "There it is! The cabin!"

Everyone cheered, and the horses, who had obviously traveled this road many times before, picked up their pace and, despite their exhaustion, trotted quite smartly through the gate and up to the stable behind the cabin.

"Quick, close the gate!" shouted someone, and one of the men leapt out of the sleigh and slammed the gate shut behind them, while everyone else piled out of the sleighs to begin unloading things and putting the horses away for the night.

As soon as the tall stockade gate had been barred, it seemed that the howling of the wind grew less, even though Slava knew that was not actually true. She and Vladislava carried the food inside, leaving the others to unharness the horses.

"The horses must be very tired, poor things," said Vladislava, who had recovered most of her spirits as soon as the gate had been shut.

"Yes," said Slava. "Very tired. I hope none of them were injured, sliding around like that all day."

"Look!" cried Vladislava, pointing up. "A star!" And sure enough, a star shone through a tiny break in the clouds for a moment, before being engulfed in their insatiable racing. The trees loomed over the stockade fence and waved frenziedly at Slava.

"Yes, a star," said Slava, looking quickly back down.

"Do you think it's good luck?" asked Vladislava.

"Oh certainly," said Slava, who thought no such thing but also thought it would do them both good to hear her say it.

"OH!" Vladislava screamed, and dropped her bundle.

"What is it!" Slava cried, dropping her own bundle and clutching Vladislava to her.

"Eyes!" said Vladislava. "I saw eyes peering out from under the porch!" She pointed at the space under the porch stairs.

Afterwards, when she thought of it, Slava was always amazed at how boldly she went to look under the stairs, but she could see no eyes, nor any sign that a creature had been there.

"Perhaps you just thought you saw them," she suggested kindly.

"No, I saw them! Eyes looking right at us!" Vladislava insisted.

"Perhaps it was a little woodland creature, taking refuge from the rain," Slava said.

"Like what?"

"Like a snow hare or a snow fox," said Slava.

"It looked bigger than that," said Vladislava doubtfully, but she seemed comforted by Slava's suggestion, and made her way up the steps, albeit with exaggerated caution, and followed Slava into the cabin, where the charms of a run-down wayside cabin and the prospect of cooking their coarse provisions into some kind of supper soon overshadowed all thoughts of the howling wind and mysterious eyes watching them from the darkness.

The cabin was too small for a party as large as theirs, and they ended up being jammed in four to a bed, which was warm if not especially comfortable.

"It's only fair," said Dunya, when Vladislava complained about it.

"We had to put some of the horses in two to a stall."

"But what if they start fighting!" cried Vladislava anxiously. "Don't horses fight with each other sometimes?"

"We'll have to hope for the best," Dunya told her. "Princess Malolesnaya's horses are very calm, and I think they're too tired to fight tonight, anyway."

"Oh good, because it would be terrible if they started fighting—but what if that creature comes in the night and starts bothering them? What will they do then?" demanded Vladislava.

"What creature?" Olga wanted to know.

This led to a very exciting description by Vladislava of the eyes she had seen.

"Probably a snow hare," said Olga. "I doubt the horses have anything to worry about. Go to sleep."

Being right on the edge of the bed with Vladislava digging into her back, Slava found it difficult to fall asleep, despite an exhaustion from the long day in the rain that made it impossible to form a single coherent thought. For a long time there was nothing in her mind except blackness, but then it seemed to her that something was watching her. She looked all around the room, but every time she thought she had turned her gaze in the direction of the eyes fixed upon her, they disappeared.

"Can't you stay still!" she finally cried in exasperation. "I only want to talk to you!"

"Over here, Krasnoslava Tsarinovna," said a faint voice, that sounded as if it must be at least two hundred years old. "Down here, in the far corner."

"Oh, there you are," said Slava, finally finding the small huddled figure in the far corner of the tiny bedroom. "What do you want?"

"I want you to come down and talk to me," said the small huddled figure. "If you can lower yourself so far."

"Of course," said Slava, climbing out of bed. The shock of the cold air made her jerk awake. She was balanced precariously right on the edge of the bed, with Vladislava digging into her back. She had an intense sensation of being watched. She searched all over the room with her eyes, but found nothing.

"It was a dream," she told herself, and shut her eyes to go back to sleep, but just then she thought she heard a noise from the far corner, where the small huddled figure had been in her dream. She opened her eyes again, and this time it seemed to her that perhaps there *was* a small huddled figure, crouched down in that corner. Slava's heart jumped in her throat, and a cold trickle of sweat ran down her side.

Perhaps it's just a bundle of clothing, or an extra blanket, she told herself. She looked at it as hard as she could in the darkness, but could come to no definite conclusion about its contents.

If I don't find out what it is, I'll think about all night and I won't get a wink of sleep, she told herself, and slid out from under the covers. She tiptoed over towards the formless dark shape in the corner, but stopped a couple of feet away from it, still unable to make out what it was, but too apprehensive to come any closer.

"Over here, Krasnoslava Tsarinovna," said a voice in her head. It was very faint, and sounded as if it were at least two hundred years old.

"What do you want?" Slava whispered.

"I want you to come down and talk to me," said the small huddled figure. "If you can lower yourself so far."

"Of course," whispered Slava, sitting down on the floor, which was extremely cold and dusty. "Who are you?"

"The house-spirit of this cabin," said the small huddled figure.

"I didn't know these cabins had house-spirits," said Slava, since it was the only thing she could think of saying.

"Most don't," said the small huddled figure faintly. "Just a few. And we are old and uncared for, as you see."

"You poor thing," whispered Slava. "How do you survive?"

"The charity of strangers," said the small huddled figure, turning to look at Slava more directly. Slava's eyes suddenly grew able to focus on it, and she saw that it looked almost like a small hairy woman who was no bigger than a little child, but also like a leshaya, and that it was very, very old. It was sitting with its back to the wall, hugging its knees.

"Is there something I can do for you?" Slava asked.

"Do you know what house-spirits are, Krasnoslava Tsarinovna?" asked the house-spirit softly.

"What?" asked Slava.

"We stand halfway between the world of women and the world of magic," said the house-spirit. "We are sisters to both women and the leshiye, and daughters of the gods themselves. Does that sound familiar?"

"Well..." said Slava, to whom it did not sound familiar, even though she could tell by the house spirit's voice that it should.

"What do you think your daughter will be, Krasnoslava Tsarinovna, should she have the good fortune to be born?"

"She will be a house-spirit?" asked Slava, trying to hide her distaste at the thought. In her mind's eye her daughter was already tall and beautiful, with hair the color of fire and eyes the color of the sea.

"No, don't worry about that, Krasnoslava Tsarinovna," said the house-spirit, laughing faintly. "She will be even more beautiful than how you picture her now. Should she have the good fortune to be born. But like me, she will be halfway between two worlds, and the pawn of both, unless she takes great care not to be used."

"I will teach her to be strong and wise!" Slava exclaimed.

"I'm sure you shall, Krasnoslava Tsarinovna," said the house-spirit. "Just as you are doing your best to teach young Vladislava who lies there in your bed. But young Vladislava, and your little daughter, would do well to learn that there is more to living than being strong and wise, which comes so naturally to them anyway. I was glad to see that Vladislava was frightened when I peered out at her from under the stairs. It is good for the strong and wise to know what it is to be fearful and foolish from time to time. I hope you teach your little Krasnoslavovna to be gentle and humble, as well as strong and wise.

"I came to you to ask you to teach her to remember us little folk too, and to remember that she is one of us. Strength, and wisdom, and courage, and a heart and mind full of fire are all very well, but so many of us lead our little lives tied to our hearths and homes, and that is all very well too. Don't let her forget that, Krasnoslava Tsarinovna. Don't let her get too proud. Should she have the good fortune to be born."

"I'll try," Slava promised.

"Only try?" asked the house-spirit. "Is that the best you can do?"

"I think that's the best any mother can do," said Slava. "So much of each new life is out of our hands."

"Well said, Krasnoslava Tsarinovna," said the house-spirit. "But now I know: there is something you can do for me."

"What?" asked Slava.

"Send your daughter to me. To us, to the house-spirits, so that she can learn about softness and kindness and service. These are things that many would do well to know more of."

"Yes," said Slava. "Is news of…Is my news spread all over Zem', then? Does the whole world of magic know of it already? Because I myself am still unsure, and you are doing nothing to increase my certainty."

"All the world of magic knew of it the day it happened," said the house-spirit. "Your humility does you credit, Krasnoslava Tsarinovna, but a possibility as great as the arrival of your Krasnoslavovna made everyone with so much as a drop of foreseeing blood in her veins stare into the future and wonder. Your little Krasnoslavovna has a bright path before her, should she have the good fortune to be born, and you may be sure that we—the house-spirits, and the leshiye, and all our sisters and brothers—will do our best to ensure that that happens. So many children are unwanted or unneeded, but your little Krasnoslavovna does not even exist yet, and already we look forward to her rule with hope, which is not often the case, I assure you. And you may be sure of one other thing as well: You will be watched over wherever you go."

"I'm not sure I like the sound of that," said Slava with a little laugh, little as she felt like laughing. The house-spirit's words were not comforting at all, even though Slava could tell she meant them to be so.

"You have nothing to fear, Krasnoslava Tsarinovna," said the house-spirit, stretching out her small wrinkled hand and stroking Slava's own hand, which seemed so large and strong in comparison. "We none of us mean you any harm. And you may count on the house-spirits, I promise you that. My sister in Krasnograd already awaits you."

"The kremlin has a house-spirit?" asked Slava. "I never knew."

"House-spirits only show themselves to the pure of mind and humble of heart," said the house-spirit. "Only those who are willing to serve are worthy of being served. Your family so rarely is worthy. But for you we will make an exception."

"I am honored," said Slava. "Although I fear that I have too much of my family in me to be worthy. Every day the fire and steel my companions accuse me of possessing shows through a little more."

"Fire and steel?" said the house-spirit. "You think you are made of fire and steel?"

"No," said Slava. "But others say I am, and sometimes I feel it coming out of me, like claws stretching forth from my fingers."

"Ah," said the house-spirit. "Well, perhaps that is so. The depths hold many things. But, Krasnoslava Tsarinovna, you and your companions are gravely mistaken if you believe you are made only of fire and steel. I fear you are made of much stronger stuff than that."

"Oh," said Slava. "Such as, for example?"

"Water, Krasnoslava Tsarinovna, water. Water is such a simple thing, is it not? And yet so powerful. After all, we fear fire and steel, but we pour water in and out of our bodies every day without a second thought. We must have it to live, and yet it can kill just as surely as any sword or flame. It takes any shape, and can tear down any wall, brick from brick and stone from stone. It can be cold hard ice, or disappear into the hottest of steam, and yet it will always return as water. You may have steel submerged within you, Krasnoslava Tsarinovna, and you may grow hot enough to scald all around you, but that is because you are made of water, and water you shall always be."

"I suppose I can see that," said Slava, "but perhaps I won't share that with the others. I think it does them better to think of fire and steel. And what about this daughter you say I will have, if she should have the good fortune to be born? Will she be made of water too?"

"What was it you thought to yourself, Krasnoslava Tsarinovna? Hair like fire and eyes the color of the sea? Perhaps that is how she shall be on the outside, but without a doubt that is how she shall be on the inside."

"That sounds difficult," said Slava. "Not that I would expect anything different, given who her parents will be. But I fear she will be unhappy and choke on all that steam."

"Oh, very likely, Krasnoslava Tsarinovna, very likely. Which is why you must send her to me and my sisters. Who better than house-spirits to teach a girl how to keep the kitchen of her own mind? Who better than house-spirits to help someone keep her fires banked and her well clean, so that she can use them for good rather than let them run wild or go bad to destroy her home and family? Promise me, Krasnoslava Tsarinovna, promise me you will send her to us!" The house-spirit's voice rose to a desperate shout, so that Slava feared it would awaken the others, but none of them so much as stirred.

"I promise," she said. "If you promise to watch over her as if she were your own. For she shall be very precious to me, should she have the good fortune to be born, and I already know I will be loath to let her out of my sight even for an instant."

"I promise," said the house-spirit, this time speaking almost in a whisper, as if she had spent all her strength on that last desperate plea. "My head for beheading, Krasnoslava Tsarinovna, she shall know nothing but health and joy when she is with us, nothing but health and joy." The house-spirit reached out her small hand, which was like an old woman's hand but also like the branch of a tree, and rested it on Slava's arm. "Health and joy," she repeated.

"Health and joy," echoed Slava, covering the house-spirit's hand with her own, much larger and fleshier one. For a moment there was a great surge of warmth where the house-spirit was touching her, as if, she couldn't help but think, she were a kettle set on a hot stove, and then they released each other and Slava felt no different than before.

"Now go back to the bed," ordered the house-spirit, sounding exactly like a fussy nanny, only much older. "You need your rest. But when you make breakfast in the morning, make extra for me, and leave some porridge in the pot."

"Of course," said Slava.

"Sweet dreams, Krasna Tsarina," said the house-spirit, and, in some fashion that Slava couldn't quite make out, slipped through a tiny crack in the wall, and disappeared.

Chapter Twelve

The next morning Slava wasn't entirely sure that she had not dreamed her encounter with the house-spirit, but she left a little porridge in the bottom of the pot anyway, feeling unusually peaceful and contented as she did so. If the house-spirit had been a dream, it had been a strangely pleasant one.

And when Vladislava inched fearfully down the steps, watching anxiously for any sign of peering eyes, Slava, instead of telling her there was nothing to fear, told her that whenever she was tempted to mock someone for being afraid of something for which Vladislava had no fear, she should remember how she walked with trembling knees while everyone else skipped blithely down. By the look on Vladislava's face, the lesson did not have much effect, but Slava felt good about saying it, at least.

Yesterday's spring had fled in the night with its racing clouds, to be replaced by a bright hard winter day. The snowy ground was covered with an icy armor that made every step treacherous, and Grisha and Sasha struggled for some time, cursing, with the stockade gate, which had frozen shut.

"It will be another long day," said Olga grimly.

"It's so bright!" complained Vladislava. "It's hurting my eyes!"

"Then keep them shut!" snapped Olga.

"Then I'll be bored!" whined Vladislava.

"We could play a game," suggested Slava. "We could try to guess what's happening by the sound of the sleigh runners."

"You're just saying that to make me stop whining!" said Vladislava resentfully.

"Is it working?" asked Slava, trying to smile as cheeringly as possible.

"NO! It's just making it worse! I hate traveling! I hate winter!"

"You're acting like a girl of five!" shouted Olga.

"*You're* acting like a girl of five, and you're much older!"

"By all the gods, how I hate children!"

"No, you hate Lisochka, and now you're treating me the same way!" screamed Vladislava, and burst into tears. Grisha and Sasha stopped struggling with the gate.

"Everyone is overwrought after our bad day yesterday," said Slava soothingly. This cost her a considerable amount of effort, as what she really wanted to do was shake both Olga and Vladislava until their teeth rattled, but much to her pride, the strain hardly came out in her voice at all.

"Yes, that's it," agreed Olga, her voice trembling. "A change of scene and company would benefit us all. Dunya! You get to tutor the little princess today! Take her in the other sleigh and teach her something!"

"I know nothing of being a princess," Dunya said.

"Good! Nothing good ever came of being a princess anyway. Teach her something useful. Teach her...teach her how to read tracks, or some such thing. Grisha can help."

"When will I ever have to read tracks when I rule Lesnograd?" demanded Vladislava, still sobbing. "That's stupid!"

Olga opened her mouth to shout something ill-considered, but Dima said quickly, "Come with me, little one, and I'll teach you how to drive a sleigh."

"Why? Why should I learn how to drive a sleigh?"

"Because it will be fun, and then you will be able to drive wherever you wish," said Dima.

This argument quelled Vladislava's quarrels and dried her tears, and by the time Grisha and Sasha had gotten the gate closed behind them, Vladislava was in Dima's lap and enthusiastically repeating after him all the parts of the harness. The men who normally rode in the same sleigh with Olga and Slava took one look at Olga's face and retreated wordlessly, leaving Slava and Olga to themselves. The rest of the party all packed somehow into the second sleigh, and they set slowly off.

"Well, perhaps that will keep her out of our hair for a few hours," said Olga. "I don't see how you can stand to be around her."

"She's very clever, and very brave, and a very wonderful child," said Slava. "I can't help but love her."

"She's a vain, spoiled brat who shouts out whatever she thinks will hurt people the most," said Olga.

"Yes, she is very clever," said Slava.

"It doesn't take cleverness to blurt out nonsense!"

"Vladislava rarely blurts out nonsense," said Slava. "Nonsense doesn't hurt people."

This provoked a long sullen silence from Olga, which was just as well, as the ice on the road required extremely careful driving. It was only after they had gone several versts, and the icy snow had softened into slush, that Olga suddenly said, as if there had been no pause in their conversation, "You don't honestly take her words seriously, do you?"

"Very seriously," said Slava. "I take everyone's words seriously."

"But most people's words are just nonsense! Trash!"

"If you're tracking a creature through the woods, then its scat is a valuable sign, even if it has no value of its own," said Slava.

"True enough," said Olga. "Well, I'll soon be rid of her, and you'll be welcome to spend as much time listening to her as you wish. Thank the gods Lisochka didn't take up your offer to come with us too! Anyone would think you wanted a child of your own, the way you keep taking in strays."

"Perhaps I do," said Slava.

"Want a child of your own? No, you don't. Or if you do, you're crazy. No one wants children."

"Most women want children," said Slava with a smile.

"Most women are fools," said Olga. "But they only realize their foolishness when it's too late. Children are a great curse—even worse than men, which half of them grow up to be, the Black God take them. Thank the gods that you have none, and keep it that way. Why are you smiling in that strange way?"

"Oh..." said Slava, who, despite her best efforts, had been unable to suppress a smile that was half pain and half uncontrollable mirth.

"You're not...expecting a child, are you? You can't be!"

"It seems likely," Slava confessed. "But it's still early yet."

"What!! How!!! Who is the father!?!"

It took Slava some time to sort through all the possible responses to this, and say calmly, "The gods had a hand in it."

"Ugh!" And Olga shuddered all over and fell into a stunned silence for several more versts.

"How!" she suddenly demanded that afternoon.

"Oh, you know," said Slava, unable to repress a grin.

"Truly?" said Olga, giving her a surprised look.

"Is there another way?" asked Slava.

"You said the gods had a hand in it," said Olga. "I thought maybe..."

"Well, it was their idea," said Slava. "But, you know..."

"How horrible!" cried Olga, shuddering all over again.

"Quite the contrary," said Slava, still grinning.

"How did they make you do it? How..." Olga trailed off, her face still filled with horror and revulsion.

"They asked," said Slava. "Many times. And every time I said yes."

"Truly?" demanded Olga.

"Truly," Slava told her. "At first I did not realize to what I was agreeing..."

"How could they!" Olga burst out.

"But then I did realize, and I agreed anyway."

"Why!!?!"

"I felt it needed to be done. Not only that, I wanted to do it. I was happy. I *am* happy, Olga. I feel...fulfilled. As if my life has purpose now, as if I have a reason for living, which I so painfully lacked before."

"You say that now, but you'll change your mind! You might think this is a blessing now, Slava, but it's a curse, a horrible curse, and it will ruin your life!"

"Olga," said Slava, speaking calmly but firmly. "I am not some little girl, caught up in someone else's greedy schemes. What happened to you was terrible, unforgiveable, and I'm sure it seemed that it ruined your life, but..."

"I'm not talking about me!"

"Yes, you are," said Slava. "Or rather, you're talking about me, but you're thinking about how your mother used you for her own ends, and how that ruined three lives—yours, Andrey Vladislavovich's, and poor Lisochka's. But my case now is different. When I faced a fate such as yours, I had the good fortune to find an herbwoman in time, and I thank the gods for it, for now I am free to welcome this child, should she have the good fortune to be born, as she deserves, of my own free will."

"They're using you!"

"Yes," agreed Slava. "They are. And I agreed to it. After all, I am getting something out of it too."

"What could you possibly be getting out of this, this, travesty of charity!"

"A child," said Slava. "A purpose, as I said before."

"Slava, listen to me." For a moment Olga's face became calmer and more focused. "I know you think that now, but a child isn't a purpose, a reason for living. Or at least, it's not enough. A child is a burden, pain and sickness, dirty diapers, cracked nipples, screaming through the night, fighting and quarreling, a constant chain holding you back...A child won't make you happy, Slava. A child won't be enough, Slava, it never is."

"No," said Slava. "I have certainly seen too many unhappy mothers and unwanted children to think that a child is the solution to all life's problems. Some, perhaps many, women should never become mothers, Olga, and no woman should become a mother as you did. But that doesn't mean that no one should ever become a mother. I don't know how to convey this to you, Olga, but as soon as it was explained to me, I knew that it was the right thing to do. I *knew*, Olga, and I still know. Have you ever just *known* something, Olga?"

"Yes," said Olga. "The moment I discovered I was with child, I *knew* it was a terrible mistake, a curse."

"And were you right?"

"Yes," said Olga.

"There you go, then," said Slava.

Olga drove on in silence. After a while she said, "I can't change your mind, can I?"

"No," said Slava.

"You're very stubborn, you know," said Olga. "You seem all soft and gentle on the outside, but on the inside you're all—fire and steel. Like your foremother."

"Which one?" asked Slava.

"Miroslava Praskovyevna. Your foremother. The queen of fire and steel. Wasn't that what she was called? It's so easy to forget that her blood flows through your veins, but it does, doesn't it? You are a direct descendent, are you not?"

"Yes, of course," said Slava. "But..." She was about to say out of habit that she and Miroslava Praskovyevna had nothing in common, but then she remembered how untrue that was. Little as Slava would like to admit it, it seemed that she and Miroslava Praskovyevna had a great deal in common, and even Olga, who had not a drop of true-seeing in her blood as far as Slava knew, had seen that truth.

"Well, I suppose it's your problem anyway, not mine," said Olga with a sigh. Then she shook her shoulders and, apparently, shook off her worry, and cried, "The father! You still haven't told me who the father is!"

"Well…"

"There is a father, is there not?"

"Of course," said Slava.

"Of course, you already admitted as much. So who is he? How did it happen? *When* did it happen? When did you find the time…The sanctuary!"

"Yes," admitted Slava.

"Those priestesses are a sly lot!" laughed Olga. "I thought they foreswore relations with men in that order."

"Yes, but I didn't," Slava pointed out.

"But how did they happen to have a man lying about, ready…" Olga trailed off and gave Slava a peculiar look. "Surely not…" she said slowly.

"Mmmm," said Slava, guessing what Olga was thinking.

"He was the only man…But how…"

"It's probably best for you not to dwell on it," said Slava, grinning again.

"You don't mean that I am to have a…a sister?"

"It seems likely," said Slava. "Are you happy?"

"Disgusted, more like," said Olga, curling up her lip but then breaking out into laughter.

"As I said, probably best if you don't dwell on it," said Slava.

"How can I not!" said Olga, but she was still laughing.

"Try," said Slava, pretending to give her a severe look. This only provoked more laughter from Olga, though, and so it was some time before she could speak again.

"So you're happy, then?" she asked.

"Yes," said Slava.

"Well, as you will, then," said Olga, shaking her head. "A sister! At my age! Can I visit her?"

"Of course," said Slava.

"She should come and be fostered in Lesnograd for a time," said

Olga.

"Well…" said Slava.

"No, you're right: not at Lesnograd. What I meant was that she should come and be fostered with me for a time. I could take her on a journey."

"It wasn't that," said Slava. "It's just that this is the third request I've had to foster her, and she has not yet even quickened inside me. I can't help but fear it's bad luck to make these plans so early."

"Oh!" cried Olga, looking remorse-stricken. "You're so right…I'm so sorry, Slava…Normally I would never so much as speak of…it…But in this case…"

"In this case there seems to be no reason to fear drawing down the ill-will of the gods upon her," Slava reassured her. "They seem more well-informed about…this matter than I am, and thus far even keener to see her come into existence. I, frankly speaking, still have little faith in her appearance, and this is all…somewhat of a dream to me. But those who came up with this scheme seem much more certain, and I believe they will do what they can to help, not hinder, her entrance into the world. But she could end up being strong-willed and difficult, and then where would we and our plans be?"

"My sister?" said Olga, laughing once more. "Strong-willed and difficult? I refuse to believe it!"

"I know," said Slava. "It seems so unlikely. But I must plan for all eventualities."

"Well…Well, in that case, Slava, I will simply say that any child of yours will always be welcome to journey with me, should she desire it. I might even take on a son, should you happen to produce one. Well, as long as he resembles his father, that is. If he turns into one of those prancing ninnies filling your kremlin, I'll probably disown him on the spot."

"Once again, I have been promised it will be a girl…Although I don't see how even the gods could have control over something like that…"

"The ways of the gods are strange," said Olga, nodding her head sagely. "Probably best not to question what they say."

"No doubt you are right," agreed Slava.

"A sister!" repeated Olga, giving Slava a look in which all her former bad temper had been forgotten.

"Don't tell the others just yet," said Slava.

"Of course not," promised Olga, giving Slava another fond look.

"We're practically sisters now! Well, I suppose you're more like an aunt to me, but I can't think of you that way. Let's just call ourselves sisters, shall we?"

"Of course, it would please me very much," said Slava.

"Frankly, you're much better than my real sister in many respects," said Olga.

"I could say the same," said Slava, smiling.

"Agreed, then! We'll be sisters!"

"Agreed," said Slava.

And just like that, Olga was back to her old self, just as she had been when they had set out from Krasnograd back before midwinter, as if the ill humor of Lesnograd were less than a bad dream.

She remained that way not only for the rest of the day, but for the next day, and the next, and the next. She even suggested that Vladislava rejoin them in their sleigh, and once she had, she asked Slava to continue her lessons, saying, "She'll need to know this if she's to make the Severnolesniye proud in Krasnograd."

For her part, Vladislava seemed to have finally absorbed some of Slava's teachings, and was able to act for longer and longer stretches at a time like a real princess, as opposed to a spoiled and abused child. Slava began to feel hope that she would be able to let Vladislava out into the company of other young princesses, and even introduce her to her sister, without the results being absolutely disastrous.

As they drew nearer and nearer to Krasnograd, the mood of everyone in the company, including Slava, continued to lift. After dreading her return to Krasnograd for so long, Slava now found herself increasingly eager to arrive and begin what she felt would be a new, important, and meaningful phase in her life. She remembered how numb she had felt as she was leaving the city, and how she had thought that she was, in a sense, going out to her death, even if she survived the journey itself. Now she thought that she had been right, that she had been going out to her death, or at least the death of her old self, and now she was returning a new woman, carrying new life with her and within her.

Sometimes she thought of the curse and her possible role in it, but she felt strangely unconcerned about it. What will be, will be, she thought every time the curse entered her thoughts, and whatever it is, it will lead to rebirth. I will go to it as eagerly as a bride to her wedding, and in fact, that was exactly how she felt. Or at least, how she imagined she felt, since of course she had never actually been married and therefore had no idea whether a bride really went eagerly to her wedding or not.

In fact, in her experience, even when brides seemed to go eagerly to their weddings, they all too often heartily regretted it afterwards. When that thought entered her head, she grinned at herself and told herself not to get so puffed up with her newfound wisdom, which was after all of rather doubtful provenance—and went right back to dreaming about how wonderful everything would be once they all reached Krasnograd, and how she would be happy for the rest of her life, and so on and so forth.

Occupied with such pleasant fantasies, Slava was content to drift along in the sleighs, letting the others worry about where they were and how far they had still to go, and so it was somewhat of a surprise when she overheard Olga telling Vladislava one morning that they were only three days out from Krasnograd.

"Only three days!" exclaimed Slava. "So soon!"

"I don't know what you mean by 'so soon,'" said Olga dryly. "It's been a week of the most disgusting rain and sleet. Traveling in early spring is no joke. And once we get to Krasnograd, we'll be trapped there for weeks."

"Weeks!" Dunya cried out unexpectedly.

"Yes, horrible, isn't it?" said Olga. "The roads will be impassable for at least a month, I'd say, and of course trying to go North will only make it worse, since you'll be traveling with the spring, not the summer."

"No...I just didn't realize it would be so long...To spend so much time in Krasnograd."

"But you'll be with us, Dunya!" said Vladislava. "It will be ever so jolly! You can learn to be a princess, like me!"

"Well..." said Dunya, her normally impassive face caught somewhere between awkwardness and amusement.

"We'll all be in an inn somewhere," said Olga firmly. "Only you and the Tsarinovna will be in the kremlin, Vladislava."

"Why?" demanded Vladislava.

"You would be most welcome in the kremlin," Slava put in.

"Is that so?" said Olga, raising an eyebrow at her. "Do you think the Empress would agree to that?"

"I have a whole suite of rooms for guests at my disposal," said Slava. "You can stay there." She refrained from adding *unless someone else has already been put there,* although in truth she so rarely used "her" guest chambers that she and everyone else tended to forget that they were, in fact, hers, and her sister often put less welcome guests there without bothering to ask Slava's permission. So Olga and the others would probably end up in them anyway, Slava told herself.

"You can't stay in an inn," she said out loud. "Princess Severnolesnaya's daughter, and the aunt to the Tsarinovna's ward! You'll have to stay in the kremlin whether you like it or not, and so will the rest of your party."

"Oh, by all the gods!" said Olga, grinning and looking annoyed at the same time. "No doubt the kremlin will be deadly dull. An inn would be much livelier, I'm sure."

"You can catch up on all the intrigues and plotting that went on while we were gone," said Slava. "That should be entertainment enough to last at least a month."

"Oh yes, that should be very jolly indeed," said Olga. "I think I'd rather join Vladenka in learning to be a princess. Dunya can tag along to make a nice threesome. Would you like to learn to be a princess, Dunya?"

"I fear it will not come very naturally to me," said Dunya gravely, much to everyone's delight.

"Well, we won't be trapped in the kremlin all day, every day," said Olga, looking quite consoled by this thought. "We can go out and about as much as we like, and then return to a nice clean bed and a warm supper. It will be just like being in an inn, only even more comfortable."

"There might be feasts and such," warned Slava. "And if my sister should call a meeting of the Princess Council, then you, at least, would have to attend."

"Oh gods, no!" groaned Olga. "Doesn't my mother have a representative there, anyway?"

"Alyona Miroslavovna, yes," said Slava. "But if the princess's actual daughter were to be in Krasnograd, then naturally she would have to attend..."

"How often does the Empress call meetings of the Princess Council?" asked Olga.

"Oh, two or three times a year, unless some special circumstance should warrant it," said Slava.

"And how often has she called it in the past year?" asked Olga.

"Twice, but she might have called another one while I was away," said Slava.

"So with any luck, she won't call another for months," said Olga, brightening up.

"Yes, but as you said, the roads will be impassable and the princesses correspondingly restless, so she could easily end up calling a meeting just to give them something to do," said Slava. "They spend most of their time eating and quarreling and bossing their children and servants around like a pack of querulous old men who have long outlived their usefulness, so sometimes my sister will call a Princess Council just to see if they can still behave like princesses. Not, it has to be said, that they ever could in the first place. But she has been known to do things like that, when she's in a particularly cruel mood."

"I'm sure I wouldn't need to attend," said Olga, pursing her lips seriously in order to repress a grin. "I'm sure Alyona Miroslavovna has been representing the family admirably, and my presence would only distract her. It would be better if I stayed out of her hair as much as possible."

"Perhaps," said Slava, who was inclined to agree with Olga, but also knew that it would be considered a terrible affront for her not to attend any meeting of the Princess Council, should one be called. She decided to join Olga in hoping that one wouldn't be called.

"Will there be more rain tomorrow?" asked Vladislava. "I hope not!"

"Tomorrow might be clear, little princess," said Grisha, sniffing the air. "Clear and cold."

"How can you tell by sniffing?" Vladislava wanted to know. This led to an unusually wordy explanation from Grisha, which left Slava to her own thoughts.

Three days to Krasnograd! she said to herself. *Only three days!* She wasn't sure what she thought about that. Somehow, when she had left, any possibility of her return had seemed so distant and unlikely that she had had a hard time believing she would ever see Krasnograd again, and yet here she was, only three days away from it. Her stomach suddenly twisted from the thought, and she couldn't tell whether that was because she feared her homecoming, or because she feared that some last-minute catastrophe would prevent it. All the terrors of Krasnograd, all the unhappiness she had experienced there, rose up before her and washed away the happy dreams she had been spinning to herself, making her wish that she still had weeks left of her journey, or that she were back in Lesnograd...Well, maybe not...But now that the Midnight Land, and Lesnograd, and all the other troubles they had faced were far away, and Krasnograd was near, Krasnograd's power suddenly loomed large in Slava's mind, and there was the little matter of the curse, as well...

"Is something the matter, Tsarinovna?" Dunya whispered in her ear.

"No, why?" asked Slava, startled. Dunya's face was very close to hers, and she could see that Dunya was worried too about their imminent arrival in Krasnograd, and that she had seen some sign of nerves from Slava, which was only making her doubly fearful.

"You're clutching your stomach. I thought you might have taken ill."

"Just hungry," said Slava with a smile that was supposed to hide her nerves. She made a conscious effort to stop clutching her stomach, and to straighten up and look cheerful and confident. She had another stab of fear when she thought that now she had even more reason to worry about pains in the stomach, but strictly ordered herself to ignore all such thoughts. "I must have had a sudden vision of the food awaiting us in Krasnograd, and my poor stomach rebelled against its diet of watery porridge."

"Ah, food," said Dunya, also smiling a smile that was meant to show that she wasn't afraid at all. "It will be most welcome after our long days on this rainy road."

"Indeed," Slava agreed, smiling even harder. "Krasnograd is a most marvelous city, Dunya, and right now it seems to me that the food is the most marvelous thing about it."

"Tell me of Krasnograd, Tsarinovna, for I know little of it," said Dunya, also smiling harder.

And so Slava spoke to her at length of the wonders of Krasnograd, the Beautiful City, the city of forty forties of towers, and they both pretended to be interested in Slava's words and to be glad to be approaching the city that they both feared. Although this did not actually make them feel any better about Krasnograd, it did occupy them until they reached a spot in the road that was so icy and muddy that they all had to get out of the sleighs and walk for close to a verst before the road became safe to drive on again. That made them so cold and wet that they had no more energy to spare for dreading Krasnograd, a welcome development.

They stopped that night at a waystation that was full up with travelers desperate to reach their destination before the roads disintegrated entirely into a muddy morass. Olga suggested, although not very seriously, that Slava announce herself and demand that the station be cleared for her, but Slava refused even to consider it, and so Olga, Slava, Dunya, and Vladislava were squeezed together in a bed meant for two people, while the men were told they could sleep in the stable. Suddenly Krasnograd didn't seem very bad at all.

The next morning the roads were solid ice. The waystation mistress, after taking one look out the front porch, announced that none of her horses would be leaving the stable until the footing softened into something less treacherous. This provoked a general wail from all the breakfasting travelers.

"Travelers come and go, but my horses are my livelihood," said the waystation mistress in response to their pleas and lamentations. "Break your own heads if you like, but may the Black God take me if I let you bow a tendon on one of my own horses."

Olga at first wanted to wait at the waystation until its mistress would permit her horses to be used, but when she asked the waystation mistress how long that would be, she was told that they would be last in line for horses when they were finally released, which would mean they would probably end up waiting at least until the next day in any case. Slava could see that she was opening her mouth to claim priority due to rank, and hastily forestalled her by saying, "What if we used our old horses?"

"They're pretty tired," said Olga, obviously irked by the station mistress's refusal. "I doubt we'll get far with them."

"But farther than we will without any horses at all?" Slava asked.

"Well...When you put it like that..." Olga suddenly grinned. "We won't be able to go above a walk today in any case, no doubt, so I suppose we might as well plod along with the old nags we've already got."

After further consultation with Dunya, Grisha, and Dima, and several forays out onto the main road to test its condition, it was decided that their party would set out directly, but that they would walk beside the sleighs until the road softened up enough to be safe.

"You must be in a powerful hurry to get to Krasnograd," observed one of the other travelers as they prepared to set off.

"We've been on the road a long time, and we have precious cargo," said Olga.

"Apparently not that precious, if you're willing to risk it on these roads," said the other traveler. "But youth is impetuous, and nobility is arrogant."

"Who said I was noble!" cried Olga indignantly, much to Slava's amusement.

"Anyone can see you're used to getting your own way, noblewoman," said the other traveler, shaking her head and preparing to return to the breakfast room. Judging by her looks, she had long left the folly of youth behind her, preferring ample breakfasts instead. "Well, life will teach you different, I have no doubt. You'll slow down one day."

"But not today, thank the gods!" said Olga. "Grisha! Where are those horses!"

Just then Grisha and Sasha brought the horses round, and they set off, with Olga hotly denying her impetuosity until she caught sight of the others' faces, and then admitted, grinning, that maybe she could sometimes be a tiny, tiny bit impetuous.

"Perhaps, but just a tiny bit, and only sometimes," said Dima, grinning at her in a way he didn't normally in front of the others. Olga only laughed, though.

Her high spirits were needed that day, for yesterday's slushy roads had frozen into treacherous ruts, which made the sleighs slide wildly in all directions, so that they all had to assist the tired horses in keeping the sleighs moving in a direction that was more or less forward. Once the roads had softened back into slush, they were able to get back into the sleighs, but the horses could do nothing more than plod along at a walk.

Their exertions meant that the morning flew by for Slava, even though they covered very little ground, and then in the afternoon Vladislava wanted to hear more about the princesses she would meet in Krasnograd, and so before Slava knew it, the day was over and they were stopping for the night in a small village.

"We didn't make much progress today, but if we can get some fresh horses here, we'll still make it to Krasnograd in two days," said Olga over supper.

"Are we likely to get fresh horses here?" asked Slava, looking around at the cottage where they were spending the night. It was sort of clean, which was the best thing that could be said about it, other than it was probably the best cottage in the village, seeing as it belonged to the village headwoman. "Are they likely to have the kind of horses we need—or any spare horses at all?"

"Oh, they'll have horses," said Olga confidently. "This time of year, before the plowing starts, they'll have lots of horses just standing around eating their heads off. I'm sure they'll be glad to loan us some of them for the right price."

Slava started to make more arguments against the likelihood of their being able to procure horses, but stopped herself when she realized she was just trying to provide reasons to herself for delaying their return to Krasnograd. She told herself not to be ridiculous, but when Olga asked their hostess if there were any available horses to take them the rest of the way to Krasnograd, and the headwoman said yes, the village had more than enough horses, Slava had to admit to herself that her heart sank at the removal of this obstacle.

Despite—no, because of—all the happy daydreams of the previous week about her return to Krasnograd, now that it was actually facing her, her happiness was turning into dread, and, what was even more annoying, quite against her will. She would have liked to be overjoyed at being so close to home, and she provided herself with many reasons why she *should* be overjoyed, but she wasn't.

She would also have liked to think that the reason she feared their arrival in Krasnograd was because of the curse, but she knew it was nothing so sensible as that—she just feared Krasnograd, and for no good reason other than it made her unhappy, which made her even more unhappy and afraid. Which, she supposed, was curse enough. If curses grew out of a person's own unhappiness, then she must have enough to curse the Krasnograd kremlin and everyone in it thrice over. Truly, she had no need of Princess Severnolesnaya and her sorceresses to cast any curses, she told herself, as she had done a perfectly respectable job all on her own. The question of whether Princess Severnolesnaya's curse had taken effect or not was probably a moot point, as Slava's own self-engendered curse was undoubtedly working away with unstoppable fervor and had no need of help from any Northern princesses to cause harm to Slava and everyone around her.

This fruitless and inescapable train of thought made her so irritated with herself that between that and the dread—which only grew, the more she tried to make it go away—she slept very poorly that night, which made her even more unhappy the next morning, when her arrival in Krasnograd was even nearer and she had to suffer the effects of a sleepless night to boot.

She spent most of the morning in a sulk, which she tried to hide from the others, which only made her even sulkier...

"Will you be going out to the Stepnoye territory this summer?" Olga suddenly asked her, breaking her sullen and self-condemnatory reverie.

"What?" asked Slava, startled.

"Since it might be yours soon. Will you be going out there this summer? Who knows," Olga raised her eyebrows, "you could even have a husband waiting out there for you."

This, while not a welcome thought in and of itself, did make Slava realize that if she didn't like Krasnograd, she could just go elsewhere! If not the Stepnoye territory, then there were many other places where she would be welcome...Krasnograd was simply where her sister happened to live, not a prison in which Slava was condemned to live out the rest of her days...

"Perhaps," she said. "Or perhaps I might go to the South—I fear you may have infected me with your love for traveling."

"You should travel this summer then, if you feel well enough," said Olga. "You won't get many chances for a year or two after that."

"Why not?" demanded Vladislava.

"Oh..." said Olga, "She'll have too many responsibilities, that's why."

"You're hiding something from me!" Vladislava said indignantly.

"How would a princess say that?" put in Slava, before Olga could deny that she was hiding anything and thereby make Vladislava even more suspicious.

"*I* don't know," said Vladislava, who seemed to have forgotten her earlier good behavior in her annoyance over having something concealed from her. "She'd probably come up with some lie."

"Not some *lie*," said Slava, although, truth be told, princesses did spend a good deal of their time engaged in something that did have a strong resemblance to lying. Even Slava was currently engaged in something that was a lot like lying, she had to admit to herself. But she plunged on regardless: "She'd tell the truth, but in a way that didn't hurt anybody's feelings."

"And helped her find out what she wanted to know!" cried Vladislava triumphantly, Slava's lessons on princessly behavior all flooding back to her, now that she was distracted from her annoyance.

"Princesses have to be very clever," Slava told her. "They have to train with their words just like a singer must train with her songs, or a warrior with his sword."

"That makes sense," said Vladislava thoughtfully. "So...Why *won't* you be able to travel after this summer? Why can you leave this summer, but only if you feel well enough, but then not in the winter or next year?"

"I may have many things I have to do in Krasnograd this winter," said Slava. "New responsibilities, as Olga said."

"Like the Stepnoye territory?"

"Yes, like the Stepnoye territory," agreed Slava.

"But shouldn't you go out there, if you end up ruling it?"

"Perhaps I will do more good ruling it from Krasnograd," said Slava, embarrassed by the feebleness of her answer but unable to think of a way to distract Vladislava and escape from the conversation. "There I will have the constant attention of the Empress, after all."

"I suppose..." said Vladislava, looking unconvinced. "But why might you not feel well enough to go out there this summer? Do you think you'll be ill?"

"It has been a hard journey," said Slava. "I might need to rest."

"But you've been doing nothing but rest in these sleighs for weeks!" pointed out Vladislava. "We've gotten far too much rest, *I* think."

"Riding in sleighs is more restful for some than it is for others," said Slava. "And it was a long hard journey before we arrived in Lesnograd."

Vladislava still looked unconvinced, but Slava was finally able to distract her with more tales of Krasnograd, and the matter was dropped. It did make Slava wonder how Vladislava would react when she finally discovered Slava's news—if, Slava added hastily in order to ward off any malevolent attention of the gods, she in fact had news to tell. Vladislava certainly looked upon Slava as her own personal property, and Slava feared she might not be willing to share Slava with a sister. In her dream, Slava reminded herself, Vladislava had quickly become reconciled to the news. Everything else in the dream had come true, so perhaps that would too.

It was cloudy all day that day, with a warm wind from the South, which made Grisha sniff and say that true spring was only a few days away.

"We're riding right into it, too," he said. "We may meet it in Krasnogorod."

"Will we reach Krasnograd tomorrow?" asked Vladislava, bouncing in her seat with excitement.

"The next morning, most likely," said Olga.

Slava's stomach twisted again at that news. She could already see Krasnograd's towers rising up before her, and hear her sister's imperious voice, demanding to know what they had accomplished and looking disappointed when she discovered how little they had learned. Slava thought of the curse, and didn't know what she would say about it. Keep it a secret? Tell her sister? Look for signs to see if it was already working? Would it even matter what she did? Princess Severnolesnaya had made it sound as if it wouldn't.

Slava had been trying hard not to think about it their whole way South, but now she was about to be forced to face it. Her return to Krasnograd, and the presence of the curse—whether the one cast by Princess Severnolesnaya's sorceresses, or the one Slava had engendered herself and now carried around inside her with no help from any outside forces—loomed before her like some dark and mysterious barrier, which she not only had no idea how to overcome, but had no desire to overcome in the first place. She would much rather run away, just as she had when she had set out on this journey.

And it had worked for a while, but now she had only created more problems for herself on her return. All the strength and courage she thought she had gained seemed to be trickling out of her with every verst she drew closer to home, until now fear was gripping her so firmly that her lungs would no longer expand properly.

I am being reborn, she told herself. *I died, and now I am being reborn. No doubt everyone chokes as they pass through the birth canal, and screams in terror when they first see the light of day. Birth must be even more terrifying than death, and it is the gods' greatest mercy that we do not remember. I am being reborn, and soon this will all be over and everything will be well with me. I am only being reborn. Thousands of people are born every year.*

And many of them die, and take their mothers with them, said another, much less comforting voice in her head.

Many survive, she argued.

Yes, but not all, said the second voice. **And there is no way to know beforehand whether you will be amongst their number.**

Then I must have courage, Slava said to herself. *My only way forward now is courage.* It was easy to say, and was also true, but that helped very little, and Slava spent the rest of the day in the claws of such dread that even she, who had sampled dread in abundance, had hitherto never suspected of existing. Every now and then she would wonder if her sufferings were leaving marks on her face and body for all to see, but no one seemed to notice any difference.

They stopped that night at another overcrowded waystation only a few versts out from Krasnograd. Slava, to her shame, could scarcely force herself to swallow her supper. Olga, thinking that her queasiness was from another source, gave her a sympathetic look and said loudly, "Saving your appetite for the kremlin table?"

"Yes," said Slava, doing her best to smile gratefully at Olga and cheerfully at the others. "My stomach seems to have become refined and picky again, this close to home."

This led to a lengthy and lively discussion on the part of the men about what kind of food they could expect to eat in Krasnograd, with many lavish descriptions of past and future feasts. After supper none of the others wanted to retire to their beds for a long time, preferring to sit in the main room and listen to the news from Krasnograd. Slava listened with half an ear for a while, but when she decided there was nothing of importance for her to hear, she was the first to leave for bed.

She thought she wouldn't be able to sleep again that night, but a dark and dreamless sleep descended upon her almost as soon as her head touched the pillow.

Chapter Thirteen

She was extremely surprised to surface from the darkness and discover that it was already the next morning, and it was time to rise and prepare for the final few versts of their journey.

"It's raining!" Olga told her. "Raining hard! A spring rain! A real spring rain—warm like a spring rain should be!" She was trying to look disgusted at this news, which meant those final few versts would be traveled in truly disgusting conditions, but the arrival of spring was too joyous an occasion to be sad about, even if it was accompanied by unpleasant inconveniences.

"It is?" said Slava, and looked out the window. Even through the thick wavy glass she could not only see but feel and smell the warm spring rain.

"How do you feel?" asked Olga. "You didn't seem very well last night."

"Much better," said Slava, rising from the bed. "Extremely well, in fact." And it was true. The dark, dreamless sleep had somehow washed away the fear, or at least—as soon as she had that thought, Slava knew that the fear was not gone, not truly—it had risen up around it and submerged it, so that she could sail safely over it.

It was strange, she thought to herself, how quickly and unexpectedly her mind could change itself. She was not only not dreading her arrival in Krasnograd, she was impatient for it to happen. Someday, she thought, she would probably laugh at herself about this. She was even eager to run out into the spring rain, although no doubt she would grow sick of it soon enough—such as within half a verst of being out in it.

They breakfasted quickly and headed out into the gray morning light. The warm spring rain was even more disgusting than Slava had imagined it would be, but no one minded. When it lashed in their faces from an extra-strong gust of wind from the South, everyone laughed and talked about the hot meals ahead of them, and when they had to get out of the sleighs and help guide them through the slushy pools on top of the icy road surface, they reminded each other, still laughing, of the warm bathhouse awaiting them when they got to Krasnograd. Once they were able to get back in the sleighs, the men broke out into a song about the rain, and sang all the way until the city towers rose up before them.

"Is that...Is that Krasnograd?!" cried Vladislava, pointing at a golden dome glimmering dully in the distance.

"Yes," said Slava. "That is the Empress Tower. It rises from the Empress's quarters in the kremlin, and is the first thing that any traveler to Krasnograd sees."

"And when will we see the rest of the city?!" demanded Vladislava.

"Soon enough," said Slava, trying to sound soothing despite the rapid beating of her heart. All the calm of the morning was gone. It was strange, she thought to herself again, with what would have been a grin if she hadn't felt so sick and her mind hadn't been circling around and around with the fevered repetitiveness of fear, how quickly and unexpectedly her mind could change itself. Yesterday she had dreaded her arrival in Krasnograd as if it were some herald of doom, then at breakfast she had been so impatient to reach Krasnograd she had wanted to run all the way there, and now that she was here she just felt ill, and wished she could lie down in the sleigh and somehow disappear and end up somewhere else...perhaps Lesnograd...No, certainly not. What terrors could Krasnograd possibly offer that would be worse than what Slava had already faced this winter? She instantly regretted trying to comfort herself with that question. Surely, she told herself, a grown woman would know better than to ask a question like that, because worse terrors could *always* be imagined.

"Will we get to go over all the city this afternoon?" asked Vladislava, wriggling with excitement.

"It would take us more than a single afternoon to go over all the city, even in good weather," Slava told her. "We'll start exploring tomorrow, I promise."

"Tomorrow!" cried Vladislava in disappointment.

"First you must see the kremlin," Slava told her. "It will be well worth your time."

"And have a bath," said Olga. "And probably be introduced to the Empress, or some such thing."

"Indeed," said Slava. "I must announce Vladislava and her position immediately."

"Will I get to meet the Empress?" asked Vladislava.

"Most likely," said Slava.

"And...what do I do?" For a moment Vladislava's usual expression of supreme self-confidence faltered.

"Bow down to your boot-tops, and say you are honored on behalf of yourself and your family," said Slava.

"And then what?" asked Vladislava anxiously.

"And then go and stand beside me," said Slava.

"Oh, that's easy enough, then," said Vladislava, her face clearing.

"Yes," Slava agreed, trying to convince herself of it as well. "Easy enough."

"Oh look! Is that the city walls?"

"Yes," said Slava.

"And is that the gate?"

"One of them," said Slava.

"Will there be guards?"

"No doubt," said Slava.

"Real Krasnograders!" squealed Vladislava. "I've never met any before!"

"I'm a real Krasnograder," Slava pointed out.

"You are? Oh, of course, but I meant real Krasnograders, not just a Tsarinovna," explained Vladislava.

"Oh, of course," said Olga, rolling her eyes.

Vladislava was about to say something angry in reply, but Slava smoothed over the difficulty by pointing out that her family was not, in fact, originally from Krasnograd but from Pristanograd, while most of the gateguards had had mothers in Krasnograd for twenty generations or more, and then they were riding up to the gate and had to end the conversation anyway.

The guards were not very keen to come out from under the gate and into the rain, and were questioning people in a rather perfunctory manner, but Olga's party was large enough, and unusual enough, to merit special interest. The guards came out from their shelter and demanded to know who they were and what their purpose was in Krasnograd.

"Olga Vasilisovna Severnolesnaya, returning from the Midnight

Land in the company of the Tsarinovna," announced Olga grandly. Slava guessed that she had been running over in her mind what to say and how to say it all morning, and was hoping to produce an impressive effect.

"Where is the Tsarinovna?" demanded the guards, giving Olga a suspicious look.

"Right here," said Olga, pointing to Slava, who was sitting beside her.

"I really am the Tsarinovna," said Slava, rising from her seat. "Returned from the Midnight Land, just as Olga Vasilisovna says. And I would prefer not to stand around in this rain any longer than I have to."

"Of course, Tsarinovna! Right away, Tsarinovna! Misha! Why are you standing around like a blockhead! Call the others, and then run and announce the Tsarinovna's arrival this instant! Come under the gate, Tsarinovna! We'll have an escort for you right away, Tsarinovna!"

"I'm sure that won't be necessary," said Slava, foolishly. The guard shuddered in horror at the thought of her going through the streets of Krasnograd without an escort, and tried to argue with her without giving the appearance of arguing with her, so that Slava was forced to give in for the sake of his sanity, and they stood there blocking the gate for what seemed like a long time but was in fact not long at all, while an escort was assembled from the guards warming themselves in the guardhouse.

And very soon they had passed under the city walls, and were in Krasnograd itself (to Vladislava's uncontainable delight), and driving through the muddy, slushy, icy spring streets. Slava's heart was beating even faster than before, much to her annoyance, and she couldn't slow it. She couldn't tell how much of it was joy at being home, and how much was dread of her meeting with her sister and everything that that entailed.

"Is that it? Is that it?" Vladislava demanded at each turn, expecting to see the kremlin around every corner, and every time that Slava told her no, they still had a ways to go, she grew even more excited.

"There it is," Slava was finally able to say. "That's the bottom of the Empress Tower."

"OH!!" screamed Vladislava.

"By all the gods!" said Olga, annoyed. "It's just a tower!"

"Every true Zemnian heart loves the Krasnograd kremlin, noblewoman," said one of the guards. "It's only natural for the little princess to feel it."

Olga looked like she wanted to say something in reply, probably something about conceited Krasnograders and their mistaken belief that they were the real Zem', when everyone knew that the real Zem' was in the far North, but she managed to restrain herself from emitting anything more than a sigh.

A guard of honor was waiting for them at the kremlin main gate, along with a crowd of curious onlookers. Slava could hear them speculating—as they bowed down to their boot-tops, just in case—over whether the Tsarinovna really was in the party, and deciding that if she was, then she must be the woman sitting next to the tall, redheaded noblewoman, and lamenting that their Tsarinovna wasn't more noble-looking, and then an argument broke out over whether or not the Tsarinovna was a good Tsarinovna, and then mercifully they were past the crowd and being handed out of the sleighs and led inside the kremlin itself.

More guards were waiting for them inside, along with the Mistress of Ceremonies, who, unlike everyone else, recognized Slava at first glance and came rushing forward with cries of joy.

"Tsarinovna!" she exclaimed, bowing down so low Slava feared she might hurt herself. "Allow me to kiss your hem!" And, much to Slava's embarrassment, she did in fact snatch up the hem of Slava's dirty cloak and kiss it before Slava could stop her.

"I am delighted to see you, Yarmila Kseniyevna," Slava told her, once she could get a word in edgewise. "And delighted beyond words, of course, to be back in my beloved native kremlin."

This led to a lengthy string of pleasantries, which finally concluded in the serious business of who Slava's companions were and where and how and for how long they should be housed.

"Olga Vasilisovna, younger daughter of Princess Severnolesnaya; her men; Yevdoksiya Anastasiyevna, our guide to the Midnight Land; and my new ward, Vladislava Vasilisovna, granddaughter to Princess Severnolesnaya and daughter to her heir."

"A ward! You have taken on a ward, Tsarinovna? Oh, how marvelous!" cried Yarmila Kseniyevna, with apparent sincerity. "Welcome to Krasnograd, little princess!"

"I am honored to be here," said Vladislava with quite respectable politeness, and even accompanied her words with a bow that was not at all bad.

"And so polite, too!" exclaimed Yarmila Kseniyevna, causing Vladislava to glow with pride. Slava wondered how often Vladislava had ever had occasion before to glow with pride over her own good behavior. Not often, she suspected. "We shall arrange a special room all for you, sweet little princess, right by the Tsarinovna's chambers."

"That sounds lovely," said Vladislava. "Truly, your hospitality exceeds even the Tsarinovna's kind descriptions of it."

"And now, if you would be so kind as to lead us to someplace where we could refresh ourselves, Yarmila Kseniyevna," said Slava, trying to speak loudly enough to cover up the sound of Olga choking with laughter over Vladislava's unusually fair words. "I fear it has been a long hard journey, and the weather has been most unpleasant for days."

"Oh, of course, Tsarinovna, of course, and the bathhouse is already heating, so your people will be able to bathe while we prepare their rooms...But meanwhile, Tsarinovna, your gracious sister, the Tsarina, is most anxious to see you, so if you come this way...Your people will be well cared for, I assure you..."

"Of course," said Slava. "Where is my sister?"

"In the Hall of Council, of course, Tsarinovna, the Hall of Council, and many of her princesses are there with her, anxious to see you... And in fact, if Olga Vasilisovna would be so gracious, I'm sure the Tsarina will be anxious to see her as well, as would her sister princesses... Did you really go all the way to the Midnight Land?"

"We did, and all the way back, too, although the leshiye, bandits, and bad weather did their best to stop us," said Olga cheerfully. Slava could tell she had intended to shock Yarmila Kseniyevna with her words, and was very pleased with herself for managing to do so.

"Leshiye! Bandits! The Empress—and the princesses—will be *most* anxious to hear your story, Olga Vasilisovna. This way, please."

Olga gave a regretful backwards glance at the others, who were being led off in the direction of the bathhouse, but could not manage to refuse Yarmila Kseniyevna's certainty in her own obedience, and so followed along behind Slava meekly enough.

"I wish we were cleaner," she whispered to Slava, as they made their way down the corridors. "I wish we didn't smell like we'd been driving in the rain for days."

"It could be worse," Slava whispered back. "We could smell like we'd been driving in the sun for days."

"So true," Olga agreed. "But it's still a bit awkward, facing down an Empress and a whole pack of princesses in dirty traveling clothes. I almost wish I were wearing a gown right now."

"Well, I'm wearing a gown—or what was once a gown, of sorts—and it isn't bringing me much comfort," Slava whispered to her. "But look at it this way: we'll be facing down an Empress and a pack of pampered princesses in the clothes of real travelers and adventurers."

"So true," Olga agreed again, cheering up. "If they're not impressed by our looks, that only shows they don't know enough to know they should be. My head for beheading, half of them have never gone farther than their estates, and then only in good weather. They'll probably even be secretly envious of our rough appearance."

"Oh, I'm sure," said Slava.

Their whispers were broken off by the sudden appearance of Boleslav Vlasiyevich, who came skidding around the corner and bowed breathlessly in a way that suggested he had run from wherever he had been in order to catch them before they entered the Hall of Council.

"Tsarinovna!" he cried, straightening up and taking a step towards her. "You returned!"

"As you see, Boleslav Vlasiyevich," said Slava.

"You are...I mean, you are most welcome to Krasnograd, Tsarinovna, and we are all overjoyed at your safe return...should you not be going to your chambers?"

"The Tsarina is waiting, Boleslav Vlasiyevich," said Yarmila Kseniyevna, giving him a stern look.

"The Tsarinovna has been traveling all morning in the rain," said Boleslav Vlasiyevich. "Time can be found for her to change into dry clothes."

Yarmila Kseniyevna began to swell up at that suggestion, and Boleslav Vlasiyevich's temerity at offering it, so that Slava felt obliged to intervene before a quarrel could break out. She knew that Boleslav Vlasiyevich was not nearly so fearful of the kremlin functionaries as they felt he should be, and he tended to rub them the wrong way. It would be embarrassing to appear before her sister after her long journey with the sounds of squabbling surrounding her.

"I thank you for your gracious concern, Boleslav Vlasiyevich," she said, forestalling whatever Yarmila Kseniyevna was about to say, "but I am not at all chilled, and I feel it my duty to greet my sister with all speed. Once I have greeted her and assured the comfort of my companions, there will be ample time for me to see to myself."

"You're soaked through, Tsarinovna!"

All the old feelings of pleasure at his obvious concern, annoyance at his assumption of the right to be concerned about her, puzzlement over his motives, and worry that he was playing some deep game against her, surfaced in Slava's chest, and made her say more curtly than she would have liked, "My duty calls me, Boleslav Vlasiyevich."

"Of course it does, Tsarinovna." She thought he might be laughing at her a little bit, and also rolling his eyes. "Well," he said with another bow, "at least allow me to escort you and your companions to the Hall of Council."

"We thank you, Boleslav Vlasiyevich," she said, and they started off again, this time with him in front. Olga was grinning and trying to catch Slava's eye, but Slava staunchly ignored her, and soon they were drawing close to the Hall of Council and Olga was no longer in a mood for laughing.

The hum of conversation was audible even from outside the closed doors of the Hall of Council. Slava's heart, which had calmed down during the initial greetings, began thumping painfully in her chest, despite her brave words. She knew that she was about to be stared at by many people, most of whom had always been happy to make her feel bad. Yarmila Kseniyevna opened the doors.

There was a noise like a strong wind in the forest as all the princesses turned to look as Slava and Olga came in. Even, Slava saw, her sister jumped to her feet as Slava came through the door.

"Slava!" she cried. "You have returned!"

Slava bowed.

"Oh, come here, come here!" Slava's sister ran to the edge of her dais. For a moment Slava thought she was even going to step down, but she stopped herself and only held out her hands entreatingly. "Oh Slava, you're back!"

Slava made her way uncertainly over to the dais and stood there awkwardly as her sister bent down and flung her arms around her, kissing her several times before pulling her up onto the dais and embracing her again. She was, Slava noted with shock, shedding genuine tears of joy. Slava had a hard time believing this was the same sister who had taken such pleasure in causing Slava's public humiliation during the murderer's trial. If she had gone tumbling down the Hall of Council like an acrobat at a celebration, her behavior could not have shocked Slava more.

"And you're well?" she demanded, holding Slava out at arm's length and examining her. "You're well? How thin and tired you look!

My apologies, sister: I'm sure it is to your honor. It must have been a long hard road. But you are well?"

"Perfectly well," Slava assured her, having found her tongue. "And so is Olga Vasilisovna. Some of our companions suffered on the journey but, thank the gods, it seems they will recover completely."

"The gods are good!" declared Slava's sister fervently. "They bless our family daily! Here!" And she turned Slava to face the assembled princesses and held her out to her side at arm's length, like a prize horse on show. "Princesses! Your Tsarinovna has returned from her perilous journey! Give her welcome!"

There was a frenzy of bowing and cheering. Some of it even seemed heartfelt. Slava stared down at them in a daze. Her sister let it go on for some time, before raising her hands and drawing an instant hush.

"And now," she said, "let us hear her story. I know you must be tired from the road, dearest, most beloved sister, but please, if you would be so kind as to deign to give us a few words, the briefest of descriptions..."

"Truly, Olga Vasilisovna should be the one," said Slava. "It was her journey, after all; I just followed along..." But she spoke too softly for anyone to pay her any attention, and her sister and all the princesses, and even Olga, who seemed perfectly happy to stand at the edge of the dais and be ignored, all stared at her in breathless anticipation until she found herself forced to speak in order not to disappoint them.

"After we set out, we traveled for many days with few difficulties," she began. To her annoyance, she could hear her voice trembling with shyness. "We overnighted with Princess Malogornaya, who, who," Slava could no longer contain herself, "who brings shame to the title 'Princess!'"

There was a brief chorus of cries in agreement, before Slava's sister held up her hands again and called for silence.

"But we were able to carry on unmolested, nonetheless," Slava continued. "We..." She decided to skip over everything that had happened before they reached Naberezhnoye. There was no need to bring up her strange dreams and visions, or the warnings of Princess Primorskaya, just yet. "We arrived in Naberezhnoye unharmed," she said after an awkward pause, "where we engaged the services of Yevdoksiya Anastasiyevna as a guide. She served us well, and has done us the honor of continuing with us to Krasnograd."

There was a murmur of approbation over this, which was silenced as soon as Slava's sister flashed her eyes over the crowd.

"Under the sure guidance of Yevdoksiya Anastasiyevna, Olga Vasilisovna set off for the Midnight Land, accompanied by her brave men and myself. We traveled many days, until we left the taiga behind and entered the tundra, where trees do not grow and the sun never rises the whole winter long."

There was a chorus of indrawn breaths at this, but everyone was too enthralled with Slava's story by now to interrupt her with any conversation.

"There we divided our party, half to stay in camp, and half to go exploring. Olga Vasilisovna and Yevdoksiya Anastasiyevna led the exploring party, while I stayed in the camp. Guarded by Olga Vasilisovna's brave men," Slava added, seeing that that last bit had not won the approval of the crowd—why should a couple of Northerners stand to gain all the glory? At her words, though, everyone nodded and smiled. Of *course* the Tsarinovna would remain in camp and under guard.

"We...We encountered many strange things in that unending midnight," said Slava. "And so we decided in the end to carry on to Lesnograd, hoping that the sorceresses there would be able to enlighten us. On our way to Lesnograd, we met with much trouble and misfortune, but in the end we arrived, only to find more trouble."

Slava stopped, momentarily unsure how to proceed. The crowd shifted restlessly, and she quickly started up again. "Princess Severnolesnaya was gravely ill, and all Lesnograd was stricken with concern and grief," she said. "We were obliged to stay there some time as a support to Vasilisa Vasilisovna, the princess's heir. While I was there, I developed a great fondness for Vladislava Vasilisovna, the princess's granddaughter and Vasilisa Vasilisovna's heir, and have brought her to Krasnograd as my ward."

There were some inadvertent exclamations of "Oh, how wonderful!" and "The Tsarinovna! So kind-hearted!"

"I am very glad to hear this, dear sister," said Slava's sister. "I look forward to making her acquaintance. And what transpired then?"

"We traveled from Lesnograd to Krasnograd, hampered by the onset of spring but without meeting any untoward difficulties," said Slava. "And as you see, we arrived today in safety."

"For which we are inexpressibly grateful," said Slava's sister. Her initial unfeigned joy at Slava's return was already sinking down beneath her Empress's mask, and her words, while more elegantly expressed, no longer contained the ring of genuine feeling that had so surprised Slava at first. "Dear sister," she continued, "you speak of encountering many strange things in the Midnight Land, things that obliged you to seek out sorceresses. What kind of strange things did you encounter? We are not poor in sorceresses in Krasnograd either, you know: perhaps they can be of some assistance. And my princesses and I thirst to hear more of your adventures, if you still have the strength to tell us."

"I had...strange dreams and visions," said Slava reluctantly. "Strange dreams and visions, that seemed also to have substance in the waking world. And when we returned to the taiga, we were pursued by leshiye, the leshiye I had seen previously in my dreams, and we barely escaped from them with our lives. And then...we encountered much magic, and those touched by the gods themselves."

"You say that you had strange dreams and visions?" asked Slava's sister, turning from the princesses, whom she had been watching with her imperial gaze, and looking at her intently. "*You* were the one who had these strange dreams and visions?"

"Yes," said Slava with a nod. "It was I."

"You and no one else?"

"Not that I am aware of," said Slava. "I was the only one who spoke of them, at least."

"The Tsarinovna was the only one," said Olga, speaking up for the first time. "And she has given a very brief description of all she saw and did. Truly, Tsarina, esteemed princesses, the Tsarinovna's gifts are strange and strong, so much so that the gods themselves desired her for their partner and ally."

"I see," said Slava's sister, continuing to stare at her intently. She had the same look that Olga had worn so many times when looking at Slava, the look of someone who had placed a bet on an unknown horse and was surprised to see the results of her boldness, only her look was tinged with a bit of fear, as well. Fear that she refused to face, so that it haunted her all the more. "I see we must speak of this further. But it will have to wait until after you are bathed, rested, and fed. Please, refresh yourselves, and this evening there will be a great feast to celebrate your safe return. Princesses, welcome your Tsarinovna back to Krasnograd, and we shall see each other again this evening!"

The princesses broke out into more cheering, and making way for her (and Olga, who was following in her wake) with the greatest apparent respect, bowed her out of the room. She must have been very tired, Slava thought, for tears prickled behind her eyes, and she was glad to escape the hall without giving them further cause to accuse her of hysteria.

But after she was out of their sight and was no longer so over-whelmed by the multitude of stares, it occurred to her that some of them, at least, had been genuine in their joy to see her home, and she had behaved most churlishly in half-running out of the room like that, looking neither right nor left.

"I should have paid them more attention," she said despondently to Olga as they were shepherded down the corridor by Boleslav Vla-siyevich, Yarmila Kseniyevna, and an ever-growing collection of ser-vants and guards.

"Whom?" asked Olga, looking around in surprise.

"The princesses," said Slava. "I hardly even looked at them...And I think they were actually glad to see me safely returned..."

"Yes..." said Olga, puzzled. "Of course they were. And it's not as if you slighted them—you came straight to them from the sleigh, with-out even stopping in the bathhouse."

"But I didn't even look at most of them," said Slava. "And I think they were actually glad to see me."

Olga gave Slava a long sideways look. "You say that as if it's a sur-prise," she said.

"Well, I always assumed they couldn't wait to see the back of me. I never thought they'd be glad to see my face again."

"You're the Tsarinovna! Of course they were overjoyed!"

"Yes, but I think some of them, at least, really were overjoyed. I mean, they weren't merely pretending. They really were glad to see me."

"And this is normally not the case?"

"No, normally they can't seem to stand the sight of me."

"Well, they've had a while to forget what you look like," said Olga bracingly. "People are always glad to see someone after a long absence. You can be fond of anyone if they're not around to annoy you. But in a day or two you start remembering all the things you hated about them, and in a week you're right back to quarrelling like bored cats."

"True," said Slava, and tried to look—and feel—more cheerful. It was all because she was tired, she told herself, but she had to admit that she was astonished at how much she had assumed the princesses disliked her, and how touched she was that today, at least, they ap-peared to like her very much. To have a hall full of people who were kindly disposed to her was almost more than she could bear. She real-ly *did* need to toughen herself up, she told herself, if she had been back in Krasnograd less than an hour and she was already growing weepy.

Of course, they said that women in her presumed happy condition could also be very weepy sometimes, but Slava knew that had very little to do with it. She was simply not used to having people like her or show her kindness, and she was still starving for it, just as she had told Andrey Vladislavovich, and all the kindness and even affection she had been shown on her journey had been no more than a crumb to whet her appetite.

She started to fear that her hunger had gone unfed for so long that now it could never be slaked, and that if she gave it free rein even for a moment it would overpower her like a raging fire...She remembered how easily she had parted with Oleg, and it occurred to her that maybe it would have been better not to have been so brave and cheerful, but to have clung to him and demanded to know when she would see him again...Perhaps she had been wrong in walking away from him so boldly...

"Have you caught a chill, Tsarinovna?" asked Boleslav Vlasiyevich, who had somehow ended up walking at her side. "You're shivering!"

"No...I'm fine, Boleslav Vlasiyevich, though I am grateful for your concern."

"Of course you've caught a chill," he said, giving her a stern look. "Yarmila Kseniyevna! Is the bathhouse ready for the Tsarinovna!"

"Why are you still hanging about, Boleslav Vlasiyevich?" Yarmila Kseniyevna said by way of reply, giving him a very sour look. "Don't you have duties to attend to in the barracks or something? The Tsarinovna doesn't need you pestering her, and I doubt the Tsarina would think this a good use of your time, either! Shouldn't you be...guarding something?"

"I am," said Boleslav Vlasiyevich, with a little bow. Slava could tell that Olga was struggling not to laugh. "I'm guarding the Tsarinovna from taking a chill, which is more than anyone else can say."

Yarmila Kseniyevna began swelling dangerously, her normal reaction to anything Boleslav Vlasiyevich said, at those words, so that Slava decided she needed to intervene again before Yarmila Kseniyevna gave Boleslav Vlasiyevich the smack she was obviously minded to give him. That, Slava thought, would not end well at all.

"I thank you for your concern," she told him, putting a hand on his arm. His muscles twitched like those of a restless horse, but he didn't try to break away. "Truly, Boleslav Vlasiyevich, your devotion to the wellbeing of my family does you great credit, but I assure you, we can make our way to the bathhouse from here. Please, do not let us detain you from attending to the press of your many duties."

He gave her a look that, as far as she could tell, since as usual she could read very little of him, was equal parts exasperation and despair at her own inability to take care of herself, with that other feeling, that inexplicable sense that they shared a secret understanding, one that was so secret not even Slava could guess what it was, mixed in. Something about it made Slava pull back from him, just as it always did.

"Very well, Tsarinovna," he said with another bow, this one rather more sincere than the one he had tendered Yarmila Kseniyevna. "I am very glad you are back in one piece."

Yarmila Kseniyevna sniffed at this, and sniffed again at his retreating back. "What a thing to concern himself with!" she said disapprovingly. "The Tsarinovna's bathing! Has he no sense of propriety? I tell you, it's high time someone took that young man in hand." She sniffed again. "I wish you would do it yourself, Tsarinovna"—Olga began choking on her own laughter at this, much to Slava's discomfort, but Yarmila Kseniyevna didn't seem to notice—"except that I'm sure you'll have more than enough on your mind, with your young ward and all. Such a good thing of you to do!"

And she carried on in that vein the rest of the way to the bathhouse, while Slava dwelt unhappily on the strange behavior of everyone they had encountered so far upon their arrival in Krasnograd—her sister's unexpected joy at their return, the princesses' glad greetings, Boleslav Vlasiyevich, bolder than ever in his treatment of her...all this gladness, coming at her from every side, made her want to throw herself in someone's, anyone's, arms in order to make it feel real, made her even more desperate for affection than she already was... she must be constantly on her guard here, constantly on her guard against trusting anyone in Krasnograd, she knew that, especially against those who should be the most trustworthy...

"Fresh clothing is being brought to you as we speak, Tsarinovna," said Yarmila Kseniyevna, bowing Slava into the bathhouse. Her words snapped Slava out of her melancholy reverie, and made her smile at her ability to sink into unhappy reflection at every opportunity.

She hoped Darya, little Dasha, would have a bolder, happier temperament than her mother...She hoped she was not bringing bad luck down on herself by indulging already in such daydreams... Darya, if she should have the good fortune to be born, would surely be strong and brave, not weak and anxious as Slava was...Slava remembered her dream, how the baby had gazed up at her with adoring eyes...Perhaps this would be the love she was hungering for so desperately...No, certainly not, Slava told herself, children took rather than gave love, she mustn't give way to any foolish fancies there...She was going to have to be doubly strong soon, because she would be doubly hungry...But perhaps it was better that way...Perhaps it was better to give love than it was to receive it...That way she would always carry it around inside her, a self-sustaining source that would never desert her...Yes, perhaps that was how it would be...

"Aren't you going to take off your clothes?" demanded Olga.

"What?" said Slava.

"You're just standing there like a block. Aren't you going to take off your clothes? It's time to steam."

"Oh," said Slava. "Yes. I was thinking."

"That's a bad habit," said Olga, shaking her head. "Especially if it gets in the way of steaming. Do you need help with your gown?"

"No...No, I can do it. I learned at least that much while we were traveling."

"Oh good," said Olga. "It's very important to be able to undress yourself. Almost as important as dressing yourself."

"Yes," said Slava. "Only I fear I will fall out of practice, now that I'm back at the kremlin."

"Well, in that case, you should use it while you can," said Olga, shrugging out of her clothes and dashing into the steam before Slava could hinder them even more with her indecisiveness. Slava shed her own clothes with rather more effort, and followed her.

Sitting in the choking clouds of steam until she thought she would faint, and then retiring to her room to be dressed by Manya and Masha, who greeted her with cries of delight, cleared Slava's mind of all the foolish fancies that had overcome it on her way to the bathhouse. In fact, after her steam she was so drained and weak that she didn't have the strength for any thoughts or feelings at all, and she allowed Manya and Masha to put her into extravagant gowns and brush and braid her hair into an extravagant style in complete indifference. It was as if all the exertions of her journey had caught up with her at once, and she desired nothing more than to collapse somewhere out of the way and sleep for days.

Even her chambers, with which she had assumed she would be reunited with sensations of inexpressible joy, seemed to her to be no more than chambers. She would have looked upon her rooms in Lesnograd or even Malolesnograd with the same feelings of disinterest. She couldn't even work up the energy to smile at herself over her lack of excitement at the momentous occasion of her return to Krasnograd. She couldn't even work up the energy to marvel at how comfortable the chair in front of her dressing table was. She had never appreciated the luxury of a chair, and a chair with cushions at that, until she had had to do without one, so she supposed—almost managing to smile at this thought, at least—that this was yet another important lesson she had learned on her journey.

She was roused from her comfort and her lethargy by the arrival of Anna Avdotyevna. Slava had forgotten how terrifying Anna Avdotyevna could be, and how her presence tended to have the effect on those beneath her of a pot of boiling water in the face.

This time was no different. Masha and Manya leapt away from Slava's hair on Anna Avdotyevna's entrance into the room as if they had been scalded, and stood there bowing repeatedly even after she had stopped paying them any attention. She preferred to speak to Slava directly, and the height of her eyebrows and the upward tilt of her nose suggested, as usual, that she was a direct extension of the Empress, and as such considered conversing with a mere Tsarinovna to be beneath her.

To Slava's surprise, this did not make her feel small and unworthy as it always had before. She wasn't sure if it was because of her extreme exhaustion, or because, compared with an angry gathering of leshiye, Anna Avdotyevna wasn't really that terrifying.

"The Tsarina wishes to speak to you," she said to Slava, making it sound as if Slava were a naughty child about to be called in and scolded by her mother.

"Right now?" Slava asked. "Before the feast?"

"There will most likely be no good opportunity to speak privately at the feast," said Anna Avdotyevna, giving Slava a look that seemed to say that even an idiot should have been able to understand that.

"I'll go as soon as my maids have finished dressing me," said Slava. "I wouldn't want to shame them by appearing at the feast ill-attired."

Masha and Manya wriggled in a way that suggested they were inexpressibly honored at her consideration, and inexpressibly horrified that she had drawn Anna Avdotyevna's attention to their existence.

"Be quick," Anna Avdotyevna ordered them, giving them the kind of look that made faint hearts flinch and run the other way. Masha and Manya flinched and tried to edge surreptitiously out of her range of vision, although that was a doomed enterprise, and only drew even more attention to them.

"I see you've grown slack in the Tsarinovna's absence," Anna Avdotyevna told them, fixing them with an even more piercing gaze. "No doubt some of the fault is my own. I have neglected you, seeing as you had no real duties to attend to for months on end. But idleness is a servant's worst enemy. I shall have to work it out of you."

Masha and Manya both bowed miserably.

"I fear I shall have too great a need of their services for there to be any time left over for their training," said Slava.

"They have grown slack," said Anna Avdotyevna impressively. "They must be taken in hand."

"And I shall do so, if I deem it necessary," said Slava. "Please go and inform my sister that I shall wait upon her when I am ready."

After staring at Slava for a moment as she might have stared at a sword-wielding sheep, Anna Avdotyevna opened her mouth to argue about something, but Slava forestalled her by rising—unwilling as she was to leave her current restful position—from her comfortable chair.

"I'm sure my sister is awaiting your reply, Anna Avdotyevna," she said. "Tell her I will be with her momentarily."

Anna Avdotyevna raised her eyebrows in something that was almost like a smile.

"I'll tell her, Tsarinovna," she said. "It is good to have you back. I can see your journey did you good. The kremlin will have need of you, I'm sure." She bowed and left, leaving the rest of the room in deep shock.

"You...you...you..." said Masha and Manya, staring at Slava in astonishment.

"You are *my* servants," said Slava, "and no one else has the right to command you, do you understand? If she should order you to do something, inform her that you are to attend *me* constantly, and have no leisure for running the errands of others, do you understand?"

"Yes, Tsarinovna, yes, yes, we understand, yes," said Masha and Manya in chorus, bobbing up and down in fervent bows. Slava wondered what they were actually thinking. They seemed perfectly sincere and she was certain that they were genuinely grateful for what she had done for them. But what else were they thinking? What was it like to be Masha or Manya? What was it like to be someone whose purpose in life was to spend her days sewing unneeded, unwanted fripperies and then putting them on and taking them off some lonely, unnecessary person you didn't understand and could never come to know?

She became aware that they had stopped bowing and were staring at her in rapidly growing apprehension, requiring some kind of order from her to restore their view of how things were supposed to be.

"And now finish my hair, so that I may go see what my sister wants," Slava told them, returning to her comfortable chair. Masha and Manya, gazing at her adoringly, rushed to finish putting up her hair.

"We're done now, Tsarinovna—will you deign to look at yourself in the mirror?" asked Manya, as she always did when they had finished with her. She held up a small hand mirror to so that Slava could see herself from all angles in the larger mirror on the wall in front of her. Normally Slava gave herself only the most cursory glance, to make absolutely sure before heading off to the Hall of Council that she was, in fact, wearing clothes (as a small girl Slava had been rather inattentive to such minor details, and had learned in her adulthood to be extremely vigilant about that kind of thing).

Looking in the mirror gave her little pleasure, and often made her feel squeamish and uncomfortable, as if the Slava-in-the-mirror could reveal to her all kinds of things she didn't want to know about herself. Even she, she now realized, had shrunk away from her own clear gaze, not wanting to expose her own heart any more than anyone else did. But now, after being away for so long, she was curious to see herself in the Tsarinovna's mirror, wearing the Tsarinovna's clothes.

She had expected to find herself very thin, but in fact, even though her gown hung on her in a way it had not before her journey, she seemed to fill it out more, as if she had grown. Everything about her seemed firmer, more defined. Her face, instead of looking worn and tired as she had expected, looked strong and sharp, like the face of someone in whose veins flowed the blood of Miroslava Praskovyevna and many generations of empresses after her. Her eyes, which seemed even larger and grayer than they had before her journey, stared back at her unflinchingly, and told her that she must have no fear, because she could neither run nor hide from whatever it was she must face, which was above all her own soul.

"You look..." said Manya. Slava waited with interest to hear what she had to say. No one, not even her maids, normally had the mendacity to call her beautiful, and to say that she looked "very fine" seemed too insignificant for the occasion.

"Like a Tsarina, Tsarinovna," said Masha. "Like *you* should be the

Tsarina."

"Perhaps the gods have other plans for me," said Slava.

"You're not going away again, are you, Tsarinovna!" cried Manya, sounding bitterly disappointed. "I'm sorry, Tsarinovna," she added quickly. "If you deign to please yourself by traveling, then that must be best."

"We shall see," said Slava. "But meanwhile I have taken on other duties. Is my ward, Vladislava Vasilisovna, being well cared for?"

"Oh yes, Tsarinovna, Lyudmila Vlastomilovna has been assigned to dress her, and little Yanochka is to wait upon her during the day and be her companion—they thought it would be jolly for her to have a little friend her own age—is that acceptable, Tsarinovna?"

"Perfectly acceptable," Slava assured them. "Run and tell Lyudmila Vlastomilovna that I will come and escort Vladislava Vasilisovna to the feast as soon as I have spoken with my sister. And now I suppose I should speak with her."

"An escort is waiting in the corridor for you, Tsarinovna," Masha told her.

"Then tell them I will be with them directly," said Slava. And, waiting just long enough for Masha to warn the guards and allow them to organize themselves into a formal escort, Slava set off to speak with her sister. She could feel her own eyes watching her steadily all the way out the room.

Chapter Fourteen

Slava was struck on entering her sister's chambers, just as she was every time, at how fine and grand they were compared with her own. Not that she envied her sister: quite the contrary. She couldn't help but wonder whether her sister didn't feel a little bit lost and awkward in such large, sumptuous rooms, which seemed designed to make their inhabitants painfully aware of their own tiny insignificance.

As far as Slava knew, her sister had no little place to call her own, some place where she could stop being the Tsarina and just be Vladya. If that were true, Slava couldn't help but feel sorry for her, and if her sister did in fact have some secret place, then Slava still couldn't help but feel sorry for her and the fact that she felt the need to hide such a thing from her only sister. Slava had often felt sorry for her sister and her faults, but this was the first time that her pity was untinged by any sense of angry resentment.

Always before, whenever she felt sorry for her, that feeling had been immediately followed by a helpless wish to change her sister's behavior, but now Slava could say to herself that if her sister wanted to improve her lot, she, Slava, would help, but if she didn't want to—and how many people couldn't or wouldn't improve their lot, even when it would require only the smallest of efforts!—then she, Slava, wouldn't worry about it anymore. Her sister's foolish unhappiness was out of her power to correct, and the only person Slava was affecting by fretting over it was herself. Now, Slava told herself, the trick would be to remember all of that when actually in her sister's presence.

"Dearest Slava!" cried her sister, sweeping into the room. "I hope you are refreshed?"

"As refreshed as I can be, after only a few hours off the road," said Slava.

"And...But I won't ask you if you had a pleasant journey, it was so long and arduous, and you already sketched so admirably for us the difficulties and dangers you faced, but I trust you will soon recover... Now, about those dangers and difficulties—but wait, first, I think, we must discuss your ward, what is her name? Vladislava Vasilisovna? She is the daughter of Princess Severnolesnaya's heir, is she not? The eventual heir of all of Severnolesnoye, isn't that so?"

"Yes," said Slava.

"And what possessed you...But I'm sure you had your reasons, and they seemed good to you at the time...The Severnolesniye, though... And the old princess is ill, is she not?...It seems not the most fortuitous time..." Slava's sister left her sentence hanging, and looked at Slava expectantly. Slava realized, with a mixture of amusement and annoyance, that once again her sister thought she (Slava, that is) had done a foolish thing, and was convinced that she (Vladya, that is) was much cleverer than Slava and that Slava had therefore made a mistake, and that she was trying to convince Slava of the same thing, and that all these notions were so firmly fixed in her sister's mind that she was not even aware of what she was doing.

"The old princess is ill, yes," said Slava. "In fact, I would not be surprised to receive word of her passing very shortly. And Lesnograd has been thrown into some disorder by all this, but that seemed all the more reason to bring Vladislava to Krasnograd. Whatever happens, Lesnograd will not pass directly into the hands of a child of ten. Vladislava Vasilisovna is a girl of high rank and, as best I can tell, even higher abilities, and I judged it best give her all the advantages Krasnograd has to offer a young princess, instead of leaving her to be raised in ignorance and neglect in a barbaric backwater province.

"Her grandmother no doubt meant to raise her to rule, but that is no longer in her power, and she is also no friend to our family. Her mother, the old princess's heir, seems to bear Krasnograd no ill will, but she is a foolish and ineffectual woman, incapable of raising a child, let alone ruling a province. When Lesnograd passes to her hands she will do nothing but wring them and dither, I am sure of it, and it will do Vladislava no good to see that. Krasnograd has need of strong and loyal princesses. Vladislava Vasilisovna may one day be such a princess, but not if she is left in Lesnograd. Let her spend a few years improving her mind and learning to love Krasnograd, and when she returns to her homeland, she will be a valuable ally."

"That is assuming that she does learn to love Krasnograd," said Slava's sister with a condescending little laugh. "Many a ward has learned exactly the opposite lesson from the one intended." She made a little face designed to show that she had just said a very wise thing.

"Then we must make her learn to love Krasnograd," said Slava.

"I fear that is not in our power," said Slava's sister, with another condescending little laugh.

"I fear we must make ourselves lovable," said Slava, looking at her sister directly in the face. Her sister squirmed slightly under her gaze. "We must gain her love by being lovable, her trust by being trustworthy, and her admiration by being admirable. In other words, we must gain good allies by being good rulers."

"I fear that only works with the few," said Slava's sister, with another little laugh that was supposed to be condescending but came out as nervous instead. "Many do not love lovability, trust trustworthiness, or admire admirability."

"Vladislava will," said Slava. "And so will many others, if those virtues arise from true strength of purpose and character."

"Why, you seem quite in love with this girl, little sister," said Slava's sister, squirming even more and trying to regain the upper hand in a conversation that was making her unexpectedly uncomfortable. "Is she such a sweet little thing, then? Is she lovable, trustworthy, and admirable?"

"No," said Slava with a smile. "Not as yet. At the moment she is more an unharnessed force than anything else, a danger to herself and all around her."

"That doesn't seem like the kind of girl we want around Krasnograd," said Slava's sister, cheering up at what seemed like the perfect opportunity to put Slava down. "She sounds more like someone we want far away from Krasnograd."

"It is the strongest currents that turn the largest mills," said Slava. "The wildest horses that win the greatest races. The boldest men who make the best warriors. One simply has to have the courage to tame them, without causing them to lose their strength and swiftness. It is the same with Vladislava."

"As long as we don't get carried off in the flood," said Slava's sister, still smiling condescendingly.

"We are Krasnograd," Slava told her. "We are the Zerkalitsy. We must trust in our own strength, if we trust in nothing else."

"Well..." Slava's sister laughed with a painful awkwardness that she was unable to conceal. "Yes...I am eager to meet this girl, since it seems she will be my guest for some time...And as for the other business...I mean the 'gifts' you claim to have manifested on your journey...Describe them. I mean, what makes you believe them to be gifts? And what made you think to go to Lesnograd to discover more about them. Surely Krasnograd would have been the better choice."

"Once we entered the forest, I began to have dreams," Slava began.

"Everybody has dreams," her sister observed, with a complacent smile.

"Yes, and so do I," said Slava. "Often. But once we entered the forest, I began to have dreams about the forest. That it was speaking to me."

"We often have dreams about the places we inhabit," said her sister. She was still smiling complacently, but there was something fixed about that smile now, as if it cost her effort to maintain it.

"Yes," said Slava. "But then one day we got lost when we shouldn't have. When we tried to retrace our steps, we ended up not where we had started. And then I saw an elk, and it seemed to speak to me, and I followed it, and it led us back to the trail."

"Many people get lost in the forest," said Slava's sister, looking relieved. "There's nothing unusual about *that*. And it's easy enough to think you're retracing your steps when you're really going farther astray. And if you're lucky enough to make it back to the path, it's easy enough to ascribe your luck to other forces. The elk was just luck, you know."

"And then I collapsed and had a great vision, that I had become the forest," Slava continued.

"You collapsed!" For a moment Slava's sister looked alarmed, but then she realized what an excellent opportunity this was to assert her own superiority, and said, "Well, that explains it all, then. You were no doubt tired and hungry. Our senses can play all kinds of tricks on us when we're tired and hungry."

"Yes," said Slava. "And then, after many days of travel, we reached the Midnight Land. There I had more visions. I dreamed that the others were running towards danger, and I begged a snow fox who was with me to turn them aside, and she did, and when they returned, they told the story of their adventures, and it was exactly as I had dreamed it, including the snow fox. And then I had a dream that the leshiye had come for me, and wanted to offer me more gifts. They wanted to seal their offering with the sacrifice of a snow hare, but I refused, and they attacked me and tore my arm, and when I awoke, there were scars—here, look." Slava unlaced her gown at the throat and pulled it open enough to show her sister her scarred shoulder. Her sister flinched and looked away, but no belief rose in her eyes.

"And so then we left the Midnight Land, and decided to proceed to Lesnograd, only we got lost again when our compass would no longer show North. But then a snow hare, brother to the one I saw in my dream, came to me and led us to the road."

Slava's sister's face was shutting up tighter and tighter at the recounting of these strange doings, but Slava carried on regardless.

"The leshiye came to us when we were on the road, and tried to take me. The others attempted to defend me, but they were unable to stand against the leshiye, and so I went to them, I gave myself to the leshiye, but they could not make use of my gift, and they let us go, but we lost our provisions and some of us were wounded."

Slava's sister shook her head disbelievingly, but said nothing.

"And then we were captured by bandits and taken to their hiding-place, and they tried to attack us and kill us, but I...I turned my gift on them somehow, I repelled them, and we escaped."

"Bandits!" Slava's sister cried. "And this was on the great road?"

"The Severnovostochnaya road," Slava confirmed.

"Bandits on the Severnovostochnaya! Attacking large parties! What has Princess Severnolesnaya been doing! Sitting with her arms folded and taking young lovers? Bandits!" Slava's sister jumped on this opportunity to express her indignation over something, and went on and on about the disgrace of bandits on one of the great roads of Zem', finally concluding, "But it was lucky you had such a large party to protect you, dear sister. Olga Vasilisovna and her men never struck me as good for much of anything, but if they were able to drive off a party of bandits, at least they served some purpose."

Slava didn't know what part of that sentence annoyed her more: the fact that her sister had apparently been willing to let her go off on a long journey with people who had never struck her as good for much of anything (although it was quite possible that she was saying that now just to say it), or the fact that she had apparently ignored everything Slava had said about what had happened with the bandits, and reconstructed the tale to suit her own fancy. After a brief pause, in which she struggled with how to frame the next part of her story, Slava continued:

"My gift for once was turned outwards, rather than inwards, and I was able to repel them long enough for us to make our escape, but only at great cost to myself and to others. Indeed, I caused almost as must harm to my allies as to my enemies. But we escaped and made our way to a nearby village, which took us in and gave us food, shelter, and care for our wounded. We were forced to leave half our party behind, as they were unfit to continue. In fact, we even feared for the lives of some of them. And so I asked...there was an herbwoman there, who seemed...more than a simple herbwoman. And I asked her if she would save them, and she said I must...she took my hand and brought me before all the spirits of the forest, and asked if I were willing to give them what they needed in exchange for my friends' lives, and so of course I agreed."

"Oh, of course," said her sister. Her face was now so full of gloating condescension that there was no room on it for anything else. Repressing a sigh, Slava plunged on.

"After we left the village, we got lost again..."

"Again!" her sister interrupted, smiling patronizingly. "I thought you had scouts and guides with you!"

"Or rather, I got lost, I strayed from the path, and I encountered...I encountered creatures from the gods. Creatures and also a man. He showed me my way back to the road, and when we were united with the group, it turned out...it turned out that he was Olga's father. Olga's father who was thought to be dead these many years. But he had not been killed, he had been taken into the service of the gods. He decided to accompany us to Lesnograd. On our way to Lesnograd, we stopped at a waystation."

"That hardly seems a noteworthy event," said Slava's sister, smiling even more patronizingly.

"At which we became entangled with sorcery, and I ended up saving a leshaya and coming before the gods themselves, and then we carried on and came to Lesnograd," said Slava quickly. She was finding it more and more difficult not to be openly rude to her sister, and decided the fight was not worth the effort. "And then we discovered that the old princess was gravely ill and everything was in disarray because of this, and I discovered that this was because of a curse she had attempted to cast on Krasnograd and our family, and then the gods revealed to me that I should conceive a child with Olga's father, so I did, and then we came home."

"So you took a lover, did you?" said Slava's sister, smiling even more widely. "Couldn't you have found someone a little younger? He must have been—well, old enough to be your father, at any rate. Frankly, it seems unlikely that you actually managed to conceive a child with him—he must have been old and tired, and you're no youth yourself anymore, you know. In fact, it seems to me to be highly unlikely. When did this take place? You're certainly not showing yet."

"Shortly before we left Lesnograd," said Slava. "It is early, yes, but still the possibility exists, so I thought it necessary to inform you immediately."

"And that would have been very proper, if you had been sure of it, but since it's still so uncertain I'd rather not have known about your... connection," Slava's sister made a grimace of distaste, "with such an old man. Some things should be kept private, you know, and it is always unwise to speak of...such things too early."

"Well, we shall see," said Slava. "Of more immediate concern is the curse..."

"Oh, surely you're not worried about that?" cried Slava's sister, waving her hand dismissively. "A curse! Even if I believed in curses, which, as I have never seen one struck effectively, I don't, I wouldn't worry about one cast by a sick old woman hundreds of versts away, especially since, according to you, she failed in her attempt by falling ill. Speak to me no more of these unfounded rumors of curses!"

Of all the reactions Slava had imagined when she had tried to envision how to break the news of the curse to her sister, this one had never crossed her mind. She had expected her sister to be wildly angry, possibly even afraid, but it had never occurred to Slava even for a moment that she would dismiss the information out of hand.

"The curse is a serious matter, sister," she said. "We must...We must consult with our own sorceresses immediately, and see what can be done to protect ourselves."

"What? And have it get out that the Empress of Zem' is afraid of a curse? Don't be ridiculous, Slava! What would people think of me?"

"They would think that you were wise," said Slava. "Many an empress has consulted with her sorceresses on magical business. It is why we keep them in Krasnograd, troublesome as they are at times."

"Nonsense! A curse! Let us have no more talk of such things! Come, I'm hungry, you must be starving, and the feast is no doubt long ready." Slava's sister stood up and held out her hand. "Let us appear in the Hall of Celebration arm in arm, to show my princesses how delighted I am to have you back."

Slava was too astonished, and still too annoyed, with her sister's behavior to be able to think up a good answer, and so she silently let her sister link her arm through Slava's and lead her down to the Hall of Celebration.

To her relief, she saw when she arrived that Vladislava's caretakers must have realized what had happened, and taken Vladislava down without waiting for Slava to meet them. Vladislava was just being seated in the place next to Slava's, but she jumped out of her chair as soon as Slava drew near.

"Slava! There you are! I was wondering where you'd been!"

"May I present to you my ward, Vladislava Vasilisovna Severnolesnaya, the only daughter of Vasilisa Vasilisovna Severnolesnaya, heir to Lesnograd," Slava said. This reminded Vladislava of her manners, and she managed quite a creditable bow to Slava's sister, and said, "Allow me to express my inexpressible honor, Empress."

Slava's sister gave her a sharp look and a curt nod, before turning and taking her own place. "Did you intend for her to be a companion to Prasha?" she whispered to Slava. "I suppose they are of an age, more or less, but I'm not sure she's a fit companion for my heir..."

"It would be a very good thing for Prasha to gain Vladislava as a friend," Slava whispered back. *If she's capable of it*, she added silently. Thus far, Prasha had shown herself to be more than adequately endowed with the imperial qualities of arrogance and self-will, so useful in issuing commands, but rather short on qualities such as intelligence and charm, which were equally useful in ensuring that those commands were fulfilled satisfactorily. Slava glanced over to where Prasha was seated on her sister's other side, and saw that she was wearing her usual expression of self-satisfied dullness. She seemed barely aware of Slava's return to Krasnograd. Looking at her face, Slava rather doubted that Vladislava would take to her—in fact, she could easily see Vladislava becoming so enraged by Prasha that an irreparable breach would follow hard on the heels of their first meeting. "But I fear Vladislava is rather behind on her education, and will need to spend all her time at first with mistresses and tutors on every subject," she said. "Perhaps Prasha can befriend her once she has caught up."

"Yes...If she catches up. And I really don't see how it would serve Prasha to have a half-wild barbarian from the North hanging on to her."

Fortunately it was so noisy in the Hall of Celebration now that Slava was sure Vladislava couldn't hear them, and she herself had the perfect excuse not to reply to such an odd comment. Her sister had never struck Slava with the subtlety of her mind, but always before Slava would have assumed her at least capable of grasping the obvious advantages to the heir of Zem' befriending the heir of Zem''s largest province. Slava tried to observe her sister out of the corner of her eye, to see if she were showing any signs of fever or other illness—perhaps that was why she had not seemed herself, ever since Slava had arrived. Thoughts of the curse floated through Slava's mind, but she tried to ignore them. She had just grown unused to her sister's blunt ways, she told herself, but received nothing but an unpleasant twinge of doubt in reply.

Slava's sister made a very lengthy and florid speech about Slava's safe return, which was greeted by many cheers, and then enormous piles of food were brought out, and consumed very slowly. Slava realized that she would have to retrain herself to eat at feasts after her journey, for she swallowed down the soup she was served before anyone else—except Olga and Vladislava—was even halfway done, and then realized that, despite the near-constant hunger that had accompanied her while she was away, she would not be able to manage much more of such rich and greasy food.

The beet soup had had yellow spots of fat covering most of its surface, and now it looked as if Slava were being served pancakes full of sour cream and caviar, and there was a whole roast pig waiting as well...Slava's mouth watered at the sight of all that food, but her stomach turned unpleasantly, and the pig's squeals as it was being slaughtered rang loud in her ears. It looked like it was going to be a very long feast.

Slava's sister ate and drank a great deal and talked more and more loudly with everyone on the other end of the table from Slava. Everyone on Slava's end of the table started drinking vodka as soon as it was poured for them, and quickly moved on to pouring it for themselves, as the servants were in no way able to keep pace with their demands. Vladislava ate for a little while, and then began to fidget in her seat with boredom, while looking at the ever-drunker princesses and princes around her with disgust.

Just as Slava was beginning to worry that she might cause a scene, little Yanochka, who was daughter to one of the Empress's serving women and therefore a valuable guide for someone such as Vladislava, who knew nothing of how to live at the Krasnograd kremlin, slipped up beside her and whispered that the younger princesses were about to leave to go dance by themselves in another room, and would the little Princess Vladislava care to join them? After the most cursory of glances in Slava's direction, seeking permission, Vladislava jumped gratefully out of her chair and followed Yanochka out of the room.

Slava was not, however, left to be lonely for too much longer, for Serafimiya Svetlanovna soon came over from the far end of the table and sat down in Vladislava's vacated chair. Of all the drunken guests at the feast, she looked to be the drunkest, or at least the closest to laying her head down on the table and weeping. She seemed much thinner than Slava remembered her, and walked awkwardly, as if too much movement was painful. There were large dark circles under her eyes.

"You're back, Ts-ts-tsalinonova," she said. "Pueasant joulney?"

"Yes," said Slava. "I hear you are to be congratulated. Allow me to offer you my most heart-felt wishes for the health and happiness of yourself and your new husband. May the gods look with favor upon your union for many years to come."

"Aaaah," moaned Serafimiya Svetlanovna, and laid her head down on the table and wept. After an internal struggle, Slava couldn't help herself, and stroked Serafimiya's head with compassion.

"You—only one who understands me," said Serafimiya, or at least she mumbled something into the table that Slava thought was intended to mean that.

"Have you had many troubles?" Slava asked kindly. "They say that a new wife's path is often strewn with rocks and thorns. Young husbands often bring much sorrow in their wake."

"But I love him so much!" wailed Serafimiya, speaking with perfect clarity, before subsiding again into inarticulate sniffling.

"They also say that it is those we love who cause us the most pain," Slava told her. It was something new brides were often told to comfort them, although why it should be comforting Slava had never understood. She thought it might be the kind of thing that Serafimiya would drink up without question, but instead it only provoked another round of sniffling, which showed that Serafimiya was not quite so stupid as Slava had always assumed.

Eventually Serafimiya's crying jag ran its course, and she raised her head from the table and—wiping her face with her sleeve in a way Slava was glad Vladislava was not present to witness—unburdened herself to Slava, laying out all the troubles that had accumulated since the last time she had poured them out on Slava's heart.

It seemed that Valery Annovich had, although with surprisingly bad grace, finally agreed to the match after months of his mother's nagging. He had even shown up to the wedding mostly sober, and cut quite a fine figure as he stood beside Serafimiya before the priestess, and then as he danced with her at the feast afterwards, and all of Serafimiya's tender hopes had rebloomed within her, as strong as on the day of their first tryst.

But as soon as they walked hand-in-hand out of the feast, things took a turn for the worse. Valery Annovich had dropped her hand as they entered the bedchamber, fallen onto the bed with his boots still on, claiming he was too tired and drunk to be a husband just yet, and gone to sleep then and there.

"I embroidered that bed cover myself!" Serafimiya sobbed. "With spells for happiness and fertility! I worked on it for a month! I thought...I thought our first child would be conceived there! And he spoiled it with his boots that very night, so I had to give it to my serving girl for her wedding! But I didn't tell him, of course I didn't scold him for it, perhaps he really was very tired...I swore to myself, when the engagement was made and again as we were standing there before the priestess, that I wouldn't be a scold like my own mother..."

"Did he...Did things improve once he'd sobered up?" Slava asked gently.

They had not, of course. It seemed that Valery Annovich spent most of his time away from Serafimiya, and when circumstances forced him to come home, he mostly sat by himself and sulked, or made unpleasant, cutting remarks to Serafimiya about how unkind she was and how unhappy she was making him. Serafimiya had tried to combat this by spoiling him like a sick child, and when that had failed, by resorting to the common tactic of hysterical scenes and tearful reproaches, but that too, strangely enough, had only made him even more sulky and unpleasant.

"He's not even...he's not even interested in...in being a husband," Serafimiya told Slava. "Most of the time he just tries to avoid me, and when he can't, he's either...either...he's either unkind, almost cruel, or, or, or...just...just...sort of limp," she finished in a horrified whisper. "He says it's my fault, I don't...interest him, and the only way is to...is if I let him...hurt me. Just a little," she added quickly.

"And of course you let him," said Slava.

"What else could I do? I don't know what I'm doing wrong. What am I doing wrong? I don't think I'm doing anything differently than I did before...before we came to Krasnograd, when I was...I was the only woman, the only person, the only thing in the world that mattered to him, but then we came to Krasnograd and he…Oh!" And Serafimiya laid her head down on the table and wept some more. Her gown opened a little as she did so, and Slava could see what looked like the bruises left by a man's hands all around the base of her neck and throat, as if Valery Annovich had grabbed her there and shaken her or choked her.

"Excuse me," said Slava, rising.

"I'm sorry," Serafimiya sobbed into the table. "I'm sorry I troubled you, Tsarinovna, but his mother reproaches me constantly for making him unhappy, and my mother says I've made my bed and now I must lie in it, every woman must learn how to rule her husband on her own, but I don't know how, I don't know how, and I love him so much, and I know that everyone despises me for my weakness, but I love him so much…"

"Of course you do," said Slava. "I understand you completely."

"You do, Tsarinovna?"

"Even Tsarinovnas know what it is like to be in love sometimes," said Slava, smiling down on her. "Even Tsarinovnas know what it is like to be weak and foolish when one needs to be strong and wise. So now I will be strong and wise for you. Go to bed, Serafimiya, if you're tired, or stay and be merry, if that will make you happier. Do what makes you happier, Serafimiya; perhaps your spells will work after all. But now I have something I must do."

"I think I'll…I think I'll just go to bed," said Serafimiya, rising unsteadily from her seat. "I feel…just terrible…I haven't been able to eat or sleep since my wedding, it seems." Slava watched as she made her way uncertainly out of the Hall of Celebration. Slava's pride tried to tell her that *she* never had and never would be anything like Serafimiya, but she knew that she was in danger of being *exactly* like Serafimiya, if she were ever to be so desperately in love. Not only that, but she was fairly certain that everyone around her thought she *was* exactly like Serafimiya all the time about everyone. She waited until she was sure that Serafimiya had made it out of the Hall of Celebration, and then set off in search of Valery Annovich.

She found him, as she had expected, drinking with a group of other young princes in a small chamber near the Hall of Celebration. They were all lolling on benches and laughing coarsely over something that, Slava was sure, did them no credit—judging from the words she managed to catch as she entered the room, something about some cruel trick on someone defenseless—and they all jerked upright in horrified surprise when they realized that Slava had entered the room.

"Tsa...Tsall...Tsarinovna," they said in drunken chorus, trying to bow without falling over. For a moment Slava was stricken with the sickening fear that all the promises she had been given that her future child would be a girl had been false. The horrifying thought that she might instead bear a son pierced through her with such intensity that for an instant she was afraid she had hurt herself. All her earlier brave words of welcoming a son with open arms fled from her at the sight of what all these other women's sons had become. The task of trying to raise a little boy to be a man, not a monster, rose up before her in all its hopelessness, and she knew that no matter how good her intentions were, no matter how much she tried, no matter how many advantages she tried to give any future son of hers, every hand would be against her in her attempt, his most of all.

She wanted to tell herself that no flesh of her flesh could ever have anything in common with the men lolling on the benches in front of her, laughing vodka-induced laughter over some cruel trick they had played on some poor servant or peasant girl, but she knew that she was just telling herself comforting lies. After all, all these men had once been someone's precious little boys. Of course any son of hers could so easily become just like his fellow princes.

She wondered how much her own father had resembled them. Probably more than she would like. She wondered if, had he survived, she would be forced to feel for him the same pity and revulsion she felt for these men lolling before her, and for a moment all she could see was the memory of her father (who, being the memory of a girl of four, was enormous) slumped drunkenly on the bench and laughing at her in vicious, thoughtless mockery. Slava shook her head to rid it of this terrifying vision, but when she looked back at the princes, they were still there in all their foolish, cruel, drunken glory.

"Ah, Valery Annovich," said Slava, spotting him as he attempted to shrink back into the far corner. "I am so glad to see you. I wished to come offer you my congratulations in person. It is not every young prince who has the happiness of calling himself the husband of Serafimiya Svetlanovna Malokrasnova. You must be the envy of all your comrades here."

Valery Annovich mumbled something unintelligible and shrank even further back into the corner, an action that looked particularly ridiculous in someone so large and handsome. Slava had to give

Serafimiya credit: she might have taken a spoiled child for a husband (although what woman hadn't?), but he was certainly one of the finest-looking men in Krasnograd. Thick hair the color of ripe wheat, clear blue eyes, strong manly features and figure...and all ruined by a petulant expression and a tendency to whine. In some other life than the one he had been given, he might have been a good man, but as it was he was just good for nothing. It was hard for Slava not to sigh over the waste, but she controlled herself and looked around the room meaningfully.

The other princes, on catching her eye, all muttered their excuses and fled. Slava waited until they had cleared the room, and then went and stood over Valery Annovich, who was slumped on his bench in a posture of equal defiance and shame.

"Welcome back to Krasnograd, Tsarinovna," he said thickly. "May it bring you joy!" He looked down at the cup in his hand, saw that it still contained a considerable measure of vodka, and drank it down to the bottom in one swallow. "More than it has me," he continued, even more thickly. "I suppose...Serafimiya has been filling your ears with talk, my head for beheading, complaining of me, I'm sure." He tried to grin at her boldly, but it came out as the most awful twisted grimace of resentment and embarrassment. "Or has Princess Malokrasnova sent you to scold me for not treating her precious darling daughter kindly enough?"

"Princess Malokrasnova would throw her daughter to the wolves at the first opportunity if she thought it might be of advantage to her, as you well know, Valery Annovich—and as your present ill-advised marriage so abundantly proves. No, I'm afraid you have nothing to fear on that score, much as I might like to be able to inform you of the opposite. It is the father's duty to keep his new son in line—peasant fathers, you know, like to beat their new sons into submission as their welcome to the family—but Serafimiya, like so many of us, has no father. I have always abhorred that peasant practice, but now, looking at you, Valery Annovich, I begin to understand it. It seems that nothing short of cruelty will cure you." Slava could feel a sweat of rage start to trickle down her back, and forced herself to stop before she began screaming at Valery Annovich, which would do no good at all.

"Princess Malokrasnova's darling daughter knew what she was getting into," muttered Valery Annovich, looking down at his boots.

"I highly doubt that," said Slava.

"Well, she was the one who insisted the match take place. *She* was

258

the one who came after *me*, *she* was the one who begged our mothers for their consent, *she* was the one who dragged us both before the priestess and got us into this mess..." Valery Annovich broke off and stared miserably somewhere off beyond Slava's left shoulder, apparently lost in melancholy, and, Slava suspected and sincerely hoped, self-critical reflections.

"You do not seem happy, Valery Annovich," said Slava, changing her tactics and sitting down beside him with a kind smile. Some part of her longed to reach out and slap his face, if not worse, but he really did look miserable, and chastising him further seemed unlikely to produce any beneficial effect, whereas sympathy was almost always a helpful jumping-off point, in Slava's experience.

"So you've come to commiserate, have you, Tsarinovna?" said Valery Annovich with a sneer. "Poor Valery Annovich! Half the women here despise me, and half pity me and are all too ready to offer me a bosom to cry on. Which half are you, Tsarinovna?"

"Neither, I hope," said Slava. "But you do seem very unhappy, Valery Annovich, and you know how unhappy that must make me."

"Why do you care, Tsarinovna?" he demanded sullenly. "I thought you were friends with Serafimiya—well, as much as either of you could ever be friends with anyone. I guess both of you like to share your sorrows, though. My head for beheading, you like nothing better than complaining to each other about your lovers."

Slava wondered how much of this he would remember tomorrow, and which would be the stronger upon remembering it: shame at having spoken so ungraciously of his wife, or horror at having spoken so insultingly to the Tsarinovna. She supposed that his feelings of both shame and fear were much blunter than her own, but she could see nonetheless that he *did* possess feelings of both shame and fear, as otherwise he would not have made himself so terribly unhappy as he had.

"The pain of others causes me pain as well," Slava told him. "And you *do* seem dreadfully unhappy, Valery Annovich. And needlessly so, if you'll allow me to say so. Think of all the advantages you have! Youth, health, riches, and a wife who loves you. How many men can boast of such good fortune?"

"Hah!" snorted Valery Annovich.

"What more would you ask for?" Slava pressed on.

"How about a wife who wasn't a burden to me?" Valery said, straightening up and growing more animated. "A wife who wasn't forced on me! A wife who wasn't a constant thorn in my side, demanding my love, always reminding me what a disappointment I am, a wife who..." He put his face in his hands, in order, Slava suspected, to hide his tears.

"Is there some other woman you prefer?" Slava asked gently.

"Any woman!"

"Her mother, perhaps?" Slava suggested with a smile. "After all, she set aside her husband years ago."

"What! Oh, that was a joke. You were joking at my unhappiness, Tsarinovna. Why do women like to laugh at men's unhappiness?" he demanded plaintively.

"Because so much of it is self-inflicted?" suggested Slava. "But think: would any other woman really be better than Serafimiya? Would you really be less unhappy with, for example, her mother?"

"The gods forbid!" cried Valery Annovich, shuddering.

"Or Princess Stepnaya, perhaps? Ailing as she is, she could use the help of a strong young man like you."

"Tfoo!" said Valery Annovich, spitting in disgust.

"Or perhaps Aleksandra Anastasiyevna?" Aleksandra Anastasiyevna was a minor noblewoman who had never married, preferring to take a succession of craftsmen and minor princes as her lovers, discarding each one as soon as she conceived a child or grew tired of him, whichever came first. How she managed to take so many lovers was a mystery to most around her, as she had a large, coarse figure (which had only grown coarser with each child), an unusually plain face, a querulous temper, and no land or riches to speak of. Slava had long since decided to put the whole thing to the unaccountability of men's tastes, but it seemed that Valery shared her opinion of Aleksandra Anastasiyevna, for he was so horror-stricken at the thought that he could manage nothing more than a shiver of distaste at the mere mention of her name.

"So you see," said Slava with a kind smile, "things could be worse."

"Yes, but..." and just as Slava had expected, the whole wretched story of his own wretchedness and all the wretchedness he had caused other people came pouring drunkenly out. Not that there was anything new to hear: it was a story Slava had heard or seen enacted in front of her many times before. From Valery's words, and from his painful silences and unhappy expressions, Slava gathered the following tale.

As far as Valery was concerned, it had all been fun and games as long as his connection with Serafimiya had been a way of defying his mother (who had talked a lot about her wish to protect his virtue and her desire to make a good match for him, without actually doing anything to promote either of those aims—but it had certainly made him *feel* deliciously disobedient to engage in an illicit relationship behind his mother's back) and deceiving his hated neighbor, Princess Malokrasnova. Serafimiya was very noble (*and* the daughter of his family's worst enemy), very pretty, and very much in love with him, and the whole thing had stroked his vanity most pleasantly.

But then, to his horror, the whole thing had gotten entirely out of hand and he had found himself a married man, with duties and responsibilities he had never been trained to assume. Still, he had allowed Serafimiya and his mother to force this upon him, because, after all, it *was* time to take up a man's station, and he *did* secretly love Serafimiya, and he *did* want this happiness forced upon him against his will. Only, as was too often the case, the forcing ruined the happiness. Being made to do something he said he didn't want to do was much less pleasant than he had thought it would be, and complaining about it eased his pain much less than he had expected.

Not only that, but the happiness itself seemed to involve a lot more work than he had bargained for. As his mother's cosseted youngest son, he was accustomed to everyone, most particularly the women of his family, catering to his every whim, and while Serafimiya was most certainly ready to do just that, she nonetheless seemed to expect some signs of affection and devotion on his side, or—even worse!—he secretly suspected that he owed her that, and that thought was more than he could bear. Gratitude for kindness and devotion! Why that would indicate that he didn't deserve that kind of treatment just by breathing!

Furthermore, he was dimly aware—no, he was acutely aware, it tortured him every hour of every day, even though he didn't want to admit it, even to himself—that his behavior towards Serafimiya caused her pain, and not only that, she would sometimes reveal this to him, a most bewildering experience for Valery Annovich, who had always been told that his very existence was enough to brighten the spirits of any woman he met.

To make matters worse, he was more and more harassed by the nagging suspicion that his own behavior was less than exemplary, a thought that had never crossed his mind before and from which he now recoiled in horror—only to have it pursue him even more aggressively. And then there was all the talk of children, the division of their estates, children (Slava had to bite her tongue to keep herself from pointing out that, as a man, Valery Annovich would be spared all the pain and sickness that would come with bearing his children, and as a nobleman, he would never have to lift a finger to care for them), the organization of their families to ensure the Yuzhnokrasnova family name did not disappear if Valery should prove to be its only heir, which seemed very likely, children, children, children...

It must be dreadful, Slava supposed, to be so terribly selfish. To have one's own self-satisfaction as one's sole source of happiness! What a slender branch on which to rest such a large burden of hope and expectation! She looked at Valery's wretchedly sullen face. It appeared his branch was long broken.

"Just the other day Serafimiya was going on and on and on about what to name the first child, and asking my opinion on the subject, and plaguing me about it till I had to leave," he related indignantly. "I went and hid out with a friend for two days, till I was sure she'd forgotten the matter—especially as I thought she wanted me to do something about it right then, about...producing a child, you know—but as soon as I returned, she was at it again, only first she cried because I'd left her for two days, and then she went right back to talking about children, until I..." Valery trailed off.

"Put your hands around her neck and squeezed until she couldn't speak?" Slava suggested.

Valery stared at her with an expression of equal parts mortification, astonishment, and sullen self-justification.

"I saw the marks this evening," said Slava. "They are plainly visible under the collar of her gown whenever she bends down. For shame, Valery Annovich! What prince could live with himself, knowing that his wife attended the Empress's feast and sat at the Empress's table, all the while wearing the marks of his own cruel, violent hands on her tender neck? And this is to be the mother of your children? This is the woman to whom you gave yourself before the gods themselves? How could you stand to soil yourself so?"

She stood back up. "I am very sorry for you and your unhappiness, and if there is anything I can do to alleviate it, you know you have only to ask and I will give it to you without hesitation, but if," she leaned in close to him, "I *ever* hear—if the thought ever even crosses my mind— that you have offended Serafimiya Svetlanovna by so much as an unkind word, you have my assurances that you will find yourself in a mine before you even have time to look about you."

"They don't send princes to the mines," said Valery sullenly.

"Oh, but they do, Valery Annovich, they do. For who do you think runs them? Someone of noble blood must oversee them, you know, and princesses have better things to do. The mines, like the battle-field, are a place for men to earn back all the food they eat from their mothers' and wives' tables. True, being the overseer of a mine is not so unpleasant as being a miner, but from what I've heard, it's not so sweet either, and for a soft little boy like you, it would seem a very hard life indeed. They say the miners make their own lives worse than that of prisoners in the most terrible dungeon, and you would be drawn down into it, whether you wished it or no. I believe you would soon find that there are self-inflicted miseries much more terrible than the ones you have already suffered. I believe you would soon long to return to your wife and her demands that you take up a husband's duties."

"I'm not a soft little boy!" cried Valery Annovich.

"So prove it! Be a man! If you can, that is. And if you do not do so voluntarily by providing Serafimiya with the husband and father she deserves, then you may be sure I will force it upon you in some rather more painful manner. I will be watching you, Valery Annovich, every day that I am in Krasnograd I will be watching you, and so you had best watch your every step. Good night, Valery Annovich, and think on what I have said to you. Think hard."

With that, Slava left him, slumped on the bench in a misery too awful to contemplate. For the first time since she had known him, he looked something like a man. Slava thought she could even see some small sliver of soul, tormenting him there somewhere. She walked as quickly away as she could, in order to prevent herself from running back to comfort him. She rather doubted that her stern words would do him any good, but she was certain that her apologies and excuses would do him a great deal of harm.

As she walked she reflected rather sadly that she seemed to have taken the place of Serafimiya's father, and beaten Valery into sub-mission so that he wouldn't dare lift a finger against his bride, even if she had used her words, not her fists. Probably for Valery words were more frightening than fists anyway. She wondered how efficacious her verbal beating would prove to me. If it worked Serafimiya would be delivered of a terrible burden, but it was dreadful to think that Valery was incapable of learning from anything other than cruelty...And he was not the only one...Slava told herself she should stop dwelling on such miserable thoughts.

She stepped back into the Hall of Celebration, but her sister was nowhere to be seen and the other guests were all dancing drunkenly. It was a shame, Slava thought, that they weren't in a condition to do better justice to the excellent performance of the balalaika player and the singer, an extremely pretty girl with milky-white skin and a cloud of flaming hair...Slava did a double-take, and her heart jumped in her chest when she realized how much the girl resembled Oleg. For a moment all she could think of was how much she wished he were there. Once she had gotten over the surprise at her own strong desire, she inched over to where some serving girls were loading up trays of beer and vodka.

"Has the singer been offered any refreshment?" Slava asked them.

"Oh! Tsarinovna! We were just on our way!"

"Allow me," said Slava, taking a tray from the girl nearest her. "I believe..." Slava quickly changed her mind about how much she wanted to reveal, and said, "Her singing is very fine, is it not? I wish to invite her to sing for me again, a private audience."

"Oh, but Tsarinovna, let me deliver the message," said the serving girl. "You'll frighten her out of her singing if you suddenly show up beside her yourself."

Slava had to admit the justice of that remark, and so, returning the tray and telling the girl to tell the singer that the Tsarinovna wished to see her the next day, retired from the Hall of Celebration and went to bed.

The next morning she received a message as soon as she awoke that Serafimiya Svetlanovna requested the honor to wait upon her at her earliest convenience.

"Send her in with the breakfast," Slava ordered, privately thinking to herself that this would be a good chance to force some much-needed food down Serafimiya's throat.

Accordingly, both Serafimiya and the food were shortly brought into Slava's sitting room. Serafimiya appeared surprised at being granted access to Slava while she was still in her dressing gown, but she was too consumed with her own troubles to be surprised for long, and after muttering the briefest of pleasantries and excuses, she thrust a note into Slava's hand.

"What does this mean?!" she demanded tearfully.

The note was a scrap of paper, on which was written *Gone to sanctuary*, and nothing more.

"Is this from Valery Annovich?" Slava asked.

"Yes! He never came home last night—well, not while I was awake, but I fell asleep, and he must have snuck in during the night, and I discovered this by my bedside this morning!"

"It appears he has gone to a sanctuary," said Slava. If it were true, she heartily rejoiced in his decision, although she had her doubts about the efficacy of a few days' prayer for someone such as Valery Annovich, if he even had, in fact, gone to a sanctuary. But everyone, she reminded herself, had to start somewhere, and leaving the note suggested some degree of remorse for his behavior, and a desire to take some step towards amendment.

"Yes, but what does it *mean*?" demanded Serafimiya. "*Why* has he gone to a sanctuary?"

"Because he feels in need of prayer and guidance?" suggested Slava.

"But *why*?" wailed Serafimiya. "Why should he need guidance? Why should he need to leave me? What did I do wrong? Do you think"—her face twisted as the horrifying thought struck her—"do you think he's run off with *another woman*?"

It was on the tip of Slava's tongue to say that if Valery had decided to run off with another woman, he most likely would have told Serafimiya directly and delighted in the pain he caused her, but she stopped herself. Just as the remark was, it would only cause Serafimiya to argue against it and anything else Slava would say after that.

"Valery Annovich has a very frank and open character," she said instead. "I believe that he would not lie to you about something like that."

Serafimiya's face cleared slightly as she contemplated the wonderfulness of Valery's frank and open character, and the fact that Slava had recognized and appreciated it.

"But do you think he really has gone off to pray, then?" she asked, once she had contemplated the wonderfulness of his frank and open character as much as—well, not as much as it deserved, but as much as she could find the time for when there were other, and sadly, even more pressing matters to discuss. "And why? Why would he do something like that?"

"Perhaps he has serious matters weighing on his conscience," said Slava, but, seeing Serafimiya's face screwing up into a pout, realized she had made a mistake and added hastily, "That is, he faces many new and unaccustomed duties, now that he is your husband. They say that sometimes facing these duties can be hard for new husbands. Perhaps he has gone to pray for the strength he needs."

"Yes, but..." Serafimiya clearly wanted to object to that, but couldn't think how.

"Think, Serafimiya!" said Slava, before Serafimiya could come up with anything to say in reply. "Just last night you were telling me of your unhappiness, all the troubles you have had with him! I know that you want him to be a man worth loving, and that is a great matter. Many husbands stumble and fall under that burden, for being a man worth loving is very hard for them. Valery Annovich is too clever not to notice such things—not to notice how unhappy you are, and how heavily sorrow and care are weighing upon you. And surely he could not help but wish to remove some of that burden from you. Perhaps he has gone to pray for the strength to do that!"

"Perhaps..." said Serafimiya hesitantly, but then, before that happy thought could take root in her head, another, less happy one crowded it out and she said accusingly, "You spoke with him! You went to him last night and spoke to him! That's where you went after you spoke with me!"

"Yes," Slava acknowledged.

"And...And...And you think he listened to you?"

"It seems possible, if he has truly gone off to a sanctuary to pray," said Slava.

"But...but...why didn't he..."—Serafimiya gave Slava a long look of suspicion and jealousy—"why didn't he speak to me, then? And how did you persuade him so easily? What power do you have over him that *I* do not?"

"I am the Tsarinovna," Slava told her with a smile.

"And you *ordered* him to go away? To leave me?"

"No, not at all. I merely represented to him how...what an unhappy situation you both had fallen into. The going away was entirely his own decision, and a very wise one, too, I think." *Much wiser than I was expecting*, Slava added to herself. Perhaps there *was* more to Valery

266

Annovich than good looks and thoughtlessness. Perhaps there was hope for him—and Serafimiya—yet.

Although, to be honest, Slava was not entirely certain how beneficial the atmosphere of a men's sanctuary would be for him. It was entirely possible that the other brothers would fill Valery Annovich's head with ridiculous notions and talk him right out of his marital responsibilities...which would at least mean he would be out of Serafimiya's hair. And it was always possible that, cut off from the life of idle pleasures he had been leading in the kremlin, he might inadvertently stumble into some serious contemplation and prayer while he was there. Stranger things had happened.

If nothing else, they were said to work the new brothers very hard at the sanctuaries. The picture of Valery Annovich cleaning stables and scrubbing floors, tears dripping down his cheeks and mixing with the washwater slopping around his sore knees, brought a lot more pleasure to Slava's inner eye than she felt entirely comfortable with... Probably it was wrong to picture another woman's husband in such a way...

"What if they overwork him?" Serafimiya wailed, breaking up Slava's happy, if indecent, fantasy of Valery Annovich dressed in rags and crawling on his hands and knees in the dirt. "He's so delicate!"

"I'm sure they will give him the gentle treatment that befits his station," Slava told her soothingly. She reached over to pat Serafimiya's shoulder comfortingly, but Serafimiya cringed away from her touch. No doubt, Slava thought, she was still covered in bruises from Valery Annovich's delicate hands.

"It is all for the best," she said, as encouragingly as possible. "Valery Annovich has made a very wise decision."

Serafimiya, however, did not see it that way at all, and it took Slava some time to convince her that it was all to the best, that Valery would most likely come back to her in good time and in much better spirits than he had been in since they had both come to Krasnograd, and that she, Slava, had no dark designs on him for herself. Slava found Serafimiya's jealous accusations to be the most painful part of the interview, as she couldn't decide whether to be mortally offended or to burst out laughing, but had to suppress both inclinations as being entirely unsuitable to Serafimiya's present delicate mental condition.

Eventually, though, she brought Serafimiya into a calm enough frame of mind that she was at least able to pretend to see sense, and they parted almost amicably, although Slava suspected that it would be a long time before the jealousy that had most unfoundedly been awakened in Serafimiya's heart would die down enough for them to be the kind of friends that, until this morning, Serafimiya had seemed so anxious for them to be.

Slava had just shepherded Serafimiya out the door and was listening to Masha and Manya discuss what gown she should wear that day, when she received another message that "the singer" had answered her summons and was awaiting her pleasure in the corridor.

"Send her in," Slava ordered.

Masha and Manya protested that she wasn't dressed yet, but Slava, knowing that once they started dressing her, they would be at it for a very long time, said that her dressing gown was certainly fine enough for Lyudmila Krasnoslavovna, and she didn't want to keep her waiting in the corridor any longer than she had to.

"Oh, she won't mind, Tsarinovna, it will be an honor for her," Masha assured her.

"But *I* will mind," said Slava. "Send her in."

Masha, Manya, and the message-girl all gave her uncertain looks, but, remembering how she had saved them the night before, Masha decided to stop protesting and let Lyudmila Krasnoslavovna into the sitting room.

Lyudmila Krasnoslavovna came in boldly enough, but lost most of her boldness as soon as she crossed the threshold and saw how fine Slava's apartment was. Slava wondered how she would have fared in her sister's chambers, and was glad at the comparative plainness of her own rooms.

"Please, Lyudmila Krasnoslavovna, have a seat," Slava said, sitting down herself.

Lyudmila bowed and sat down hesitantly, watching Slava all the while. She was, Slava thought, the absolute spitting image of Oleg, even more like him than Olga was, and it was strange and wonderful to see those features on a girl who had not yet reached her twentieth summer.

This morning she had pulled back her flaming red tangle of hair, and all the hollows around her eyes and nose were blue from last night's exertions, but even that could not dampen the restless energy that rose from her like heat from a stove. It was less focused than the strength that poured out of Olga and Oleg, but Slava could still feel it, and she understood why Andrey Vladislavovich could have fallen so badly in love with her. She was like a smaller, softer version of Olga, but with the charm of a performer, not the charisma of an adventurer.

Slava wondered if Andrey Vladislavovich had realized that. Probably not. And of course, he had not had Slava's advantage of knowing that they were half-sisters. Slava remembered what Mirik had said of the village women's distaste for a gift from the gods like Lyudmila, and wondered what kind of scorn her own daughter would receive, should she be gifted with Lyudmila's beauty. It was not impossible...Oleg was fine-looking...and so was Slava's sister...her daughter could be a great beauty...but none of that mattered a jot to Lyudmila, who was still gazing fearfully up at Slava.

"I thank you for answering my invitation so promptly, Lyudmila Krasnoslavovna," said Slava, shaking off her thoughts.

"How did you..." said Lyudmila. "I mean, I hope I am not too early. Tsarinovna," she gulped.

"Perhaps you do not know this, but we share many connections," said Slava. "But I know your name because I became acquainted with your brother in my time in the North."

"With Mirik? Then he's well?!" cried Lyudmila. "Tsarinovna," she added, bowing in her seat.

"As well as can be expected," Slava told her. "You know that it is generally assumed amongst your family that you are dead."

"Yes..." Lyudmila's face twisted up. "I was afraid of that...But I was afraid of being followed if they all knew I wasn't...I guess...I mean, perhaps you heard my story, Tsarinovna?"

"Yes," said Slava. "From both sides. Meaning: I heard your brother's version, and I heard Andrey Vladislavovich's version. I have not, of course, heard your version yet, but my greatest concern for the moment is to know that you are well. Well and happy. And to assure you that you have nothing more to fear from Andrey Vladislavovich's side."

"Yes..." said Lyudmila, looking down at her feet in embarrassment. "It was all so...I was sorry I ever went to sing for him, but I never thought he would take such a fancy to me...And it just couldn't be, it couldn't be, my Misha is the only man for me, I knew it as soon as I laid eyes on him, and there was never any question of...But then my mother became so set on it, and he was so insistent, and the next thing I knew, I had to run off to Krasnogorod. Tsarinovna."

"Sometimes these things happen," said Slava sympathetically. "But I am glad it seems to have worked out so well for you. And you are doing well? There is enough work for you?"

"Oh yes, Tsarinovna," said Lyudmila, now starting to smile. "We play almost every night, sometimes at two different places—we are so lucky! We never go hungry. In fact, my Misha likes to joke, the only thing we're short on is rest. That and...We miss our families, Tsarinovna. And we wish we could tell them about our situation, and have their blessing, so that we could be married properly. Of course, in our hearts we're married, but in the eyes of the world I'm just a flighty-headed girl and Misha is just another man I've stolen away from his mother, and that's very uncomfortable for both of us. We get so many strange looks, sometimes, and the innkeepers wink at me and laugh so rudely! Tsarinovna."

"That must be very uncomfortable," Slava agreed. "So you do intend to be married?"

"Oh yes! Tsarinovna."

"I am very glad to hear it," said Slava. "And it is right that you should wish to be reunited with your families. Do you intend to return to the North anytime soon?"

"Oh...well...we'd like to, but things are going so well for us here in Krasnogorod..."

"I understand," Slava told her. "But perhaps you could write to your families? I assure you, there is no danger now in your being discovered. Vasilisa Vasilisovna and Olga Vasilisovna know all, and so you can rest easy on that score."

"Oh...I am glad to hear that. Tsarinovna. Is Olga Vasilisovna...She must be terribly angry with me? Tsarinovna."

"Not at all," Slava assured her.

"Oh, but...But if you say so, of course it must be true, Tsarinovna."

"She may even wish to see you herself," Slava said.

"Oh! No, that would be very awkward...but of course, if she wishes it, I would not oppose her, Tsarinovna, I certainly wouldn't dare."

Lyudmila smiled up at Slava in a manner that was intended to be both beseeching and fetching, and Slava was certain that there were few, especially of the male sex, who could have withstood such a look. She was also certain that such a look had rarely, if ever, crossed either Olga or Oleg's faces. They were much more likely to laugh heartily at anyone who contradicted them, or possibly vanquish them through force.

She supposed that Lyudmila had gotten at least some of her winning ways from her mother, which made her wonder what of her would be preserved in her own daughter. Something good, she hoped. She also couldn't help but remember how Mirik had said that there was something about her that reminded him of Lyudmila, but now that she was looking at her, she saw that there was very little in common between them. Slava was, when it came right down to it, no charmer as Lyudmila was, of that she was certain. It must have been just another of Mirik's fancies.

"Olga Vasilisovna bears you no ill will," Slava told her. "But my most pressing concern of the moment, as I told you, is to ensure that you wanted for nothing, and reassure you that you had nothing to fear on the score of, of anything that had happened in Severnoles-noye. And as I see that you are faring most prosperously in your chosen trade, and as proof of it that you appear quite tired, I will let you return to your rest, Lyudmila Krasnoslavovna. But please," said Slava, rising in order to let Lyudmila know that she could get out of her chair too, "if you need anything, send for me immediately, and you may be assured of my assistance."

"Th-thank you, Tsarinovna," stuttered Lyudmila, bowing deeply again.

"It is very possible that I will call for you again," Slava told her. "To know that you are continuing to do well, and to have the pleasure of hearing you sing, if you would be willing to oblige me."

"Oh! Of course, Tsarinovna, of course! At any time!"

"Thank you again for your prompt answer to my summons," said Slava, and let Manya show Lyudmila out the door.

Now she was finally able to release Masha and Manya from their impatience, and allow them to dress her, as they had been longing to do for at least an hour. As they fussed over her and consulted each other on what would suit her best—they knew better than to consult with Slava on such a subject—Slava thought over whether or not she would see Lyudmila again, and what she would tell her.

She wanted to bring together as many of Oleg's daughters as she could, and make them sisters to each other and most particularly to her own daughter, so that when Darya Krasnoslavovna arrived in the world, should she have the good fortune to be born, she would have a family ready-made, a family more congenial and reliable than the one she would gain from her mother's side.

Slava was afraid that her sister would not make the kind of aunt, and her niece not the kind of second-sister, that she would wish for her daughter to have. And now that she had seen Lyudmila, she began to suspect that she wished to gather as many of Oleg's daughters as possible in order to have yet another piece of him around her. Slava feared that this was another manifestation of her excessive soft-heartedness, but as she could see no immediate harm from indulging in it, she decided to hold off on giving up on her plan for the time being.

Thinking of this, a sudden sharp desire for Oleg to be by her side through all her coming ordeals rose up in her. She wondered if she had let him go too easily, if she should have put her foot down when they parted and insisted that he come back to Krasnograd with her and take his place at her side, as was fitting for the father of her child. The others—Gray Wolf, the leshiye, all of those responsible—would have agreed if she had demanded it, she was certain, and Oleg most likely would have agreed as well.

In fact, he had half seemed as if he had wanted her to do just that. His refusal of her invitation had been nothing more than a moment of faint-heartedness, or something of that nature, and had he had more time to think it over, he surely would have agreed, Slava told herself. She imagined him trapped with her in the Krasnograd kremlin. Perhaps not, she thought.

She imagined him growing ever more miserable and bad-tempered, as Olga had done during their time in Lesnograd. Certainly not, she said to herself. Perhaps Oleg would come, but he would have to come willingly if she was to accept him by her side. Otherwise there was no point, and she would have to learn to do without him, just as she had her entire life. It wasn't even as if she were so desperately in love with him...That was most surely not the case...Slava sighed and told herself to stop thinking about it. The worst thing she could do would be to fancy herself in love with some vision of him until she truly was, and then suffer dreadful disappointment when he failed to come, or did come and failed to be what she had fancied him to be... He had seemed so scared and miserable on their parting...

"Stop!" said Slava out loud.

"What, Tsarinovna?" cried Manya, jumping in shock at Slava's sudden outburst.

"I was thinking of things that are no use thinking of," said Slava. "I had to tell myself to stop."

"Oh." Manya paused for a moment, and then, in an outpouring of candor, said, half-shyly, half-eagerly, "I do that too sometimes, Tsarinovna. Think about things I shouldn't, I mean, like Valya from the night shift...Well, it doesn't matter." She broke out in what Slava knew had to be a very painful blush.

"I understand," said Slava. "That's why I had to tell myself to stop."

"Oh, Tsarinovna...I mean, oh, I'm sorry."

"Nothing to be sorry for," said Slava. "It's not worth worrying about. There's nothing I can do about it anyway." She found this thought so cheering that she really was able to stop dwelling on her imagined problems, and prepare herself to face whatever real problems were coming her way.

Slava expected to be summoned to her sister's side again, probably for more painful attempts on her sister's part to humiliate and put her down, but by the time Masha and Manya had finally decided that she was fit to go out in public, there was still no message for her, so she went to visit Vladislava instead.

Unsurprisingly, she found Vladislava wild with impatience to go explore the kremlin and see the rest of Krasnograd, and so, in the absence of any more official duties, Slava spent most of the day giving Vladislava a private tour of the kremlin. She concluded with a promise to take Vladislava around Krasnograd tomorrow, and then to arrange for her to start her lessons the next day. Slava was not sure what Vladislava was imagining her lessons to be like, but for the moment she was extremely keen to start them. Slava only hoped she wouldn't be too terribly disappointed when they actually began, and resolved once again to make sure that Vladislava had the very best teachers in Krasnograd, as anything less would certainly draw from her nothing but bored contempt and probably outright rebellion.

As Slava had still not received a summons from her sister by the evening, she and Vladislava had supper with Olga, Dunya, and the men, and then Slava, feeling unaccountably tired after her uneventful day, retired early to bed.

Chapter Fifteen

The next day, though, Slava's sister made up for her earlier neglect by sending Slava a message before breakfast, demanding that Slava come see her this instant. Accordingly, and filled with a mixture of curiosity and dread, Slava, still in her dressing gown and escorted only by the two guards stationed outside her apartment for the night, went to her sister's chambers.

"What is this!" Slava's sister demanded as soon as Slava entered her room. She was standing by the fire, but even that could not explain the hectic flush of her cheeks, and Slava could see that she was furiously angry, and probably a bit drunk besides.

"What?" Slava asked her.

"This...This report I hear that you called the singer in for a private audience yesterday morning!"

Of all the things Slava had expected to be challenged on, this was not one of them.

"She is a fine singer, and from Severnolesnoye," Slava said mildly. "I merely wished to express my admiration, give her news of her kin, and make sure that she wanted for nothing."

"You...! You're plotting with the Severnolesniye!"

Slava was so surprised by the leap her sister had taken that for a moment all she could do was laugh, which made her sister even angrier.

"I assure you," Slava said, as soon as she had regained control of herself, "I am not plotting with the Severnolesniye. And if...well, Lyudmila Krasnoslavovna has no connection with that family." As she said it, Slava realized that it was not quite true, but it was, she was sure, true in the sense she meant it, so she plowed on. "She's just a poor peasant girl, come to Krasnograd to make her fortune with her song. I happened to become acquainted with her brother during my journey—he joined our party briefly—and I decided I would look her up, once I was back in Krasnograd."

"Lyudmila Krasnoslavovna!" cried Slava's sister, as if her name had some particular significance.

"Yes," Slava confirmed, puzzled. "That is her name."

"And yet you claim to have no connection with her!"

"Her mother and I are namesakes, it is true, but how many Krasnoslavas are there in Zem'? Almost as many as there are Vladislavas or Miroslavas...Why, Dunya's sister asked to be allowed to name her daughter Krasnoslava while I was in Naberezhnoye..."

"Dunya's sister! So her family is part of this too! All the North is rising against me!"

"No, not at all," Slava told her, still puzzled, and starting to grow alarmed as well. "Surely naming a child after the Tsarinovna could not be construed as an act of rebellion against the Tsarina." Slava thought about adding that most people in the North did not think much about the Tsarina from one month to the next, except on tax days, but decided against it, fearing that in her present state of mind, her sister would construe that as a threat, too. Slava took a step closer to her, and caught the smell of both old and new vodka rising from her skin. Her clothing, while as rich as ever, appeared wrinkled, as if she had spent the night in it.

"Are you sure you are well?" she asked, filling her voice and her eyes with concern. "You do not look very well at all. Perhaps you have caught a chill—your duties must be a great burden on you, and it would be no wonder if you were to fall ill."

"I knew it!" Slava's sister's voice was almost a shriek. "You *are* trying to take the Wooden Throne from me! You'd like nothing better than to claim I'd fallen ill, and take power for yourself—just like your friend Vasilisa Vasilisovna did with her mother, I have no doubt! Well, it won't work on me!"

"Vladya!" cried Slava in horror. "What has come over you! What are you saying! You must be unwell, it is the only explanation!" She reached out and, pushing aside her sister's feeble attempts to fend her off, felt her forehead. It was burning up, from fever or drink Slava couldn't tell.

"You *are* ill," she told her. "Come, you *must* lie down, you simply must, Vladya, before you do yourself even greater harm. Where is your night-maid?"

"I dismissed her," said Vladya, looking down at Slava with a confused expression. "I was afraid...I thought she was in league with Masha and Manya..."

"And Anna Avdotyevna?"

"I don't know...Slava! I can't remember! I can't remember what I did or said!"

"Shhhh...Come, come lie down on the bed...Anna! Anna Avdotyevna! Anna Avdotyevna! Come here this instant!"

As Slava had guessed, Anna Avdotyevna was in the next room, along with Vladya's night-maid, and they both came running in as soon as she called for them, and in very short order her sister was in clean nightclothes, in her bed, and Krasnograd's best healers and herbwomen had been sent for.

At least half-a-dozen healers and herbwomen came to Slava's sister's bedside that morning, and, after bowing and expressing their gratitude for the immense honor that had been vouchsafed them, they all felt her pulse and looked into her eyes and nodded gravely, before telling her it was but a passing indisposition and, if she drank the infusions they recommended, she would be sure to recover in a day or two. Slava's sister accepted this with incurious relief, but Slava, after she had heard the same thing from five different people, followed the sixth one out into the front room and demanded to know the truth from her.

"The truth, Tsarinovna?" repeated the healer. "The truth is that the Tsarina will almost certainly recover within a day or two."

"But why did she fall ill in the first place?" Slava pressed. "What ails her?"

"The strain of a Tsarina's duties must be great, Tsarinovna," said the healer evasively.

"And so?"

"And so...Sometimes one may treat one symptom, only to cause more."

"You mean she's been drinking," guessed Slava.

"Well, Tsarinovna..."

"Don't lie to me, for I've witnessed it myself, and I've only been back in Krasnograd two days," said Slava. "How grave a danger does it pose her?"

"Well, Tsarinovna..."

"The only thing you have to fear is a dishonest answer," Slava said.

"I will forgive you any truth, no matter how bitter, but don't lie to me about my own sister's health!"

"Well, Tsarinovna, in that case...Luckily your sister has already produced an heir, and seems unlikely to produce more...Until this morning, I would have said that the Tsarina was in no great danger, but this sudden attack...You should watch her, Tsarinovna, watch her and see if she has more attacks, or if her condition worsens...It is so hard to tell what will happen, when a person takes to drink. One woman will drink a bottle of vodka a day for years without any ill effects, and another will drink herself into an early grave within half a year, and one simply can't tell which it will be."

"I see," said Slava. She thanked the woman for her honesty, and sent her on her way, before returning to her sister's bedside, where she spent a long and anxious day. Luckily there was no important business to attend to, and so Slava was free to sit by her sister's bed and think dark and serious thoughts from breakfast until suppertime. After the parade of healers had finished, her sister, to Slava's relief, fell asleep, and Slava, having sent away Anna Avdotyevna to deal with all the questions that her sister's absence would no doubt provoke, was left entirely on her own for many hours.

The most important conclusion she came to, after a morning of sitting with one eye cocked towards her sister's movements, and another towards her own idle ruminations, was that it seemed entirely possible that this was the work of Princess Severnolesnaya's curse. If so, it was most cleverly disguised as simply an extension of her sister's folly, but Slava remembered what Anastasiya, Sonya's second-sister, had said about how curses only had the power that their victims gave them, and that they always ran downhill, like water.

The curse had been for Slava's sister to be betrayed by those nearest to her, and that was what her fearful fantasies seemed to be telling her—thereby making it all the more possible that they would become reality. Although Slava was certain—well, fairly certain—that she would not betray or attempt to usurp her own sister—well, not unless, Slava admitted to herself uncomfortably, she continued behaving in this hysterical and irrational fashion—Slava knew that people who were treated as untrustworthy tended to become untrustworthy, even if they had not been so before.

And if—Slava had to confess to herself—her sister's mind was somehow affected, and she became unfit to rule, Slava would have no choice but to replace her, no matter how bitter her objections—

both their objections—would be to such a step. Prasha was still far too young to take her place on the Wooden Throne. Slava even wondered if Prasha would *ever* be ready to take her place on the Wooden Throne, for woe betide Zem' if she should not show more promise as a ruler than she had hitherto...It occurred to Slava that she could find herself Zem''s most qualified ruler in a very short time...Or that the rule could someday pass down to her daughter, and she could be the Tsarina's mother...She wasn't sure that she liked that picture very much, but she liked the picture of Prasha's selfish petulance on the throne even less...

"Is it daytime?" Slava's sister asked groggily from the bed.

"Midday," Slava told her gently. "You've slept all morning, the gods grant that it did you a great deal of good. Do you want anything to eat?"

"Tfoo," Slava's sister made a face at the thought. "Just...is there something to drink?"

"The healers recommended watered wine with healing herbs," Slava told her, holding up a jug of it. "Would you care for some? Shall I help you sit up?"

"Oh...I suppose...I suppose I can't drink it lying down...If you give it to me...No one else but you...And you won't leave me, will you?"

"Of course not," Slava told her. She helped her up to a sitting position and gave her a cup of watered wine, which she drank down thirstily. Slava offered her more, but she refused, saying weakly that she still felt too unwell to trust her stomach to anything more. She tried to say something else, but fell back asleep before she could finish her thoughts. Slava continued to sit at her bedside, struggling against the desire to fall asleep herself. At one point she did in fact start to nod off, but was startled back to wakefulness by the sensation that a shadow was watching her from the corner of the room. When she went to investigate it, though, nothing was there.

Vladya awoke again in the late afternoon, jerking up in her bed with a start.

"Slava!" she cried. "Are you still there?"

"Right here," Slava assured her.

"You didn't leave me, did you? You won't leave me, will you?"

"Of course not," Slava promised.

"Oh Slava! And I used to laugh at your dreams! Slava, Slavochka, I had the most terrible dream! A dark cloud full of rain was hanging over Krasnograd, and I said, 'Good, here come the spring rains,' and then it opened up and let loose so much water, and I was washed away,

Slava, I was washed away!"

"It was only a dream," Slava told her soothingly.

"No, Slava, it was terrible, terrible! I always used to laugh at your dream-fears, but now I see! It was much more than a dream, much worse! Slava, I don't see how I will ever be free of the fear again!"

"You will," said Slava. "Not entirely, of course, but in a few hours it will start to fade away, and in a week it will be no more than a distant memory, like the pain of your sprained ankle from when you were ten."

"Oh Slava! You promise!"

"I promise," Slava told her solemnly. "It has been so for me, many, many times."

"Really?" asked Vladya, looking up at Slava with a face full of uncertain hope.

"Really," promised Slava. "How many times when we were children did I come to you with a bad dream, crying and shaking? And yet here I am."

For a moment Vladya's face filled with horror at the thought of Slava's childish suffering, and then even more horror at the thought that Slava could ever have possibly felt the same things that she had, when she was so sure that they were so different—already the old Vladya was coming back—and then all the horror drained away at the realization that, of course, Slava was lying, and she exclaimed, "A child could never have had such a terrible dream! I was so afraid! I still am!"

"Who knows fear better than children?" said Slava. "And yet I got over it every time. It is very hard to die of fear, whatever we might like to think to the contrary."

"What should I do, Slava?" For a moment Vladya looked as lost as when she had first awakened. "Should I go back to sleep? I'm so afraid of sleep now!"

"Try to get up, if you can," Slava advised her. "If you go right back to sleep after a bad dream, often as not it will just come to reclaim you."

"But I'm so tired! And yet I don't think I could dare to close my eyes, even so!" Vladya's face was now filled with the dreadful awareness of her own suffering, something she had hitherto had very few occasions to contemplate. The knowledge was so unusual and so crushing that for an instant Slava wished she could be spared it, even though she knew that there was nothing her sister needed more than the awareness of her own and others' suffering.

"Perhaps if you get up you will wake up a bit," Slava told her. "And it will help you forget the dream."

Vladya, after a bit more wavering and doubting, saw the sense in that, and allowed Slava to help her out of bed and into the front room, where she cheered up so much that she took a bit more watered wine and even some white bread. This brought about an even greater improvement in her spirits, so that she decided to get dressed and walk about the kremlin. This was even more beneficial, and by evening she was almost her old self again. Slava could tell it was so because she, Slava, was dismissed in favor of the servants and flatterers whose company her sister normally preferred to her own.

As Slava watched her sister's face regain its usual expression of confident and unquestioning self-satisfaction under the influence of these more congenial companions, she realized with painful clarity that her sister preferred them to Slava, her own flesh and blood, precisely because they were servants and flatterers, and therefore would pose Vladya no threatening questions, nor fill her head with frightening doubts. Slava feared that the dream, which three hours ago her sister had claimed would haunt her forever, was long forgotten. By Vladya, anyway. Slava, although she had done her best to soothe her at the time, feared that the dream was just as significant as Vladya had initially felt it to be, and she retired to her own chambers full of all the terrors for the future that by rights should have been Vladya's, but had somehow ended up as her own lot instead.

The next day Slava's sister was able to make her triumphant return to the Hall of Council and the Wooden Throne, and reassure all her anxious subjects of her complete return to health. To celebrate it she declared another feast, which set her recovery back considerably, although this time she suffered nothing worse than a day of misery and ill humor.

Over the next few days she continued to leave Slava to her own devices, which suited Slava just fine. Slava, for her part, busied herself with finding tutors for Vladislava and showing Dunya the sights of

Krasnograd, or at least the sights of Krasnograd that were best shown by the Tsarinovna and not Olga's men.

Slava suspected that they were also showing Dunya the sights of Krasnograd, but that they were the kind of sights that she, Slava, was supposed to pretend ignorance of. Taverns, she guessed from Dunya's occasional remarks, made up the bulk of the Krasnograd known to Olga's men. She also guessed from Dunya's brief comments that she, Dunya, did not care overmuch for spending so much time indoors, especially in such doors, but that in her own quiet way she also found all this merrymaking to be quite amusing, and so allowed them to drag her along and be their chaperone whenever they needed the appearance of a woman's steady hand guiding and watching over them—some innkeepers refused unsupervised parties of men admittance to their establishments, out of a well-founded fear of destructive and licentious behavior.

In fact, it seemed that Dunya had become a great favorite of several of the innkeepers, who had taken to treating her like a daughter, and Dunya, in turn, had taken to imitating, quite unconsciously, their turns of speech, which caused Slava much internal merriment. It was quite odd, and even more amusing, to see someone as self-possessed as Dunya be taken over in this way, which was how Slava thought of this encroachment of the slurred speech of the common folk of Krasnograd onto Dunya's clipped Northern voice. She wondered what people would think of it when Dunya returned to Naberezhnoye, but promised herself she would never mention it, much less laugh about it, in Dunya's presence.

Dunya had also, Slava gathered, seen Lyudmila Krasnoslavovna and her Misha perform at several of the taverns, always with great success. Slava was glad to hear it, and half-wished that she could join Dunya and the others one evening and see Lyudmila herself, but decided it would be better not to, as it would certainly raise a number of questions in a number of heads, including in the head of Slava's sister. Slava did not want to provoke another such outburst as she had already witnessed on that score if it could possibly be avoided, and so she contented herself with listening to Dunya's descriptions of the songs Lyudmila sang, the applause she received for them, and the fullness of her hat after it had been passed around.

Unfortunately, Slava could not spend all her time only in the company of Dunya and Vladislava. Although, just as Olga had predicted, much of the original joy at Slava's return had died down within two days of her arrival at the kremlin, all the princesses currently in Kras-nograd still seemed to want to see her, and it was a rare day that she did not receive a request for the honor of her company for dinner, tea, or supper. Disinclined as she was to spend so much time amongst wom-en whose society she had for the most part previously always found excruciatingly painful, and whom she now suspected of inviting her out of boredom and a vague desire to alleviate it by the always-pop-ular sport of mocking the Tsarinovna, she could not bring herself to refuse them.

She went to the first meeting full of dread, and was pleasantly surprised to discover that Princess Glubokostepnaya, whom she had always found irritating to the point of tears, was now no more than a minor annoyance, and even on occasion a source of amusement, as when she began to argue vehemently with Slava over the location of various villages along the Severnovostochnaya road, which she had never visited and which Slava had passed through just this winter.

Although part of Slava could not help but see that this was, exact-ly as she had suspected, nothing more than a desire to pass the time pleasantly by making Slava look foolish, part of her could not sum-mon up the energy to become angry at such stupidity. Sitting there listening to Princess Glubokostepnaya's fatuous, erroneous, insulting, and deeply, deeply illogical arguments, Slava realized (as she grinned to herself over her own overwrought reaction) that, while she might be trapped amongst such women, she did not have to take them seri-ously. At least not when they were making absurd statements over tea. They were still a scourge to the Princess Council and no doubt spread misery and suffering amongst their families, servants, and peasants, but right now, over tea, Princess Glubokostepnaya and her ilk were do-ing nothing worse than wasting Slava's time and making themselves look foolish.

And then when Darya Marinovna spent the entire tea-time exhib-iting her own beauty and denigrating Slava's (although in the most subtle, delicate fashion, of course), Slava first found comfort in the thought that Darya Marinovna might have good looks but that she, Slava, had been the one chosen to bear the gods' blessed child, and then, as the visit finally drew to a close, she realized that Darya Mari-novna was not so beautiful after all, but that she simply wore very fine gowns, did her hair in a very elaborate manner, painted her face, and walked with the air of someone who was very pleased with herself, which for most people was, of course, just the same as beauty.

Slava was at first a bit hurt at this discovery, hurt, that is, at the discovery of how foolish and blind people could be, but as she was used to discoveries of that sort, she quickly got over the hurt and ended the visit in high good humor, even as she chastised herself for being so pleased for noticing that Darya Marinovna's face was too long and thin and her eyes too small and closely-set. Slava knew it was very wrong of her to rejoice at this, but she quieted her conscience by telling herself it was private enjoyment only, and went away with a smile on her face and a spring to her step that she had not exhibited since, she was sure, the age of fifteen.

All the other visits were of a piece with those two. The meanness, narrowness, and folly of so many of the greatest women of Zem', while it could not fail to raise Slava's ire on a deeper level, was no longer capable of reducing her to misery and tears on the surface. If she found it too hard to take, she simply made her excuses and left as quickly as was acceptable, but more often than not she was able to sit there and make polite comments while silently laughing to herself.

She thought back to how she had once thought of these people as wolves clothing themselves in the remnants of rotting lambskins, and saw that, while it was still true, in her eyes now the lambskins had fallen away completely, leaving behind nothing but what turned out to be fawning dogs. Annoying, yes, and sometimes even dangerous, but most of the time they were not nearly so menacing as they had seemed at first glance. Not only that, but they often responded well to a sharp word from their mistress, or someone who was willing to assume that office, because what they wanted more than anything was for someone to take up the burden of being human for them.

And, what was even more gratifying, in some cases she was able to look past the surface irritants and see that some of the princesses, at least, possessed merits that could not be denied; that those who were foolish could also be gentle and good-hearted, and those who were bossy could be acting out of genuine concern and affection for others, and those who were sharp and unpleasant could be motivated by quickness of thought and firmness of principle.

This did not, of course, negate the evils of their outward behavior, but Slava found that she could with remarkable ease look past these trifling annoyances and appreciate the greater merits that stood behind them. She was glad that she did not have to live with any of them, but she found that she could spend an afternoon or evening in their company with tolerable comfort and even enjoyment.

Other than providing entertainment for bored princesses, and overseeing Vladislava's education, which was proceeding in fits and starts—all her tutors agreed that she was the brightest and most difficult princess they had ever had the privilege of teaching, and every day brought new stories of her rapid progress and her intolerable manners, which made even the most stalwart of nannies and mistresses cringe away from her in mingled fear and rage—Slava also spent some of her time looking for the kremlin's house-spirit, of which she had been promised a glimpse.

She couldn't help but suspect that the watchful shadow that had awoken her at her sister's bedside had been it, observing her and gathering its courage to make itself known, but for some reason it had changed its mind, and had remained in hiding ever since. Slava tried to find excuses to wander alone through different parts of the kremlin every day, but ridding herself of her maids and guards proved, as usual, next to impossible, and it was a rare day that she was actually able to accomplish her task. That must be, she told herself, why the house-spirit still refused to reveal itself to her. Although she would have liked to have found it and spoken with it, not finding it meant that she was not disturbed by whatever words it might have for her, and wandering about the kremlin was diversion enough without it, and so all in all Slava was not sorry not to have found it yet.

Sometimes, when it was not too slushy out, Slava went riding. She was delighted during one visit to the stable to discover that Skvorets and Ogonyok had returned from Naberezhnoye, after working their slow way down from there as waystation mounts. They were both much thinner than they had been when Slava had last seen them, which was distressing, but other than that they did not seem to be much worse for the wear, and when Slava took them out, they trotted forward readily enough and seemed glad to explore the sights, scents, and sounds of the woods behind the kremlin. As no one objected, Slava declared them to be her horses, along with Rozochka, and even on days when it was too wet to go outside, she would sometimes slip out of the palace and visit them.

When she was riding, or searching, or waiting for princesses who took delight in making the Tsarinovna wait, she sometimes found herself talking to Oleg, as if he were there and he, too, would find all this interesting and diverting. Slava knew that this was a silly thing to do, that he probably wouldn't find this interesting and diverting, and would probably be offended if he knew what use she was making of him, and that thinking about him as if he were a friend would probably make him even more disappointing if he ever did come to Krasnograd, and that if she wanted an imaginary friend, she should imagine one, instead of using a real person for her own ends, but their imaginary conversations were so pleasant in reality that she couldn't seem to stop herself.

And so, despite having learned on many occasions that imaginary friends were not nearly so satisfactory whenever they manifested themselves as flesh-and-blood people, she allowed herself this indulgence. With so much of Zem' between them, making it so easy for him to forget her, it seemed very unlikely that she would ever see Oleg again anyway (she would tell herself), and, she couldn't help but sense, there were unpleasant trials awaiting her, so she should gather her strength from whatever sources she could. Sometimes—well, more often than sometimes—she found herself regretting not having put her foot down and insisting that he come back to Krasnograd with her. The memory of his fearful face and hunched shoulders when she had suggested it had a hard time holding its own against her much more flattering fantasies.

Whenever the regret would grow too strong, she would remind herself of that warning twinge that had told her to let him go, and return to her daydreams. At least imaginary Oleg was a rewarding person to talk to, and often gave excellent advice—much better, no doubt, than that of the real Oleg. The real Oleg probably would have suggested facing any problem with shouting, fisticuffs, and running away, and not necessarily in that order. Slava tried not to smile too much whenever that thought occurred to her.

The only thing disturbing these pleasant fantasies were the moments when Boleslav Vlasiyevich suddenly came across her path and did something thoughtful for her, reminding her, albeit unintentionally, that while the father of her child, if she should have the good fortune to be born, had run off, this man seemed determined to stick doggedly by her side. If only, she found herself thinking from time to time, the better qualities of both of them (what those better qualities were, exactly, escaped her, but never mind) could be combined into one person, along with a little bit of wisdom and some morals. Now *that* would be a man worth having...but even Slava recognized this fantasy as wild overindulgence, and did her best to rein it in, at least when her conscience pricked her particularly hard.

Several weeks passed in this pleasant manner, bringing with them not only Slava's peace of mind, but also confirmation that the gods had not lied to Slava, and that she was, more than likely, with child. When water ran continuously from the roofs, and the streets became a muddy morass, she became certain enough in her own mind—because she felt so terrible that she decided she must be either with child or dying—to summon a healer to examine her. She called the same woman who had spoken to her so honestly of her sister's condition, trusting her more than she did any other healer in the kremlin.

"It is still early to be proclaiming it at every street corner, but, Tsarinovna, you are most definitely with child," the healer told her, after looking her over and asking her many questions. "May I offer my congratulations?"

"You may," said Slava, who was blushing much more than she would have expected. "Such happy news! I am so glad to have it confirmed!" And she was, even more than she thought she would be. The healer, recognizing her mood, congratulated her heartily and offered many pieces of advice and encouraging stories. She was the first person to be unequivocally glad for Slava and her condition, which was so gratifying that by the time she left, Slava was a little bit afraid she might cry with joy. She had to walk about her rooms for a while, grinning like a fool, before she could trust herself to go out in public.

She had sobered up some by the time she went to join Olga and Dunya and the others, with whom she was dining that evening, but even so, Olga said, "Good news?" as soon as she caught sight of her.

"Yes," said Slava, blushing and, despite her best efforts not to, grinning like a fool all over again.

"It is certain, then?" asked Olga, giving her a sharp look. "Have you had a healer look you over?"

"This afternoon," Slava told her. "It's still early, but for now it's certain."

"What..." began Dunya, and then trailed off, also giving her a sharp look.

"It's still too early to speak of," said Olga firmly.

"Really?" said Dunya, *almost* raising her voice in her excitement.

Slava nodded, blushing even harder.

"Well then I won't...My best wishes! My best wishes! But not a word more."

"Thank you," said Slava, trying to compose her face before they joined the men for supper. She succeeded in that, at least at first, but then when the food was brought in she was unable to eat hardly any of it, provoking tremendous concern amongst all the men, and when she tried to assure them that it was nothing to worry about, she did so with such a self-conscious air that they—well, Dima and Grisha; the others were entirely mystified—instantly guessed what was wrong with her, and gave her such looks of mingled concern and approbation that she sank into a state of wordless confusion and was unable to extricate herself from it all evening.

Slava woke up the next morning still with a smile, which only slipped slightly when she found herself unable to swallow even a bite of breakfast. It seemed that the curse of future mothers would not be passing her by. She assumed that she would grow tired of this sickness very soon, but today it was such an encouraging sign that she was even pleased by it.

Masha and Manya, on the other hand, were overcome with horror at her refusal to eat. After begging, pleading, and representing to her in the strongest terms they dared use the dangers of not fattening herself up again after the rigors of her journey, they backed out of the room with downcast faces, carrying the untouched tray as if it were a viper.

Slava had hoped that they would leave her in peace, but instead, as it turned out, they went straight to Anna Avdotyevna. While Slava was moved by such evidence of their devotion—only the most desperate need would have caused them to brave the presence of Anna Avdotyevna—she rather wished they had not done it, for Anna Avdotyevna came marching in directly and demanded to know what was ailing the Tsarinovna.

"I'm just not hungry," Slava said evasively. "I had a large supper last night with Olga Vasilisovna and her party...And there was a lot of drinking..." Which was true, just not in Slava's case, as the mere sight of beer and vodka had been enough to make her stomach turn.

"You don't look hungover, Tsarinovna," said Anna Avdotyevna, peering sharply into her eyes. "You look the picture of health, only too thin. Have a pie."

"No, thank you," Slava told her, smiling politely. "I'm really not hungry."

"In that case, Tsarinovna, how about some porridge," said Anna Avdotyevna. The tone of her voice made it clear it was not a suggestion. "With plenty of butter."

"By all the gods, no!" cried Slava, hastily putting her hand to her mouth to prevent herself from heaving the meager contents of her stomach all over Anna Avdotyevna's fine gown.

"You *are* ill, Tsarinovna," said Anna Avdotyevna, giving her a very stern look. "Why will you not admit it?"

"I told you...just the effects of last night..."

"You had a healer come to you yesterday afternoon, did you not, Tsarinovna?"

"A mere trifle...And I wanted to ask her about the Tsarina's health," said Slava, regretting that she had not thought of that excuse earlier.

"If you wanted to inquire about the Tsarina's health, you could ask her yourself, Tsarinovna," said Anna Avdotyevna, giving her another witheringly stern look.

"No I couldn't," said Slava, forgetting herself and her indisposition for a moment, and giving Anna Avdotyevna an equally withering look in reply. She immediately wished she could take it back, but Anna Avdotyevna merely said, with the faintest hint of a smile, "And perhaps you are right, Tsarinovna. But I still don't believe that is why you called the healer to you."

Her voice changed, taking on a reassuring, confiding tone that Slava had never heard before. "You are suffering from something, Tsarinovna, I can see that plainly enough. If it is something you fear to broadcast about the kremlin, I understand that perfectly well. But you have no need to hide it from me. I promise you, Tsarinovna, that I will keep your confidence, and aid you in whatever way I can. You were right not to let Masha and Manya in on your secrets. They are good-hearted girls, but they are not fit to be the confidantes of a Tsarinovna. I know you have no one else to turn to here in Krasnograd, except possibly Olga Vasilisovna, and she would most likely be of little use to you. Accept me as your advisor, Tsarinovna, and let me in on your secrets. I assure you, you will not regret it."

Slava vacillated for a moment in indecision, but she could see no dishonesty in Anna Avdotyevna's face, and in all the years she had known her, she had never witnessed a single instance of Anna Avdotyevna being untrustworthy or underhanded. Anna Avdotyevna was many things, most of them unpleasant, but deceitful was not one of them.

"I have..." Slava began, and had to stop in order to gain control of her blushes. "I have hopes...hopeful expectations..."

"Tsarinovna!" cried Anna Avdotyevna. "Truly?! And what did the healer say?"

"She confirmed my expectations..."

"Tsarinovna!!" cried Anna Avdotyevna again. "Is this true!?"

"It is early yet, but so far…"

"Tsarinovna!!!" repeated Anna Avdotyevna for a third time. "This is wonderful! The most wonderful news. Oh, Tsarinovna! Does your mother know yet…Oh, but of course not, she would not have had time to receive your letter…But your sister…! Oh, Tsarinovna, the most wonderful, wonderful news…" And she had to stop in order to compose herself. Her face was flushed with tears of joy, a sight Slava had never seen before, nor ever expected to see. "Let me…will you deign to permit me to embrace you…Oh, Tsarinovna!!!!" She threw her arms around Slava and hugged her tightly, before saying, "Oh, but I mustn't crush you too much…But let me kiss you…" She kissed Slava on each cheek.

"Oh, but Tsarinovna, you're crying," she said, letting her go.

"I'm so happy," said Slava. "I'm so happy that you're happy for me."

"Oh, but of course I'm happy for you, of course! Another Zerkalitsa! And high time, too! After we had long given up all of hope of you ever settling down and…But you have! Oh, Tsarinovna!" And she hugged Slava again.

"Your mother!" she suddenly cried, letting Slava go. "Have you written to her yet?"

"Not yet…" said Slava weakly.

"Oh! Tsarinovna! This instant! Sit down this instant and write!"

"It is still so early…" Slava objected feebly. "I wouldn't want to raise any hopes and then disappoint them…"

"How early, Tsarinovna?" Anna Avdotyevna asked, giving her a sharp look that was much more in character with her usual self. "How many months has it been?"

"Two, more or less," Slava told her.

"And you're sure, Tsarinovna? You're sure it was…That is, it is possible to be unsure in these matters…Exactly when it happened…One may confuse one event for another…"

"Not in my case," said Slava firmly. She grinned and blushed at the same time. "In my case I may be extremely certain about the timing of the event."

"Oh, well, that is good, very good, I am glad you are not so light-minded as some women in your situation, although I would have expected nothing less from you…And, if you will permit the question, Tsarinovna…" She trailed off delicately.

"The father?" Slava asked.

"Pardon my only too natural curiosity, Tsarinovna. And I will not be the last to ask you, you may be certain of that! You had best have your story ready. Although I see by your smile that it must be a happy one." She gave Slava another most un-Anna-Avdotyevna-like affectionate smile herself.

"Well, the story is a long one..." began Slava, and fell silent. Now that she came to tell it to someone who was, for all the trust she placed in Anna Avdotyevna, neither friend nor close family, she didn't know what to say. The business with Oleg was awkward enough to explain, and the reason for their liaison was even more so. Slava realized that she must decide right now whether or not she wanted to share the task the gods had given her with the world, or not.

"We came together on the journey," she said. "The hardship and danger, you know, and, well...And it is high time I had a child, as you yourself have said...But he could not return with me to Krasnograd. Or rather, well, he is not of noble birth, you see, and, well...But I am sure he will provide good blood for the child, despite his humble origins."

"I'm sure, Tsarinovna," said Anna Avdotyevna. "After all, many noblewomen take commoners as lovers, to strengthen the stock. Even Empresses. Even Miroslava Praskovyevna, when you come right down to it. You would only be following in her footsteps—although admittedly she married her peasant lad."

"Yes, well..."

"But that is no reflection on you, Tsarinovna, far from it," Anna Avdotyevna added hastily. "This is even better, for you are still free to marry if need be, without first having to go to the trouble of setting a husband aside. I know your sister has spoken of strengthening your claims to the Stepnaya lands." Seeing by Slava's expression that the idea was not to her taste, she went on, inflecting her voice with as much persuasion as possible, "I know it may not appeal at first, but think of the advantages, Tsarinovna! Your own lands and home, to visit whenever you wished to escape from Krasnograd—and something to bequeath to your daughter, should the gods grant you with one! *That* is nothing to turn down lightly."

Slava had to agree that Anna Avdotyevna had painted a very attractive picture. A place to raise her daughter that was all her own, far away from Krasnograd! Even if it meant marrying a Stepnoy, it might be a prize worth gaining. And Princess Stepnaya's son had seemed handsome enough when she had met him, and not ill-spoken...he might make a passable husband...almost certainly better than Oleg, it had to be said...and perhaps it *would* be good to have a proper husband, in order to put an end to her sister's ceaseless scheming in that quarter, and to give her daughter a proper father...Disquiet rose in her as she contemplated this picture, and she knew, unfortunately, that it was not to be.

"And if Princess Stepnaya's son's first wife should produce a daughter?" said Slava instead. "Then I would be in a fine mess."

"Oh, but ten to one it will be a son, or die before it draws its first breath, Tsarinovna," said Anna Avdotyevna encouragingly.

"That is a happy thought," said Slava.

"It is the kind of thought you must learn to have, Tsarinovna, if you are to be a good mother to your child. You must learn to be ready to sacrifice a thousand other mothers' children for the sake of your own. And even if, by some mischance, Princess Stepnaya's son's wife should produce a healthy daughter, it can always be disinherited easily enough. Inheritance through the male line is such an unchancy, uncertain sort of thing—I'm sure the Tsarina will find a way out of it."

"Thus creating a lifelong enemy for my own daughter," said Slava.

"Oh, not if we pack her off with her mother to the Tribes where they belong," said Anna Avdotyevna.

"I still would prefer not to entangle my daughter in such a messy business," said Slava. "She will have friends enough, without the Stepnaya lands. Not only will she be *my* daughter, but...When I said she would not be of noble birth on her father's side, I did not entirely speak the truth. Or rather...She will be close kin to Olga Vasilisovna, you see. Surely *that* will be worth something."

"I see, Tsarinovna!" said Anna Avdotyevna, giving her a long look. "Will she have any claim to the Severnolesnaya lands, then?"

"No," said Slava. The look Anna Avdotyevna had given her made her see, with horrible clarity, that she should have not under any circumstances revealed her future daughter's, should she have the good fortune to be born, kinship with Olga. She was already trying to come up with some tale to explain the relationship, but no matter what it was, she could see that in the eyes of the Krasnograd kremlin, close kin to Olga Vasilisovna Severnolesnaya meant a strong claim to Lesnograd.

"They will be related through the male line," said Slava quickly. "You know that Olga Vasilisovna's father was not of noble birth—and neither"—she suddenly remembered the story about Oleg they had used at the waystation, and snatched at it gratefully—"is his fourth-brother. She will have no claim on the Severnolesnaya lands at all."

"Olga Vasilisovna's fourth-sister once removed through the male line will still have a claim to the Severnolesnaya lands if your sister thinks she does, Tsarinovna," said Anna Avdotyevna. This time the look she gave Slava was half sympathy, half warning. "Not that I blame you—I never saw Oleg Svetoslavovich in the flesh myself, but stories of his handsomeness stretched all the way to Krasnograd, when Princess Severnolesnaya married him, and I have no doubt his fourth-brother was just as fine to look upon—but you could have done better to choose either a great prince whom you could marry, or a real peasant whom you could discard without question. A connection with Olga Vasilisovna through the male line is a complication."

"Yes," said Slava, first cursing herself for not thinking of that sooner, and thinking to hide it, and then realizing that there was a strong possibility the child would be the spitting image of Olga, so that the truth would have to come out sooner or later anyway. She told herself that at least this way she would have plenty of time to get her story straight and explain away as many inconsistencies in it as possible.

"But enough speculation on the future, Tsarinovna," said Anna Avdotyevna briskly. "You must write to your mother! No, first you must speak with your sister, and then you must write to your mother. News of this magnitude cannot be hidden for long. I wouldn't be surprised if your mother ventures out of her sanctuary all the way back to Krasnograd, once she hears of it."

"Do you think so?" asked Slava.

"It wouldn't surprise me," Anna Avdotyevna repeated. "Which is why you must write to her directly, Tsarinovna. But first your sister. Let us go to her at once—I know she is not occupied at the moment."

Slava followed Anna Avdotyevna obediently out into the hall, wondering how her sister would take the news, but too wrapped up in her hope of seeing her mother again—and at such an important moment!—to care overmuch about the reception awaiting her.

Slava thought that a man might have whisked out of sight upon her entrance into her sister's chambers, muttering something in—had that been a Western accent?—but she decided not to ask about it or even speculate too much on it privately, tempting as it was. Vladya was lounging on the low couch that some Southern dignitary had given her, contemplating a tray of sweets and a half-finished bottle of Southern wine on the little table in front of her.

"What is it?" she snapped as soon as she saw Slava. "I was busy. Important business. Our foreign concerns...important business!"

"I'm sure," said Slava.

"What is that supposed to mean?" demanded Vladya, flushing even more than she was already flushed.

"Nothing," said Slava. "I'm sure you were busy, that is all, and I'm sorry to draw you away from your important business."

"Oh." Vladya straightened up on the couch, looking slightly mollified. "So why did you, then? Draw me away, that is."

"Important business of my own," said Slava. "I thought you should be the first to know"—she was about to add, *well, except for Anna Avdotyevna, Olga Vasilisovna, and Dunya*, but stopped herself just in time, guessing that her sister would not care to discover that Anna Avdotyevna and a couple of Northerners were more privy to Slava's affairs than she was—"that a healer has confirmed my...my expectations."

"What expectations?" demanded Vladya.

"Of a child," clarified Slava.

"What!" screamed Vladya, sitting bolt upright and losing the look of a woman who had been interrupted in the middle of a dalliance. "A child!"

"Yes. If you remember, we spoke of the possibility before..."

"Yes, but you weren't *serious* about that, Slava, it's just not possible! You don't really mean to say you are with child!"

"It is early yet, but yes," said Slava.

"I refuse to believe it!"

"It is already starting to show, when I am in the bathhouse," Slava told her.

"Let me feel," ordered Vladya.

Slava went over and let Vladya feel her stomach. Vladya squeezed her for a long time before admitting that yes, it was already starting to show.

"But how!" she demanded, once she had conceded that point.

"The usual way," said Slava, smiling slightly.

"And you don't really mean to say...Didn't you say last time that the father is...is Olga Vasilisovna's father?"

"Yes," said Slava.

"Does Olga Vasilisovna know?"

"She knows of the possibility," said Slava.

"And what does she say to that?"

"She is willing to treat the child, should it have the good fortune to be born, as a sister," said Slava, and then wished she hadn't. Just as with Anna Avdotyevna, the kinship with Olga was giving rise to all kinds of speculation that Slava would prefer to suppress, and she certainly didn't want to go fanning the flames by stressing their sisterhood.

"The circumstances surrounding the conception are so strange and complex that I thought it best to conceal them from the world at large," she added. "I intend to announce that the father is a distant relation to...to the actual father. Oleg—the father—his reappearance was of short duration, and he may not wish to have it bruited about. And besides, who would believe me?"

"Not I," said Vladya. "Frankly, Slava, your story is so incredible that I can't help but wonder if you are trying to make a name for yourself in the kremlin, to...to...I don't know." She waved her hands to show Slava's vague but sinister intentions.

"I already have a name for myself," said Slava. "I'm the Tsarinovna."

"And so is Prasha!"

"True," said Slava. "But she is still young, while I have been known as the Tsarinovna for many years now. I have no need for extra fame, Vladya. Do not impute your followers' shallow and selfish motives to me, Vladya. Have a little faith in your own sister."

Slava spoke as earnestly as possible, but instead of imbuing Vladya with more faith in her, it only made her draw back and narrow her brows at Slava.

"You're up to something, Slava," she said.

"No," Slava said. "Nothing. Nothing but what I have told you."

"You always were a sly one, Slava," said Vladya, eyeing her even more narrowly. "Who knows what's going on behind those big eyes of yours?"

"Very few, it seems," said Slava. "But that's still no reason for you to suspect me of anything now. I am with child, and that is all. Have you not been encouraging me for the past ten years to take a lover and bear a child? And I have not forgotten your earlier attempts to coerce me into this…but that is no matter now. What's done is done, and I have finally done so, and I have to say, I think you were right in your advice. It just took me a long time to find the right lover, that's all—good ones are in such short supply here in Krasnograd. But now I've taken your advice and it seems you will gain a second-sister for Prasha, just as you wanted. As you keep reminding me, we need to breed more Zerkalitsy—there are just the two of us and Prasha. So I have finally done something about it."

"But why now?" demanded Vladya. "And don't give me that stupid story about the will of the gods and all that nonsense."

"Then I don't know what to tell you," said Slava. "Should I give you the story I intend to feed the kremlin? A handsome lad, a distant land, the hardships and dangers of the journey, and so on and so forth?"

"I don't believe it," Vladya repeated. She got up and started pacing around. "You're hatching something, I know you are!"

"Vladya! How often have you ever known me to 'hatch something,' in all the years that you've known me?!"

"You're hatching something," repeated Vladya. She was staring at the far wall with a strange, distant look in her eyes. The hairs on the back of Slava's neck rose.

"Vladya!" she cried. "Are you well?"

"Go back to your rooms, Slava," said Vladya, still staring at the far wall. "Go back and stay there until I summon you…No, until I make my decision regarding your fate."

"Vladya!" cried Slava again. "What has come over you?!"

"Nothing," said Vladya, still not looking at Slava. "Don't let me see you here when I turn around. I have no place for traitors in my kremlin."

"Traitors!" cried Slava.

"Yes, traitors!" Vladya suddenly swung around to face Slava, despite what she had just said about not wanting to see her when she turned around. "Traitors who go behind my back, attempting to usurp my throne and the throne of my daughter—traitors! That was your plan! Yours and Olga Vasilisovna's! Everyone knows she is Princess Severnolesnaya's less-favored daughter! You…you plotted this together with her! Now I see it! If the father really is her father, then it was a plot with her to put her half-sister on the Wooden Throne! There is no other explanation.

"And if he *isn't* Oleg Svetoslavovich—no, he couldn't be! It's impossible! You're double-crossing Olga Vasilisovna as well, I know you are! You *did* get this child off some handsome lad, just as you are claiming in your story, but you've made Olga Vasilisovna believe it was off of her father, miraculously returned from the dead, in order to gain her support! And now you plan to install this child on *my* throne, and rule through her! I know you, Slava, and I know what you're capable of! You'll stop at nothing to get your way, I know you, I know you will!" She stopped just as suddenly as she had started, panting. Her eyes were large and staring, and there was a trickle of spit in the corner of her mouth.

"Vladya!" cried Slava again. "I don't...I don't know..." she fell silent, not knowing how to respond to such a ridiculous concoction of accusations.

"The gods," she finally said, deciding to ignore the bulk of her sister's fevered fantasies entirely. "It really was the will of the gods, just as I told you. How can I prove that to you?"

"You can't! You can't because it's impossible! Now go, go back to your chambers or I'll have the guards drag you back! Get out of my sight! Tfoo, I can't bear it! I can't bear the sight of your traitor's face and your traitor's swelling belly another instant! Get out!"

Slava, the hair on the back of her neck now bristling like a dog's from horror, turned and left. Instead of going to her rooms, though, she went to the guest apartments in search of Olga.

Chapter Sixteen

She found Olga pacing around restlessly, cursing the spring rains. She brightened considerably at the sight of Slava, who was a fresh face to complain to.

"Can you believe it!" she cried as soon as Slava entered the room. "Three days of rain! We'll never escape Krasnograd at this rate!"

"By next month the roads will be passable for more than foot traffic again," Slava told her soothingly. The back of her neck, which was still bristling like a dog's from the horror of the scene it had just witnessed, was astonished to hear her speak so smoothly.

"Next month!" cried Olga in disgust.

"Next month!" Dunya echoed, more quietly. Slava could see that Dunya was also ready to leave Krasnograd and head back for the safety and comforts of the North. Right now she couldn't blame her.

"Yes, next month," Slava told them. "But that's not why I came here. Olga...Dunya...I don't know...Something very peculiar has happened..." She had to stop to regain control of her voice.

"What?" demanded Olga, trying not to appear too happy at the thought of something peculiar happening, and failing.

"Well, I spoke to my sister of my hopes," said Slava, and then had to wait for Olga and Dunya to pour out all their effusions of joy and good wishes.

"But that's not peculiar," said Olga, having exhausted for the moment all the felicity she felt on the possibility of a half-sister who was also third in line for the Wooden Throne arriving by the fall.

"No, no, but what is peculiar is my sister's reaction to the news," said Slava, and described the scene she had just participated in.

"That *is* peculiar," agreed Olga. "I suppose I can see her not being overjoyed, but I can't see anyone with a grain of sense supposing that you're planning to usurp her and plant your own child on the Wooden Throne—and in collusion with me! Anyone who thinks that's possible must not know either of us at all."

"My sister *doesn't* know you at all," Slava pointed out.

"But she knows you rather well," Olga pointed out in return, although wrongly. "I can see her suspecting me of all sorts of underhanded dealings—although if she took the slightest trouble to inquire into my character, she'd know how ill-founded such suspicions would be—but I don't see how anyone who's spent her entire life with you could think for a minute that you would do something like that. Your sister must be a half-wit. I can see *her* doing something like that, but not you."

"Yes," said Slava. "It is very strange. Always before she would complain of my lack of talent for such things. I can't see the sister I left behind in Krasnograd when I set off for the Midnight Land saying something like...like what she just said. It is as if she is a different person since I came back—a caricature of her former self. Where she used to be strong, now she is shrieking, and where she used to be forceful, now she is fearful. I do not know what to make of this new Vladya, and I do not know how to handle her either. But I have a feeling that returning to my rooms and awaiting her judgment would be a very bad idea."

"I have the same feeling," said Olga. "I think this is the curse at work."

"I agree," said Slava. "But I do not know how to fight it."

"I don't think you can," said Dunya softly. "I think it runs downhill, like water," she went on, speaking more strongly, "and you cannot regather it any more than you can regather water spilled from a bucket, just as we were told. I think we must face the fact that your old sister is gone, and this new, dangerous sister has been put in her place." She stopped abruptly, looking abashed at her sudden outburst—and at its contents, which, Slava could see, were much too close for comfort to what one of her despised seer-sisters would say.

"Yes," agreed Slava, giving Dunya a smile designed to reassure her that her words were welcome. "How unfair that I should be the one to face all the dangers, and she should be the one to get hurt! But I cannot let her hurt me, just because she is suffering. So what should I do?"

"Run away," said Olga instantly.

"I was afraid you would say that," said Slava.

"Of course that's what I'd tell you," said Olga. "It's what *I* would do." She looked as if she didn't know whether to be proud or ashamed of such an admission.

"I was even more afraid you'd be right," said Slava. Now that the danger and the curse were out in the open, she felt calmer, and able to face them squarely. "But the question is, where shall I run to? Where can I go that will not put me in even more danger than I am already in—and that will not endanger those around me? Half of me tells me I should disappear right now, with nothing more but the clothes on my back, and half of me tells me that if I do that, there will be no turning back and I really will be marked as the traitor my sister believes me to be."

"Well, *all* of me tells me that if you go back to your rooms, you're dead," said Olga. "I say we snatch up the little princess and sneak out before anyone thinks to stop us. Dunya, you spirit Slava out of here right now. I'll take care of Vladya. We'll meet in the inn in the evening."

"Yes," said Dunya. She stood up, looking much more decisive than she had since they had arrived in Krasnograd. "Let's go, Tsarinovna. I've found us a back way out. It turns out that all that late-night merry-making was not wasted, after all."

"The hidden corridors?" Slava guessed. She almost smiled. "I don't think my foremothers had them built with this kind of thing in mind."

"Oh, I'm sure some of them had them built with *exactly* this kind of thing in mind," said Olga. "They were a crafty bunch, your foremothers. And since Dunya and I haven't had anything better to do since we arrived, we've been exploring them. We could get you from one end of the kremlin to the other without anyone being any the wiser."

"Some of them are guarded," Slava pointed out.

"Yes, and we know which ones," said Olga. "Now go! No doubt your sister has dispatched guards to your room already—if she still has her wits about her enough to think of something like that. And if not—well, the gods help us all!" She stepped into what appeared to be a closet, and disappeared.

"Fortunately I have an extra spring cloak, Tsarinovna," said Dunya, opening a wardrobe and pulling out outer clothing for the both of them. "And you'll just have to try to keep my extra set of boots from falling off."

"Thank you," said Slava, pulling on Dunya's spare outer clothing. It was too big, although not as big as Olga's would have been. At least it disguised her well, she thought. "I am sorry to have drawn you into this."

"Not your fault, Tsarinovna," said Dunya with a shrug. "Now come! We mustn't lose any time." She stepped into the same closet that had swallowed up Olga. Slava followed her.

As she had guessed, it was not a closet, but the entrance to one of the hidden passageways that ran through the kremlin. Dunya began moving down it with swift confidence. Slava did her best to keep up.

It took a long time—much longer than Slava would have liked—for them to make their way from the guest quarters on the third floor to the exit Dunya had chosen, which came out behind the barracks. Slava had never realized until that moment just how large the kremlin was, and how many parts there were to it. In some places the passageways passed through thick stone, so that they could have been many versts underground for all Slava could tell, and in some places there was nothing more than thin boards between them and the people on the other side of the wall, and they had to time their movements with the sounds from the outside, in order not to give themselves away.

They passed her own quarters, and the quarters of other noble visitors, and maids' chambers, and the kitchens, and more servants' quarters, and storerooms, and great rooms of state, and many other rooms, until Slava began to fear that they would be lost forever, despite Dunya's confidence in her ability to lead them to freedom.

As they passed by the kitchens—unmistakable for their heat and noise—Slava overheard some of the undercooks speculating about the rumor that the Tsarina had ordered a search for the Tsarinovna, who was said to have run away after her treasonous schemes had been revealed. The wall between the secret passageway and the outer world was very thin here, and even had cracks in places, allowing them to look out into the kitchen if they so desired.

Slava and Dunya froze for a moment and stared at each other in horror, and then began inching ever so quietly down the passageway again. Slava couldn't speak for Dunya, but her own heart was pounding so hard it hurt to breathe.

Her escape, which up until that moment had been something unreal and faraway, even as she was participating in it, suddenly struck her for what it was: a desperate flight for her life, in which she would be branded a traitor by everyone she encountered and pursued by her own sister until she was caught or this dreadful and ridiculous misunderstanding could be cleared up. For a moment she considered turning back, but when she remembered the strange look that had filled her sister's eyes as they spoke, she knew that she would find no safety in the kremlin while her sister still ruled.

"Do you think the search has already started, then?" whispered Slava, once they had reached the reassuring safety of stone again.

"It seems so," Dunya whispered back. "So let us be quick!" She turned to look ahead again and began leading Slava down the passageway at twice the pace they had been going before.

When they came out behind the barracks, after, as far as Slava could tell, crossing the square in an underground tunnel and emerging from an empty storeroom hidden in the barracks' back wall, they could hear soldiers being mustered on the other side of the building. Probably, Slava realized with a sick feeling, in order to search for her. The empty space between the back of the barracks and the kremlin wall yawned before them. Even worse, the wall was blank. If they reached it, they would be outlined clearly against it. Slava wondered what they would do now: try to walk across the square without being seen? Give themselves up on the spot in order to cut this hopeless flight short?

The penalty for treason is death by boiling, Slava suddenly thought to herself. *But surely Vladya wouldn't*...she tried to convince herself, but a vision of her sister as she had last seen her rose up before her, and she knew, with a sickening certainty more sickeningly certain than any previous certainty that had ever sickened her that her sister would most likely toss her into the boiling oil herself, and with the same thoughtless sureness that she had once tossed the live shellfish they had been brought as a tribute from Pristanograd into boiling water. Slava had to stuff her hand into her mouth to keep from screaming. Living creatures were boiled alive all the time, and one of them could be her. It would be terrible, she knew, like scalding herself with hot tea only a thousand times more terrible. And yet people would do it and stand by and watch as she died. It would be a thousand times more terrible than her worst nightmare, and yet people would do it if they could.

Dunya looked at her to see why she was standing there with her hand in her mouth, and Slava made a "where-do-we-go" gesture with her free hand, while still keeping her other hand firmly on her mouth to prevent any sound from escaping.

Dunya, not daring to speak, nodded in the direction of what appeared to be a small privy wedged in the space between the corner of the barracks and the kremlin wall. A long time ago someone had carved a big X—as one did with a privy that was no longer usable—on the door.

Walking as quickly as they dared, they crossed the vast stretch of ground—probably at least ten paces, the longest ten paces of Slava's life—between them and it, and slipped inside. It was so tight inside that they were jammed up against each other, and Slava could tell that Dunya's heart was racing too. Somehow the cramped space made Slava feel even more desperate and vulnerable—if someone were to come upon them now, they would have nowhere to run.

Moving slowly and carefully, so as not to make any unnecessary noise, Dunya reached over and pulled on a loose board in the back wall. A whole section of the wall came away, revealing a passageway just large enough to fit someone of Dunya's size down it, if she crawled on her belly.

"You'll have to put it back in place behind you, so they don't know which way we've gone," Dunya whispered in Slava's ear. "So you'll have to start going backwards. I'll go first, headfirst, to scout. Follow right behind me. There will be a place to turn around in a few yards."

Slava nodded, feeling, if such a thing were possible, even sicker than before. She had never before had occasion to squeeze into something so narrow, and so had never realized how much she disliked cramped spaces. The very thought of crawling down that passageway made her whole body hurt with fear. What if she became trapped there...The soldiers mustering on the other side of the barracks shouted something, something about searching for her...

I have to I have to I have to, Slava told herself. Dunya stood on the seat of the privy and climbed into the passageway. Once she had gotten far enough down the passageway for there to be room, Slava climbed up on the privy seat and, very slowly and awkwardly, and with her skin prickling with fear, climbed up into tiny passageway, turned herself around, reached down and picked up the section of wall, lifted it, her arms trembling with terror and strain, fitted it into place, and then began crawling backwards down the passageway.

It took her so long, or so it seemed, to reach the place where she could turn around that she began to wonder if Dunya had lied in order to get her to come along, or if she had somehow taken a wrong turning and was crawling backwards down the wrong tunnel, or if this whole thing were a nightmare and she was doomed to crawl along until morning...Suddenly she came out into a junction of two tunnels.

Sure enough, there was room for her to turn around. Dunya was waiting for her on the far side.

"Almost there," Dunya whispered. "We've passed through the kremlin wall, and we're going to come out one street down from the kremlin, in a back alley. I'll go first, to see if the coast is clear."

Dunya, Slava thought to herself, even though now was no time for such a trivial insight, was from a coastal settlement, and so would of course use phrases such as "the coast is clear." Slava reminded herself to stay focused on the task at hand, because you could only embroider what was currently in your frame...She had to stop thinking about folk sayings, now was not the time...For a moment, Slava was afraid she was going to burst out into hysterical laughter at the inappropriate manifestation of her own hysteria...Dunya set off down the passageway, still crawling on her belly, and Slava set off after her, and was soon, thankfully, too breathless to laugh, although by the way her shoulders kept shaking, she knew that as soon as she was safe, her body would want to start laughing or crying uncontrollably.

Even though it was cold in the passageway, Slava was sweating heavily from fear and exertion, and wished she could take off the heavy cloak that Dunya had so kindly lent her, and which was now, she was sure, ruined forever. But it was too tight in there for her to attempt such a thing.

Despite Dunya's claim that they were almost there, they crawled for even longer than they had before, or at least so it seemed to Slava, before Dunya stopped and whispered over her shoulder for Slava to wait while she scouted ahead. Slava lay there on the cold dirt floor and prayed more earnestly than she had ever prayed before that Dunya would find their passage safe, and that her, Slava's, tender new-mother's stomach would not betray her at this crucial moment and cause her to vomit up all its scant contents on the ground in front of her, because then she would have to drag herself through her own sick, and who would be willing to take them in and hide them then ...

"Come," Dunya whispered. "Everyone has run to the kremlin to see what the fuss is about—some kind of proclamation is being issued. If we're quick, we should be able to go quite far without being seen."

Probably a proclamation declaring me a traitor, Slava thought to herself, but didn't waste any time or breath saying it out loud. She heaved herself forward the last few feet, and dragged herself painfully out of the tunnel and into what appeared to be a deserted storeroom.

"I think it's a deserted storeroom," Dunya whispered. "No one ever comes here, as far as I can tell. Now quick! Quick but calm. Follow me, and don't draw attention to yourself, and don't look back."

They climbed up the steps out of the deserted storeroom into another deserted storeroom, this one at ground level. Dunya peered out of a chink in the wall, and then motioned for Slava to follow her. She opened the door very softly, and then stepped out into the empty street. Slava came along after her, trying to copy her air of indifference. She knew that looking nervous or furtive would only draw attention to them, but she found it very hard to seem calm, and to match Dunya's calm pace.

They walked, briskly but not too briskly, down the street in the direction away from the kremlin. A great shout arose from the kremlin square, and Slava glanced back before she could stop herself. But all she saw was the old storehouse. It had been built in such a way that it blocked the view from the street to the kremlin—and, Slava hoped, from the kremlin to the street as well.

They walked down the empty alley, and turned onto a larger street, also empty. Slava tried to brush some of the dirt off the front of her cloak.

"Pull your scarf up a little higher, Zhenya: you'll catch cold," said Dunya. "You need to take better care of yourself, you know—tripping and falling like that." When Slava did nothing, she repeated, more impatiently, "Pull your scarf up a little higher, Zhenya."

"Oh," said Slava, understanding what Dunya was doing. "Like this, Masha?" she asked, pulling her scarf up so that it covered her mouth.

"Just like that, Zhenya," said Dunya.

"You should pull your own scarf up higher, Masha," said Slava. "This spring weather is treacherous." A hysterical laugh threatened to burst free, and she clamped her mouth down on it just in time.

"You're so right, Zhenya," said Dunya, covering her face with her scarf too. She turned down another street. This one had people on it. Slava would have stopped and run away, but Dunya continued moving briskly away from the kremlin, her apparent confidence pulling Slava along behind her. To Slava's relief, the laughter welling up inside her receded at the sight of all these people, and was replaced by a surprisingly steely calm. Although no one was paying them any attention anyway. They were all heading towards the kremlin to find out what the fuss was about.

They went down another street, and another. Everyone they met was going in the other direction, towards the kremlin. One person stopped Dunya and tried to get her to join them to see what was happening, but Dunya said, "Zhenya and I don't want anything to do with the troubles of nobles," in such a cold voice that the woman let them go and they were able to carry on their way, unmolested by any further such attacks of unwanted curiosity.

After the fifth, or maybe the sixth—Slava had kept her eyes so firmly fixed on the ground that she wasn't even sure where they were—street Dunya led them into a tavern. No one was there except the tavern mistress.

"In the back, second room," she said, nodding to a door behind the counter. Dunya nodded and walked Slava through the door.

They went down a narrow corridor, lined with doors—probably, Slava thought, rooms for guests. At the second door Dunya stopped and knocked softly.

"Who's there?" called a voice that was unmistakably Dima's. The relief of hearing him was so great that Slava's knees started to tremble, so that she almost staggered where she stood.

"It's me," said Dunya. "With our leshaya-girl. No other guests, though."

"Just a moment," said Dima. There was the sound of latches being unlatched, and then Dima cracked open the door and peered out. He glanced up and down the corridor, nodded once to Dunya, and stepped back to let them in.

"Slava!" screamed Vladislava, as soon as Slava crossed the threshold. She leapt up from the bed on which she had been sitting and threw herself into Slava's arms. "You made it!"

"SHHH!" hissed Olga and Dima, even more loudly than Vladislava had screamed.

"This is Zhenya," said Dunya, nodding towards Slava.

"And this is Masha," said Slava, nodding towards Dunya. She felt an urge to laugh again, and quelled it only with difficulty.

"Very wise," said Olga, catching on immediately. "In that case, I'm Liza, this," she nodded towards Vladislava, "is Varya, and he," she nodded at Dima, "can be..." she thought for a moment, "Kiryusha."

"Whom should we be?" asked Slanik and Olik together.

"Whomever you want," Olga told them. "No one knows who you are anyway."

Slanik and Olik looked a little put out about this, until Grisha whispered to them that it was for the best, since that meant they could serve "Liza" and "Zhenya" much better than if they were known in the kremlin and about Krasnograd.

"Now that we're all here, and have our new names, let's turn to the important business," said Olga. "Where to go?"

"Or should we go to ground in Krasnograd itself?" suggested Dima. "It's the easiest city in all of Zem' to hide in."

"Yes..." said Olga uncertainly. "Very true, but the Ts...but Zhenya's face is well-known here. I would feel safer somewhere farther from her sister's long arm."

"Getting out of the city will be dangerous," warned Dima.

"Yes..." said Olga. "And then we will have to choose a direction to travel in, too. But I'd still leave, if we think there's any chance at all of us making it out of here."

"We could return to Naberezhnoye," suggested Dunya hopefully.

"We're all too well known there too," said Olga. "All it would take would be one loyal subject sending word, and we'd find ourselves right back in the kremlin, only in rather less comfortable accommodations. The same goes for Lesnograd and Vostochnoye Selo. Besides, the roads will still be well-nigh impassible to the North for another week at least."

"Princess Malogornaya is no friend to the Empress," said Dima speculatively.

"But she's no friend to us, either," said Olga. "I don't trust her any farther than I can see her, and even then I'd rather not have anything to do with her."

"Princess Malolesnaya was very kind," Vladislava put in.

"Yes, but I don't think we should test her loyalty like that," said Slava. "I don't think she should be tried too hard."

"I'm afraid you're right," agreed Olga.

"We could always disappear into the woods," said Dunya.

"Correction: *you* could disappear into the woods, and so could I, and Dima and Grisha, and Slanik and Olik and Sasha would probably be able to make it too, but the Ts...but Zhenya and Varya would never survive."

"We will if we have to," said Slava.

"Not in your condition, not if I can help it," said Olga. "We need some sanctuary...A sanctuary! Perhaps...By all the gods!" She stopped and stared at her own inspiration for a moment.

"Zhenya!" she said, once she had recovered herself and collected her thoughts sufficiently. "*Your mother lives in a sanctuary! We must go* to *your mother* immediately!"

"My mother?" repeated Slava foolishly.

"Sl...Zhenya! Who is the one person who has the power to protect you? Who is the one person who has the authority to overrule your sister? *Your mother*. We must enlist her aid!"

"I suppose..." said Slava, who was so startled by the idea that she was unable to form a clear response.

"Could we write to her, do you think?" suggested Dima. "It might be easier to smuggle a letter out of the city than the Ts...than Zhenya."

"We should write to her, that's true," said Olga, staring off at the wall again for more inspiration. "But I don't think it's safe to remain here. No doubt there'll be a search for us."

"We could hear the soldiers forming up outside the barracks as we escaped," said Slava.

"So you took the barracks way out, then? Varya and I slipped out behind the laundry, and the maids were abuzz with the story of your treason. Sorry, Zhenya, but it's true."

"They were in the kitchen as well," said Slava. "I'm afraid all of Krasnograd will be abuzz with it by tomorrow morning."

"Yes, and so I fear it's too dangerous to remain. But you're right, ah, Kiryusha, in suggesting we send her mother a letter. If we can't make it out, perhaps the letter will still reach her, and perhaps she'll even still be able to rescue us. Zhenya, you should write the letter right now. Sasha can try to smuggle it out, and see what the lay of the land is, so to speak, as well."

And so, unexpectedly, Slava found herself perched on the narrow and uncomfortable bed, trying to write a letter to her mother that would explain her situation without putting them in any danger, should the letter be intercepted.

This proved to be a challenging task, and so Slava was unable to participate in the argument over whether they should stay where they were or move on before night came, and when and how they should make their attempt to escape the city. She was only able to rejoin the rest of the party, sealed letter in hand, once they had decided to send Sasha out, to scout and to attempt to deliver the letter to any caravan that might be heading East. It was early yet for travel, but the road East tended to dry up the soonest, so some enterprising caravan-mistresses might already be heading out. In good weather Slava's mother's sanctuary was no more than a week's ride away, which always before had seemed quite close, but now seemed like an impassable distance, especially the journey from their current position to beyond the city walls.

Sasha went off to the Haymarket with the letter, leaving the rest of them to wait anxiously for his return in their tiny uncomfortable room. Olga suggested that they try to pass the time more pleasantly by eating some of the provisions with which Grisha had provided them when he had taken the room for them, but only Vladislava, Olik, and Slanik had any appetite, and even they put down their food after a few bites. So the provisions were packed away again, and Olga, Dunya, and Dima turned back to trying to make plans in low voices, while the rest of them tried to keep quiet and find a more tolerable position to sit in. Slava and Vladya were given the bed, but Olik, Slanik, and Grisha all had to sit on the floor, which was dirty and cold. At one point Slava offered them her place on the bed, but they all turned her down in horror.

Olga, Dunya, and Dima debated for what seemed like—and probably was—hours on the relative merits and risks of staying where they were, trying to hide out in a different inn, attempting to find shelter with some princess friendly with the Tsarinovna or the Severnolesnaya family, or making a break for it that very night.

The longer that they debated, and the longer that Sasha failed to reappear, the more heated the discussion became, and the less clear it became to all of them what they should. Slava could see that Olga was on the verge of some disastrous explosion, and tried to deflect as much of her ill humor as possible from the others, but with limited success. She tried to convince herself that this was not the most miserable afternoon of her entire life, that she had experienced worse and survived, but her assurances rang hollow, even in the privacy of her own mind.

Having very little to contribute to this discussion, and unwilling to be drawn into the arguing even if she did, Slava had nothing to do that whole long dreadful afternoon but think about the curse and her own role in bringing it about. She remembered her vision of the sleigh sliding through the forest, bearing evil inside it, and that evil had been herself...she had been cursed already, cursed maybe from birth...And nonetheless she had agreed to the gods' and the leshiye's mad plan, and borne the curse right back to Krasnograd...

She remembered what Princess Severnolesnaya had told her, that stopping the birth of the child she was carrying inside of her would do nothing to prevent the curse from being carried out, but she was unable to believe it...Her impending motherhood had certainly been the cause of Vladya's madness, and even if it had already been lurking there inside of her, waiting for an opportunity to come out, Slava's news had been that opportunity, she and her impending motherhood were the ultimate reason...Whatever happened, however this turned out, Slava knew that she would always have to know that she had chosen the leshiye and their offer over her own sister...her only sister, who was so frightened...Who was probably plotting her death this very instant...they must escape, they had to, they had to, where was Sasha...

It was well after dark when Sasha finally returned. "The whole town is alight with the news of the Tsarinovna's treason," he announced as soon as the door had been closed behind him. "And there are soldiers everywhere with torches, searching. The Haymarket was crawling with them, and they even came up to everyone in the line for letters, wanting to know who we were writing to. I said my aunt in the sanctuary, and they told me to watch out for, for..." he nodded in Slava's direction, "and then went on their way."

"So the letter went off, then," said Olga.

"The first caravan of the spring heading East took it," said Sasha. "They don't set off until tomorrow, so who knows what will happen to it by then."

"Don't say such things," Olga told him severely.

"We have to be ready," said Sasha with a shrug.

"Sasha is right," said Slava, before Olga and Sasha, who were both on edge—although no more than the rest of them—could start quarreling. "We cannot count solely on that letter, pleasant as such a thought might be. We have to have other plans."

"What do you say, Sasha?" asked Olga. "Do we attempt to escape Krasnograd tonight, or wait? You were the one most recently out on the streets: is it possible, do you think, for us to make our way to the gates unnoticed, or do we run too great a risk by being out of doors?"

"The risk would be great either way," Sasha told them. "They're patrolling every street they can go down, like I said, but I also heard they were going to start going through all the inns, so I wouldn't give much for our chances if we stay here, either."

"We should split up," put in Dunya. "A large group like us will surely draw attention, and if we try to go out in pairs or threes, then we have a better chance of getting at least some people through the gates. Even if only one person gets through, she should try to make it to the sanctuary at all speed—perhaps her"—she nodded at Slava—"mother will still be able to save the rest of us. At least she will be informed of what has happened."

And so, after surprisingly little further debate, considering the hours they had spent agonizing over it before, it was decided that they would go out in groups of two or three, each to a different gate, and meet up outside the city.

"But what if they shut the gates?" asked Slava. She was loath to re-start the debate, but this seemed an important point. "The Krasnograd gates have never been shut in my lifetime, but for something such as this, they very well could be."

"They hadn't shut them when I was out," said Sasha.

"It would be very bad if we were to arrive there, and discover that they had been shut," said Dima. "Very bad. We would have left our shelter here, and have nowhere to go all night—if they even reopen them in the morning at all, that is."

"From what I heard, it sounded as if the Tsarina didn't expect her"—Sasha nodded at Slava—"to flee. She thinks she's going to try to take her throne, and for that she needs to be in Krasnograd. From what I overheard, everyone assumed she had taken refuge with one of her princess-accomplices."

"Well, that rules out taking refuge with a princess, then," said Olga with a certain grim relief at having their path simplified by at least one choice. "And it sounds like our way out won't be as difficult as we feared."

"Let us hope so," said Slava, trying to quell a ridiculous feeling of annoyance with her sister for being so foolish. If Sasha really was tell-ing the truth—for a moment Slava was overcome with the panicked thought that perhaps he had been caught and turned to her sister's service while he was out there, and he was now leading them straight into a trap, but she stifled the thought as quickly as possible—then Slava's sister was behaving in a truly irrational fashion.

Slava knew that it would be better for her, and that she should take advantage of this as much as she could, but she still couldn't help but feel a tiny spark of irritation with her sister's stupidity. For some rea-son, her sister's failure to close the city gates seemed much worse than her declaration of Slava as a traitor. It was only then that Slava realized with shock just how badly her sister's mind had been affected by the curse. Even if they escaped and were able to reach the sanctuary and enlist her mother's aid and have everything turn out all right, Slava thought, her sister might never be fit to rule again. Someone, probably

Slava, would have to step in and rule in her place...

"Let's leave now," Olga said, interrupting Slava's unpleasant thoughts. "There's no point in standing around like bulls for the chop if we could be making our escape right now. The longer we wait here, the more likely we are to be found here. We'll split up, as we planned, and each go out our separate gates. Dunya, you take Slava out of the East Gate"—she seemed to have forgotten their new names, or decided it was no longer worth keeping up the charade—"it's the closest and, I hope, the safest. Dima, take Slanik and Olik out the South Gate. Grisha and Sasha, you'll have the longest walk from the West Gate. I'll take Vladya and test our luck at the North Gate. We'll meet at that big oak tree on the East Road—it's the only landmark around for versts and versts."

And so, once again much more quickly than Slava would have expected, given all the talking they had been doing up to that moment, she found herself slipping out of the room as secretly as possible. They all left the room at once and walked as quickly and quietly as they could down the corridor and out a back door without, as best they could tell, drawing anyone's attention, even that of the tavern mistress.

Sasha, as the last to have been outside and therefore suddenly the most knowledgeable of them (a position he was not used to having, as was evident by his hesitancy when Olga sent him out), went out first onto the street, and summoned the rest of them once he saw that everything was clear. Then they all went their separate ways, Olga and Vladislava in one group; Dima, Slanik, and Olik in another; Grisha and Sasha together; and Dunya and Slava as the final pair. Dunya took Slava by the arm and set off towards their gate without a backwards glance at the others, and Slava tried to copy her calm as they disappeared around the corner.

"I have an idea, Zhenya," said Dunya in a low voice, once they were several streets away. "We're supposed to go out the East Gate, but there's a way out one street down from it."

"Really?" Slava whispered back doubtfully. "I've never heard of it."

"You know how the wall makes a little jog where Malaya Vostochnaya street dead ends into it?"

"Yes..." Slava whispered hesitantly, as she didn't actually know the streets of Krasnograd very well at all. "I think they rebuilt the wall there a generation or so back," she added. "After the last invasion by the Hordes. The wall was smaller, and Malaya Vostochnaya used to be the main road." She fell silent and looked determinedly at the ground as a patrol of soldiers passed by. One of them tried to hang back and make highly improper—what would his mother think!—remarks to Dunya, but his leader called him on, and they all hurried off, the other soldiers consoling Dunya's potential suitor with promises to find him some proper-looking women, not "some little wisp of a girl and a dried-up old aunty."

"Soldiers," said Dunya when they were out of earshot and she and Slava could breathe again. "Ruined forever, all of them. What woman would ever marry the likes of that?"

"Some do," said Slava.

"And live to regret it," said Dunya, sounding as if she were thinking of many particular instances.

"Many live to regret marrying non-soldiers, as well," said Slava, thinking of Serafimiya Svetlanovna.

"Well, once we're out of here, we'll have plenty of time to worry about that sort of thing," said Dunya, shaking her head and turning back to the matter at hand. "I slipped out of the city at Malaya Vostochnaya last week—there's a little unguarded gate at the jog, where the wall was mended when they made it bigger, I suppose. They must have left it there as a back way out, but hardly anyone ever seems to use it. It's barely big enough for you or me to slide through it, so I guess they don't think it's worth guarding—you'd never fit a horse down it, or even an armed soldier. But it's worth a try, don't you think?"

"What if it *is* guarded now, and we're caught trying to go through it?" objected Slava. "Surely there's no good reason for people to be lurking about there, and there probably isn't a good way to escape."

"We'll say...We'll say you're my nanny, smuggling me away from my cruel mother and into the arms of my lover," said Dunya. It was hard for Slava to tell in the dark, but she thought Dunya might have been grinning a little. She was glad someone was enjoying this.

"It's worth a try," Dunya repeated. "We'll be able to see the East Gate before we make the last turn, and we can make up our minds then, but the little gate will be the best choice, I'm sure of it."

"Very well," she agreed, and she and Dunya hurried on arm-in-arm, past flocks of excited people and patrols of enthusiastic soldiers, none of whom paid the slightest attention to "a wisp of a girl and a dried-up aunty."

They came in sight of the East Gate and saw that there was a great crowd gathered there, all shouting and complaining to each other and to the soldiers who were trying to stop everyone and search them.

Many were people who lived in outer Krasnograd, on the other side of the wall, and were afraid of being trapped inside the city for days.

"Madness," whispered Slava. "They should have shut the gate hours ago."

"They've heard you!" Dunya whispered back, as the soldiers did, in fact, turn from their searching in order to shut the gate. A loud groan rose from the crowd in protest. Soldiers started fanning out from the gate, whether to quell the crowd or search it, Slava couldn't tell. Probably both. Probably it would be very, very bad if they were to come across the two of them, because probably someone among them would recognize them for who they were, and not just take them for some aunty and her niece out for an evening stroll.

"Quick!" whispered Dunya. "Malaya Vostochnaya! The other gate!" She pulled Slava after her in a half-jog away from the main road and down a little alley onto Malaya Vostochnaya. As soon as they were off the main street, she glanced both ways and, not seeing anyone, pulled Slava after her at a dead run towards the end of the alley and the little gate she said was there.

To Slava's intense surprise, they encountered no one as they raced the few yards down the alley and up to what looked like a blank corner where the two walls met.

"Left!" hissed Dunya. "There, to the left!"

Slava turned to her left, and saw a little alcove, barely large enough for her to fit into and too dark to see anything more. She threw herself into it, and collided with what was undeniably a man's body.

Chapter Seventeen

"O h!" they both cried.

"I'm sorry!" Slava said instinctively. "We were..."

"*Tsarinovna?!?*" said the man's voice incredulously.

"Oh!" cried Slava again, forgetting in her panic even the name of the man she had just crashed into, the man she saw every day in the kremlin, how could she have forgotten his name, oh, by all the gods, this was worse than anything she could have possibly imagined, oh, they were done for, it was all over now, if only Dunya would have the presence of mind to turn and run while he was still standing there in shock, run Dunya run, oh, it was all over now...

"Tsarinovna!" repeated the man, grabbing her arm and pulling her out of Dunya's grasp—Dunya had also gone limp with shock, it seemed, oh, how unlucky, how unlucky, how unlucky—and into the alcove where he had been standing. "What are you doing?"

"We..." said Slava, and stopped, unable to think of anything else to say.

"This is all the escort you have?" he demanded. "All the protection you have?"

"Well..." said Slava, not sure whether it would be better to confirm or deny it. There was a sound of metal sliding over metal behind her.

"Let her go if you want to keep your blood in your body," said Dunya. The edge of a very long and sharp-looking knife appeared uncomfortably close in Slava's field of vision.

"You're running, aren't you?" the man demanded. "Out of Krasnograd." He paused, apparently in thought. "And I don't blame you," he said, now speaking slowly. "The Tsarina is not...not in her right mind. Anyone could see it by the commands she's been issuing today. Treason! You! It's impossible. But then to let you escape from the kremlin... and to refuse to close the gates until just now...Honestly, I thought you might have left the city already. I even...I even hoped it was so. If only, I said to myself, she has the presence of mind to flee to her mother's protection! That would solve all her problems. I was just stepping out to see what was happening beyond the walls, before assigning someone to guard here. Lucky for me. Lucky for both of us. Tell me true, Tsarinovna: are you a traitor?"

"No!" said Slava. "Of course not! But I...when I was with the Tsarina earlier...she is not in her right mind, as you said, and I...I began to fear for my own life, and...and rightly so, it seems!"

"Rightly so," agreed Boleslav Vlasiyevich. "And what shall we do about it now?"

"Oh! Ah, well..."

"What should *I* do, Tsarinovna?" he asked thoughtfully. Dunya's knife was really very, very close to Slava's neck. Slava wondered if it came down to it, who would win in a straight fight: Dunya or Boleslav Vlasiyevich. Dunya had acquitted herself handsomely against the bandits in Severnolesnoye, while Slava had never seen Boleslav Vlasiyevich raise his hand against anyone more threatening than a bound prisoner, but she knew that he had won his post for conspicuous bravery, and that his men still considered him one of the finest swords in Zem'. Plus, he was wearing chainmail, and Slava did not like her own chances if it came to fight between him and Dunya, being that she herself was unarmed, unarmored, and standing between them. She decided that it might be best to try cunning and charm before resorting to cold steel.

"What is in your heart to do, Boleslav Vlasiyevich?" she asked, leaning a little closer to him. He was really, she thought, not so very much bigger than Dunya, or even herself. The hulking lads he had serving under him would never have been able to conceal themselves in the corner between the walls, but he fit in easily. It should have made him seem less dangerous, but somehow it made it worse. Someone that neatly made would probably be quick and agile, like a cat. Behind her, Dunya shifted uneasily, as if she were thinking the same thoughts.

"In my heart to do?" He smiled strangely, and also, she couldn't help but notice, sadly. "Many things, Tsarinovna. They say you see into the hearts of women; is it also true of men? Can you not see for yourself?"

"I would hear it from your mouth," said Slava, shifting a tiny bit closer to him and looking into his eyes. They were the same color gray as her own. She tried not to think of that. If she could just grab his hands, even for an instant, then perhaps they would have a chance... "Tell me what it is you wish, and I will do all I can to help you in it."

"What do I wish?" repeated Boleslav Vlasiyevich slowly. "I wish you to say..." He gazed inwards at his own desires, and continued more firmly, "I wish you to say: Help me, Boleslav, I need you. You're the only one who stood up for me before, and you're the only one who can save me now."

"Help me, Boleslav," said Slava, stepping even closer to him and gazing into his eyes with every ounce of pleading charm she could summon up. As she was desperate, and she was telling the truth, it was quite a lot. Lyudmila Krasnoslavovna would have been envious. "I need you: you're the only one who can save me. Help me, Boleslav." She put her hand on his chest, and he instinctively clutched at it with both of his. Slava could feel herself go faint with relief.

"Well..." he swallowed and shook his head. "Well." His voice sounded rough. "Come...I can't believe I'm going to do this...but I've thought that before about you. Come this way. You can slip through here."

He moved back, although still holding her hand, and Slava saw that there really was a gap between the old and new walls, which a thin person, such as herself or Dunya or even Boleslav Vlasiyevich if he took his chainmail off, might be able to slip through.

"Wait!" he cried, as she moved to take her hand from his. "Where are the others? I know you have more accomplices than just your knife-girl here."

"I don't know," she said honestly.

"Are they escaping too?"

"I don't know," she answered, still honestly. After all, right now she had no idea where they were or whether they were succeeding in their escape.

"But who are they? Don't you have anyone to help you? Surely you're not running off on your own! You'll be helpless out there!"

"It's better if you don't know," she said. And that, too, was completely true: it really would be better if he didn't know, because then he couldn't reveal their identity to anyone else—not, Slava thought, that it was likely to remain a secret for long.

"And where are you going?"

"That, too, is something better for you not to know," she told him, beginning to weary of his insistence on holding her when she needed to be running away.

"Well...I suppose you're right..."

"Thank you," she said, trying to slide past Boleslav Vlasiyevich and towards the gap.

"The only way you can thank me is by thinking of me," he told her, clutching her hand like a child clutching at its mother.

"I will," she said, and then she was through the gap and out on the other side the wall, her hand finally free of Boleslav Vlasiyevich's, she couldn't say how, and Dunya was behind her, and they were making their way as quickly as possible down the dark alley in which they had found themselves.

They went down the alley and turned onto a larger street, which was full of torches and people. This part of outer Krasnograd was heavily built up and populated, so that it was almost the same as being inside the city proper, only here, Slava noticed, the people were much more poorly dressed, and seemed to have taken the occasion of the Tsarinovna's treason as an excuse to celebrate, or so she assumed by all the animated groups that had gathered at every street corner, standing over bonfires and laughing loudly. Once again, Slava had to quell the urge to be annoyed at something that was in her favor. While it was undeniably a blessing, a wonderful blessing, to be able to pass through the throngs of outer Krasnograd unnoticed, if she truly had been a traitor!..

"This way," said Dunya, steering her by the elbow. "And by all the gods, that was impressive. How did you do that?"

"I don't know," confessed Slava. "I've never been able to do anything like that before, and I doubt I'll ever manage it again. But it needed to be done, and so...I guess all the charm I ever possessed was summoned up in that moment. But I feel bad for him, now. I always assumed he was too much my sister's man, or just too lightminded, to be trustworthy. I'm sorry if he's suffered because of it."

"Oh, I doubt he's suffered half as much as he thinks he has," said Dunya absentmindedly, looking up and down the street. "This way, I think." They hurried down another street full of torches and people laughing the kind of laughter that only comes after several glasses of vodka. Several times parties tried to stop them and make them join in on the merrymaking, but Dunya always shook her head and moved on in a way that brooked no argument, and everyone they encountered was too drunk to care whether they stayed or went.

Despite the need to flee, Slava spent a while worrying about the possibility that she had hurt Boleslav Vlasiyevich's feelings, and that perhaps she should have asked him to join them...But then she remembered that he could have offered to join them and hadn't. He had let her go, but not offered her any other aid, even though he had said she would be helpless out there.

But on the other hand, he had let her go, even though he was sworn to serve her sister, and what aid could he have lent her that would not have made her even more conspicuous than she already was? And what had he meant about standing up for her before? She puzzled over that for a while, but could think of no special example. Oh, many times he had been solicitous; for years he had acted as if there were some special bond between them, but why he thought so she was no closer to guessing than she had ever been, except to note that there was some incident in his mind that was important to him, something about which she knew nothing, despite whatever he might think. She resolved to worry about it as little as possible and concentrate on her escape instead. Whatever would be with Boleslav Vlasiyevich, would be, and he was out of her control now.

They walked farther and farther through outer Krasnograd, until the torches died away and they were passing the darkened huts of people who could hardly even be termed Krasnograders anymore, and then they were out amongst fields, and the city was nothing but a dark presence at their backs.

"I can't believe we escaped!" Slava whispered. Somehow she felt much more exposed on the empty road amongst the empty fields than she had in the city.

"We haven't gotten there yet, Zhenya," Dunya hissed back fiercely. "I won't say we've escaped until we've put at least a day behind us—and found the others as well. I think we've got at least three more versts before we reach the rendezvous point."

"Should we get off the road?" Slava asked.

"There's nowhere to hide," Dunya pointed out. "There's nothing but fields for versts and versts around. We'll attract more attention if we leave the road than if we stay."

Slava saw the sense in that, and concentrated on keeping up with Dunya's brisk pace as they tried to make as much time as possible without looking suspicious, in case anyone else should be about. Slava would have expected people to be out, even at this time of night, as the Vostochnaya Road was the main road connecting Krasnograd with the bulk of the country, but it seemed that no one else cared to travel on a damp spring night. After slipping and sliding her way through a verst or so of the mud pit that was the road this time of year, Slava had to say she couldn't blame them. It started to drizzle.

"How much farther?" Slava asked.

"At least another verst," Dunya told her.

"Very well," said Slava, trying to sound cheerful and brave. She reminded herself the road would have been much worse a week or two ago, and that they were lucky to be able to use it at all, and that wading through mud in a cold drizzle was still infinitely preferable to being locked up in a dungeon at the bottom of the kremlin. Probably preferable. It might be preferable if she had some food and better boots, not to mention a good night's sleep under her belt...*Stop whining!* she told herself. *You're falling behind Dunya!*

After three or four eternities they reached the large oak that was their meeting place. It was the first tree they had encountered since they had left Krasnograd, and so it was unmissable, even in the darkness of a rainy spring night. No one else was there.

"I thought we'd probably be the first to arrive," Dunya told her, trying to sound confident. "The others all had to travel around Krasnograd before getting onto the Vostochnaya. Let's just settle here and get comfortable."

"Of course," said Slava, trying to sound as if Dunya's false confidence had been transferred to her. "I'm sure they'll be here shortly." She and Dunya went around to the far side of the tree, in order to be less visible to any unwelcome passersby on the road, and leaned against the trunk and waited. Slava wished that the leaves had started coming out already: it was very damp, standing there in the rain, and the bare branches offered little protection. It was that most unpleasant part of spring when winter's beauty was truly gone, but the land was still dead and barren—and extremely muddy and wet.

And cold, too. Slava suspected that one of her boots had developed a slow leak. She tried to direct her thoughts elsewhere, and found them wandering over to her back, which was pressed most uncomfortably against the cold rough bark of the tree. She wished she had some place to sit down. She wished she had some water. She wished she were almost anywhere other than under this tree, waiting anxiously to see if her friends had made it out of the city...

"Someone's coming," whispered Dunya. "Stay quiet and still."

Slava tried to stay as still and quiet as possible, while they waited for the passersby to draw near enough for Dunya to make out who it was. Positioned as she was, Slava was unable to see the road at all, and so she had to take Dunya's word that someone was coming, and wait for her to decide whether they were friend or foe. It was a long wait.

Eventually she heard footsteps, the footsteps of several people. She froze even stiller than before, holding her breath.

"Who's there?" called Dima softly.

"Di—Kiryusha!" called Dunya. "It's us! Masha and Zhenya!"

"Thanks the gods!" said Dima fervently, and he, Slanik, and Olik ran over to join them.

"We made it out just before they closed the gates," Dima told them once he had joined them under the tree. "No one even looked at us twice."

"We slipped out the side gate at Malaya Vostochnaya," Dunya told him. "Someone was there, but...He let us through."

"A guard?" Dima asked incredulously.

"I know him well," said Slava.

"By all the gods! That was a stroke of luck!"

"The Ts...Zhenya sweet-talked him into letting us go," said Dunya, still sounding impressed at Slava's feat.

"Ai-da Ts...by all the gods! What a stroke of brilliance! You truly are the gods' chosen!"

"I suppose," said Slava. "Although I'm not sure if or for how long he'll keep our departure a secret."

"Surely he couldn't dare reveal such a thing!" said Dima. "How could he explain letting you go?!"

"I don't know," said Slava. "But I still wouldn't count on his secrecy for too long."

"Well...You're probably right, of course. Any sign of the others?"

"Not yet," said Dunya. "But we haven't been waiting for long."

It seemed to Slava that they had already waited half the night, at least, but she supposed Dunya had some better way of marking time than her own discomfort, and also that Dunya was probably much less uncomfortable than she was anyway. She tried to resign herself to waiting a while longer.

After another three or four eternities, during which Dima and even Dunya began to grow restless and uneasy, Grisha and Sasha joined them under the tree.

"Thank the gods!" said Dima when he saw them. "We thought..."

"We had to make our way through the docks and up the bluff and then come all the way around Krasnograd, once we'd gotten through the gate," explained Sasha. "And we heard...we heard...We heard as we were coming through outer Krasnograd..."

"We heard that some of the traitors had been captured," said Grisha.

There was a horrified silence.

"It could be wrong," said Slava. "Rumors in a crowd...Ten to one it was wrong, nothing but rumors..."

"Olga and the little princess aren't here yet, though," said Dunya soberly.

"Vladislava can't walk as fast or as far as the rest of us," said Slava. She knew she was only saying it because she didn't think she could bear the alternative, but she couldn't seem to stop herself from coming up with excuses for Olga and Vladislava's continued absence. She thought of Vladislava stumbling along, tired and cold, and her heart squeezed so painfully she thought she might be sick.

"She still should have made it by now," said Dunya, and Dima nodded his grim agreement.

"We still don't know what happened, though," said Slava. "Perhaps they are hiding somewhere..." This time she thought of Vladislava hiding, crouched somewhere...but where? There was nowhere to hide between here and the North Gate...unless they had managed to take refuge in some alley in outer Krasnograd...That was what they must have done...

"We can't wait here much longer, though," said Dunya. "We need to be in the woods by morning, and the night is already more than half over...We must move on shortly, or our risk of being captured will become too great."

"And leave them?" demanded Slava. Her whole body flinched away from the thought of leaving Vladislava behind, alone and unprotected. At that moment she thought that she would have sacrificed anyone else, even Dunya or Olga, in order to keep Vladislava safe.

"We won't be doing them any good here," said Dunya.

"And even less good by being captured," said Grisha. Dima remained silent, but Slava knew that he was thinking the same thoughts as Dunya and Grisha, and fighting them even harder than she was.

"But to leave them..." argued Slava, even though she knew that it was not only pointless, but that the others were right and she was wrong. Somehow, though, even though she knew it perfectly well, she still could not force herself to give up on rescuing Vladislava yet. She couldn't leave Vladislava, who was in part responsible for all this, and was still the dearest person in Slava's life, now and perhaps forever. If something terrible were to happen to Vladislava, Slava didn't see how she would be able to go on living...it was strange, but she had never thought that about another person...and for it to be Vladislava to inspire such a thought...And so they could not give up on her, they could not abandon her, absolutely not, not now, not ever.

"If they are not captured, then they can make their own way to the sanctuary—Olga knows where it is as well as I do," said Dunya. "Rather better, in fact. And if they are captured, then it seems to me our best hope is to carry on with our plan, go to your mother, and beg her aid. Returning to Krasnograd will only make things worse."

"Little as I like it, I fear D...Masha is right," said Dima. He spoke with the voice of someone who has confronted unpleasant thoughts, and not run away from them. It was a rare sound to hear in a man's voice, but in Dima's it sounded almost natural. He stood up a little taller, as if Olga's courage and decisiveness had flowed across those fields and into him, making him her stand-in for this dreadful decision. "I fear we have no choice but to go on. O...She would insist on it, I know she would."

It was a terrible moment. Slava knew Dunya and Dima were right, that their best hope was to try to reach her mother, and that Olga would insist on it were she there to make the choice for them, but every drop of blood, every fiber in her body, screamed at her not to leave, not to abandon Vladislava and Olga, and it was only with the most awful dragging reluctance that she was able to detach herself from the tree and follow the others down the road.

From their slow, stumbling progress, Slava guessed that the other felt much the same. She didn't dare look at Dima. She wanted to offer him some kind of comfort, but what comfort could she offer him? He knew, probably much better than she did, the dangers Olga faced, and what Olga would want him to do in such a situation, and there was nothing Slava could say or do that could make it any better for him. Her only way to help was to walk as quickly and boldly as possible in the opposite direction from Olga, and to remind herself over and over again that she wasn't abandoning her, she was going to get help, she was going to rescue her. Her and Vladislava.

When she thought of Vladislava, Slava thought she might turn around and run all the way back to Krasnograd...force her way through the gates...into her sister's chambers...turn herself in, as long as Vladislava would remain safe…but surely, surely, surely, Slava told herself, her sister would not harm Vladislava. As far as she knew, Vladislava was nothing more than Slava's ward, an innocent girl of ten who had gotten caught up in something much larger and more dangerous than she should have…Surely even her sister would not harm a little girl…surely, surely, surely—and they would rescue her. They would arrive very soon at the sanctuary, they would find her mother, and she would immediately return to Krasnograd and restore order and sanity and Olga and Vladislava would be rescued. All they had to do was make it to the sanctuary in time, and everything would be right again.

They walked for a long time through field after field, until finally, at long last, they came to a stand of trees. According to Dunya, it was almost morning.

"There's a village on the far side of this little woods," said Dima. "Someone should go scout ahead while the rest wait here."

Slava instinctively looked around to see what Olga would make of this suggestion, and then remembered that Olga was not there. It was only then that the full tragedy of Olga's failure to escape the city hit her: not only was Olga trapped and in danger, but she was not there to guide them, either. Slava had been so caught up in the misery of leaving Vladislava behind that she had not spared too much thought to the practical significance of losing Olga, which was twice as bad as losing anyone else. Much as Slava trusted Dunya, Dima, Grisha, and the others, they were not the same as Olga's comforting presence.

"Sasha: you should go," continued Dima. By the heavy tone of his voice, Slava suspected he was suffering from the same doubts as herself. "Take Olik with you. See what's what. And if you can get us some food, or blankets, or anything to help us survive our journey, do so. But don't put us at risk. If you think people are suspicious, run away. And think up some kind of story."

"I'll say that…that Olik and I are brothers, who…"

"Came to Krasnograd to seek our fortunes," put in Olik. He had looked frightened and distraught ever since they had decided to leave the oak tree without Olga and Vladislava, but now he was cheering up again.

"Yes," said Sasha. "Only we had to leave, because, because…"

"Our sister's new husband took a dislike to us and kicked us out of the house without clothes nor bread," said Olik, sounding more and more inspired.

"Yes, yes, and we have to make it all the way back to…"

"Bolshoy Stepnoy Prud," Olik finished for him. "It's at least four hundred versts from here, so we'll need a lot of provisions to make it."

"I see you should have been a bard, not an adventurer," said Sasha, giving him a look that was somewhat impressed and somewhat suspicious at this sudden ability to tell lies.

"There are a lot of bards in my family, it's true," said Olik, now sounding almost his old cheerful self again. "But I wanted a wilder life."

"Well, lucky you," said Sasha sourly.

"And lucky us," said Dima, before Sasha could lose his temper or Olik could take offence. "Now go, and be careful! And don't forget how to find us!"

"Yes, mother," said Olik, and set off after Sasha with a jaunty step that gave no hint of his desperate flight and many versts of walking. Slava wished she could be so hale and bold. But as she couldn't, she settled for collapsing on a tree root that was slightly less muddy and damp than the ground all around them.

"I think there's a stream just over there," announced Dima. "And look! I have a wine bottle I snatched up from our room as we were leaving. I'll go fetch us some water." He left, probably, Slava guessed, as much to be alone with his grim thoughts as to fetch water. She hoped he wouldn't get lost in the dark: she wouldn't have cared to venture deeper into the woods without a torch for anything.

After a while he did come back, though, and with the bottle full of water. They all drank gratefully: despite all the mud, sources of clean water had been scarce on their walk. The sun began to rise.

"I wonder how long they'll be," said Slanik anxiously.

"A while," Grisha told him. "First they have to scout the place, and then they have to wait until people are up and about, and then they have to tell them their story, and see what provisions they can get...It will be a while. Try to get some rest."

There was, of course, no such thing as rest while perched on a muddy root on a damp spring dawn while fleeing, possibly for their lives, from the Tsarina, unless one defined "rest" as "not walking," which, Slava supposed, it was. Her legs certainly thought so, although the rest of her body disagreed.

The sun had already long risen, and some travelers had even slogged by, much to Slava's alarm, when Sasha and Olik returned, bearing a sack full of provisions.

"Bread!" exclaimed Olik exultantly. "Pies! And blankets!"

"The villagers were truly generous," said Sasha more soberly. "The gods grant that we meet such generosity elsewhere—and that we deserve it."

"If I am able, I will return and reward them," Slava promised, touched by Sasha's uncharacteristic thoughtfulness.

"You will, Krasna Tsarina?" he said, cheering up.

"Best not to call her that," warned Grisha.

"We're unlikely to be overheard here," said Dima comfortingly. "But Grisha is right: we mustn't reveal the... 'Zhenya's' true name."

"My true name is Krasnoslava," said Slava with a smile. "You can call me that, if it would make you feel better. I doubt anyone would guess: no one calls me anything except...well, my title."

"Can we call you...just Krasna? Krasnochka?" asked Olik. "It would be better than Zhenya." He suddenly remembered whom he was addressing, and, blushing profusely, fell into silent confusion.

"Of course you can call me Krasnochka," Slava told him. "It would be an honor. And now...Do we carry on?"

"We should breakfast first," said Dima. "And then...How far does this little patch of forest extend, Sasha?"

"To the village. Then there are fields again, although there are more woods off in the distance."

"Does the road go through the village?"

"Unluckily, yes."

"Do you think we could skirt around?"

"If we were quick and careful, Dmitry Marusyevich."

"Well then, we'll just have to be quick and careful," said Dima. "And now let's sample the delicacies of our benefactors from the village."

But when Slava tried to eat a pie, her stomach turned and she was unable to swallow so much as a crumb. All the men hovered around her in helpless anxiety, and refused to be soothed when both she and Dunya assured them that this was normal, perfectly normal, for women in her condition.

"They say it is a test by the gods," said Dunya. "To see who is truly fit to be a mother."

"Then the gods are cruel!" said Slanik indignantly. "Tormenting the...Tormenting our Krasnochka like this, and at such a bad time!"

"No one will deny that the gods are cruel, especially to new mothers," said Dunya. "I've seen my sisters go through this too many times to disagree. Will you be fit to walk, do you think?"

"I'll make it to the sanctuary if I have to crawl on my hands and knees, vomiting all the way," said Slava, with such unexpected firmness that she surprised even herself, and made all the men take a step back.

"Let us go, then," said Dima, after a moment. "Quickly and quietly! And Grisha..."

Grisha took Slava's arm before Dima could even finish the sentence.

As soon as they set off Slava realized that she was even more tired and weak than she had thought, and very shortly, despite all her intentions to support herself and not be a burden to the others, she found herself clinging desperately to Grisha's arm.

"I'm sorry," she said at one point. "It seems like you're always having to pull me along. Someday I'll learn how to carry myself on my own two feet, I promise."

"You're no burden, Krasna," he told her. "And you'll make it to the sanctuary if I have to crawl all the way with you on my back, I swear it."

They had to skirt well around the village to avoid being seen, which took up most of the day. They stopped once to rest and eat, but out in the fields they felt exposed and uneasy, and there was little rest or nourishment to be had under those conditions. Only by late afternoon did they reach the safety of another little clump of woods, and were able to stop and eat in relative security.

Dunya, Dima, Grisha, and Sasha all debated at anxious length about the road in front of them, the benefits and dangers of traveling at night versus day, and whether they should risk approaching any settlements. Slava felt that she should contribute something to the discussion, but she was so tired that she was having a hard time focusing her eyes, let alone talk. She felt as if she were in some never-ending trial by walking, that she had been condemned to walk ceaselessly until she collapsed, and even that was little hope, because her body refused to collapse, the Black God take it, it kept going long after she would have liked to give up and lie down and never rise again. It was hard to believe that she had fled from Krasnograd only the day before: it seemed like a lifetime ago, some other life in which she did not keep putting one foot in front of the other, no matter how desperate she was to stop and rest.

It was decided that they would keep going, at least for a while, after dark, and so as soon as the sun set they took off again, moving slowly and tiredly down the empty road between the trees, but moving nonetheless. Dunya walked in front, guiding them in the dark, and Grisha took the rear, listening for the approach of travelers, since travelers could be soldiers from Krasnograd. Dima took Slava's arm, to keep her from swaying off the road in her dazed condition.

They walked and walked and walked, until it was decided that they were approaching the edge of the woods and they should stop and rest while they could still do so in the safety of the trees. They stumbled off the road until they found a fir grove that offered shelter and secrecy, where they wrapped themselves up in the blankets the kind villagers had given Sasha and Olik, and tried to rest for a while. They would, Dunya and Dima agreed, set off again at dawn, as their need for speed was greater than their need for secrecy, now that Olga and Vladislava had been captured.

Slava gathered from their discussion that they would have little chance at a full night's sleep until they reached the sanctuary, so intent were Dunya and Dima on reaching its safety as quickly as possible. She could not disagree with their plan, tired as she already was and doubtful as she felt over her ability to keep up such a pace for near on a hundred and fifty versts, especially as she seemed unable to take in any form of nourishment most of the time. Surely she should be past this sickness already? Or perhaps it was just nerves? Not that it really mattered in the end.

Slava wasn't sure how much of her rest was spent in dazed wakefulness, and how much in restless dozing, but when the others rose and shook her awake, she came to with the sensation that she had been dreaming, and that the forest had been talking to her in her dream, telling her not to worry, that it would watch over her on her journey. But when they set off again in the dawn light, Slava had no sense that eyes were following her, as she had on their way North. She wished she had: for once it would have been comforting.

They walked out of the woods and through fields and into another little patch of woods, where they came around a corner and suddenly heard voices. Everyone froze.

"Travelers—get off the road!" hissed Dunya.

But the road there was old and sunken into the muddy ground, so that there were slick chest-high walls of dirt on either side. Olik vaulted up out of the road, but when Slava tried to follow him, she only slid against the slippery dirt and almost fell down. She and Dima stared at each other in horror, and Slava could see that he was exhausted too, too exhausted to lift her off the road to safety and climb up after her himself. They started scrambling back as quickly as their weary legs would carry them, looking for an opening in the banks hemming them in.

The group was moving towards them, not very fast, but faster than they were escaping themselves. Slava could see Olik run along the top of the bank, back the way they had come, looking for a way out, and then run back to where they were, shaking his head. So it seemed their discovery was imminent. If only, Slava thought, the group coming towards them would prove to be incurious, if only they would pass them by without a second glance...

Two members of the group were talking; it seemed to be an older woman and a younger woman. The younger woman had a soft, shy, and oddly familiar voice...Slava was sure she had heard it somewhere, if only she could remember where, if only she could recognize it and know whether it were friend or foe, whether they still needed to run...

"Do you think the Tsarinovna is back from her journey, Svetlana Alinovna?" asked the soft voice shyly. "Do you think she's in Krasnograd by now?"

"I know she is, Yevgeniya Marislavovna," said the older woman comfortingly. "I heard of her return from a sister merchant. Don't you worry: you'll see your Tsarinovna soon enough."

"If she'll see me," said the soft voice doubtfully.

"If she's as kind as you say, she will, I'm sure of it," said the older woman, still speaking comfortingly. "Especially if she gave you a handkerchief, as you said she did."

"I hope she won't mind that I came...I got on the first merchant caravan I could, that's why I'm coming from the wrong direction...My mother doesn't know...You don't think she'll send me back, do you? The Tsarinovna, I mean?"

"*Zhenya!*" gasped Slava, recognition shocking her into alertness where fear had failed. "Princess Malogornaya's daughter! Do we...do we reveal ourselves?"

"We agreed Princess Malogornaya was untrustworthy," whispered Dima.

"But not Zhenya! She's running from her mother to find me!"

"We can't escape anyway," said Dunya quietly. "What fools we were, to stay on the road and not see the danger!"

"You didn't see it because you could climb out to safety," Slava pointed out. "It's only I who can't. But now...Here they come!"

Olik, who was still standing on the bank above them, moved as if to come down and join them on the road, but Dima shook his head furiously and mouthed the words *run to safety*, and Olik, after an equally furious silent argument with Dima over the advisability of that action, retreated out of sight.

Two wagons came walking slowly around the corner. Zhenya and an older woman were sitting in the first one. The older woman pulled her horses to a stop on seeing Slava and the others.

"Hello, travelers," she said cheerfully. "It's muddy weather to be out walking."

"And to be out driving," said Slava, since no one else seemed to be capable of speech. "But spring is a muddy time."

"So true, traveler, so true," said the older woman with a smile. "Where are you headed, my dears?"

"East," said Slava. "And yourselves?"

"Krasnograd, of course, where else? I'm from the steppe myself, but my passenger here comes from Malogornoye, don't you, my dear? Not coming by the most direct route, are you, sweetheart? But she was desperate to get to Krasnograd, weren't you, darling?"

"Yes," said Zhenya. Her eyes were fixed on Slava.

"But do you know each other, my doves? I can tell that you do. What a chance meeting!"

"*Tsarinovna?*" whispered Zhenya. "Is that you?"

"Yes, Yevgeniya Marislavovna, and in dire need of your help, or at least your silence," Slava told her.

"Tsarinovna?" repeated the older woman, giving Slava a sharp look. "Truly?"

"Truly, Svetlana Alinovna," said Zhenya softly.

"Should I get out and kneel?" asked Svetlana Alinovna, sounding bewildered.

"No, no, no need for that," said Slava hastily. "But Zhenya! It is imperative that no one, especially no one in Krasnograd, finds out that you saw us. Do you understand? Please, Zhenya, if you have any care for my life and the lives of my companions, please tell no one, absolutely no one, that you saw us."

"Are you in trouble, Tsarinovna?" asked Zhenya slowly.

"Yes, and Zhenya, if you…"

"Do you need help, Tsarinovna?" Zhenya interrupted her.

"We need your silence, Zhenya, your complete and absolute silence about meeting us here, and…"

"Where are you going, Tsarinovna?" said Zhenya before Slava

could finish her plea.

"It's better if you don't know, Zhenya, so that no one can force you..."

"No one will force me, Tsarinovna," said Zhenya, with more conviction than Slava would have thought possible from such a poor beaten-down creature. "But I can see you are heading East, with no horses, no carts, and hardly any weapons or provisions worth speaking of. So I am asking you: do you have far to go? Do you need help reaching your destination?"

"Well..." said Slava, since Zhenya's assessment of her situation was all too accurate, but she was still reluctant to ask for her help.

"I can see that you do," said Zhenya. "Svetlana Alinovna! We must assist the Tsarinovna and her companions!"

"Of course, Yevgeniya Marislavovna," said Svetlana Alinovna, respect pushing out all the motherliness that had previously filled her voice. Slava couldn't blame her. Zhenya's transformation had been quite impressive.

"We will take you East, Tsarinovna, don't you worry," said Zhenya. "Here: climb in with me."

And so, quite unexpectedly, Slava found herself in a cart next to Zhenya, and soon they had gathered up Olik from his hiding place on the bank, and he and all the others had seated themselves in the two carts as well, and the carts had been turned around—not without difficulty and nearly getting stuck on the muddy banks—and they were heading East.

"We're taking you in the wrong way," Slava whispered to Zhenya, as they set off.

"My only direction is with you, Tsarinovna," Zhenya whispered back.

"Well, then, we're taking Svetlana Alinovna in the wrong direction," said Slava.

"Svetlana Alinovna will be glad to serve you," said Zhenya.

"I will try to see she is well rewarded," said Slava with a sigh. "If it is in my power at all, I will make sure she is not put out of her way for nothing."

"Why are you fleeing, Tsarinovna?" asked Zhenya.

"I...the fewer who hear of it, the better, Zhenya, so now is not the time."

"Well then, *where* are you fleeing, Tsarinovna?" said Zhenya. "That, at least, you must tell us, if we are to take you there."

"Gluboky Prud sanctuary," said Slava apologetically.

"Gluboky Prud sanctuary, Tsarinovna?" said Svetlana Alinovna. "I was just there. And now I suppose I'll be seeing it again. Ah well, I'm sure they'll be glad to have me back, for we always have a nice little chat and I give them a few nice things. I picked up some blankets at our last stop; I was going to bring them to Krasnograd, but perhaps they'll need them at the sanctuary—perhaps they'll need them even more than in Krasnograd—they get so few visitors there, while merchants in Krasnograd are simply crawling around every street corner."

"You were just there?" asked Slava, surprised, gratified, and amused at how readily and graciously Svetlana Alinovna was allowing them to take over her caravan and cause her to return exactly to the place from where she had just departed. "And how...how were things there?"

"The same as always, Tsarinovna: peaceful and quiet. Although— you know they have a men's sanctuary there as well? Well, it was all abuzz with the latest news." Svetlana Alinovna seemed to be recovering from her shock and returning to what Slava could see was her usual cheerful, motherly, talkative self.

"And what was that?" asked Slava.

"That some new nobleman had arrived, some new young prince, straight from Krasnograd and all distraught over something, and spends all his time laboring and praying, so that even the hardiest of the brothers are amazed. They say he's terribly handsome, but heartbroken, Tsarinovna, utterly heartbroken and sick with himself. I only caught a glimpse of him out of the corner of my eye, as I was unloading my goods, but I could tell they were telling the truth; he was as handsome and sad as they said. He was chopping wood. They say he fell into some great guilt before his wife, and is now committing a most awful penance." Svetlana Alinovna sighed. "Romantic, is it not, girls?" she said.

"Yes," said Slava. "You don't happen to know his name, do you?"

"No, Tsarinovna, and more's a pity, for it's a great story, isn't it? All the sanctuary was full of it, as I said—well, as much as it could be, being a sanctuary and concerned with other things and trying to keep silent—I'm glad I'm not a sister, aren't you? Give me traveling any day over prayer, that's what I say. But other than that there was nothing of interest at all—a sanctuary's a sanctuary, after all, you know."

"Yes," agreed Slava. She couldn't help but suspect that the newest arrival at the men's sanctuary was Valery Annovich. She would like to think so, anyway.

Soon she forgot to think about Valery Annovich or anyone else, and stared off at the trees, and then at the empty fields, through which they were traveling. For a while she was too apprehensive of meeting another traveler to get any rest, but after they had been going for a few hours and not seen another soul, she found herself dozing off on the cart bench, despite the lurching and the jolting.

"Rest your head on my shoulder, Tsarinovna," said Zhenya, after Slava lolled over and then jerked awake for the third time.

"I don't want to bother you," said Slava hesitantly.

"Nonsense, Tsarinovna, you won't be bothering me at all," Zhenya told her. "Rest your head on my shoulder and get some sleep while you can."

And so Slava rested her head on Zhenya's shoulder and drifted off to a kind of semi-sleep. She stayed in that condition for what she guessed to be several versts, until she suddenly heard Vladislava calling for help, and snapped awake, her heat racing and sweat running down her sides.

"What is it, Tsarinovna?" asked Zhenya, as Dunya asked, "What's the matter?" at the same time.

"I thought I heard Vladislava calling for help," Slava told them. "Vladislava is my ward," she explained to Zhenya.

"It was just a dream," Dunya told her comfortingly. "It's natural you're worried for her, so it's natural that you're dreaming of her. Think nothing of it."

"Yes, think nothing of it, Tsarinovna," Zhenya echoed.

"I suppose you're right," said Slava, but she couldn't shake off the awful impression of Vladislava's plea for help all the rest of the day.

They stopped for the night in a small village whose inhabitants accepted the return of Svetlana Alinovna with an added retinue without question. Slava could see by their faces that they considered the ways of all travelers incomprehensible, and that if Svetlana Alinovna wanted to come back their way only the day after she had set out, with a party of noblewomen and their guards, that was her business. They were all fed and given beds, and in the morning, they were fed again and sent on their way without further questions.

Slava could only marvel at how easily everything had turned out for her: two days ago she had been fleeing for her life, and now, while she was still in fact fleeing for her life, she was doing so with a minimum of trouble and inconvenience. She wondered if the gods had had a hand in it, or if it was only her own good luck. She supposed she was due a little good luck, and decided not to view it with too much suspicion, although she knew that was a decision easier made than upheld.

They passed very few travelers that day, and those whom they did encounter also showed very little interest in them. They greeted Svetlana Alinovna, remarked briefly on the size of her party, and then carried on towards Krasnograd without a backwards glance. It was apparent that Slava had outrun the news of her treason, and no one they met had reason so much as to look twice at her. She hoped that none of them remembered her once they arrived in Krasnograd and heard what had happened.

They traveled for several days in that fashion, with, Slava couldn't help but think, the most unaccountable ease. It was as if the world were making way for them. Slava, abandoning her earlier decision not to treat their good fortune with too much suspicion, wondered what ill fortune their current good luck presaged, and had to tell herself to stop wondering such things immediately. It did no good at all, and only made her unhappy. She passed most of the journey in a haze of tiredness and morning sickness.

Chapter Eighteen

A week after they had set out from Krasnograd, they arrived at Deep Pond sanctuary. As might be expected from the name, it was on the banks of a deep pond in a small clearing in the midst of a thick woods. A sister came out to greet them.

"Svetlana Alinovna," she said in surprise. "What brings you back so early?"

"Travelers your way," said Svetlana Alinovna. "I decided to give them a ride."

"That was kind of you, Svetlana Alinovna," said the sister. "Welcome, travelers. What brings you to our sanctuary?"

"The Tsarina," said Slava, speaking for the first time that day.

"The Tsarina is in Krasnograd, sister," said the sister with a faint smile.

"You know whom I mean," said Slava impatiently, and then, embarrassed at her rudeness, added quickly, "I'm sorry, sister. But you know whom I mean. I must speak with her this instant." Having arrived at the sanctuary, Slava's earlier dazedness had suddenly given way to a frightening urgency that was making her heart jump in her chest and sweat trickle down her back.

"The woman of whom you speak has chosen to retire from the world of women, sister," said the sister, calmly but firmly.

"I'm her daughter," said Slava. "Surely she'll see me."

The sister started at that announcement, and stood there for a moment in speechless surprise before bowing and saying, "I'll see that she's informed. In the meanwhile, please, come in and refresh yourselves. Sisters will take your horses, and show your men where they can rest."

They all climbed out of the carts, and Slava, Dunya, Zhenya, and Svetlana Alinovna followed the sister inside the main building, Svetlana Alinovna hanging back to the rear and looking very uncertain about her place in things now that it had become clear that she was about to encounter the Tsarina.

"Of course," Slava heard her whisper to Zhenya as they took of their boots and slipped on slippers, "I saw her before, but somehow it was different: she was always just another sister then. But now—the Tsarina! I know there's another one ruling in Krasnograd now, but our little mother Marislava will always be the Tsarina in my heart. The good-hearted Tsarina, that's what we always called her! And now here's the Tsarinovna here to see her! It makes a difference, somehow, don't you feel it, Zhenechka my dear? It makes a difference, and my heart's beating so that my hands are shaking—just look! I don't know if I'll have the nerve to face her, if she should appear."

"We'll just stand back here," Zhenya whispered back to her. "I doubt she'll have eyes for anyone except the Tsarinovna."

And then they were in a small side room and there was the sound of someone walking quickly down the corridor towards them, and then her mother was there in the room with them, wearing a brown sister's dress and looking very surprised, and also a little bit different than Slava remembered her looking two years ago, when they had last seen each other, but mostly she looked surprised, more surprised even than pleased.

"Slava?" she asked disbelievingly. "Is that you?"

"Yes," said Slava.

"What...What brings you here?"

"It's a long story," said Slava.

"Oh...well...there will be time, I'm sure...are you here for long?"

"I don't know," said Slava. "Did you not receive my letter?"

"Oh, that...Well...Come here, then...I haven't hugged you in so long..."

And when her mother put her arms around her, Slava saw that tears suddenly came to her eyes, and that she was now, finally, really glad to see her. Her face looked older than it had when she had left Krasnograd, but also softer and happier, more like the face of an ordinary woman and less like the remote mask of an empress.

"Are these your companions, then?" she asked, after she had hugged Slava for a long time, squeezing her almost painfully hard. She was much bigger than Slava, almost as big as Vladya, and Slava could feel how she had filled out in her time at the sanctuary—probably she had to work in the garden and the stables every day.

"Some of them," Slava told her. "The men are putting away the horses, and the others..." She thought of Olga and Vladislava, and her throat closed up, so that she had to stop for a moment, confused. "It's a long story," she said again. "But an urgent one. Oh mother! Did you not receive my letter? Vladya...I come to you with no good news!"

"Vladya!" cried her mother. "Is she...ill?" Slava could see by her face that she was really thinking *dead*, since surely nothing else would bring Slava herself all the way out here.

"She is...Oh mother! She seems to have fallen under a curse!"

"A curse!" exclaimed her mother. "How?"

"It's a long story," said Slava again.

"I can imagine," said her mother dryly, and for a moment they both smiled, despite the gravity of the situation. "What signs does she show?" Slava's mother asked.

"She mistrusts me...Oh mother! I am here because she declared me a traitor, and I had to flee Krasnograd, perhaps for my life...We slipped out the secret corridors and then out the old Malaya Vostochnaya gate...Soldiers were searching for us everywhere...And two of my companions never met with us at the meeting point, and we think they were captured...Olga Vasilisovna, Princess Severnolesnaya's younger daughter, and Vladislava Vasilisovna, her granddaughter—I took her as my ward, and I am afraid...But we couldn't go back, what could we have done? And so we came to you—actually it was Olga's idea, and we decided to carry it out even after she was unable to join us, she must have been captured—we came to you, as the only person who could manage her, who could do anything...And here we are..."

"You *fled* Krasnograd?" said Slava's mother, taking a step back. "Vladya declared you a *traitor*? What did you *do*?"

Slava stared at her mother. In that moment she saw that her mother desperately did not want to be dragged back to Krasnograd, and even more desperately did not want to hear anything against Vladya's rule, as she had always feared that Vladya would be a poor ruler but was too eager to give up her throne to admit it. She had told herself she was doing the right thing by turning the throne over to Vladya while they were still both of sound mind and body, and if Vladya had ever been fit to rule, she would have been right, but Vladya never had been and, Slava thought, most likely never would be fit to rule.

But her mother had never been able to bring herself to see that, and now she was looking for an excuse, any excuse, to avoid becoming entangled in her daughters' problems and being dragged back to Krasnograd, and if that meant throwing Slava to the wolves, then so be it. Slava supposed she couldn't blame her—in fact, she, too, would have done almost anything to avoid being dragged back to Krasnograd—but she also knew, with the most sickening certainty, that her mother was not going to save her.

"I made her afraid of me," said Slava, telling herself that she was wrong, she had misjudged her mother and that she mustn't give up now, now that they had made it all the way to the sanctuary, outstripping even her letter. At that thought, Slava felt a strong twinge, and she knew she was lying to herself, but she tried to cover that up with even more lies.

"Afraid of you! How!?"

"She's never been very brave," said Slava. "I didn't even mean to, but I did it anyway. But really it was the curse—or rather, the curse took the easiest route…"

"You must be tired," her mother interrupted. "And no doubt hungry as well. Let's sit down and have something to eat. This way."

Her mother led them to another, slightly larger, room with a table and benches. They all sat down silently, except her mother, who went off and came back a little later with tea, and then, after another trip, pies.

"It's simple fare," she said. "It's all we have here."

"Of course," said Slava. "Thank you."

"So tell me your long story," her mother commanded. "I did receive your letter, it came in yesterday, but it seemed so outlandish…I decided it was a joke, or the work of a halfwit. Sometimes people send me letters begging for my help, but they are all halfwits, and I have learned to ignore them. The good-hearted Empress—did you know that's what they called me? When I ruled I answered petitions day and night, but I no longer rule. I retired to this sanctuary for a reason. So I have learned not to listen to such petitions, and besides, as I said, it was obviously the work of a halfwit. It couldn't possibly be true. Our Vladya would never do anything like that. It had to be the work of an imposter, someone seeking to play on my fears for her own ends."

"But I wrote it with my own hand!" cried Slava, her heart sinking even deeper than before.

"You never did have a very clear hand," said her mother. "How was I to know? And your news seemed so far-fetched—I knew it couldn't

337

possibly be true. So tell me your story."

For a moment Slava wondered if her mother had been struck by the curse as well, or if she was just much more slow-witted than Slava remembered her. But as there was nothing to be done about it now, Slava told a very shortened version of the story of her journey with Olga, and finished with her return to Krasnograd, Vladya's strange behavior, and their final scene together and Slava's decision to run. Perhaps, she told herself, once her mother heard the truth from Slava's own mouth, she would come to her senses and offer her help.

"But what provoked her?" her mother asked when she had finished. "Why would she think you had designs on her? You have never shown the slightest aptitude or appetite for rule, and it's not as if you have any heirs for whom you would want to take the Wooden Throne."

"Ah, well..." said Slava, blushing deeply. "As I mentioned in my letter..."

"Slava!! Really?!?" Now her mother straightened up and began to look animated.

"Really," said Slava. "In the fall, if the gods are kind," she added.

"Slava! And the father?!!"

"Is in Severnolesnoye," said Slava.

"Oh," said her mother, sounding disappointed. "Aren't you going to marry him, then?"

"That seems unlikely," said Slava.

"But to abandon him like that...Men cannot take care of themselves, you know, they're not strong like women...What does his mother think? Didn't she insist he be turned over to a wife's care?"

"I don't think she's around anymore," said Slava, who had not until that moment thought for an instant about what Oleg's mother would think of their connection, and had a hard time not laughing, now that she had.

"Oh...That's too bad..."

"He is older than I am," said Slava. "He already has daughters with other women."

"Oh...Well...Well, that's good too. A man isn't really a man until he's had a few daughters, although a man who's been shared with other women...It's not natural, you know: men were made to belong to one woman and one woman only, in order to continue the line. They're not like women, always needing to seek new blood for their children..."

"I did suggest that he come back with me," said Slava. It was much harder to confess that than she would have liked, or expected. "But he wouldn't...He has other duties..." As she said it she knew, even more strongly than she had when she had actually asked and Oleg had refused, that that was just a convenient excuse, and of course he hadn't had other duties, he had just been too afraid to come back with her, but she resolutely refused to say that, or even keep thinking that thought.

"He's not *already* married, is he?" her mother demanded. "Because *that* would be a complication. The wife could claim that the child was her property...Although in this case she would surely lose."

"No," said Slava, and then realized that Oleg was, in fact, already married. "He was," she added. "But the wife is no longer an issue. No, he has other duties...He did not want to abandon them to come with me to Krasnograd...What I mean is that he couldn't..."

"Oh nonsense," said her mother. "What could be more important than a child, and the heir to the Tsarinovna? He probably just wanted to be talked into it properly. You should have put your foot down and insisted—he would have thanked you later. You know how men never know what is good for them—or can make up their minds to accept it, even if they do know. Sometimes they have to be forced for their own good. They'll just keep running away from you if you won't learn that lesson. But that is neither here nor there...What I mean is: *why?* What came over you?"

This led to a second, and much longer, description of Slava's journey, after which her mother sat in stunned silence for a long time.

"You're joking," she said, when she finally spoke.

"No, I'm not," Slava told her. "I really am with child, and Vladya really has gone mad and driven me out of Krasnograd."

"Are you *sure* you haven't done anything to provoke her?" Slava's mother repeated. "You can be very provoking at times, Slava my dear, you know, and Vladya has many cares upon her shoulders—you mustn't burden her even further with your own selfish troubles. And it's not as if you've never threatened to do something that might be... might be deemed to be treasonous. I haven't forgotten how you...how you threatened to," her mother flushed with old hurt and suppressed shame, but carried on, "threatened to raise the steppe princesses if you didn't get your way."

"And I haven't forgotten why I made that threat," said Slava. "But in the end, both you and Vladya saw sense, and there was no reason for me to carry it out. Mother! You must intercede! You *must* make Vladya see reason, or I fear the realm will be drawn into open rebellion and war. If Vladya really has taken the heir of Severnolesnoye into captivity, and if she makes her threat to me known to the whole country—or if, the gods forbid, she were actually to carry it out—then ten to one both the North and the steppe would rise against her."

"Oh Slava!" said her mother, looking very tired. "If you would only stop provoking her..."

Slava saw, even more clearly than before, how little her mother wanted to be dragged into this quarrel, and how little she wanted to admit that Vladya was a poor ruler, and how much she, Slava, would have liked to join her in that denial, and how impossible that would be for her, Slava, to do so. She had left her mother's care a long time ago, like it or not, and now there was no one to stand up for her but her.

"I provoke her just by breathing," said Slava. "And if she were to manage to do away with me, I'm sure I'd provoke her by not breathing, too. But now she has provoked *me*."

"You know," said her mother, "I always thought you were like me, Slavochka. But now I see you grow more like your father with every passing year, in both mind and body. You look like him now, you know, and you act like him, too. So much wildness! So much fierceness!" She smiled painfully. "I would be glad, but it brought him to no good end. The wild ones rarely end up well."

"I look like him?" said Slava, surprised. "I thought he was huge..."

"So he was—to a girl of four," said her mother. "But you never saw him from any taller height. To a grown woman he was barely of normal size. That didn't stop him from being the boldest man in Zem'—everyone said so. Until he got himself killed, that is."

"He was a hero," said Slava. "Everyone says so." For a moment she was overcome with disorientation, overwhelmed as she was between this new, unexpected connection between herself and her father, one that she had never thought of before. Everyone said *he* had been a hero, and now they were saying that *Slava* was a hero, too.

The mental seasickness was so strong that Slava had to resist the temptation to grab hold of the table to steady herself. And then the vision she had had of him lolling drunkenly and laughing at things that were a fitter subject for tears rose up before her, and she wasn't sure which was her real father, and she knew that she would never know, and she would have to be a hero on her own, whether or not he had been. For after all, his heroism had consisted in running away, running away from her, his only daughter, whom he had said he loved more than anything else in the world.

So if Slava were to be a hero, as perhaps her father had been, she too would have to take in some of that thoughtlessness, that callousness, that heedlessness of others, that had allowed him to leave her and go off on his final journey. Only she would have to use it to run towards, not away. She wasn't sure yet what she would have to run towards, rather than away from, but she knew that she would, because, as she had been told, she was meant to be a hero.

"Yes," said her mother. "A hero. Hacked to pieces by Horde warriors, somewhere far to the East. They sent me back the shattered bones. You don't know," her mother smiled painfully again, "how many times I wished I'd put my foot down then and not let him go on that journey. I learned my lesson then, and I wish you'd learn it from me. If you wish your child to have a father, you had best drag him in and keep him close to you, because like as not he can't be trusted to stay by you on his own."

"I don't think I want my child to have a father whom I have to keep tied to my side," said Slava. "Let him run off and leave us if that's how he is. A bad father is worse than no father at all. And my own father died so that his companions might live. Everyone says so."

"So fierce," said her mother, still smiling painfully. "I don't know whom you resemble more, Slava: those hot-headed steppe warriors like your father, or our very own Miroslava Praskovyevna. I always thought you were like me, but now I see I was wrong. And who knows which is worse, a bad father or no father at all? You certainly never had the chance to find out. Neither of my girls did.

"Vladya's own father never gave three straws about her, and your father loved her even less. No wonder that she chose that awful man as her husband—after all, I chose one just as bad for her father, and one hardly better for yours. Not that he couldn't have been worse. He loved you well enough—when you were clean and dressed and smiling prettily while everyone told him how much the little Tsarinovna took after him. I don't think he would have thrown you to the wolves, if they were circling about you, but he as good as did so when he went off on his final adventure. Sometimes foresight is worth more than heroism. You lost your father forever, and the Tsarina's husband died so that lesser men, men whose only duty was to die defending him, might live. An unfair trade, some might say."

"Those men's wives, and sisters, and mothers, and daughters, might not," said Slava. "They might say their men's lives were bought cheaply."

"Slava! Your own father! Your own father, who died when you were still a child!"

"Yes," said Slava. "*I* might say so. But *you* might say that he never loved me all that much anyway, so it was best that I never found out. And those other women might say that their men's lives were bought cheaply, and that my father died a hero."

"Well, perhaps he did," said her mother. "But they still sent me back the shattered bones, and I buried them next to your sister, the one who died before she drew her first breath. Oh Slava! If only you'd had another sister! Sometimes I think...Sometimes I think how much happier things might have been for you, if she had lived."

"Yes," said Slava. "Because if she had lived, then you would have had no need to marry my father and get another daughter, just in case something happened to the ones from your first husband, and I never would have been born at all."

"Slava!" cried her mother.

"It's true," said Slava. "Everyone says so, including you. You told me directly that I was born to be the Tsarinovna, and it's true. It's what I am. I was born because she didn't live."

"Slava! You can't...You can't say that! You can't replace one person with another!"

"Yes," said Slava. "You can't. Who knows what she would have been, if she had lived? Perhaps everything would be much better than it is now. But she didn't live, so I had to be born. And here I am, a thorn in Vladya's side. Poor Vladya! If only her full sister had survived! Perhaps she would be much happier than she is now."

"You should try to explain everything to her," said Slava's mother, with an obtuseness that was much more like Vladya and much less like the mother that Slava remembered. Slava could see that she was already forgetting much of what she and Slava had just said to each other, as thoughts that were much too unpleasant to be remembered. And there was that strange business with the letter...curse or no, Slava could see, more clearly with every passing breath, that there was little help to be had from that quarter.

"I did explain," said Slava. "But you can only explain things to people if they are willing to hear you." She thought she spoke rather pointedly, but her mother did not seem to take the hint.

"Well..." she said instead. "You'll be safe here, at any rate. Stay here for a while, and we'll see what happens. Perhaps news will arrive soon from Krasnograd."

"Yes," said Slava. It was not as active a plan as she had hoped for, but they would, at least, be reasonably safe for a few days. Slava wondered what would happen if—when—the sanctuary received the command to return Slava to Krasnograd. She would like to think they would refuse and give her refuge, but she could not, alas, be certain of that. So far she had not seen anyone of Vlastomila Serafimiyevna's strength of character, and the more she spoke with her mother, the less faith she had in her ability or even willingness to protect Slava from her sister. Far from being willing to return to Krasnograd and make Vladya see sense, her mother seemed ready to hand her over to Vladya without a second thought.

Their evening together only reinforced her opinion. While it was clear that her mother was delighted to see Slava, and overjoyed by the news of her happy expectations—although she would have been even happier had Slava had a new husband in tow as well—it was also clear that her mother was very happy at the sanctuary, and had no intention of ever leaving. The Tsarina that Slava remembered from her childhood was gone, to be replaced by a woman whose main pleasures in life were working in the herb garden and contemplating her grown daughters' successes in life.

Furthermore, it was apparent that she had no intention of allowing anything to disturb her tranquility, especially if that involved disturbing thoughts that perhaps her daughters were not so successful as she had hoped, or that she had made a mistake in leaving them to their own devices, or that, worst of all, they were now irreconcilably opposed to each other and one would have to make way for the other. But—Slava could see her mother thinking—if that really were the case, then clearly Vladya, as the Empress, would have to get her way, and Slava would have to give way, especially as she was so much better at it. She could come and live in the sanctuary and work in the herb garden too, and they would all live very peaceful and happy lives.

Once she realized that this was the help her mother intended to offer (providing Vladya did not press too hard for Slava to be dragged back to Krasnograd in irons, of course), Slava tried to tell herself that, despite her annoyance at her mother's decision to let this be one of those moments when she would fall into a selfish panic and fail Slava at a crucial juncture, perhaps that really was the best thing to do.

After all, she had no love of Krasnograd, while she did prefer quiet and retirement. Much as they might all talk about her unexpected resemblance to her father, she was first and foremost her mother's daughter, and as such would almost certainly be happiest here by her mother's side, hiding from the world and its many, many evils. She could write Vladya a letter explaining that she had decided to renounce her position as Tsarinovna in favor of Prasha, and promise to move permanently to the sanctuary and live as a simple sister. It would solve all their problems. All her other plans—to adopt wards, to bring up her daughter, should she have the good fortune to be born, to be the gift she hoped her to be, and so on and so forth—those had just been the kind of idle daydreaming to which Slava was so predisposed, and which she should have put behind her years ago. This was a good, sensible plan, and she should do her best to bring it to life.

Slava repeated this to herself several times that evening, ignoring the disquiet that rose up in her whenever she told herself that it was what she should do, that it was a good plan, a sensible plan, a plan that would fix everything and make everything right and everyone happy again. She could even, she thought, make Olga and Vladislava's release a condition of her retirement to the sanctuary. Surely Vladya would have no objection to that...Surely even she would see no hidden evil in such a move...She would write the letter tomorrow, Slava decided.

She informed her mother and the others of her intentions at the end of the evening, as they were preparing for bed, and everyone agreed that it was a good plan, the best plan. Her mother was overjoyed, and hugged her again, and told her that they had very fine herbwomen and healers there, and it would be a fine place to bear and raise a child, and no one would mind, and her daughter would be the pride of the place, and so on and so forth, and everyone went to their rooms that night in high good humor and hopes, thinking that everything was right again. Everyone except Slava, who still couldn't quell the voice inside her telling her it was the wrong thing to do, but, she assured herself over and over again, that voice was wrong. She would write and send the letter tomorrow, and soon everything would be fixed and it would all be behind them and she could start her new, quiet life as a sister in the Deep Pond sanctuary.

Chapter Nineteen

Slava slept restlessly that night, but she told herself that that was to be expected, a strange room and strange home and strange people and so many adventures in the past week. She arose the next morning determined to go to breakfast and eat at least a bite or two, and then sit down and write her letter without delay.

There was a new person at breakfast that morning, a quiet thin woman who looked like an older version of Dunya, and who proved to be a tracker traveling from Krasnograd back to the steppe. Her name was Nadya and she sat in silence for most of the meal, only breaking her silence when Anastasiya Tatyanovna, the sanctuary mother, asked her straight out for the latest news from Krasnograd.

"They say that the Tsarinovna has plotted some black treason against the Tsarina, and fled the city with the help of her dark accomplices," said Nadya.

Slava tried not to look like someone in the midst of plotting black treason. Fortunately, Nadya had no idea who she was—she had merely been introduced as "Our guest, Krasna."

"But they say that the Tsarina has managed to capture some of her fellow traitors," continued Nadya, warming to her subject. "One was only a child. They say the Tsarina plans to have them put to death if the Tsarinovna doesn't show herself soon."

"WHAT!!!" Slava screamed.

Everyone stared at her in horribly mild surprise.

"WHY?" Slaved demanded, still, she could tell by the others' faces, screaming.

"They're traitors, sister," said Nadya calmly. "And the Tsarina hopes that the Tsarinovna will return for them. Some say it's a little harsh, putting a child to death, but the Tsarina says that a traitor's a traitor—best to get rid of them before they're grown, like vipers."

The chair knocked against Slava's legs as it fell over, but she didn't feel it, just as she didn't feel all the stares as she ran out of room, or the door slamming against her, or the cold rain hitting her face as she left the building and ran across the muddy yard to the prayer wood, or the wet ribbons slapping her face as she ran through a thousand other women's silent, useless prayers, or the cold mud squelching over her legs as she fell to her knees in front of the largest of the prayer trees.

"Save her!" Slava heard someone shouting over and over again. "Save her, save her, save her!" The person shouting was herself, but she couldn't make herself stop, nor did she want to. "Anything—anything you ask! Just save her!"

"Do you think you are the first with that prayer, little woman?" said the cold wind in her face. "Many women have knelt before us, just as you have, and begged us to save their daughters, but so rarely is that prayer answered."

"I don't care!" cried Slava. "Just save her!"

"Yes, many women have said that too," said the cold wind. "All of them would have been happy to sacrifice the lives of a thousand other mothers' children, or even their own life, for the one of the person they wished to save, but it so rarely happens. What makes you think you are any different from them?"

"Because I'll FIGHT HARDER!" screamed Slava. "I'll FIGHT HARDER—fire, and steel, and magic, and blood, and great flooding tides, and everything else inside of me! Whatever it takes to save her!"

"It will take more than you have, little woman," said the cold wind. "Even you don't have enough to save her."

"You told me last time that I would succeed where others had failed! And I will!"

"Even so, you cannot save her, little woman. Her fate is her fate, and it is a dark one. She is doomed by the curse that she caused to be brought down on your family. And her own, too, of course—after all, you are all blood kin. So by destroying herself she will be fulfilling the curse that she herself caused to be cast against her. She must die, and then the curse will be broken, and you and your sister will be free. But you cannot save her."

"Then you have to!" Slava sobbed. "You have to save her! I'll give anything...Haven't I already given you so much? And I'll give you more, I promise! I've already promised you my own blood—take it!

Anything you ask! Just save Vladislava!"

"Why?" asked the cold wind. "The world is full of little girls like her."

"No! Not like her! There's only one Vladislava!"

"That is not true," said the cold wind, its laughter blowing in Slava's face. "The world is full of Vladislavas."

"Yes it *is* true! There is only one of her, never to be repeated! And now my sister will destroy her! Save her, save her, save her!"

"She's not even your own flesh and blood," said the cold wind. "Well—not as your sister is. And she truly is a traitor. How fitting that your sister's delusion should lead her to administer real justice. No, Slava, we cannot save her, and neither can you: you turned down our offer, remember? You lost all your chance to be strong, to be a hero. But don't worry: our later bargain will work to your advantage. You will stay here and have your baby, and soon you will forget all about Vladislava. Your own real daughter will be a more than adequate replacement for the little traitor who is only the most distant of blood kin.

"And then your sister's madness will run its course, and after she demonstrates the danger she poses our land by executing the granddaughter of Princess Severnolesnaya, everyone will call for you to replace her, and you will become Tsarina, and your daughter after you. It will be so easy—so much easier than you think now. A year from now Vladislava will be barely even a sad memory. Even her own mother will not grieve for her overmuch—or rather, she will enjoy grieving for her dead daughter much more than she ever enjoyed caring for her when she was alive. Everyone will be well served by her death, and it will be so easy to let it happen."

For a moment Slava could see how that was true. It would be easy, so easy, to stand by and let justice take its course. Vladislava was no one to her, no one but a little traitor. It would be so easy for Slava to stay here in this sanctuary and bear her own daughter in peace and quiet, the peace and quiet she had always longed for, and a year from now Vladislava would be nothing but rotting bones and a sad memory.

Slava could already see the happy outcome of Vladislava's death: Vladya would administer justice, thus putting the Severnolesniye in their place and restoring order to the realm, and no one would even mourn Vladislava's death more than was proper. Her fate was, as the gods and Vlastomila Serafimiyevna had said, her fate, and it was, without question, a dark one, but there was nothing Slava could do about that. Not even she could save someone who was destined for a dark fate, and it would be unnatural for her to try. It would be in the nature of things for Slava to sacrifice some other mother's child without a second thought, and even Vladislava's own mother had thrown her to the wolves long ago. No one would miss her too much, and as it was she was nothing but a nuisance. It would be so easy, and so right too. It would be what everyone would tell Slava was her duty.

For the first time Slava realized, truly realized, how heavy a burden her gifts had laid upon her. For far from the first time she felt she might be torn apart, as her desperate desire to save Vladislava, dark as she was, tore in one direction, and her desperate desire never to return to Krasnograd, never to look its dreadful people in the face again, never to be faced with all the pain that came from their own irremediable dreadfulness, tore in the other. It was as if wild horses were tearing off in opposite directions, with her heart tied to their tails. Whatever she did, she knew, her heart would not escape from this dreadful, dreadful, thrice-dreadful ordeal whole and unharmed. Her fate was her fate, and no one could save her from it.

"NO!" she screamed. "I won't! I'll never forget her! You can't replace one person with another! No one will ever replace her! If you try, I'll...I'll hate that child you demanded I have for the rest of my life! I'll make her a curse, like Lisochka! No, I'll...I'll end it now! It's still early—these things happen all the time! I won't have her! I'll sacrifice my own blood! My own blood! Anything for Vladislava!"

"You don't mean that," said the cold wind, but it sounded uncertain.

"Watch me," said Slava quietly. At that moment she knew, more surely than she had ever known anything, that she really would do anything for Vladislava, even if it meant sacrificing the child-to-be she had been told she was carrying around inside her, because no future child could ever, ever replace Vladislava, no, not ever. Not even all those happy dreams she had had of a daughter of her own, all that potential joy she had wanted, that she had been starving for. Nothing mattered now except Vladislava. Without Vladislava the rest would be a lie, would be like ashes and wormwood in her mouth.

Slava didn't know yet how she would save her, but she knew that she would, and that nothing could stand in her way. The easy path, the right path, was the wrong one, and she could never take it, no matter how much others might think that she should, or even how much she might want to herself. Even if everything in her was screaming at her

348

to take the easier course, even if she was begging herself to turn aside and give up, she could not. She was the one who had to stand in front, who had to take the hard path, because there was no one else who could or would, and no one could stop her, not even herself.

Something moved in the corner of her vision. Slava whipped around. A leshaya with golden eyes was standing there.

"The gods are cruel," it said. "Even when they mean to be kind, they often give their gifts in unwelcome packages, and things turn out other than as you'd hoped. Don't put your faith in them, Krasnoslava Tsarinovna. Put your faith in us instead."

There was more movement, lots of movement, so that it seemed as if the whole forest were uprooting itself and moving in protective ranks around Slava.

"What..." said Slava, and fell silent.

"The gods are cruel, Krasnoslava Tsarinovna," repeated the golden-eyed leshaya. "One shouldn't turn to them for help too often. We, their daughters, should turn to each other instead. You showed us that."

"I did?" said Slava, and then, thinking it would be unwise to show too much surprise at the leshiye's willingness to help her, asked quickly, "Are you the one...The one I...met before?"

"A sister, Krasnoslava Tsarinovna," said the golden-eyed leshaya. "One day you will learn to distinguish us from each other, just as you distinguish your human sisters by their faces."

"I see the difference now," said Slava, and it was true, she did: this leshaya was smaller and slenderer than the one she had encountered on the Severnovostochnaya road. It came up and laid a branch on Slava's shoulder, and all the forest seemed to draw up around them.

"You showed us," the leshaya repeated. "When we tried to take your gifts, and thought we had failed—we succeeded. It was just that your gifts came in an unwelcome package, and things turned out other than as we'd hoped. We saw the world as you do, Krasnoslava Tsarinovna, and we saw how weak and frail we all are—and how we must help each other. You helped us, Krasnoslava Tsarinovna, and so now we will help you. We will help you save this Vladislava you hold so dear."

"Thank you," said Slava. "You won't regret it, I promise you."

"As to that, I can't say," said the leshaya. "Vladislava has already started down a dark path, and it is very likely that an even darker path still lies before her. Her fate is her fate, and if we avert doom now, it will come to find us later. But we will help you help her nonetheless, as otherwise we are all doomed for a certainty."

"Thank you," said Slava again, rising to her feet despite the lesha-ya's heavy branch on her shoulder.

"It is the least we could do," said a huge wolf, stepping out from the gathered ranks of trees.

They threw me to the wolves, Slava thought to herself, and almost smiled. She gave a tiny wave to Gray Wolf, and he grinned his toothy grin back at her.

"Indeed," said an elk, stepping out and sniffing Slava's face with surprising delicacy for so enormous a creature.

"Indeed," said a bear. "You haven't saved any of my kin yet, Krasno-slava Tsarinovna, but I'm sure the day will come."

"As it already has for me," said a snow hare.

"And for me," said a snow fox.

"I..." said Slava, as animals continued to appear from between the trees. "I don't know what to..."

"I see our daughters have grown rebellious, as daughters so often do," said the cold wind, and laughed. "Much good may it do you! Well, daughters, if you must rush off to Krasnograd, then rush off—we won't stop you. And Krasnoslava—remember what you were told before. You would do well to consider the price of any help they offer you."

"It will still be lower than the price you demanded," said Slava.

"If that is what you think! We will be watching over you, Krasno-slava."

"Thank you," said Slava.

"For what? They have done nothing," demanded the golden-eyed leshaya.

"Thanking the gods is always wise," said the cold wind. "You have the look of your foremother, Krasnoslava Tsarinovna. Much good may it do you!" And then Slava could feel it disappear from the space around her, leaving nothing but an empty ringing in the air.

"Come, Krasnoslava Tsarinovna," said the golden-eyed leshaya. "We must set out for Krasnograd."

"The others!" said Slava. "We should see if the others want to come with us. Dima will want to come for sure."

"Then let us go, Krasnoslava Tsarinovna," said the golden-eyed leshaya, stepping back so that Slava could lead the way. The trees all stepped back to form a path for Slava to go down, their leaves making a rustling sound as they moved.

Dima, Dunya, Grisha, Sasha, Slanik, Olik, and Slava's mother were all standing on the sanctuary porch, staring anxiously into the moving forest.

"Slava!" cried her mother as soon as she appeared. "Slava, where have you been? What happened?"

"I asked for help," said Slava. "And it was given to me."

More people were appearing on the sanctuary porch. Sisters were running out from inside the building, and brothers from the nearby men's sanctuary were making their astonished way through groves of trees that had not been there the last time they had come this way.

"We're going to Krasnograd," Slava said, speaking mostly to Dima and Dunya. "To save Vladislava. And Olga, of course, too. Will you join me?"

Dima, Dunya, and the others all stepped forward without hesitation. "When do we leave, Tsarinovna?" asked Dima.

"As soon as you're ready," said the golden-eyed leshaya.

"We're ready now," said Dima, and the others all nodded.

"Good," said Slava. "Sisters!" she called out to the sanctuary porch. "Are there any brave women willing to send out messages?"

Zhenya pushed her way to the front of the ever-growing group of astonished sisters. "I will, Tsarinovna!" she cried. "Where do you bid me to go?"

"I need messages sent to Lesnograd and Princess Stepnaya," said Slava.

"I will go to Lesnograd," said Zhenya.

"And I to Princess Stepnaya," said Nadya, also stepping forward, much to Slava's surprise.

"It's a long way for one woman to travel," said Slava.

"I shall make it with all speed, Tsarinovna, have no fear," said Zhenya.

"Your message will be delivered, Tsarinovna, don't you worry," agreed Nadya. "I never did hold with killing children, even if it's the Empress herself who orders it. And I'm going that way anyway."

"Then tell whomever rules in Lesnograd that their heir has been imprisoned in Krasnograd and threatened with death, and that the Tsarinovna has gone to rescue her, but that they should send...whatever force they think best down to Krasnograd at all speed. Tell Princess Stepnaya or whomever rules in her stead that baseless accusations of treason have been leveled against her kinswoman Krasnoslava Tsarinovna, and that her life is in danger."

"Slava!" cried her mother in horror. "You know what the Severnolesniye and the steppe princesses will do..!"

"Yes," said Slava. "I do."

Someone else stepped forward to join their group, interrupting whatever her mother was about to say in response to that. Slava saw, with only slight surprise, that it was Valery Annovich.

"Take me with you too, please," he said, speaking to Dima. Slava could see that he was still much too ashamed to look at her, but that he desperately wanted to go back to Krasnograd and prove his worth, possibly even redeem himself somehow.

And, she thought, even if his reasons for coming with them were personal, he still represented two of the most important Krasna princesses. If she could get Malokrasnovskoye, Yuzhnokrasnovskoye, and the other Krasna princesses to support her, along with Severnolesnoye and the steppe princesses, Vladya would have no choice but to give way. If only she could be certain of their support, and that they would arrive in Krasnograd in time...little chance of that...so they must make all haste while they could. Dima glanced her way, asking what she thought of including Valery Annovich in their party, and she nodded her permission.

"Of course," said Dima. "Are you ready?"

"I am," said Valery Annovich.

"It seems we are all ready, then, Tsarinovna," said Dima.

"Let us be off, then," Slava told the golden-eyed leshaya.

"Slava!" cried her mother again from the porch. Slava looked up at her expectantly, hoping just for an instant that her mother really was about to save her from what she had to do, as she had hoped when they had set off from Krasnograd.

"Slava, you know that what you do—it could lead to war!"

"Only if Vladya is foolish," said Slava.

"Slava, be careful!"

"I make no promises," said Slava. She knew then that she had been foolish to hope for anything. Foolish and wrong. Her mother could not save her from what she had to do, because she, Slava, had to be the one to stand in front and be brave. "This is not a moment for caution," she said. "This is a moment for courage."

"Oh Slava!" For a moment Slava thought her mother might start to cry, but instead she smiled and said, "So much like your father, Slava. He was always so headstrong too. Headstrong and foolhardy."

"Sometimes you have to be headstrong and foolhardy to do what must be done," said Slava. "Sometimes there is no choice. Sometimes someone has to be the one to stand in front and do what no one else will do, even if that is the foolish thing to do. I wish I could be wise and sensible, but I cannot. Not and save Vladislava. So I must be headstrong and foolhardy, because I have nothing left. Sometimes one has to be headstrong and foolhardy to be a hero, and it seems I cannot evade my fate. It seems I must be a hero, whether I will it or no, and so I must be headstrong and foolhardy in the bargain."

"Then...Remember, Slava: Vladya is your own blood sister. Your only blood sister. Those others—they are just Severnolesniye."

"Yes," said Slava. "Women who took me in and cared for me and protected me. Unlike my own family. My own blood sister. My only blood sister. I cannot let her kill them."

"Slava!" cried her mother. "Have mercy on her!"

"When am I not merciful?" said Slava sadly. "If only Vladya had thought to have mercy on me. If only all of you had thought to have mercy on me. But no more. I will wield a sharper kind of mercy now. And so...before I go. I forgive you."

"Forgive me?" Her mother's face twisted. "Forgive me for what?"

"For what you had done to me. I didn't think I could—but I forgive you."

"Slava...Slava, I..." her mother's face was still twisted up, and Slava knew it was the grimace of denial, not remorse, that distorted it.

"Stop." She held up her hand. "Even if you were to apologize, which you will not, there is nothing to be done. At least not by you. I can forgive you, but you can never take it back. So I will forgive you, as that is the only thing that either of us can do. Now let us be off."

The golden-eyed leshaya swept her up in its branches, and they set off. Her mother stared after them, her hand at her throat, her mouth opening and closing as if she were crying, or screaming, but could force no sound out. Slava wished...she wished her mother had never put them in this position, but as she herself had said, the past could not be undone, no matter how much both of them might wish it. The way only was forward, with Slava at the front.

Slava had expected their progress to be slow, but within moments they were out of sight of the sanctuary. She tried to look back and find the others, but the golden-eyed leshaya held her tightly, and it was impossible to see back through its fir boughs.

"The others are behind us, never fear, Krasnoslava Tsarinovna," the golden-eyed leshaya told her. "The wolf, in his arrogance, has felt a great bond with them and has taken charge of their safety. Do not concern yourself about them. Concern yourself with what lies ahead."

After one last futile look back, Slava decided to follow the leshaya's advice, at least as far as not concerning herself over the others, who were out of her power to help now anyway. But when she tried to think about what lay ahead, she could see nothing but darkness. She leaned back against the leshaya's trunk and tried not to be sick instead. Apparently even the leshaya could not save her from morning sickness.

Whether they traveled for a long time or a short time she couldn't say, but when the leshaya stopped later in the day to let Slava rest for a moment, she recognized the place they had stopped two days before their arrival at the sanctuary. Slava looked back, and saw that the woods seemed rather thicker this time than when they had been there before. Dunya came up to her from out of a particularly thick grove.

"The leshiye and the animals have been trading us off," she told Slava. "How are you? Are you well?"

"Yes," Slava assured her. "And the others?"

"All well. Hungry, but well."

"We'll need to procure some food soon," said Slava, struck by this new difficulty.

"We will stop later outside some village, Krasnoslava Tsarinovna," said the golden-eyed leshaya. "You can send someone for provisions. But you will not need much, as we will be in Krasnograd by tomorrow afternoon."

"Tomorrow afternoon!" cried Slava, who, despite having seen the evidence of their speedy passage, had still not grasped the pace at which they traveled. "How so quickly?"

"We leshiye are not so closely bound to the earth as you women," the golden-eyed leshaya told her. "The same magic that lifted our roots from the soil allows us to skim over it more lightly than those of you who are so tightly tied to the clay from which you are made."

"Oh," said Slava, seeing that she would have to content herself with that explanation. The golden-eyed leshaya stretched out its branches for her, and she climbed back into them and tried to settle herself as comfortably as possible.

The rest of the day passed in another blur, which Slava supposed was only natural, as they were traveling faster than a galloping horse. They did, as the golden-eyed leshaya had promised, stop outside of a village so that Sasha and Olik could go ask for food for them, but then as soon as they had returned, the leshaya swept Slava up in her branches again, and after that they left the road entirely, and spent the night racing through dark forests, where, Slava was sure, she was the first human to pass that way in many a month.

Sunrise found them approaching another village, where once again they stopped and sent Sasha and Olik for food, and then they set off again at their madlong rush. Slava leaned against the leshaya's rough trunk, and let her thoughts stream past her just as the scenery was doing. She was vaguely aware of the others behind her, although she couldn't tell if she were truly seeing and hearing them, or if it were all in the vision of her mind's eye.

It seemed to her that Dunya was lost in silent conversation with the elk, who was so clearly a sister to her, and that Dima and Valery Annovich spent many hours in serious conversation, but perhaps she only dreamed all of that, just as she had dreamed away so much of her life. And now she had dreamed herself to where she was now. She thought of all the plans she had made, ever since she had decided to leave Krasnograd, and all the dreams she had had of a better future once she returned from the Midnight Land, and how it seemed that they had all been in vain and how none of her happy fancies and grand plans would come to be, because the future was just as dark and mysterious as it had been a year ago. Slava nestled herself more deeply into the golden-eyed leshaya's branches, and went back to dreaming.

Sometime around noon they came to an abrupt halt.

"We are within a couple of versts of Krasnograd, Krasnoslava Tsarinovna," announced the golden-eyed leshaya. "What is your plan?"

"My plan?" repeated Slava dazedly.

"Shall we storm the city by force, Krasnoslava Tsarinovna?"

"Would it work?" asked Slava doubtfully.

"The city would be torn apart, brick from brick and stone from stone," the golden-eyed leshaya assured her.

"That seems a little drastic for an opening tactic," said Slava. "Perhaps I should try to reason with Vladya first."

"Will that work, Krasnoslava Tsarinovna?" asked the golden-eyed leshaya doubtfully.

"Most likely not, but I would feel bad if I tore the city apart brick from brick and stone from stone without first at least trying it," said Slava. "I wouldn't want to give into my baser impulses at the first provocation. Will you...Will you come in with me?" she asked hesitantly. She realized it was silly, after accepting the leshaya's help to storm her own city, but she felt embarrassed to inconvenience it any further than necessary.

"Its walls will not be congenial to me, Krasnoslava Tsarinovna," said the golden-eyed leshaya. "You will have to be brave for me."

"Then I will," said Slava.

"Then let us set off," said the golden-eyed leshaya. "Those who do not enter the city can wait within sight of the city, so that your sister will know we are not bluffing. We can call for them if necessary, and they will be at our side in moments."

They moved at little more than walking pace until Krasnograd rose up before them, when they came to a halt again.

"We should enter the city in numbers," said the golden-eyed leshaya. "A few of my sisters should join us, and so should Gray Wolf and Elk and Bear."

"And me!" said the snow fox, trotting forward boldly from amongst the tree trunks.

"And me!" cried Dima, coming forward.

"And me," said the snow hare quietly, loping over to stare up at Slava meaningfully.

"Yes," said Slava. "Here: jump into my arms." She stretched out her arms, and the snow hare bounded into them. He was even warmer and heavier than she had expected, and she could feel his heart racing in his chest.

"Don't be afraid," she whispered to him.

"I'm not afraid, Krasnoslava Tsarinovna," he whispered back. "I am here to give you courage, just as my brother did before."

"What would I do without you?" asked Slava, holding him to her closely.

"Not much, Krasnoslava Tsarinovna," he told her. "Now, enough of this sentimental rambling! Let us be off!"

"Wisely spoken, snow hare," agreed the golden-eyed leshaya, and they set off again. The smallness of their group, Slava noted, did nothing to diminish its strangeness; in fact, each member of it seemed much stranger, with so much more empty space around it and so many fewer similar companions. Even Dima looked strange, striding between Gray Wolf and Bear, although Slava couldn't put her finger on why. Perhaps it was because, for the first time since she had met him, his face was grim and sad.

They came to outer Krasnograd and started down its streets. Screams rose up from all around them, and Slava could sense, even half-hidden as she was in the leshaya's branches, movement on all the streets as people ran for cover, or ran to inform the Empress of what was invading her city. But no one attempted to stop them.

The gates were still closed when they arrived at the city walls, and there were no guards on the outside to open them or hold them against their assault. The golden-eyed leshaya banged on the gate with her branches, and when that failed to summon anyone, called forward an oak-leshaya with long bare arm-like limbs, who reached out and ripped through the gates with one motion. Suddenly Slava began to believe, as she had not truly believed before, that they were indeed capable of tearing the city apart, brick from brick and stone from stone.

A knot of frightened soldiers was waiting for them on the other side, swords drawn, and the sound of boots running towards them could be heard, signaling the arrival of reinforcements.

"Do not attack!" cried Slava, pulling aside the leshaya's boughs in order to be seen more clearly. "We come in peace!"

The soldiers all gave her a look that suggested that, in their experience, people who tore through city gates as if through paper did not normally come in peace.

"I am here to speak with my sister!" Slava continued. "The Tsarina! I am the Tsarinovna, and I must speak with her most urgently!"

This did not appear to comfort the soldiers in any way. The only good it did was to make them take a hesitant step back. It was apparent that none of them wanted to be the one to strike down the Tsarinovna, no matter what orders the Tsarina might have given to that effect.

The running boots came around the corner and proved themselves to be Boleslav Vlasiyevich and about fifty guards.

"Tsarinovna!" he cried, sliding to a stop on the damp cobblestones. "What are you doing here?!?" Some strong emotion worked across his face; if it had not been so unlikely, Slava would have said it was joy and pride, comingled with fear and horror. The latter she was perfectly willing to believe, while the former, she told herself, was merely the result of her overactive imagination, showing her what she wished to see.

"I come in peace, Boleslav Vlasiyevich," Slava repeated. "But I must speak with my sister. I have heard of her intentions regarding Olga Vasilisovna and my ward."

"And you, what, came to trade yourself for them?" demanded Boleslav Vlasiyevich. Now the horror was unmistakable.

"No," said Slava. Gray Wolf raised his hackles and showed his teeth. Slava was fairly sure that several of the soldiers whimpered.

"If they are set free, then no one will come to any harm," said Slava.

"I can see how peaceful your plans are, Tsarinovna." said Boleslav Vlasiyevich. "Why did you not stay with your mother! I thought you were headed there, I thought you would be safe there, I thought…"

"I know what you thought, Boleslav Vlasiyevich," Slava told him, before he could finish his sentence. "You thought I had no intention of harming the Tsarina. And you were not wrong. But this threat to Olga Vasilisovna and Vladislava Vasilisovna changes everything. Deliver them safe and sound into my hands, allow us to walk free out of Krasnograd, and I swear to you, you need never concern yourself about me again. I will retire to the most distant sanctuary in Zem', and spend the rest of my days there, praying and tending my herb garden. Simply give me Olga and Vladislava, and all your problems will be solved." Once again disquiet twinged through Slava at that thought, but she quelled it and did her best to look like someone whose greatest desire was to retire to a distant sanctuary and tend to her herb garden.

"Well…" said Boleslav Vlasiyevich. Several of the soldiers unwisely chose that moment to raise their swords in what Gray Wolf interpreted as a threatening manner. He growled at them again, and they quickly lowered their weapons with shaking hands.

"How do I know your intentions are what you claim them to be?" Boleslav Vlasiyevich demanded, giving Gray Wolf a wary and unhappy glance. "How do I know this will not end in…in…" He could not seem to put words to the dire images in his head.

"I will enter my sister's chambers with no more protection than these two companions," said Slava, holding up the snow hare and nodding at the snow fox. "Surely you cannot suspect *them* of deadly danger."

Oh, you would be surprised, said the snow fox in Slava's head. *Especially when others make decisions for us without consulting us first.*

Oh, be quiet: you know you want to go, Slava said back to her.

True, so true, agreed the snow fox with a grin. *I've never seen a Tsarina before. I hope she's much grander than you are.*

You'll find out soon enough, Slava told her, and turned her attention back to Boleslav Vlasiyevich.

"Well…" he said, fidgeting a little and then stopping himself, aware that the eyes of all his men were upon him. Once again there was a very strange expression on his face, one that Slava could not read and that was not what she would have expected to see on him.

"Let me down, please," Slava said to the golden-eyed leshaya. It released her, and she slid to the ground. "Boleslav Vlasiyevich," she said, stepping closer to him. "You trusted me before; trust me again! I mean no one any harm, I swear it, I swear it by anything you will have me swear it by, but I cannot stand by while Olga Vasilisovna and Vladislava Vasilisovna are in danger! And surely you cannot stand by either, when the life of an innocent child is under threat! If you do not let me save Vladislava Vasilisovna, and she comes to any harm, then her blood will be on your hands!"

"Well…" said Boleslav Vlasiyevich, and then, clearing his throat, said more firmly, "You may go, Tsarinovna, but only on the condition that I and my most trusted men accompany you."

"We will accompany Krasnoslava Tsarinovna to the palace walls," said the golden-eyed leshaya.

Boleslav Vlasiyevich opened his mouth to argue, but before he could say anything, the golden-eyed leshaya told him, speaking surprisingly kindly, "We will reach the palace walls whether you wish us to or not. Better to let us make our way there peacefully rather than by force. You have nothing to fear from us, as long as Krasnoslava Tsarinovna is safe."

"Please, Boleslav Vlasiyevich," said Slava. She looked into his indecisive eyes and tried to pour all of her need, all of her conviction, into him. "Please help me. I cannot stand idly by while the life of a little child is in danger. Please help me."

"Very well," said Boleslav Vlasiyevich, swallowing heavily. He looked closely into her face, as if trying to discern what her plans were, and added, "Your 'companions' will need to stay under guard on the main square, if you wish to gain her trust. And I make no promises that the Tsarina will see you—or that she will listen to you if she does. But I will do what I can for you, Tsarinovna."

"Thank you, Boleslav Vlasiyevich," said Slava. "Let us be off, then."

They started walking down the street. Boleslav Vlasiyevich walked in silent uncertainty next to Slava, who clutched the snow hare to her chest like a shield. The feel of his soft fur against her chin and soft little body in her arms made her feel, rightly or wrongly, as if she were capable of protecting others, since she was protecting him. The snow fox trotted at her heels, looking around and grinning at everything that caught her eye. The golden-eyed leshaya and Gray Wolf stalked right behind them, followed by the others of Slava's party, and surrounded by Boleslav Vlasiyevich's men, who were so terrified Slava thought she could hear their ragged breath and racing heartbeats over the sound of their heavy boots.

People came out of their homes to see them, but immediately screamed and ran back in. News of their arrival made its way ahead of them, so that by the time they had taken the second turn, the streets had cleared of all but the occasional foolhardy urchin, hoping to catch a glimpse of the monsters and traitors, and having no mother handy to forbid it.

They walked in silence, except for the running commentary that the snow fox and Gray Wolf kept up in Slava's head about everything they encountered and how tasty the street urchins looked, until finally the snow hare told them to be quiet and stop fooling around and bothering Krasnoslava Tsarinovna. They both fell into a mock offended silence, and the rest of the journey was completed to the sound of nothing but their footsteps and the cries of those they encountered.

They had to stop and wait for a while at the kremlin gates, while Boleslav Vlasiyevich spoke with the guards inside and arranged for word to be sent to the Empress and for a guard to be set over those who would remain outside while Slava was with her sister. Then they had to wait a while longer until Slava's sister sent word that she would speak with her. The longer they waited, the more Slava could feel her courage and her certainty ebbing out of her, and the more rash and improbable this ill-thought venture seemed. When word came that Slava's sister would deign to speak with her, but only if she, Slava, came to her alone, Slava had to fight off a wave of dread, and remind herself that she had volunteered for this, she had insisted that the others come along, and that this was what she must do, there was no backing out of it now.

"When should we expect you back, Tsarinovna?" asked Dima, once they had been told that the Empress was waiting for Slava in the palace.

"I don't know," said Slava. "Who knows how long this will take."

"Well, how long should we wait before coming in to rescue you, then, Tsarinovna?" asked Dima.

"If I am not out by dusk, I suppose you should come looking for me," said Slava.

"My fox-sister will keep me informed of all that takes place around her," said Gray Wolf.

"And my hare-brother will do the same for me," said the elk. "So we will know what happens to them, and also to Krasnoslava Tsarinovna, as long as she is with them."

Slava couldn't pretend that she didn't feel heartily relieved at that information. Bravely as she had set off on this mission, she had rather less faith than she would have liked in Vladya's good will and her own chances of getting herself, Olga, and Vladislava out of there alive. But as soon as she thought that, she knew that she *would* get them out alive, no matter what it took.

Boleslav Vlasiyevich and what seemed a very large number of soldiers, but was probably no more than a dozen, surrounded Slava and her two guardians, and they started towards the doors. Slava started to think about how this was the most important walk she had ever made in her life, that her own life and the lives of all her companions and those under her protection depended on what she was about to do... The snow hare squirmed in her arms, and she reminded herself not to think those thoughts. She pressed her cheeks against the snow hare's soft, soft fur, and thought only about that.

Even Boleslav Vlasiyevich's puzzled and unhappy gaze failed to draw her out of her concentration, although some part of her supposed that she was making a very strange picture for someone who had fled under a cloud of treason and then returned threatening to tear the city apart brick from brick and stone from stone...probably such people should not snuggle their cheeks against snow hares. Slava did not pull herself away, however.

More guards greeted them, or rather, lined the corridors looking stern and nervous, once they were inside the palace itself.

People live here? the snow fox asked incredulously. *It's so stuffy!*

Aren't your holes? Slava asked in reply.

Too true, agreed the snow fox, and grinned at the soldiers. The snow hare burrowed his head under Slava's arm, and refused to look out. All of a sudden, Slava's courage returned tenfold.

Slava had expected to be led to the Hall of Council, or perhaps the Hall of Justice, or possibly to her sister's private chambers, but instead she found herself being led to Imperial guest chambers. They encountered no one on their way, and she assumed that everyone had been cleared out and been given strict orders to stay away.

They were brought to an ostentatiously furnished but unpleasantly unwelcoming guest chamber. There was a lengthy arrangement of the guards, during which the snow fox became bored and began wandering around the room, frightening all the men.

"Sit, Tsarinovna, sit down and the Tsarina will be here shortly," Boleslav Vlasiyevich told her, once all his men had been arranged to his liking. "She is resting in her chambers in anticipation of your arrival."

They only want you to sit so that you'll have to stand when your sister comes in, the snow fox told her. *They want you to feel smaller than her.*

Yes, I know, Slava answered back. "Thank you, but I prefer to stand by this fire," she said out loud.

This caused some consternation amongst the guards which confirmed the snow fox's supposition, but once it became clear that Slava had no intention of sitting, Boleslav Vlasiyevich told his men rather sharply that the Tsarinovna knew her own mind, and if she wished to stand by the fire, she would stand by the fire, and he took up a position near her. Slava couldn't tell if he were guarding the others from her, or her from the others, and she thought that perhaps he didn't know himself. One of the guards was sent to inform the Empress that Slava had arrived, and, after some more running back and forth and worried whispered consultations, Slava heard the unmistakable sounds of her sister's footsteps, and then her sister came in through a side door.

Slava's first thought was that her sister's entrance through the side door meant that she had not been resting in her chambers at all, but waiting in the maid's quarters next door, which meant that this whole thing had been staged in order to make Slava wait as long as possible. Slava suppressed both the smile and the sigh that this thought caused, and turned to greet her sister.

"What do you want!" her sister shrieked as soon as she had swept into the room. Her high, harried voice formed a shocking contrast with the arrogant glide of her walk, and Slava saw that, despite her high head, she was so close to hysteria she was almost trembling.

"To negotiate," Slava told her, seeing that there was no point in wasting time on pleasantries. "Give me Olga and Vladislava, and I will leave in peace and never return. I will renounce my title and retire to a sanctuary. You will never need concern yourself over me again."

As she said it, Slava felt an uneasy sense of wrong, and the thought arose in her mind, ten times stronger than any disquiet she had previously felt on entertaining such plans, that she would not be allowed to carry out her intention, or if she were successful, it would be a mistake. She knew, as she had known back at Deep Pond, that retiring to a sanctuary, alas, was not the path she was meant to take, no matter how sensible and attractive it seemed on the surface. But perhaps she was wrong, she told herself, and in any case, she had little else she could offer her sister in exchange for Olga and Vladislava.

"Why are you carrying that stupid rabbit around?" her sister demanded. "This is hardly the time for pets!"

"He is here as a witness," Slava told her. "For my allies. Vladya! This need not be difficult! I have no desire for a quarrel! Please, release Olga and Vladislava, and we will be on our way!"

"And what is that stupid fox doing?" her sister continued, as if Slava had never spoken.

"Also a witness," Slava said. "Vladya! Please! What quarrel do you have with Olga and Vladislava? They have never done anything to you, and Vladislava is only a little child! Set them free, and it shall be as if none of this had ever happened!"

"You're so sure I took them prisoner! You're so sure I would do that!"

"Everyone said…Vladya! Is it a lie? Have they maligned you? Oh, Vladya! Please tell me it is a lie!"

"Of course I took them prisoner! I had them caught at the gate and brought here! Of course I did! They were plotting against me! Of course I had to!"

"Oh Vladya! They mean you no harm! None of us mean you any harm!"

"No no no," said Slava's sister, staring off at the wall and wringing her hands. "No no no, what are you doing here? No no no! You shouldn't be here! You're plotting against me! Plotting against me! Ever since…you've always been plotting against me! This is just another plot!"

"Vladya!" cried Slava. "This is not a plot! Vladya! Do you remember your dream?"

"My dream?" repeated Vladya, puzzled.

"Of the water," Slava clarified.

"Oh…" said Vladya, and something like a real person looked through her eyes for a moment.

"Do you remember, Vladya? You were afraid of being washed away! Well, you are being washed away! Vladya! It is the curse! All of these thoughts, all of these fears of plots and treason—it's all nothing but the curse! Vladya! These are not your thoughts! They are the curse, Vladya, nothing but the curse! Don't let it wash you away! Hold onto me, Vladya, hold onto me and don't let them take you!"

"Why do you always have to be so emotional!" shrieked Vladya. "Look at you! You're crying! It's disgusting!"

"Of course I'm crying," said Slava, hugging the snow hare to her even more tightly. The snow fox came and wrapped her bushy tail around Slava's ankles. "Vladya! Please, please, please see sense! Free Olga and Vladislava, and let us all walk out of here! Don't do this terrible thing you are thinking of doing!"

But as soon as Slava said that, she saw it was a mistake, for Vladya's face twisted into an even more hateful expression than it had worn before, and she screamed, "Why are you always the good one! Why do you have to be the good one! Why do you have to be the good one!"

"Oh Vladya!" cried Slava. "I don't have to! Let us all go, and you will be the good one! All you have to do is let us go, and you will have done a wonderful deed, a kind and merciful act..."

"No!" Vladya interrupted her. "No! I don't have to do anything you tell me to!"

This stopped Slava short, and for a moment there was silence as she tried to regroup and think of what to say next.

"Oh Vladya," she said eventually. "Of course we are both free to do as we choose here, but let us not quarrel, let us resolve our differences and be sisters again! You are the only sister I have, Vladya; let us not quarrel. Think of the suffering it causes our mother..."

"Hah!" said Vladya. "She only cares for you!"

"No, Vladya, no, she cares for you, she said so herself just now..."

"You went to see her!" cried Vladya.

"Yes of course, Vladya, I went straight to her from Krasnograd, and she begged me to stay with her in the sanctuary and leave you in peace, and I would have, Vladya, I would have, but then the news of Olga and Vladislava came..."

"You went to her!" Vladya shrieked. "And you asked her for help, I suppose? Help against me?"

"Of course I asked her for help, Vladya; that is why I went there. And the help she offered me was shelter in her sanctuary. She would not turn against you for anything, Vladya, not even for me."

"She wouldn't help you?" said Vladya, and for a moment her face glowed with gladness.

"She offered me shelter in her sanctuary," Slava repeated. "But she would not move against you for any reason. Oh Vladya! We all know you are the one who was meant to rule! No one argues with that. Just let Olga and Vladislava go, Vladya, let them go! Let them go, and go back to your rule. Your country needs your judgment, Vladya. You have more important matters to attend to than a small child and the younger daughter of a Northern barbarian."

Once again, unease twinged in Slava's stomach when she offered to leave Vladya to her rule, but she told herself she must ignore it, no matter what. There was more at stake here than her own fancies, she told herself, and if saving Olga and Vladislava meant sacrificing the voices in her head, then so be it. There were worse sacrifices to make. The voices screamed out in protest, but Slava ignored them.

"You may be right..." Vladya was saying slowly. Sensing that she was about to decide something, and that any interruption would be dangerous, Slava waited, hardly daring to breathe, and willed with every ounce of strength she possessed that Vladya would decide to let them all go, so that she could return to the sanctuary and never come back to Krasnograd again. Something inside her screamed twice as loudly than before in protest at that thought, but she clamped down on it as hard as she could, and went back to willing Vladya to accept her offer.

"You're trying to control me!" Vladya cried suddenly.

"What!" Slava said, before she could stop herself. "How could I possibly do that?" She managed to close her mouth before adding *don't be ridiculous*, but she must not have closed her face fast enough, for Vladya's own face twisted back into its earlier expression of hate.

"You are!" she insisted. "You're using your gifts on me, just like you always do!"

"My gifts give me no ability to control others," Slava said.

"You're lying! You're lying, just like you always have! You've always lied about your gifts in order to, to use them behind other people's backs! You're a liar and you always have been!"

Both the snow hare and the snow fox turned angry, hate-filled gazes at Vladya. Even the snow hare had forgotten his fear in the face of her shrieking rage, and was filled with an answering anger. Slava wanted to tell them to stop looking at her that way, it would only make things worse, but before she could summon up the concentration to do so, Vladya broke the silence by bursting out, "Come with me!"

"Where?" asked Slava.

"To see your friends! Come! Come see your friends!"

For an instant Slava was filled with the hope that Vladya intended to free Olga and Vladislava immediately, but one glance at her twisted face, her hunched shoulders, and her shaking hands, told Slava that her hope was in vain. Following her to wherever she was holding them was probably, the pit of Slava's stomach told her, a bad idea, but refusing was probably an even worse one. The snow hare and the snow fox gave her questioning glances. She nodded at them, and after a moment, they both blinked their eyes in agreement.

"So you take advice from animals now?" Vladya asked. She tried to say it sarcastically, to assert her superiority over Slava, but it came out as more of a hysterical shriek.

"Sometimes," said Slava. "Sometimes they have good advice."

"You think you're so smart!" said Vladya. "Come! I'll show you how smart you are!"

She set off at an angry and erratic walk. There was a fair amount of confusion behind her, as Boleslav Vlasiyevich and his men tried to organize themselves quickly around Vladya and Slava, but Vladya didn't seem to notice it at all, so intent was she on showing Slava how smart she, Vladya, was.

Slava had, foolishly and naively, imagined that Olga and Vladislava were being kept in some guest apartment, perhaps the one down the corridor from where Vladya had received her. They would have been under guard, of course, but they would have been kept in a manner befitting their status as noblewomen from one of the greatest families in Zem'. But Vladya led her right past all the guest apartments and down some stairs and along a corridor and down some more stairs and along another corridor and down some more stairs, and Slava realized they were going to the kremlin's dungeon.

Chapter Twenty

"**Y**ou put them in the *dungeon*?" she blurted out before she could stop herself.

"Where else should traitors be kept?" Vladya demanded angrily. "You're so smart: you should be able to see that, surely!"

As there was nothing sensible that could be said in response to that, Slava said nothing. They walked down another corridor in silence, or in as much silence as could be made in such a large party as theirs. In fact, the sound of the guards' boots was loud enough to drown out most speech, anyway. Slava wondered what they thought of this: just a few days ago they had been guards to the most powerful person in the Known World, and now they were guards to a person with all the inner stability of a child who had just learned to walk, but with rather less charm. Slava also wondered what they thought of her. It occurred to her that she might need their support if she was unable to make Vladya see reason—which now seemed an almost hopeless task—and she wondered if she had any chance of gaining it. It seemed so terribly unlikely...Everyone always supported Vladya...something flitted past the corner of her eye.

"What are you looking at!" demanded Vladya.

"I thought I saw something...Someone went down the other corridor," said Slava.

"Some maid," said Vladya. "You always see things that aren't there!"

"I also see things that are there," said Slava. She immediately regretted her words, but Vladya had no time to do anything more than angrily toss her head, and then they were at the door to the underground corridors that led to the dungeons.

When they came to the dungeon doors, Vladya ordered that half the guards remain behind to do their duty and stand guard. There was an unpleasant scene when she tried to demand that the snow hare and the snow fox stay behind as well, but Slava, urged on by their voiceless voices, adamantly refused to agree to that, and Vladya was too eager to bring her into the dungeon and show her Olga and Vladislava to quarrel over it for long, so after a few nasty remarks and ill-tempered glares, she appeared to forget about the matter in the excitement of watching Boleslav Vlasiyevich open the doors for her.

Having won the argument over her companions, Slava tried to stand in the background and remain as unseen as possible as Boleslav Vlasiyevich fiddled with the keys with unusual clumsiness, as if staying unnoticed would save her from whatever trap she was about to fall into. Something was telling her that something terrible was about to happen, and that she would not walk out of those dungeons a free woman.

She tried to convince herself that it was no more than what anyone would feel, standing at those doors, but she feared that that was not true. Going into there was an irrevocable step, and something that was even worse than what she was envisioning was waiting for her at the other end of it. For a moment Slava considered begging off this whole enterprise, or even just turning and trying to run away, but her stomach twisted at those thoughts, and she knew that she had to go through with it, no matter what the consequences that awaited her were. Boleslav Vlasiyevich and one of the other guards pulled open the doors at last. They all stepped through, with Slava in the middle of the group, making any thought of escape impossible. She glanced back, and it seemed to her that a small shadow flitted in with them, behind the last guard's boots.

After spending her entire life trying to forget that the dungeons even existed, Slava supposed it was fitting that she was being dragged down there now. When she did think of them, she envisioned something dark, dank, and horrid, fell into despair over her inability to get rid of them or even free the poor souls held inside them, and ended up by resolving to forget that they existed, because she could as soon destroy them as she could destroy Krasnograd itself. Krasnograd was built on cruelty and killing, as much as she and everyone else would like to ignore that fact. Only now, she thought, she was finally being forced to confront their existence. She hoped she would not be forced to regret a lifetime of weakness in the face of evil. She hoped that the dungeons were not as bad as she had always imagined.

Her imagination, she realized as soon as she entered, had, as was all too often the case, not let her down. The dungeons were just as dark, dank, and horrid in reality as they had been in her mind's eye. And they smelled even worse, too. Slava thought of Vladislava being kept here for days and days, helplessly awaiting her fate, and a rage swelled up inside her so strong she didn't know how she managed to contain it. A lifetime of weakness, she knew, was about to end.

Wait a little more, Krasnoslava Tsarinovna, the snow hare whispered in her mind. *Wait until the moment is right.*

The snow hare is right, Krasnoslava Tsarinovna, agreed the snow fox. *Wait until your prey is truly in your power before striking. Wait just a little bit longer.*

Something flitted past the corner of her eye again, but when she turned her head, it was gone, even though there was nowhere for it to go.

Pay it no mind, Krasnoslava Tsarinovna, said the snow hare, and so Slava made herself look forward again and move along with the others.

They walked down a long narrow corridor with cell doors every few feet. Some of the cell doors held people behind them, Slava could tell. Some part of her was overwhelmed by the horror and misery of so many people in such horrible and miserable conditions, but that part was carried along by her determination to rescue Vladislava, and she walked past all the doors without even a second glance.

"I'm *bored,*" a childish voice said from behind the last door on the left. "And I'm *hungry*. But mostly I'm *bored.*"

"Thank the gods you have nothing worse to complain of," said Olga's voice, from behind the same door.

"We've been here for *days,*" said Vladislava. "When do you think they'll let us out?"

"Not soon, I hope," said Olga grimly, and Slava could tell that Olga was sure that they would only be let out in order to be led to their execution, and even though at this point she might have welcomed that for herself, as something that would at least break up the tedium, she couldn't bear to think of that for Vladislava, and was praying with all her might that they be left in their little cell for years, if that was what it took to keep Vladislava alive.

"Slava will come to save us," said Vladislava confidently.

"No!" said Olga. "She has to stay away, Vladenka, she has to! And she will, if she has any sense."

"She'll come save us," repeated Vladislava. "She's a saver. She won't be able to help herself. She'll come for us, and she'll figure out a way to get us all out of here."

"Vladislava!" cried Slava, pushing ahead of the others. She sensed Vladya make a move as if to grab her and pull her back, and Boleslav Vlasiyevich also make a move as if he were trying to catch her, but really he was keeping Vladya from stopping her. "Olga!" she shouted. "Olga! Vladislava! Are you all right!"

"What are you doing here!" cried Olga, running up and putting her face against the tiny barred window in the cell door, just as Slava came running up to it from the other side. "What are you doing here!"

"I came for you!" Slava told her. "You and Vladislava! I came as soon as I heard! Are you all right?"

"Fine," said Olga. Slava could see that it was not true: her face was badly bruised, and when she spoke, her mouth revealed missing teeth. Suddenly the cold damp of the dungeon seemed too hot for Slava. The snow fox growled a little, and the snow hare jumped down from Slava's arms and looked back towards Vladya and the guards in a way that made the cleverer of them take a step back in fear. Vladya was not, alas, among that number.

"Why did you come back?" Olga demanded angrily. "Why didn't you just stay away?"

"And leave you to...to your fate?" Slava said. "Never! Under no circumstances!"

"You shouldn't have come back," said Olga. She looked much more tired and defeated that Slava had ever seen her. She supposed that being beaten up, dragged into a dungeon, and sentenced to death would do that to a person.

"Boleslav Vlasiyevich!" said Vladya sharply. "Open the cell door! Prepare to bring out the prisoners!"

Boleslav Vlasiyevich bowed silently and unlocked the cell door with a key on his belt.

"Bring them out!" ordered Vladya. "Let my sister see the results of her treason!"

Slava stepped back to allow Boleslav Vlasiyevich to pull open the cell door and usher Olga and Vladislava out. He gave her a brief, private look as he did so. She couldn't tell whether it was supposed to be pleading or warning. Both, perhaps.

"Slava!" cried Vladislava, as soon as the door was open. She rushed out and threw herself into Slava's arms. "You came back for us! I knew you would! I knew you would, Slava, I knew it, I knew it, I knew it!"

"I see even this *child* recognizes your capacity for foolishness," said Vladya, giving Vladislava a poisonous look.

"What now?" demanded Olga. "I don't suppose you're letting us go out of the goodness of your heart?"

"WHY DOES EVERYONE WANT ME TO BE MERCIFUL!" screamed Vladya, in the voice of a woman rebelling against the cruelties of fate. Slava, her heart squeezing painfully at the thought, recognized it as the same voice she had used to cry out to the gods to save Vladislava. "WHY DOES EVERYONE TRY TO TELL ME WHAT TO DO?!!"

"No one would dare tell you what to do, Tsarina," said Boleslav Vlasiyevich, with a quickness of wit Slava would not have suspected in him. She supposed he had had to develop it, in order to stay alive. "Everyone stands in awe of your power, and therefore they beg for mercy, as befits such humble subjects."

"Yes," said Olga, with a pitiful attempt at humility that, Slava could see, was brought entirely about by her desperate desire to save Vladislava. "We beg for mercy, O gracious Tsarina."

"You do?" asked Vladya, her eyes shining greedily.

"Oh yes," said Olga, her voice so flat and false that Slava was sure Vladya would call her out on her falsehood in an instant, but instead, Vladya's eyes only shown even more greedily.

"How will you prove it?" she asked.

"How do you want me to prove it—O gracious Tsarina?" said Olga. She was staring off into the darkness of the dungeon corridor, and Slava could see that her thoughts were somewhere else entirely, somewhere where there was a chance, no matter how remote, of saving Vladislava.

"Kneel!" said Vladya.

Olga got down, slowly and gracelessly, onto her knees, still staring off into the darkness. She had her right arm clutched against her chest as if in pain, just as she always did when she was afraid, and Slava knew that she was thinking, even if she didn't know it, of that terrible day when she had tried to save herself and failed, and broken only her arm. Vladislava tried to pull away from Slava and stop her, but Slava held her tightly and wouldn't let her go. The scene was so strange and horrifying that even Vladislava was cowed, and gave in to Slava's embrace with only the briefest of struggles.

"Now beg!" commanded Vladya. "Beg for mercy!"

Something flitted behind the guards' boots, and then faded back into the shadows. No one other than Slava seemed to have noticed it.

"I beg for mercy, O gracious Tsarina," said Olga, in the same strange flat voice. She rubbed her arm and flexed her fingers in remembered pain. "Mercy for my young kinswoman," she added. "My young kinswoman Vladislava."

"WHAT!!" screamed Vladya.

"Mercy," repeated Olga dully, still rubbing her arm. "Mercy for my young kinswoman, Vladislava Vasilisovna. Spare her life, gracious Tsarina, little mother, spare her life out of the bottomless goodness of your heart."

"And yourself?!" cried Vladya. "Won't you beg for mercy for yourself?"

For a moment Olga's gaze fixed sharply on Vladya's face, and, reading the repellent message there, she hastily added, "Oh yes, gracious Tsarina, spare my life too—I beg you."

"Beg louder!" screamed Vladya. "I don't believe you!"

"Mercy," repeated Olga, slightly more loudly. "Mercy for myself and my young kinswoman."

"Why!?" shouted Vladya.

"Why?" repeated Olga in confusion.

"Why did you beg for her life first! Why! What's so special about her?!"

"She is my only niece, gracious Tsarina," said Olga.

"Many an aunt would sacrifice her niece gladly if it meant saving her own skin! What makes you so much better than the others? What makes your heart so much more motherly than that of other women?!"

"My heart is not very motherly at all, gracious Tsarina," said Olga. "I walked away from my own daughter, not once but many times. I knew I was abandoning her to that nest of jackals, and yet I could not force myself to stay. Every time I look at her, I feel ill with hatred, and I wish she had never been born. I will never love her, or even protect her from others, no matter how desperately she needs me. I am a failure."

"You did?" said Vladya, her face suddenly smoothing out. "You do? You won't? You are?"

"Oh yes, gracious Tsarina," said Olga. Slava could tell she was puzzled by Vladya's sudden change of mood, but was willing to go along with it if it meant getting them out of here alive. "I am a terrible mother. I have no love for my only daughter, I admit it freely, and I walked away from her without a backwards glance, over and over again, even though she was suffering and in need of a mother's care and protection, even though I knew I was betraying her just as my own mother betrayed me."

Olga's voice actually trembled as she said those words, and Slava could see that for once, she was truly moved by the thought of Lisochka's suffering and her own guilt before her. She was squeezing her right arm with her left so tightly Slava was afraid she might break it all over again. Even here, at this desperate moment for herself, Slava wished that there were something she could do for Olga, something that would ease the pain, but she knew that, even if they should get out of this alive, there was nothing she could do. Olga had been broken a long time ago, by her mother and her daughter, and there was nothing Slava could do to fix her. Perhaps there was nothing even Olga could do to fix herself. Perhaps she had been broken so badly she was unfixable.

"Yes, I see: you are a terrible mother," said Vladya, with deep satisfaction. For a moment, Slava could see, her desperate hunger to avenge herself on the fate that had made her who she was had been appeased. Slava hoped that it might last, but, knowing as she did the depths of her own particular hunger, she knew that her sister's much deeper and more terrible hunger would not be slaked so easily.

"Yes, Tsarina," agreed Olga. Already her voice was stronger: her own failure had already been considered and discarded.

"And yet you still pleaded for her life before your own!" shrieked Vladya, pointing at Vladislava. Her face had twisted up again in rage, as if whatever thoughts that were floating through her head had floated into some new, more hateful configuration.

"Yes, Tsarina," said Olga. "I suppose I wanted to make up for some of my past. I suppose I wanted to save someone, my niece if not my daughter."

"NO!" screamed Vladya. "That can't be it! It's a plot! It's all a plot! I see clearly now! You, my sister...you all want to save this little girl! It must be a plot! There can be no other explanation! Well...Well...I show you! I'll teach you to plot!"

"NO, Vladya!" shouted Slava. "It's not a plot! How could it be a plot? We just want to save her and leave! Just let us save her and leave! We'll leave now, leave now and never come back, just let us go! We only want to save her!"

As she was saying the words, Slava again felt a deep sense of wrong, so strong that, when Vladya shook her head in furious denial of what she was saying, her first feeling was not despair, but relief. Something was telling her, louder and louder, that she would not be able to leave this dungeon and walk away a free woman, and all attempts she made to do so would and should be met only with failure.

The little shape flitted back out from the shadows and stood behind the guards' boots, catching Slava's eye even as she tried to look only at Vladya.

"You're lying!" Vladya insisted. "Lying again! You can't even look me in the face! You've always been a liar, and a cheat! You've always been able to get your way with others, you, you, you liar!" This pulled Slava's attention away from the little shadow and focused it only onto Vladya, much to Vladya's satisfaction—but that lasted only for a moment. Feeling the force of Slava's gaze, her face twisted up even more, and she said even more loudly, "You play tricks on their minds and you get your way with them! I don't know how you do it, but you do, and, and, and YOU'RE DOING IT RIGHT NOW! YOU'RE PLAYING TRICKS ON MY MIND! YOU'RE TRYING TO CONTROL ME!"

"Yes, Vladya," said Slava quietly. "Of course I am. You have declared me a traitor and threatened to kill the people I care for most in the world. Of course I am trying to control you."

"YOUR KNIFE!" Vladya screamed, turning suddenly to Boleslav Vlasiyevich.

"Gracious Tsarina..." he said in a faltering voice. "Whatever you do...give me your command, gracious Tsarina, and I will carry it out gladly. Do not sully your own fair hands with tasks that are beneath you."

"YOU ALL TURN AGAINST ME!" Vladya screamed.

"Gracious Tsarina," said Boleslav Vlasiyevich, drawing himself up straight. "Merely give me your command, and it shall be done in an instant."

"Oh?" said Vladya. The rage of a moment ago had left her, and now that she was calm again, she was even more terrifying than before. All the hairs on the back of Slava's neck rose, and she knew that now was the moment, now the thing that had brought her down here was about to happen. She gently pushed Vladislava aside, and Vladislava, feeling it too, allowed herself to be pushed.

"Of course, gracious Tsarina," Boleslav Vlasiyevich was saying. "Whatever you command."

"Then kill her," said Vladya, pointing at Vladislava.

Olga lunged to her feet, shouting something that was not words. A dozen guards snapped out of their chained state and grabbed her. The little shape took a step closer to Boleslav Vlasiyevich, who somehow failed to see it, even though Slava was certain he had looked right at it.

"Hold, boys, hold," he said. "Hold her, and hold steady. Don't do anyone any harm." He looked up at Vladya. "Are you certain, gracious Tsarina?" he asked.

"Of course I'm certain," said Vladya. "I gave the order, did I not?"

"She is nothing but a small child, a slip of a girl," said Boleslav Vlasiyevich calmly. "Little threat at present. And killing her could enrage the princesses."

"What do I care of the princesses' rage?" asked Vladya. "I am the Tsarina. And it is your duty to do as I command without question."

"True," agreed Boleslav Vlasiyevich. "But it is also my duty to protect you, gracious Tsarina, and I would be remiss in my duty if I did not point out the dangers in any course of action you had deigned to take."

"Noted," said Vladya. "Thank you, Boleslav Vlasiyevich. I thank you for your concern. I know you always act only in my interest, Boleslav Vlasiyevich, and I thank you for it. Thank you. I have taken your remarks under consideration, but I believe the gains outweigh the risks. The girl must die before she causes any more trouble. And so must my sister. Dispatch them both at once, and let us be finished with this tiresome business. I have an empire to run."

"As you command, gracious Tsarina," said Boleslav Vlasiyevich.

"Wait!" cried Vladya. For a moment Boleslav Vlasiyevich's face twitched as if with hope, but then it was gone and he looked up at Vladya with an expression of calm devotion.

"Kill the girl first," said Vladya. "I want my sister to watch. It will do her good. But wait! Don't kill my sister just yet. I have just remembered that she is a traitor, and the proper punishment for traitors is boiling. We should save her for her own fate."

"You are all-wise, gracious Tsarina," said Boleslav Vlasiyevich. He turned and took one slow step in Slava's direction, and then another. He was walking as if moving through honey. The little shape was dogging right at his heels, but he seemed not to see it, or not to want to see it. One more step and he would be within Slava's reach. He stopped and looked straight into Slava's eyes, and she saw that he was pleading with her, begging her to save him and save them all, because there was no other way out of the dungeon for any of them.

"VLADYA!" screamed Slava. "STOP! STOP THIS MADNESS!"

"Beg all you want," said Vladya with extreme satisfaction. "It won't do you any good. The time for begging is long over."

Slava leaped forward, brushing past Boleslav Vlasiyevich, who made a slow and feeble motion as if attempting to stop her, but stumbled with uncharacteristic clumsiness over the little shape that had suddenly gotten itself tangled in his feet. Somehow, as Boleslav Vlasiyevich failed to rise and stop her, Slava's hands found themselves around Vladya's throat. That only lasted for a moment, though, because Vladya pried Slava's hands off with her own, much stronger and larger hands, and forced Slava to her knees. Suddenly Boleslav Vlasiyevich was on his feet again, his sword drawn.

"Come here, Boleslav Vlasiyevich," said Vladya. "I've changed my mind. Kill my sister first. I want to watch her die in my arms. I want to see what she thinks of me with her last thoughts."

"No need to wait," said Slava, and looked into Vladya's eyes.

For a moment Vladya was still, and then she shook her head, and then she tried to pull away, but even though she was the one holding onto Slava, even though she was the one holding Slava down, she was unable to prise herself free, and everything Slava had seen of her, everything Slava had thought of her, came pouring into her like a flood, like the time the Krasna had broken its banks when they were children and washed away half of Krasnograd, and no matter how hard she struggled to hold onto solid ground, onto a wall, a post, anything solid and familiar, she couldn't stand against the onslaught of Slava's thoughts, and in the space of a few breaths she, too, was washed away.

Boleslav Vlasiyevich was standing an arm's length away, but had somehow failed to stop her or drag her away from Vladya. The other guards had not even made the half-dozen steps it took to reach them before it was over. Slava stood up. Vladya was still holding onto her.

"Slava?" she said faintly.

"Yes?" said Slava. "Vladya! Are you still there? Do you see me!?"

"Where is mother?" said Vladya, and began to cry.

"Shhhhh," said Slava, putting her arms around her. "Shhhhh. Everything is all right now."

"Yes," agreed Vladya, and stopped crying. "Everything is all right now."

"We should leave this place and return to the palace," said Slava. "We have no need of this dark dungeon anymore."

"Yes," agreed Vladya. "We should leave this place and return to the palace. We have no need of this dark dungeon anymore."

"Olga and Vladislava should accompany us," said Slava. "There is no need to keep them here anymore, now that we know they are not traitors."

"Olga and Vladislava should accompany us," repeated Vladya. "There is no need to keep them here anymore, now that we know they are not traitors."

"You heard the Tsarina!" cried Boleslav Vlasiyevich. "Boys! Free Olga Vasilisovna! Someone watch over the little princess! We're leaving!"

The guards looked back and forth at each other. "Ah, Boleslav Vlasiyevich…" a couple of them ventured cautiously, and Slava could see that they had their doubts about the Tsarina's sudden change of heart.

"You heard the Tsarina!" said Boleslav Vlasiyevich. "Let it not be said that we stood here gaping when she gave an order!" He started striding briskly in the direction of the dungeon doors, and the guards, with hesitant and puzzled looks, let go of Olga and formed up around Slava and Vladya. The little shape slipped back into the shadows. Slava was sure that it was the house-spirit, revealing itself to her at last.

Slava started walking after Boleslav Vlasiyevich. She was unable to match his pace, though, hampered as she was by Vladya's fumbling, wavering steps. Vladya clutched at her arm and pressed up against her as they walked, as if she were terribly cold, or terribly afraid. She was shivering.

"Slava!" she whispered urgently. "Where is our mother? I want her, Slava, I want her!"

"She is away," Slava told her gently. "But you will be able to see her soon. Perhaps she will even come to Krasnograd."

"She has to, Slava! I want to see her! I need her!" Vladya started crying, and pressed up even more closely against Slava's side. Slava wondered if she would ever feel more guilty, or more wretched, in her entire life than she did now, supporting her broken sister after being the one to break her. She hoped not. She didn't see right now how that could be possible.

They made their way up the stairs and corridors to the palace proper. "Where to, Tsarina?" asked Boleslav Vlasiyevich, but he looked at Slava.

The Hall of Council, the snow hare whispered in Slava's mind. *Everyone should see the state your sister is in, so that you may claim her place unopposed.*

And don't you dare refuse, added the snow fox. *It's the only right thing to do, and you know it.*

"The Hall of Council," said Slava out loud. She wished the snow fox were wrong, but she was, unfortunately, right. Just as Slava had known on her way down to the dungeons, she would not be able to leave them a free woman.

"The Hall of Council," repeated Vladya feebly. "What will we do there, Slava? Will our mother be there?"

"Not yet," Slava told her soothingly. "But soon. We'll only spend a short time there, and then you can retire to your chambers."

"I want to sleep," agreed Vladya. "I'm tired. But I'm afraid of bad dreams."

"Everyone fears bad dreams," Slava told her gently. "But you have no reason to fear them anymore, Vladya."

"I don't?" asked Vladya, brightening.

"No," Slava told her. "No reason at all. Nothing bad will ever happen to you again, Vladya."

"It won't?" said Vladya, cheering up even more.

"It won't," Slava promised. "You can live in your chambers and…" Slava trailed off, not knowing what innocent pastimes her sister might take up, since she had never had any before. "And rest," she concluded. "You've earned a long rest."

"Yes, I have," agreed Vladya. "I'd like a rest. Can't I go to my chambers now?"

"Shortly," Slava promised. "First the Hall of Council."

"If you say so, Slava," said Vladya obediently. "But only for a short while, yes? I'm very tired, and I don't feel very well."

"Only for a short while," agreed Slava.

The others would like to come in, the snow fox told her. *Tell that man there to call off his guards and let them in.*

"Boleslav Vlasiyevich!" Slava called. "My companions would like to come in!"

"Into the Hall of Council, Tsarina?" he asked doubtfully. "Will they fit?"

They will fit, the snow hare said. *Their form is not so fixed as your own.*

"They will fit," Slava assured him. "Tell your guards to let them in."

"Yes, let them in," seconded Vladya. "I'd like to see them!"

"As you say, Tsarina," said Boleslav Vlasiyevich, bowing in their direction. "Mariyich! Miroslavych! Relay the message!"

A couple of guards broke away from the main pack and took off down a corridor leading to the outside. The rest of them continued their inexorable march to the Hall of Council. It seemed to Slava that it was much farther away than usual, and she wished they would hurry up and arrive, so that she could get this over with.

The seemingly magical communication system of the kremlin was apparently still in place, for word had obviously gotten out that it was safe to walk the corridors again, and people were sticking out their heads here and there, and even scurrying back and forth, so that there was the impression of a hive coming to life again after the danger had passed.

As they approached the Hall of Council, Slava could see people going in the doors, and the hum of a crowd of voices. She tried to conceal her cringing.

The more witnesses, the better, said the snow fox.

My sister is right, said the snow hare.

I know, agreed Slava.

Then don't forget and lose your nerve, said the snow fox.

"Why are all the people there, Slava?" asked Vladya anxiously. "I don't want too many people!"

"They have come to see us," Slava told her soothingly. "They're glad that we are all right, and they've come to see us. There's nothing to fear: we'll let them look at us, and then we'll leave."

"I want to go to my chambers," said Vladya fretfully.

"Soon, Vladya, soon," Slava told her. "We'll just go into the Hall of Council for a moment, and then you can go to your chambers, I promise."

This appeased Vladya briefly, but as they made to enter the Hall of Council, she hung back like a frightened child, and Slava had to half-coax, half coerce her to come into the Hall of Council with her.

It was, Slava had to admit, frighteningly full of princesses and other onlookers. Slava wondered where they had all come from on such short notice. There was a great deal of whispering, and the crowd was slow to make way for Slava and Vladya to pass between them to the Wooden Throne. Not, Slava thought, out of any disrespect, but because they were so eager to see what had become of the Tsarina and the traitor-Tsarinovna who had been let back into the fold.

They climbed up onto the dais where the throne was stationed, and there was an awkward moment as they both stood uncertainly in front of the chair.

"Sit, Vladya; sit on the throne," Slava whispered into her ear.

"I don't want to," Vladya objected. "I want to go to my chambers."

"Sit just for a moment," Slava told her.

"Do you think that's wise?" Boleslav Vlasiyevich whispered to Slava from the other side of her sister.

"I think it must be done," Slava told him.

Vladya sat down reluctantly on the throne and looked out on the crowd, which looked expectantly back.

"They want you to say something," Slava whispered to her. She felt wretched about what she was about to do, but every time she thought about doing something else, her stomach lurched, and she knew that she must do this thing and no other. There was no escape for her from this distasteful duty.

"What do they want me to say, Slava?" asked Vladya anxiously.

"Anything," Slava whispered to her. "Say you are glad to see them."

"I'm glad to see you!" Vladya shouted, in the voice of a shy child suddenly forced to perform in public.

There was a ripple of surprise through the crowd. None of them had ever seen the Tsarina like this before, and Slava could see that they didn't know what to make of it, other than that they didn't like it.

"Now what, Slava?" asked Vladya.

"Tell them you've forgiven me, that it was all a misunderstanding and that there are no more differences between us," Slava told her.

"Forgiven you for what, Slava?" asked Vladya, frowning.

"For thinking I was a traitor," Slava told her. "It was all a misunderstanding. I wasn't a traitor at all. You can see that now, and all is forgiven and I can come back to Krasnograd."

"Slava!" cried Vladya in horror. "You weren't a traitor!"

There was another ripple through the crowd.

"Yes," said Slava. "And now all is forgiven, and I can come and go from Krasnograd as I please, and there is no bad blood between us."

"Who said you were a traitor!" demanded Vladya, becoming more and more agitated.

"You thought I was a traitor, but it was all a misunderstanding," Slava told her patiently.

"No!" insisted Vladya. "I would never say that! You weren't a traitor, Slava, that's impossible! Slava!" She looked up at Slava, and something like consciousness peered out from her eyes. "Did I say you were a traitor? Oh Slava!" The spark of consciousness slipped away from sight. "No Slava, no, I didn't, I didn't say you were a traitor, I didn't,

Slava, I didn't! I want our mother, Slava! Where is our mother!" She started to cry.

"Shh, shh," Slava told her, bending over from where she was standing beside the throne and kissing Vladya's head. "Shh, Vladya, stop crying. This will all be over soon enough."

"NO!" shouted Vladya. "I want to go to my chambers! I want to go to my chambers! I want to go to my chambers! Why are all these people here!? Send them away! They're hurting me! They're hurting me with their eyes!"

"The Tsarina is overwrought, and will retire to her chambers now," said Slava firmly, helping Vladya up from the throne. "This audience is over."

"No, Krasnoslava Tsarinovna, it isn't," said a voice from the doors, and the golden-eyed leshaya came in.

Chapter Twenty-One

You *can talk,* said Slava stupidly.

Out loud, too, said the golden-eyed leshaya. *And I summoned some more of my friends for this audience—and yours.* "Make way for my companions," she said out loud. "We are rather large."

She was followed into the Hall of Council by Gray Wolf, and Elk, and Bear, and several more leshiye. Dima, Dunya, and Valery Annovich slipped in behind them.

For a moment, as they entered, the only sound was dozens of indrawn breaths, as all the princesses gathered there gasped in astonishment, but that was soon followed by cries of fear and delight, and then demands to know what was happening.

"Make way for my companions," Slava found herself shouting, as the crowd milled about in confusion, but then Gray Wolf snapped at them, and the golden-eyed leshaya blinked in their direction, and suddenly there was a large clear space by the doors.

"We would walk up to the Tsarina," said the golden-eyed leshaya.

All the guards looked to Boleslav Vlasiyevich, who looked to Slava.

"Let them come unhindered," Slava ordered. "They are my allies, and will do you no harm."

"As long as you deserve none," said Gray Wolf cheerfully.

"Even those who deserve it shall not be harmed," said Slava.

"Kindhearted as always, Krasnoslava," said Gray Wolf. "Are you sure that is wise?"

"There is more to wisdom than being wise," said Slava. "Come up to the throne, and harm no one on your way up."

The crowd shuffled nervously towards the walls, clearing a path for Gray Wolf, who stalked happily down it. *My wolf*, thought Slava, even though he was most certainly not her wolf. *They threw me to the wolves, and this is what we all got for it.* He was followed by the golden-eyed leshaya, who made her stately way between the fearful princesses; Elk and Bear, who looked around with frank curiosity; and Dima, Dunya, and Valery Annovich. Dima appeared overwhelmingly relieved to see them all still alive, Dunya appeared indifferent to the fuss around her, and Valery Annovich appeared stunned at finding himself where he was, and extremely uncertain about joining the others on the dais, but not seeing any better choice.

"I see you saved your little princess—and your friend," said the golden-eyed leshaya, looking at Vladislava and Olga.

"Were they in danger?" asked Vladya, surprised. She seemed to have calmed down for the moment, but Slava could see that another outburst could happen at any instant.

"It is of no matter," Slava told her gently.

"Does she not remember, then?" asked the golden-eyed leshaya.

"It seems not," said Slava.

"Our brother and sister shared with us what they saw, but they could do no more than see," said the golden-eyed leshaya. "I would hear your story in your words."

"We went down into the dungeon," said Slava slowly.

"So I saw," said the golden-eyed leshaya, when Slava stopped. "And then the Tsarina threatened to kill the little princess, and your friend, and you yourself, did she not?"

"Yes," said Slava reluctantly, as the crowd gasped.

"No!" shouted Vladya. "No I didn't! I didn't, I didn't, I didn't! Oh Slava! Did I?"

The crowd shifted uneasily in the silence that followed.

"Yes," said Slava, with what even she could recognize was agonizing slowness.

The crowd gasped again. The golden-eyed leshaya ignored them.

"And she ordered this man here"—she stretched out a branch towards Boleslav Vlasiyevich—"to kill all of you, did she not?"

"Yes," agreed Slava reluctantly.

"And she wanted to save you for last, so you could watch the little girl die and then be boiled as a traitor, did she not?"

Slava realized with horror that, true as that all was, she could not force herself to open her mouth and agree with it. Saying such a thing of anyone, let alone her own sister, no matter how true it might be, was too terrible even to think of right now, let alone pronounce out loud in front of witnesses.

"No!" cried Vladya, saving Slava from having to speak. "No, no, no! I would never do something like that! Slava, where is our mother?"

"Soon," Slava promised her.

"And so, to save all of you, you were forced to reveal the true nature of your gifts to her, were you not?" continued the golden-eyed leshaya.

"I suppose," said Slava.

"You hurt me!" Vladya cried accusingly. "You hurt me with your mind! You're mean! Slava, where is mother? I want her! I want her!" She started to sniffle, which quickly turned into full-throated sobbing.

"What do you think, Krasnoslava?" asked the golden-eyed leshaya, still paying no mind to either Vladya or the crowd. "Do you think the people in this hall believe your story?"

"I don't know," said Slava.

"Then look out, Krasnoslava, look out onto them and tell me."

Slava looked out onto the crowd. Mostly, she saw, they were astonished and terrified by the presence of her companions, and horrified at the sight of Vladya breaking down and crying on the throne. There did not seem to be a lot of belief in their faces. They could see that something magical and shattering had happened, but they did not want to believe in anything that would shake up their lives so terribly, and they were also slightly sorry for Vladya's suffering, which was clearly Slava's fault.

Well, many of them were. Some of them were secretly—because they would rather die than admit it inside the Hall of Council—delighted to see the proud and fearsome Tsarina humbled like that, but that did not endear Slava to them in any way—quite the reverse, in fact. Anyone who could make the Tsarina cry was someone who needed to be sent as far away as possible.

"They don't believe me," said Slava. "They don't believe me because they don't want to. They wish I would go away and stop bothering them."

"What will make them believe, Krasnoslava?" asked the golden-eyed leshaya seriously.

"I don't know," said Slava. "Perhaps if they saw things through my eyes for a moment."

"Then show them, Krasnoslava," said the golden-eyed leshaya.

"How?" asked Slava.

"Reach out to them, Krasnoslava. Reach out to them, and I will help you touch them."

Slava looked out onto the crowd again, and thought of what she saw there: all the pride, and greed, and fear, and sympathy, and concern for others, and petty envy and jealousy, and the need to be strong and brave, and the desperate wish to be, even for an instant and even if carefully hidden away from everyone, even themselves, a better person—a hero. Someone who saved others. That, she saw, was the way into their hearts. They all, even if they would never, ever say it, even if they didn't know it themselves, wanted to be a savior, just for a moment. Only saving others was hard, so much terribly harder than it should be. But they all wanted it, nonetheless, and Slava could give it to them, just for that precious instant.

The crowd gasped.

"Your head!" cried Vladya. "Like light!"

The golden-eyed leshaya's golden eyes seemed to fill the whole hall.

"Not again!" screamed Vladya. "Not again! It hurts too much!"

The crowd screamed too. It was made up of dozens and dozens of individual women, but just then it screamed with one voice, one voice begging for mercy.

"Krasnoslava!" said the golden-eyed leshaya sharply. "Enough!"

Suddenly Slava could see with only her own eyes again.

"You were losing yourself, Krasnoslava," it said, just to her. "Sucking in the crowd's feelings, like a tree taking in sun and water. Beware of that, Krasnoslava. A little is more than enough. There is more to their feelings than just sun and water. Poisonous evil lies there too. You must not suck in too much of that, or you will be poisoned by it too. You see, your gift runs both ways—always. You cannot give without receiving."

"Yes," said Slava faintly. "Will...will I be able to reach out again, like that? Do I have that gift now?"

"You always had that gift, Krasnoslava," said the leshaya. "Just as all women do. Anyone can raise her voice and reach out to her sister. You just have to be willing to speak up. There is no magic to it. You have no need of my magic for that."

"But..." said Slava. "How will I make them listen to me now? No one has ever listened to me!"

"That is not true, Krasnoslava," said the leshaya. "Perhaps it seemed to you, and to them, that no one ever listened to you, but they did. They did because you listened to them. Hearing others, seeing others, *being* others—that is your gift, and it always, always runs both ways. You have nothing to fear, Krasnoslava. They will listen to you, as long as you are willing to let them hear you. Everyone is always listening, Krasnoslava, whether they know it or not. You just have to find the right words to reach their ears. But that is your gift—the other edge of its double-edged blade. The fact that you hear them so clearly means that you know, in your heart of hearts, how to make them hear you. You just have to listen, to yourself as well as others, and then you will know."

"The Tsarina!" said a voice in Slava's ear, before she could respond to the leshaya's words, or even make sense of them. She looked around. Boleslav Vlasiyevich was tugging at her arm and pointing. Vladya was folded over double, her face in her knees, and sobbing bitterly.

"Take her to her chambers," Slava ordered. "You and..." she looked at her companions. Valery Annovich was standing to the back of the dais, behind all the others, looking even more bewildered and miserable than everyone else. "You and Valery Annovich can take her to her chambers." She went over to Vladya.

"Vladya," she said softly. "Vladya, it's all right. Vladya, there's nothing wrong."

"It hurts too much," said Vladya into her knees, rocking back and forth.

"I know it does, Vladya, but you can go to your chambers now."

"I felt like I was being washed away, Slava! I was washed away, and there was nothing left of me!"

"I know, Vladya, I know. You can go to your chambers now. Boleslav Vlasiyevich and Valery Annovich will escort you."

Vladya raised her head and looked directly into Slava's face. "How do you stand it, Slava?" she asked, and something like her old sharp determination peered out from her eyes for a moment. "How do you keep from being washed away?"

"You have to find the part of you that's made of stone, not sand," said Slava. She wondered if Vladya's mind was really returning, and if so, for how long.

"Even stones get ground down into sand with enough water," said Vladya.

"Yes," said Slava.

Vladya's face collapsed, and her head sank back down to her knees.

Some distant part of Slava couldn't help but be surprised at her sister's agility: she was folding into a pose that would have done credit to a child of two, let alone a grown woman. Slava supposed despair had made her boneless.

"Help my sister to her chambers," she ordered Boleslav Vlasiyevich and Valery Annovich. They helped her to her feet, Boleslav Vlasiyevich with alacrity and Valery Annovich with deep uncertainty, and led her to the door in the wall behind the dais. Slava was pleased at this evidence of thought on their part: the last thing Vladya needed was to be paraded past all her princesses. The hidden passageways were much more appropriate for her now—and were likely to remain so, she reflected.

"Well, Krasnoslava," said the golden-eyed leshaya, once Vladya had been escorted off the dais and into the passageway behind the wall.

"Yes," said Slava.

"You appear to be the only one left here," said the golden-eyed leshaya.

"And them?" asked Slava, nodding towards Olga and Vladislava. She knew she was only pointlessly trying to delay things, but she couldn't stop herself.

"They do not count, and you know it," said the golden-eyed leshaya. "Not here. The only person who matters on that dais is the descendent of Miroslava Praskovyevna, as you well know. And so, Krasnoslava, many-times Miroslavovna, what are you going to do?"

"Vladya is unfit to rule," said Slava.

"Yes," said the golden-eyed leshaya.

"Prasha is too young—she is still a child."

"Yes," said the golden-eyed leshaya.

"My mother has refused to return to Krasnograd and resume the throne."

"Yes," said the golden-eyed leshaya.

"I am the Tsarinovna. It is my duty to rule in Vladya's stead, at least until she recovers."

"She will not recover," said the golden-eyed leshaya.

"You can't know that! She could recover—the damage to her mind could be but slight."

"She will not recover," repeated the golden-eyed leshaya.

"How can you know that! You can't possibly know that!"

"I know," said the golden-eyed leshaya, and blinked her large eyes slowly.

"Krasnoslava," she said, once her eyes were open again. "Krasna Tsarina. Let us stop pretending. Let us stop playing games. Your sister will never rule in Krasnograd again. You ensured that the moment you brought us through that gate. No—you ensured that the moment you accepted our bargain, and agreed to bear the child we offered you. And many other times as well. You have been asked to choose between two sides many times, Krasnoslava, your sister's and another's, and every time you have not chosen your sister's. You traded her life for Vladislava's, and for the chance to have a daughter of your own. So now you must take your sister's place. It is the price you must pay for what you have done."

"But..." said Slava, and then, realizing that she was starting to whine, stopped herself. "Yes," she said. "It is the price."

"Doubly over," said the golden-eyed leshaya. "It is the price for defeating your sister, and it is the price for enlisting our aid to do so. You must rule now, Krasnoslava, and the daughter you will be given must rule after you. It is the price."

"Yes," said Slava. "And a heavy one it is, and one that will be paid by more than just me. Just as the price for my rule is my rule, and my daughter's rule after me. Is that a price you are willing to pay?"

"It is a gamble," said the golden-eyed leshaya soberly. "You are a dangerous woman, Krasnoslava. I have no doubt that as Krasna Tsarina you will be even more dangerous, and your Darya, your gift from the gods, will be doubly dangerous, if not worse. But it is a gamble we are willing to take. Gambling on your mercy is a risk worth taking: that is why you are here."

"And if they"—Slava gestured towards the crowd—"deny me? If they are loyal to my sister, and demand her return to the throne?"

"They will not," said the golden-eyed leshaya. "They are not so loyal as to turn against a sorceress of such great power as you. You have defeated your sister, Krasnoslava, and exercised your power over your subjects in no uncertain fashion. You are a woman to be feared, Krasnoslava—a worthy Tsarina."

Slava looked out onto the crowd. "True," she said.

"Princesses!" said the golden-eyed leshaya, turning to the crowd. "Bow down to your new Tsarina!"

The crowd sank to its knees and knocked its forehead against the surely-dirty floor. "Tsarina!" cried out many voices. "Ai-da Tsarina! Our Tsarina! Little mother! Have mercy, little mother!"

"Rise," said Slava. Out of the corner of her eye she saw that Olga and Dunya had both sunk to their knees as well, and pulled Vladislava down with them.

"Rise," she repeated. "I have no need of your prostrations. It is your loyalty I demand."

"You have it!" someone shouted out, to be seconded by many more. "You have it, little mother! Our loyalty! Our loyalty is yours!"

"Take the throne, Krasnoslava," said the golden-eyed leshaya. "You must take the throne."

Slava sat down on the Wooden Throne. Bizarrely, for a moment all she could think of was the one time she had sat in it before—as a child, in her mother's lap. It was more comfortable than she had expected. She rested her hands on the armrests. The wood was soft and welcoming, and the spells carved into it made a soothing shape under her hands. She felt as if she had finally found the place she was meant to be, the place that was her true home. She could feel the tree it had once been, and through that, all the trees of Zem', and the earth they grew from, and the animals that lived in their shade and protection, and the power that her connection with them gave her.

"Where are my faithful companions?" she asked. "Snow hare! Where are you? And snow fox! I would have you at my side."

"Here, Krasna Tsarina," said the snow hare, loping across the dais and leaping into her lap.

"Here, Krasna Tsarina," said the snow fox, trotting across the dais and curling up at her feet.

"And Elk? And Gray Wolf? And Bear? We have not spent much time in conversation, Bear, but I value your presence greatly."

"Here, Krasna Tsarina," they said, and arranged themselves behind her, the dais creaking in protest under their weight. Elk reached her head over the throne and rested her soft nose on Slava's shoulder.

How lucky for all of us that you saved my sister, she huffed into Slava's ear.

It was not luck, Slava told her in reply. *It was meant to be.*

You are no doubt right, Krasna Tsarina, agreed Elk. They waited for a moment in companionable silence while Bear and Gray Wolf snapped at each other and quarreled over who got to stand where.

Pay no mind to them, Krasna Tsarina, said Elk. *They must have their little differences, just to show themselves that they know how to think.*

I know, said Slava.

The leshiye arranged themselves in front of the dais, on either side of the throne.

"Let it be known," said the golden-eyed leshaya. "Zem' is full of souls and spirits, many of which do not wear the form of women. But we have chosen to ally ourselves behind one who does wear the form of woman, Krasnoslava Tsarina. Any who go against her go against us as well."

"I thank you for the confidence you have entrusted in me," said Slava. "And Zem' will thank you too one day for your support."

"I have no doubt, Krasnoslava Tsarina," said the golden-eyed leshaya, turning to her and eyeing her gravely. "And now we will leave you to it. We have done all we can for the moment. We must return to our forest homes."

"Thank you again," said Slava. "I shall never forget what you have done for me."

"I am certain of that, Krasnoslava Tsarina. Neither shall we." The golden-eyed leshaya blinked her golden eyes in one long slow blink, and when she opened them, for a moment Slava thought she was drowning in golden light. But then she blinked her own eyes, and the feeling disappeared.

"Come, let us go," said the golden-eyed leshaya. "Let us leave the Tsarina to her rule. She has many matters to attend to."

"We would stay," said the snow hare. "At least for a little while."

"Yes," said the snow fox. "My brother and I would stay. *Someone* must keep an eye on this innocent, at least until her full teeth come in."

"Stay as long as you wish," Slava told them. "You are always welcome."

"We weren't asking *you*," said the snow fox.

"Anyone who wishes to stay with me in my kremlin must ask me, nonetheless," Slava told her with a smile.

"Well said!" said the snow fox. "I see my fears are already partially put to rest."

"Even so, I would stay," said the snow hare. "Even the best of travelers can lose her way from time to time."

"Stay," said Slava. "I wish it greatly."

"Then let them stay, to be our eyes and ears, as well as your strong support," said the golden-eyed leshaya. "The rest of us must be on our way."

"Stay strong, Krasnoslava Tsarina," said Bear. "Whenever you need a little of my strength, call for me."

"I thank you," said Slava, bowing from her seat.

"Stay strong, Krasnoslava Tsarina," said Gray Wolf. "Whenever you need a little of my good friend Oleg Svetoslavovich, call for me, and I'll bring him. Just call very soon or not until next year, because this summer you're going to be too fat for any man to want you."

Slava tried to thank him for that, but she was laughing too much to get the words out.

"That's all right, Krasnoslava Tsarina," said Gray Wolf, seeing her problem. "On second thought, never underestimate the willingness of men, even for very fat women. Call for me whenever you want him. I'll make sure he comes."

"You are too kind," Slava told him. "When you stepped out of the woods, back in Deep Pond, I thought of how I had been thrown to the wolves, and how lucky I was to have been thrown. You are a good, kind wolf."

Gray Wolf tried to snarl at that, but it only come out as a snort. He retreated from the dais in mock offense.

"Stay kind, Krasnoslava Tsarina," said Elk. "Whenever you need a little of my shy spirit, call for me."

"Of that you may be sure, sister," Slava told her. Elk snorted softly into her ear, and walked off the dais.

"Call for me," said the golden-eyed leshaya. "And I shall call for you. But for the moment, Krasnoslava Tsarina, farewell."

"Farewell," said Slava, and watched as they all walked out of the Hall of Council, between the kneeling princesses.

There was a moment of silence.

"Ai-da Krasnoslava Tsarina!" someone suddenly shouted.

"Ai-da Krasna Tsarina!" someone else shouted, and Slava realized it was Dima.

"Krasna Tsarina!" a hundred voices joined in. There was another flurry of bowing, which filled the Hall of Council with the rustling of a hundred dresses and the scraping of two hundred boots.

"Sisters," said Slava, rising from the throne. "I thank you for your welcome. I am sure that none of you will forget this day, and what you have witnessed. But now I must retire. I have much to attend to, not the least of which is the sorry situation of my own sad sister."

"Go, little mother!" voices called from all sides. "Go and see to your sad sister! The gods watch over you and her, little mother!"

"I thank you for your kind wishes," said Slava, and began retreating towards the same door behind the dais through which Vladya had been taken. Dunya, followed quickly by Dima and Olga, jumped to open the door for her and escort her through. Vladislava followed close behind, one hand clinging to Slava's skirt.

"Will you hold my hand?" she asked as soon as they were all through the door and in the narrow passageway between the walls. "I'm—I'm—I'm—"

"Don't bother the Tsarina, little princess," said Dima. "And speak to her properly when you do speak."

"Give me your hand, Vladislava," said Slava. "You have been through a terrible ordeal—you and Olga both."

"It was nothing...Tsarina," said Olga, starting off as herself and finishing with the puzzled voice of a woman whose house has just crumbled to the foundations. She eyed Slava in the semi-darkness, realized that Slava could probably see her eyeing her, and looked away quickly.

"Nonsense," said Slava briskly. "It must have been terrible. I am sorry I could not have arrived sooner."

"How long did it take you to get here?" asked Vladislava, her voice filling with curiosity. "Did you travel with those leshiye?"

"Yes," Slava told her. "It took me two days to travel here from Deep Pond."

"And how long does it normally take?"

"It took us a week to go the distance the other way," Slava told her.

"That's quite fast, then, two days," said Vladislava, sounding impressed. "Did you run the whole way?"

"The leshiye ran," said Slava. "I just sat as they carried me."

"I wish *I* had been carried by leshiye, instead of stuck in that dungeon," said Vladislava.

"Vladislava!" said Olga sharply. Vladislava pursed her lips in a sulk.

"I certainly hope you're not planning to shout at Vladislava every time she asks a question," said Slava with a smile. "Because if so, you'll never get anything done at all."

"True," agreed Vladislava, cheering up. "And I have *lots* of question—Slava! Are you really Tsarina now?"

"It seems so," Slava told her.

"But what about Prasha?" Vladislava asked. "The Tsarina's—the other Tsarina's—I mean the former Tsarina's—daughter. What about her?"

"It is good that you reminded me," Slava told her. "Prasha must be dealt with."

"You're not going to let her be Tsarina, are you?" Vladislava asked anxiously. "She'd be *terrible*, I'm sure!"

"I fear you are right," said Slava. "I must think on this, and perhaps take council."

"Which means no more questions from you!" Olga told Vladislava.

"Vladislava's questions are always welcome," said Slava. "Sometimes they lead straight to the heart of the matter—as in this case. But now you should rest."

"I've had enough rest!" said Vladislava. "I've just spent more than a week locked inside a cell! I'm tired of rest!"

"In that case, take a pony and go riding," Slava told her. "The park is no doubt ankle-deep in slop, but you could still stretch your legs a little."

"Can *I* take a pony and go riding?" asked Olga, perking up and looking less fearful of Slava's sudden elevation, now that she had spoken such sensible words.

"By all means," said Slava, smiling. "All of you should go out, if you wish."

"Maybe *you* should take a pony and go riding, too," Olga suggested.

"I'm afraid I might throw up on its neck, poor thing," said Slava. "All my morning sickness has just come rushing back, even though it's afternoon."

"Oh! Well, in that case, you should rest. You're no doubt tired after your...exertions." Olga suddenly seemed to remember everything Slava had just done, and fell back into confusion.

"Yes, and very hungry, too, in between the sickness," said Slava with a smile, in order to dispel the confusion before it became awkwardly permanent. The thought of losing Olga's good-humored affection was more than she could bear right now, or probably ever, but she knew that if she told Olga that directly, she would just embarrass Olga even more, so she held her tongue and satisfied herself with grinning and raising an eyebrow. Olga grinned back.

"I'm hungry too," said Olga. "I don't think I've had anything but stale black bread for days now."

"It was so hard, we had to hold it in our mouths to soften it up before we could chew it," Vladislava confided. "At first it was fun, but by the second meal it wasn't so fun anymore, although we tried to make a game out it. We also tried to make a game out of how often the guards would come, and when, and how often your sister would come see us."

"She came to see you often, then?" Slava asked.

"Oh yes, every day, sometimes twice. She'd come and shout threats and so on at us, and then she'd get all upset and sometimes cry. She really hated us."

"I see," said Slava. She didn't even feel that guilty that her first thought at this information was that it meant there were witnesses to Vladya's craziness—not only Olga and Vladislava, who as witnesses were rather suspect (or so the princesses would think), but probably lots of guards as well. She thought of her sister making such scenes in front of the guards, and tried not to cringe. She asked herself how there had not been a rebellion before she had even arrived. Because the guards wouldn't know how to rebel if you explained it to them in words of one syllable, she answered. And apparently the princesses didn't know how to take action, either...And this was the empire she had inherited.

They came to a door that led out from between the walls to a small side corridor. "If you go down that way, you'll come to some back stairs, which will take you to the kitchens, which open out onto the stable yard," Slava told the others. "I'm sure if you tell the grooms you have my permission, they'll let you take some ponies—horses, even."

"I'm sure—Tsarina," said Olga, giving her a slightly odd look. At first Slava thought it was because, of course, Olga knew the kremlin rather better than she did by now, having spent the past several weeks—before she was put in the dungeons, that is—exploring it, while Slava had merely been mooning about, fantasizing about futures that now would never come to pass, but then she realized that it was because she had said "I'm sure." A Tsarina didn't need to state something so painfully obvious. "I'm sure" implied that there was a possibility of doubt, and there could be no possibility of doubt in any of Slava's statements, from this day forward.

"Enjoy your ride," Slava said. "Rest yourselves after your bitter ordeal. And join me for supper this evening. We have much to talk of."

"We will be honored, Tsarina," said Olga, and shepherded Vladislava away. Dima followed, after giving Slava a glance that was both considering and sympathetic. Slava smiled in reply, and, after a moment, Dima smiled back, before turning and going after Olga and Vladislava.

When Slava arrived in her chambers, she discovered Masha, Manya, Anna Avdotyevna (Masha and Manya were cringing on the far side of the room from her), Yarmila Kseniyevna, and Boleslav Vlasiyevich (who had been relegated to a corner near the door, so that he wouldn't dirty Slava's carpet with his boots) all waiting for her in the front room.

"This is a fine gathering," she remarked as she entered.

"Tsarina!" cried Anna Avdotyevna, and bowed down to her boot-tops. All the others hastily copied her, although, Slava noticed, they all looked more at the snow hare and the snow fox than at her as they did so. The snow hare and the snow fox quickly sized up the room, and made their way without any hesitation over to the fire, where they curled up on the floor in evident enjoyment of the warmth.

"Tsarina!" repeated Boleslav Vlasiyevich, coming out from his corner, in complete disregard of the state of his boots and her carpet. "Where is your escort! Why do you not have an escort!"

"I had an escort," said Slava cheerfully. "But I sent them to go pony-riding, so I could return to my chambers in peace. A vain wish, I see."

There was an awkward and unpleasant silence. Slava reminded herself that Tsarinas were generally advised not to joke, in case they confused their subjects. And she also remembered the leshaya's words, and allowed the feelings that were pouring in all sides from those around her be transformed into what they needed to hear, and suddenly the right words came spilling out.

"Truly, Boleslav Vlasiyevich, your concern for my safety is commendable, but it so happened that I had to a walk a corridor on my own. But it is of no matter, I assure you. Today is a day of great changes, and we cannot expect all the ordinary patterns and protocols to be observed."

"About that, Tsarinovn...Tsarina," said Anna Avdotyevna and Yarmila Kseniyevna together.

"Yes?" said Slava.

A lengthy discussion on the advisability of her moving into her sister's chambers followed. Anna Avdotyevna and Yarmila Kseniyevna argued that it was both right and proper that she should transfer to the Empress's chambers as soon as possible. Whenever he could get a word in edgewise, which was rarely, Boleslav Vlasiyevich seconded their opinion, saying that the Imperial chambers were more easily guarded than the Tsarinovna's rooms. Slava attempted to convince them that she preferred her own apartment, at least for the present, but, despite their excessively respectful language and their many bows, they seemed incapable of hearing a word she said, and Slava saw that though she could make them hear her, she would have to speak very strongly, too strongly for the present moment, to open their hearts and their ears, and decided to let the matter rest for the moment.

"What of my sister?" she finally asked instead.

"I beg your pardon, Tsarinovn...Tsarina?" said Anna Avdotyevna.

"What of my sister?" she repeated. "Where is she now? I would not cast her out of her own chambers without ensuring she has somewhere to go. And who is attending to her? What state is she in?"

"She is in her chambers, Tsarina," said Boleslav Vlasiyevich. "Valery Annovich and I brought her there ourselves, and left her in the care of two maids, a healer, and half-a-dozen guards."

"And Valery Annovich?" Slava asked, temporarily diverted from the matter at hand by her curiosity over his fate.

"I released him, Tsarina. I hope you are not displeased."

"Not at all," said Slava. "I merely wondered what had happened to him, that was all."

"No doubt he has gone off in search of Serafimiya Svetlanovna," said Boleslav Vlasiyevich. Slava thought she detected a slight eye-roll as he said it.

"No doubt!" said Yarmila Kseniyevna. "Poor thing, she's been pining for him desperately ever since he left. It was so cruel of him to leave her like that..."

"In my opinion, he came back much too soon," said Anna Avdotyevna sharply. "I saw the bruises on her neck—and the rest of her body."

"And you did nothing about it?" cried Slava. "You just stood idly by with your arms folded, wondering how the story would end?"

"I believe your new *Captain*," Anna Avdotyevna gave Boleslav Vlasiyevich a mistrustful glare, "attempted to reason with him, or rather, he battered him a few times in the practice yard, but of course it did no good, and we soon put a stop to it. Valery Annovich is son and husband to princesses. He deserves better than to be bruised and shamed by some...some peasant's son."

"Merchant's; peasant's sons don't train with swords in boyhood," said Boleslav Vlasiyevich, but only Slava seemed to hear, or to notice the sour look he gave Anna Avdotyevna. Slava had to resist the urge to slap herself in the face. Her reign was only a few hours old and already her councilors were at odds.

"Besides, every woman must learn to rule her own husband," continued Anna Avdotyevna, warming to her theme. "Otherwise she will never be anything but a sniveling little girl. We are not Westerners, to let our men do what they please, simply because it pleases them."

"But that is *exactly* what we do!" said Slava. "We raise them to be spoiled and vicious, like mistreated dogs, and then we set them upon our daughters and wait to see how things will turn out. It is unkind— no, it is *wrong*—for all parties. Serafimiya's own mother would not step forward and save her...And now you..." She suddenly remembered that Boleslav Vlasiyevich was present, and that her words must give him pain, and stopped, but when her gaze inadvertently strayed his way, for once she could read him easily as he shrugged as if to say, "You're right."

"I see you take your princesses' welfare to heart," said Anna Avdotyevna. "That is a good thing, as long as it does not go too far. We cannot allow them to go soft, out of a misguided sense of pity. Boleslav Vlasiyevich! I command you to watch over him—and her. Neither of them can be trusted to look after their own good. But you are to not to lay a hand on Valery Annovich, do you understand?"

Boleslav Vlasiyevich looked at Slava.

"Anna Avdotyevna is right," said Slava, calming herself as much as possible. "Watch over them, if you please, Boleslav Vlasiyevich, and, er, try to avoid doing anything to Valery Annovich unless he really, really deserves it. But above all let us keep an eye on them. I fear that neither of them can be trusted in this matter."

"Or any other," muttered Anna Avdotyevna, flaring her nostrils and pretending to ignore Boleslav Vlasiyevich's amused look.

"No doubt you are correct," agreed Slava. "But back to more important business"—she waited until they had all wrenched their minds away from contemplating the idiocy that was the romance between Serafimiya Svetlanovna and Valery Annovich—"where is Prasha?"

"I beg your pardon, Tsarinovn...Tsarina?" asked Anna Avdotyevna and Yarmila Kseniyevna together.

"My niece," Slava explained. "Praskovya Vladislavovna Tsarinovna."

"Tsarinovna no longer, Tsarina," said Anna Avdotyevna.

"Exactly, Anna Avdotyevna," said Slava. "Where is she? This has been a terrible day for her; I would not have her left alone and neglected. She should be given access to her mother. And I would speak with her myself."

"Excuse me, Tsarina, but I must ask..." said Anna Avdotyevna. "Are you still...These recent trying events...Are your hopes..."

"Still intact, to the best of my knowledge," Slava assured her.

"Thank the gods, Tsarina!"

"Yes," said Slava, somewhat dryly. "But you see what this means for Prasha. At the moment she is still my heir, and therefore heir to the throne, but if I should...if all my hopes should be rewarded with an heir..."

"Surely the gods will send you a girl, Tsarina!"

"So they say," said Slava. "But this is a terrible blow to Prasha."

"Praskovya Vladislavovna was never meant to sit a throne of any size," said Anna Avdotyevna decisively. Yarmila Kseniyevna and Boleslav Vlasiyevich both nodded in agreement, and then stopped guiltily.

"She has never, perhaps, shown those qualities one would hope for in a Tsarina..." said Slava. "But nonetheless this is a terrible blow to her. I would have her found and brought to her mother, and I will visit them both shortly."

"It shall be done, Tsarina," said Boleslav Vlasiyevich. He bowed and left. He seemed rather less upset about the day's events than Slava would have expected, but why that would be so she could not say. Perhaps he had never had any particularly deep loyalty to her sister. She wondered how deep his loyalty to her would go, and wrenched her mind away from that painful thought.

"Meanwhile I would change," she said instead. "These clothes have seen rather hard wear, and are not fit for a Tsarina."

"Masha! Manya!" snapped Anna Avdotyevna. "What are you cowering there in the corner for! Go!"

Masha and Manya fled to the bedroom with the air of people fleeing a forest fire.

"The people will be wishing to see you, Tsarina," said Yarmila Kseniyevna. "A public appearance...Perhaps an audience, and a feast...A proclamation to the square..."

"Tomorrow," said Slava. "You are right, but let it be tomorrow. Today I will see my sister and my niece, and then I will sup with my companions in my chambers, and retire. It has been a long day."

Yarmila Kseniyevna looked as if she were about to argue, but before she could get anything out, Anna Avdotyevna said briskly, "And quite rightly, Tsarina. Go change, and when you are ready to see your sister, I will make sure your niece is also there waiting for you. Come, Yarmila Kseniyevna: let us leave the Tsarina in peace. There is much to be done." She put her hand on Yarmila Kseniyevna's shoulder and ushered her out of the room in a way suggesting that any resistance was futile. Yarmila Kseniyevna, after a quick bewildered backwards glance at Slava, allowed herself to be led away.

Slava wondered with amusement how much of the governing of Zem' had been accomplished by Anna Avdotyevna under her sister's reign, and how much was likely to be accomplished under her own. Quite a lot, she suspected. She started over towards her bedroom. The snow hare and the snow fox leaped up and trotted after her.

We want to see our new quarters, the snow fox told her. *We should ascertain whether they are fit lodgings for us, or if we need something a little finer. Perhaps you will have to move to the Imperial apartments after all.*

I thought you lived in a den in the snow, Slava replied.

So? asked the fox. She darted ahead of Slava and into the bedroom. Masha and Manya shrieked.

"It is nothing; it is only my companion," Slava assured them.

"Like a pet, Tsarinovn...Tsarina?" asked Manya, and turned bright red and bowed down to her boot-tops three times before Slava could stop her.

"Sort of," said Slava. "They will be lodging with me, it seems."

Feathers, said the snow fox, with a deep sigh of happiness, and leapt onto the bed and curled up on a pillow. Masha and Manya shrieked again and twitched in a way that suggested that their intense desire to protect Slava's pillow was warring with their intense fear of the snow fox.

"She can sleep there," said Slava.

Of course I can; who would dare stop me? said the snow fox, snuggling deeper into the pillow. The snow hare leapt up onto the bed and took a position on another pillow. It was a good thing, Slava though, that her bed had more pillows on it than any sane woman could ever possibly want or need. There would be enough for both her new companions, and to spare.

"Won't they...won't they...fight, Tsarina?" asked Manya, bowing nervously.

She means, won't I try to eat the snow hare, explained the snow fox smugly, rejoicing in her own mental acuity.

She won't, said the snow hare.

The snow hare is right, alas, said the snow fox. *I won't try to eat him. He is a brother, or something like that, so I can't. Those of us in the gods' service cannot do harm to each other. Well, not easily, anyway.*

And if she tried, she would fail, added the snow hare.

The gods would stop her? asked Slava.

No, I would.

*You **think** you would*, said the snow fox.

"They won't fight," Slava assured Manya. "They're in the service of the gods, and therefore must live in harmony." She wasn't entirely sure herself what that meant, but Masha and Manya seemed to find the words very wise and comforting, and so, nodding their heads sagely, they turned away from the bed and the animals luxuriating in it and to the important business of dressing Slava for her private audience with her sister (now presumably half-witted) and niece.

This turned out to be a complex process, with much agonizing on the part of Masha and Manya, and many disparaging comments about Slava's current gown, which she had borrowed from her mother.

"It is a sanctuary robe," Slava told them as they held it out at arm's length and pursed their mouths disapprovingly. "It is not supposed to be fine. It is supposed to keep me from being naked. And riding in the arms of a leshaya has left it rather worn."

"Yes, of course, Tsarinovn...Tsarina," Masha bowed hastily, "but I think it should be...be..."

"Put to better use," suggested Manya.

"The scullery maids always need more rags," said Masha.

"Well..." said Slava. She knew that they were right and that she couldn't go around wearing it, now that she was Tsarina, but the thought of turning her mother's sanctuary robe into scullery rags seemed somehow indecent. "I would rather save it," she said finally. "It has served me well, and on a day of great import. Set it aside and keep it safe."

"Yes, of course, Tsarina," said Masha and Manya together, eyeing the robe with new interest. "Perhaps people will want to see it, and pay their respects."

For a moment Slava thought they must be mocking her, but then she looked at their solemn faces and realized that they were speaking perfectly seriously. "Perhaps," she said. "Let's not turn it into kitchen rags just yet, in any case."

Masha and Manya reverently folded the ragged robe and set it aside, before returning to dressing Slava.

"Do you think this is fine enough?" Masha asked Manya, holding up a gown she had dug up somewhere, probably from one of the chests that filled the wardrobe room next door to overflowing. Slava had never seen that particular gown before, but there was nothing unusual about that, as Masha and Manya were constantly producing new gowns out of nowhere. She suspected they stayed up late at night and sewed them in their own time, which was both touching and horrible. This one was so encrusted with gold and precious gems that Masha was having a hard time holding it up high enough to keep it from dragging on the floor.

"It has a headdress somewhere to go with it," said Manya. "Very large and gold. If we could find that..."

"And two or three stout guards to carry me," Slava put in.

Masha and Manya stopped and gave her looks of confusion and terror.

"It will be very heavy," Slava said with a gentle smile. "Let's save it for an audience with the Princess Council, shall we? And that way you can search out the matching headdress—I would hate to appear ill-dressed"—Masha and Manya flinched so horribly at that thought that Slava knew she had gone too far, and added hastily—"not that I ever would, with you two to dress me. Do find the headdress, if you can, and see if needs burnishing or dusting or something. Meanwhile, something simple would suit me better for this simple evening with my friends and family."

"Of course, Tsarina, of course, of course," said Masha, bowing three or four times and scurrying, or rather dragging herself and the massive gown, off to the wardrobe.

"You are very kind, Tsarina," said Manya. She gave Slava a surprisingly shrewd look. Slava had occasionally suspected that there was some kind of intelligence lurking behind Manya's eyes, if only she would take the trouble to let it out. Pleased to see it peeking out again, Slava smiled as encouragingly as possible and said, "Much can be accomplished with kindness, Manya."

"I see that, Tsarina," said Manya, giving Slava an even shrewder look.

"Will this gown suit, Tsarina?" asked Masha anxiously, trotting back from the wardrobe with a gown in her arms that was so plain it was almost wearable.

"Excellently," said Slava, giving her a smile as well. For a moment Masha smiled in return with the smile of the genuinely good-hearted.

"Did anyone try to harm you while I was...gone?" asked Slava, suddenly wondering if anyone had attempted to take revenge on her through her maids. She could feel her cheeks flushing at the very idea.

"No, no, not at all, Tsarina," Masha assured her.

"There was some talk of locking us up, and we got some queer looks from the guards, and once Vova who guards the lower stairs said that we'd get what was coming to us and pinched my waist so hard I got a bruise, but other than that nothing. Tsarina," said Manya in one long hurried breath.

"Vova pinched me, too, and twisted my arm so hard I thought I'd sprained it," whispered Masha, looking down.

"Vova was sent to do night watch at the East Gate," added Manya with great satisfaction. "I told Allochka in the kitchen, who told one of the cooks, who told Anna Avdotyevna, who told Boleslav Vlasiyevich if any of his guards ever laid a hand on her maids again, she'd..." Manya paused in unusual confusion, and concluded, "and Vova was out doing the coldest night duty the very next evening, with a black eye to boot."

"She said she'd cut off his balls and eat them in the Hall of Celebration," said Masha with a giggle.

"Really?" said Slava. "I suddenly feel a new respect for Anna Avdotyevna. I knew she ruled with an iron fist, but truly..."

"I don't think she'd've had to make good on her threat, Tsarina," said Manya with a grin. "Because everyone knows that she already did it once. Or something like it."

"Everyone is *very* afraid of Anna Avdotyevna, Tsarina," said Masha, with an expression that said she counted herself most emphatically amongst that number.

"Every now and then she likes to remind people they shouldn't stop being afraid, Tsarina," said Manya. "Not that they need much reminding. And the guards are even more afraid to cross Boleslav Vlasiyevich now than they were before."

"I shall keep that in mind," said Slava. "Now, my gown..."

Although clearly full of misgivings about allowing Slava to go out in such unpresentable attire, Masha and Manya dressed her in the very plain dress they had found, and, with only feeble attacks at her hair and face, let her go.

A large gang of guards was waiting for Slava as soon as she stepped out of her chambers, and they all closed silently around her as she began walking down the hall. Slava tried to smile at them in an encouraging fashion, but they all resolutely refused to meet her eye. Some of them, she recognized, were the same men who half a year ago would share gossip with her from the kitchens. Those guards appeared particularly keen not to catch her gaze.

Anna Avdotyevna suddenly swept in from a side corridor and, sliding in some mysterious fashion through all the guards, joined up with Slava. Everyone, including Slava, twitched in uncontrollable terror at her unexpected appearance. Somehow, from one step to the next, the guards were all walking two paces farther away from Slava than they had been an instant before. Anna Avdotyevna really did bear a strong resemblance to Vladya in both mind and manner, Slava thought as they walked through the suddenly-empty air around them. She wondered, uncomfortably, how strong a resemblance Anna Avdotyevna bore to her.

"I see I have not spoken in vain," said Anna Avdotyevna with satisfaction, breaking the terrified silence. Slava could see that she was thinking of the story Masha and Manya had just shared with her, and that she knew that everyone else there was also thinking of the same story. "Bear that in mind, Tsarina, for when *you* must command the respect of those you rule."

"Perhaps I will let you do it for me, Anna Avdotyevna," said Slava. "You do it so much better than I ever could, I think."

"Some Tsarinas do employ other women to do their dirty work for them, it is true, Tsarina," said Anna Avdotyevna. Slava couldn't tell whether she approved of this or not.

"I am coming with you, Tsarina," Anna Avdotyevna continued. "You should not have to face...what you are about to face alone."

"Is my niece there?" Slava asked.

"I brought her to her mother myself, Tsarina," said Anna Avdotyevna. "I judged no one else so fit to perform that sad task."

"And...How is she? How has she taken it?"

"I cannot tell, Tsarina," said Anna Avdotyevna thoughtfully. "Or at least, I could not when I left them. Your niece did not appear to have grasped the enormity of what had happened. Or even what had happened at all. I am not sure that she understands the change undergone by her mother, in both mind and station."

"I'm not sure I do either," said Slava.

"Well, whatever you do, Tsarina, do not let your niece know that. At the moment I think you have little to fear from her, but even at her tender age she possesses some cunning and little honor, and there are those who would support her claim to the Wooden Throne, I am sure of it."

"Like whom?" Slava asked.

Anna Avdotyevna gave her an approving look. "You should have the matter looked into, Tsarina," she said. "Soon. By someone you trust. But in the meantime, do not let your guard down around Prasha. She might seem like a mere little girl, but because of who she is, she is much more dangerous than that."

"Yes, I know," said Slava.

"Then make sure you do not stop knowing it, Tsarina, when you see your sister and your niece before you. I know how tender your heart can be, but in this you must steel it against the claims of others. Do not forget with whom you are dealing."

"My heart is more than tender, Anna Avdotyevna," said Slava. "I will not forget. I will do what I consider necessary, you may be sure of that."

"Then be sure that you consider keeping your sister and your niece off the throne necessary, Tsarina," said Anna Avdotyevna.

"I was the one who stopped my sister when no one else would," said Slava evenly. "I will not forget."

By then they had reached the doors to her sister's chambers, preventing Anna Avdotyevna from saying more, but Slava could see from her face that she had nothing more to say, as she had tested Slava and not found her wanting. Slava wondered how often she was going to do that, and what Slava would have to do to stop her. She knew that to Anna Avdotyevna's firm mind, Slava's own softness seemed like weakness, and that it would be very hard to disabuse her of that notion, as in Anna Avdotyevna herself, softness *would* be weakness. Slava knew that the argument she had been given, up there in the North, that the world needed more people like her, would hold little weight with Anna Avdotyevna. She needed some other argument, something that would appeal to Anna Avdotyevna...

"Anna Avdotyevna!" said Slava abruptly, making the guard at the door freeze in mid-knock.

"Do not confuse me for you, or anyone else," Slava said. "The blood of both Lyubov the Kind and Miroslava Praskovyevna runs through my veins. Thus far you have only seen Lyubov's granddaughter, but Miroslava's granddaughter is there just as surely. Be assured that she stands behind me, stiffening my backbone and strengthening all my actions."

"Truly, Tsarina?" asked Anna Avdotyevna.

"I hear her speak to me every day," said Slava. "Sometimes—often—I force myself to be soft and gentle in order to drown out her voice, which calls for blood and fire. Her voice is not a kind one, Anna

Avdotyevna, and should not be given too much say, especially in the Hall of Council. It whispers sweet things to the evil that lurks in all of us, urging us to do terrible deeds. You do not want me to do terrible deeds, Anna Avdotyevna. But be assured that I could. I am not so soft as you think, Anna Avdotyevna."

Slava could see by the look on Anna Avdotyevna's face that she had accomplished her aim, and made Anna Avdotyevna believe in her. Anna Avdotyevna, Slava thought, was a lot less like Vladya than seemed at first glance, because Anna Avdotyevna could, on occasion, actually hear what other people were saying when they spoke. Even if what they were speaking was barely more than nonsense. Once again she marveled at how easy it was to win people over by telling a certain kind of truth, a truth that skirted dangerously close to stupidity and lies, a truth that she had not known existed until that moment, but as soon as it left her mouth, she knew that it was not only true, it was exactly the right thing to say.

"They say that even the strongest wept when you looked into their hearts in the Hall of Council, Tsarina," said Anna Avdotyevna. "The kitchens and the maids' chambers are afire with the news. Is it true?"

"I have no doubt that the kitchens are afire with gossip," said Slava. "They always are. But in this case it is true. My own sister lost her wits when I let her look into my heart, and the Hall of Council was nearly undone when I looked into theirs. You do not want me to do terrible deeds, Anna Avdotyevna."

"Perhaps not," said Anna Avdotyevna. "But I want you to remember that you can do them. Guard! Open the door!"

The guard, who had stood there in frozen terror during the entire conversation between Slava and Anna Avdotyevna, let his hand reach the door and knock.

"Who is it!" cried a voice. Slava realized it was Prasha's.

"The Tsarina demands entry!" called Anna Avdotyevna.

"The Tsarina is already here!" shouted Prasha back through the door.

Anna Avdotyevna flared her nostrils.

"Boleslav Vlasiyevich!" called Slava quickly. "Are you there?"

"I'm opening the door as we speak, Tsarina!" shouted Boleslav Vlasiyevich. There was a rattling of bolts, and Boleslav Vlasiyevich pulled open the door.

"How is my sister?" Slava demanded.

"A healer is with her, Tsarina," said Boleslav Vlasiyevich, stepping back with a bow to let Slava in. "She appears...as she was, but she does not appear to suffer."

"That is good," said Slava. "I would see her."

"She is in her bedroom, with her daughter and the healer, Tsarina," said Boleslav Vlasiyevich. "I will take you to her."

"Don't you dare! Don't let her near us!" cried Prasha from the next room.

"Prasha!" called Slava. Part of her was aware how ridiculous this was, to be conducting this delicate and terrible conversation with her niece at the top of her lungs, in front of at least a dozen onlookers, but there didn't seem to be any way around it. "Prasha!" she repeated. "I would speak to you!"

"NO!" screamed Prasha, making Slava flinch.

"Tsarina..." said Anna Avdotyevna warningly.

"I know," said Slava softly. She brushed past the guards and went into her sister's bedroom.

"HOW DARE YOU!" screamed Prasha from where she was sitting on the bed, next to Slava's sister, who was lying propped on pillows. Slava couldn't tell if she was awake or asleep. Perhaps she couldn't tell herself. "HOW DARE YOU COME IN HERE! BOLESLAV! WHY IS SHE NOT ARRESTED?"

"It is good that you care so for your mother, Prasha," said Slava gently. "You are a good daughter."

"GET AWAY! GUARDS! GUARDS!! ARREST THIS TRAITOR!!" Prasha's face, never, alas, very handsome, crumpled into pitiful tears. Slava spared a moment to wonder how her sister, who despite all her flaws had always been a great beauty, and her handpicked husband, who on his wedding day had been counted the handsomest man in the empire, had managed to produce a girl so ill-favored as Prasha. Truly, the gods were cruel. Of course, a sweeter temper would have sweetened her face considerably.

"Healer!" said Slava. "Is there nothing you can do for my niece?"

"I can give her watered vodka, Tsarinovna...Tsarina!" added the healer, after catching the menacing eyes of both Boleslav Vlasiyevich and (much more terrifying) Anna Avdotyevna. "But it may only make her more excited. A nervous trouble of this sort..."

"I understand," said Slava. "Prasha, my dear niece, dry your eyes. Your mother needs you. Someone must be strong for her, since she cannot be strong for herself."

"NO!" screamed Prasha.

"Prasha?" said Slava's sister, raising herself feebly from her pillows. "Did you say something, Prashenka?"

"Mama!" cried Prasha. "Mama, send her away! Send them all away, the traitors!"

"Who is here?" asked Vladya. "Is that Slava?"

"Yes," said Slava, stepping closer to the bed. "How do you feel, Vladya?"

"My head..." said Vladya feebly. "But it doesn't matter, as long as you're here. Come lie beside me, Slavochka. I want you to lie beside me. Do you remember when we were little girls?"

"Of course," said Slava.

"I don't remember...I don't remember much today, for some reason. But I remember when you were born. I remember when you were a little baby. Lie down beside me, Slavochka."

Slava lay down beside her, on the other side of the bed from Prasha, who was radiating rage and pain like heat from bathhouse stones. Vladya reached over and pulled Slava close to her, so that Slava's head was resting on her shoulder.

"I used to hold you like this, Slavochka, when you were little. I loved you so much. Mother told me to watch over you always. You were fragile and special, she said, and I must watch over you always."

On the other side of the bed Prasha gave a great sob and buried her face in the bedclothes.

"And then I had Prasha, and I knew exactly how mother felt. Only Prasha is strong, like me, isn't she?"

"Yes," said Slava.

"So she'll have to watch over you always, won't she? Because you're still fragile and special."

"I am a woman grown now," said Slava. "It is my turn to watch over Prasha."

"But you are still fragile and special. I can feel it. Our hearts...Our hearts were torn apart for a long time, Slava, but now they are joined again. I looked into your heart, and I was washed away, just as the dream warned me, wasn't I?"

Slava looked up at Vladya. Her eyes were bright and clear.

"Vladya!" cried Slava.

"I am washed away, Slava," said Vladya serenely. "You can't call me back. But I have a piece of your heart with me."

"No, Vladya! Try to stay!" Out of the corner of her eye Slava saw Anna Avdotyevna shake her head in warning.

"I am washed away," repeated Vladya. "I can no longer watch over you. Prasha will have to take my place. Prasha!" She sat up. "Swear to me."

"What, mama?" asked Prasha, raising her tear-rumpled face from the bedclothes.

"Swear to me you will watch over Slava always. Swear your allegiance to her."

"What! No! Mama, no!"

"Swear it, Prasha. I will not be able to ask this of you again. Already the flood is taking me. So swear it now."

"I..." Prasha gave Slava a look of such bitter hatred that Slava half-feared she would be forced to call the guards to restrain her. "I swear it."

"My sweet girl," said Vladya, kissing Prasha's hand. She stroked Slava's hair. "Fragile and special..." she murmured.

"Vladya..." said Slava, but before she could say anything else, Vladya had fallen back onto the pillows. When Slava looked into her eyes, they were closed.

"It didn't have to be like this," Slava said, mostly to herself. "It didn't have to be like this. We both had the same gifts...the same sight. You just never cared enough to use them. You never wanted to make yourself weak enough to accept them. And then when they washed over you, you broke instead of bending, and were washed away." She looked over at the healer. "What ails her now?" she asked.

"Her mind has wandered...Tsarina," said the healer. "Sometimes people who are sick in the head, their minds wander back and forth. Sometimes it's like they're right in the room there with you, and sometimes it's like they're somewhere across the Middle Sea, and you never know when it's going to be which."

"Do they ever get better?" Slava asked.

"Sometimes, Tsarina."

"But sometimes not," Slava concluded.

"Often not, Tsarina."

"I thought not. Guards! Escort the others to more comfortable quarters for a moment. I would speak with my niece alone."

"No!" cried Prasha.

"We must have this conversation someday, Prasha," said Slava. "Let us have it now."

"Boleslav Vlasiyevich!" pleaded Prasha. "Surely you won't leave me here with this traitor!"

"She is your Tsarina now," said Boleslav Vlasiyevich, looking rather more resolute than Slava had ever seen him before.

"I will do you no harm, I promise," Slava said. "You have no reason to fear me."

"No? Then why is my mother lying here in this bed?"

"Boleslav Vlasiyevich! I would speak with my niece in private."

Slava waited until Boleslav Vlasiyevich and Anna Avdotyevna had shepherded everyone—including themselves, although it was clear that Anna Avdotyevna found leaving painful, and was in grave doubts about Slava's ability to handle Prasha—out of the room.

"Dry your eyes, Prasha," she said once they were gone. "You will do no one any good with your weeping, least of all my sister."

"How dare you call her sister!" cried Prasha.

"Because I have known her for three times as long as you have, my dear. Like it or not, she is my older sister, and I have spent my entire life by her side."

"And yet you...you..."

"Prasha," said Slava firmly. "What do you know of your mother's rule? What do you know of her actions of late?"

"What is it to you?!"

"Do you know what happened to her, Prasha?"

"You...You cursed her!"

"No," said Slava. "Others did. Only...Do you know how a curse works, Prasha?"

"Why? No, of course not," said Prasha sullenly.

"I have little knowledge of it myself, but I have been told that curses take the easiest way, like water running downhill. And it seems to me, from what I have seen of them, that the easiest way for them is through our weaknesses. It seems to me, from what I have seen of curses, that they merely make use of what is evil in us already. We let them in. I do not know whether it is possible to withstand them, but everyone I have seen who was brought down by one let it happen through their own evil actions. We bring them upon ourselves, at least in part. Or so it seems to me, from what I have seen of them."

"This isn't her fault!"

"No," said Slava. "And yes. Do you know what happened today, Prasha?"

"You...You came back with your monsters, and you attacked my mother, and usurped her place!"

"Do you know why I came back, Prasha?"

"To attack her!"

"I received word that she intended to kill my friends. Even Vladislava Vasilisovna, Prasha, who is younger than you, and a guest in this kremlin. So I came back, and word had not deceived me. She did intend to kill them. And me too. She gave the order to have me killed, Prasha. I heard the words issue from her own mouth."

"You...You're a traitor! The Tsarina said so herself!"

"I do not think that one can condemn someone for treason so easily..." said Slava, staring thoughtfully off at the wall. She shook her head and brought herself back to the matter at hand. "You see, Prasha, it was the curse, eating at her mind, making her say such things, but she could not have said such things if she had not been thinking them anyway. A curse, it seems to me, will not make you act against your will: quite the reverse, in fact. It merely brings out what you have been secretly willing all along. And so she ordered to have me killed, and so I let her look into my heart."

"And it was that evil! She looked in, and the horror struck her down, it was so evil!"

"Prasha," said Slava. "If you look into my heart, the only thing you will see is yourself. It is my gift."

"That's not true!" cried Prasha.

"I fear that it is. But it is true that when she looked into my heart, and saw herself, she was indeed struck down with horror, and her mind was broken. I fear it will never recover. And I fear that she should never rule again, even if her mind should return to her. She is not fit to rule."

"And you are! You just want the throne to yourself! You *are* a traitor!"

"Prasha," said Slava patiently. "You must see that this means my sister's line has ended. Your sole duty now is to care for your mother. Do you understand what I am saying, Prasha?"

"Yes! You've usurped the throne from my mother *and* me! I understand perfectly!"

"I think it might be best if you went with my sister to Deep Pond sanctuary," said Slava. "To your grandmother. They will care for you both there, and you will want for nothing."

"And now you're exiling me!" cried Prasha. "Exiling us both!"

"There can be no other way," said Slava. "I will ensure that you both have the best of care, but my sister's line is ended." She rose from the bed. "It will do you good to spend time with your grandmother,

Prasha. There is much that you could learn from her, and I am sure that she longs to be with you."

"I..." Prasha's mouth suddenly twisted and her face turned such an alarming shade that Slava had already shouted "Healer!" before the shriek was able to leave Prasha's mouth.

Anna Avdotyevna and the healer came rushing in. Prasha was still shrieking incoherently.

"See if you can calm her," said Slava. "If she appears to be bothering my sister, have her moved."

The healer bowed silently without looking up from Prasha's quivering form.

"Send word if you have need of me," said Slava. "I will leave you to your work." She swept out of the room, with Anna Avdotyevna hurrying behind her.

"I take it that did not go well, Tsarina?" said Anna Avdotyevna, once they were out in the corridor. Boleslav Vlasiyevich and half-a-dozen guards formed up around them.

"Was there ever any chance that it would?" said Slava. "But I had to tell her of her new position with my own mouth. I think I shall send both of them to Gluboky Prud, to my mother. It will do them good."

"You are disinheriting Praskovya, then?" asked Anna Avdotyevna approvingly.

"Yes," said Slava. "It is the only way."

"I know it is, Tsarina, but I feared you lacked the ability to do it. Are you sure Deep Pond is far enough away?"

Slava stopped and turned to face Anna Avdotyevna. "It was far enough away to keep my mother from the throne for many years," she said. "It is far enough. I believe I have little to fear on that score, for the moment at least. The princesses will be plunged into confusion by this sudden change in power, and Prasha is still too young—and frankly, too incompetent—to organize an uprising any time soon. I think they will be safely contained for many years there."

"If you say so, Tsarina," said Anna Avdotyevna, sounding more agreeable than Slava had imagined possible. "But now, if I may make a suggestion..."

"Yes?" said Slava.

"Return to your chambers and rest. The throne, and the princesses, and your troublesome family, will still be waiting for you tomorrow. You must refresh yourself for your coming labors, especially considering..." she looked meaningfully at Slava's waist.

"Wise advice," said Slava.

"Good. Boleslav Vlasiyevich! Escort the Tsarina back to her quarters! Ensure that she has everything she might need. Good night, Tsarina, and may your sleep be restful." Anna Avdotyevna bowed and walked off back towards Slava's sister's chambers. Slava suspected that she meant to spend the night there, watching over Vladya and Prasha. Anna Avdotyevna was, under her terrifying outer surface, a kind person, Slava thought. Rather kinder than she was herself, in fact, or at least softer. She, after all, unlike Slava, had not traded away her own sister's life for that of some Northern slip of a girl and the possibility of a daughter.

Boleslav Vlasiyevich and the other guards walked Slava the rest of the way back to her chambers, and, after a knock failed to raise either Masha or Manya, Boleslav Vlasiyevich opened the door and led her in himself. The room was dark and empty, except for a small fire in the fireplace.

"Go find the maids!" Boleslav Vlasiyevich told the other guards. "I'll light some candles while we wait, Tsarina," he added, once the others were gone.

"Thank you," Slava told him. "And...Boleslav Vlasiyevich?"

"Yes, Tsarina?" he asked, staring hard at the candle he had picked up off the table.

"I have two questions."

"Only two, Tsarina?" She thought he smiled despite his best efforts to stop himself.

"Only two. Why did you let us go?"

"At the gate, you mean, Tsarina?"

"Yes, at the gate. Why did you...why did you let us go but not go with us?"

"Are you angry about that, Tsarina?" he asked, no longer smiling but still staring hard at the candle, as if afraid to meet her gaze.

"No, just puzzled. You see, I never could tell where your loyalty lies, Boleslav Vlasiyevich, and I still can't. So why did you let us go?"

"My loyalty is always to Zem', Tsarina."

"I'm very glad to hear that. How did...doing what you did at the gate serve Zem'?"

This time he glanced up for a moment and then quickly looked back down, as if scalded or...shy. It was such an odd thought to have of him that Slava wanted to dismiss it out of hand, but nonetheless she could sense some reticence in him she had never sensed before, as if he were fighting hard to hide something from her.

"If your sister had caught you, Tsarina..." he said eventually, turning the candle over and over in his hands.

"Yes?"

"If your sister had caught you, it would have torn the realm apart. I knew she was mad that day, not in her right mind, and I knew...I knew that she mustn't catch you, not for anything. I had hoped and hoped that you had slipped out already, but when you ran into me..." his breath caught for a moment, "...when you ran into me, I knew that I couldn't turn you in. But if I had also gone missing...well, that would have been even uglier. The guard would have descended into chaos, and...it was too much of a risk. Are you angry that I didn't go with you, Tsarina?"

"Of course you couldn't just disappear," said Slava by way of answering. "That was well done on your part."

"Thank you, Tsarina." He played with the candle a bit more, and then asked, in a voice that in another man Slava would have called apprehensive, "And your second question, Tsarina?"

"What would you have done?" she asked.

"About what, Tsarina?" he asked, squatting down to light the candle from the fire in the fireplace.

"Today," Slava said, even though she knew that he knew what she meant. "Down...down there. What would you have done, if I hadn't done anything?"

"If you hadn't saved us, you mean, Tsarina?" he asked, standing back up. The candle in his hand blossomed with fire, shedding an unsteady light on his face.

"Yes. What would you have done?"

"Speaking truthfully, Tsarina?"

"Of course."

"Speaking truthfully, Tsarina, I don't know what I would have done. I didn't know what I was doing the whole time we were down there. All I could think was that I had to buy us more time, buy you more time. All I could think of was not to let her kill any of you—all of you—especially you—for as long as possible. When she gave the order and I started walking towards you, I don't know what I was thinking. I wasn't thinking anything at all, except that the house spirit was walking with me, and so maybe I had a chance. All I could think was that as long as I hadn't killed any of you, especially you, there was still a chance. Because I knew that I would never shed your blood, nor the little princess's.

"But I couldn't see how not to do it. Your sister...well, you saw how she was, and half the guard will do whatever they're told without a second thought. I knew I couldn't tell her no, not straight out to her face, without there being bloodshed, but I didn't know what else to do. All I could think of was that as long as I hadn't done it yet, there was still a chance. When the house spirit tripped me it was the happiest moment of my life. I never went down so easy in my life. I knew it was my chance."

"Did you ever consider yourself loyal to my sister?" asked Slava.

Even in the flickering candlelight Slava could see the shame-faced smile that flitted across his face at that question.

"I was loyal to what your sister should have been, Tsarina," he said finally. "I wanted to serve a great Empress, someone to be proud of. Even guards and merchants' sons have pride. I wanted to serve a great Empress, and be proud of that service. Only..."

"You could not take pride in my sister's service?" Slava asked.

"No...Sometimes...Of late, not much. Tsarina."

"And mine?" asked Slava.

He smiled a strange smile. Slava couldn't help but be struck again by how hard it was for her to read him, when most other people were open books to her.

"Thus far your wavering has served me well, Boleslav Vlasiyevich," she said. "I cannot criticize you for it too harshly. But I will not hold with you wavering in your service when it is *me* you serve, do you understand me?"

For a moment she thought he might laugh, or perhaps shout at her in anger. "You have to ask?" he said. "After...after everything I've done for you? How many times do I have to prove myself?"

"What have you ever done to prove yourself to me, Boleslav Vlasiyevich?" she asked sharply. "You...you let me escape, true enough, and you stood by while I...did what I had to do, but truly, I don't know why. How should I know you will not do the same to me, if some other woman should ask it of you? What have you done, that you think I should trust in you? For I will need to have people around me I can trust, in the coming days. Why should one of them be you?"

"How could you doubt me, Tsarina!" he cried, now truly angry. "After...after..."

"After what, Boleslav Vlasiyevich! After what?"

"You don't..." His voice changed from anger to bewilderment, and something softer. "You don't know," he said. "You never knew, did you Tsarina?"

"Know what, Boleslav Vlasiyevich?"

He put the candle down on the table, hiding his face in darkness. For a moment there was silence.

"I smashed his hands," he said eventually. "I found out who he was and I smashed his hands so that he would never work again. He used to beg by the North Gate until he disappeared a few winters ago, probably frozen to death."

"Whose..." Slava's voice cracked, and she had to swallow and try again, even though she knew the answer already. "Whose hands did you break, Boleslav Vlasiyevich?"

"The man...the guard your mother and your sister...it was the week after I was taken into service here. You had already been so kind to me, Tsarina, although perhaps you don't remember it. You gave me money to send word to my mother of what had become of me, because I wouldn't receive any pay for a month and I hadn't a grosh to my name. And you told me you were sure I would bring great honor to my family with my service. Already I knew, knew that...well, anyway. And then one night when I was standing guard, I saw you running away from the kremlin in the dark, and you were bareheaded and crying and your clothes were torn, and I know something terrible had happened, so I left my post and I followed you, and I heard...I heard what you told the herbwoman, and I kept watch while you were there, and I heard what passed between you and your mother and your sister.

"I waited till I was sure you had gone home before I returned to the barracks, and after my punishment for deserting my post was over, I found out who it was and I caught him when he wasn't expecting it and I smashed his hands so that he would never use them again. And after my punishment for that was over, word got out that I was the man for brutal work, and I rose higher and higher because of it. No one guessed why I'd done what I'd done, and I...it was not my secret to share.

"Except with your mother. One day when she offered me the chance to be her Captain, I told her that I knew, and asked her what restitution she would make to you, what the Stepnaya family would demand in retribution, and she stepped down from the throne rather than answer." He smiled bitterly. "I'm afraid I didn't serve you very well in that, Tsarina. I know that many had cause to love her, but I hated her every day of my service to her, and I thought anyone would treat you better, even your sister. But it seems I was wrong about that."

"Who can tell," said Slava softly. "My mother loved me more, of that I am sure, but we do not always serve the ones we love very well. And what will you do about it now, Boleslav Vlasiyevich?"

"What would you have me do, Tsarina?"

"Keep your secret, Boleslav Vlasiyevich. Does anyone else know?" He shook his head.

"Then let us keep it that way. I would not tarnish the reputation of my kinswomen even more than I have already done. The Stepnaya family's retribution would be...unhelpful, I fear, especially with the succession in such disarray now. And I would have my mother re-membered as the good-hearted Empress. She...she did help many people, even if she failed me. And even me—it's not as if she failed me entirely. She did what she thought was best, and much of what she did was good."

"As you wish, Tsarina." He was staring at her as if expecting some-thing more from her, but said nothing more.

"And...so you say he is gone, Boleslav?" she added, to fill in the si-lence, but urgency suddenly overcame her. "Gone from this city?" she asked, her voice cracking again, to her shame.

"Tsarina..." Boleslav Vlasiyevich came and, to her surprise, knelt down before her and kissed her hand before she could stop him. "By all accounts, he is dead. And, Tsarina?" He smiled up at her. "He suf-fered greatly."

Slava knew she should say something, thank Boleslav Vlasiyevich for his service, express joy that this man whose face she only remem-bered in nightmarish snatches had suffered and died in order to give her peace of mind, but instead she found herself sitting on the floor, crying as she had that night so long ago when she had slipped out of the kremlin and run bareheaded through the frosty streets. Boleslav patted her back until she was done.

"Are you sure you don't want my sister back?" she asked when she had stopped. "Or someone with a little more steel in her backbone? Someone who...wouldn't cry over trifles all the time? As you told me yourself, I am made of such fine, soft stuff. Perhaps this is all wrong... perhaps I should go back to the sanctuary..." She tried to make herself shut up, but she couldn't, and babbled on for several more breaths, un-til Boleslav took a handkerchief out of his pocket and wiped her face.

"Your maids are coming, if I guess rightly, Tsarina," he said. He got up and helped her to her feet. "And Tsarina?"

"What?" She tried to arrange her hair and her clothing to make it seem as if she had not just been crying her heart out and—it had to be admitted—practically lying on the floor in the dark in the arms of her own Captain of the Guard, but it was a hopeless task. The best she could hope for was that her appearance would be no more disheveled than usual, and Masha and Manya would put it down to her general carelessness about such matters.

"Two things. One, your secret—your mother's secret, that is—is safe with me, but only on one condition."

"What?"

"Don't feel too sorry for him, Tsarina. You were hardly the first he...treated as he did. All the maids and guards walked in fear of him. He volunteered for the duty, knowing the trick your mother was planning to play on you, and he..." Boleslav Vlasiyevich's cheek twitched, "bragged to me of your tears when I questioned him."

"Oh. How...how terrible."

"For him, Tsarina, yes. So don't feel too sorry for him."

"I'll...I'll try not to, I guess. But...will you forgive me for forgiving him?"

"Forgive him? Why would you do such a thing?"

"I don't know. No, I do. I always thought...I always thought I could never forgive him, or my mother, but now...now *I* am the one with the power, *I* am the strong one, and so...so I can forgive him, and her too. I...I can feel the strength, for the first time in my life, I can feel the strength to forgive."

"Neither of them deserve it," said Boleslav Vlasiyevich bluntly.

"If they deserved it, it wouldn't be forgiveness. The question is whether or not they need it."

"I doubt they need it either."

"But I do. I need to forgive them so that I don't spend the rest of my life wringing my hands over wrongs done to me and by me. But what was the second thing?"

"Oh." He gave her a considering look, and wiped off a few more tears. "To the best of my knowledge, Tsarina, your *sister* never made a ruling Empress kneel at her feet and beg forgiveness when she was still a slip of a girl. Your *sister* never raised a magical army and threatened to sack Krasnograd with it."

"I also called on Severnolesnoye and the steppe princesses to join me," said Slava through her sniffles. "Who knows what kind of an army we might have at our gates next month."

"I suppose I'd better be prepared, then," said Boleslav Vlasiyevich, crooking one corner of his mouth. "Do you think they'll actually send an army?"

"I wouldn't put it past them; that's why I sent my messages to them," said Slava. "The Severnolesniye have always been rebellious, and the steppe princesses have let me know that they would only be too happy to see someone of their blood sit the Wooden Throne. I am just afraid that—that the realm be will divided over this. But I could never have lived with myself if I had just sat back and let my sister harm Vladislava."

"You see, Tsarina?" said Boleslav Vlasiyevich. "Your *sister* never... your sister never did anything that frightened her, simply because she knew that she could never live with herself if it were not done. I always knew who the true Empress in the family was, and so did many others. It was never your sister."

"Thank you," said Slava, and started to sniffle again.

"Keep the handkerchief, Tsarina," he said, folding it into her hand, just as she had with Princess Malogornaya's daughter, so many months ago.

"Thank you," she said again.

"Think nothing of it, Tsarina," he said. He turned to go, and then stopped. "And in case you had any doubts, Tsarina, I will never waver when it comes to you."

"Why?" she demanded, and then could have kicked herself for asking such a question and for encouraging him when she shouldn't, as she so often seemed to do, but it was too late. He turned back to her, no longer showing any signs of intending to leave, and gave her another considering look in the semi-darkness.

"I told you, Tsarina. I wanted to serve a great Empress, someone I could take pride in. A child of ten could see that that Empress would be you."

"And what if I fail?"

"You won't, Tsarina."

"I am weak and foolish, Boleslav Vlasiyevich. Just now I was sobbing on the floor over a cruel trick played on me some fifteen years ago, one I barely remember. I doubt that is the behavior of a great Empress."

"You are wrong, Tsarina."

"*And* my own Captain of the Guard contradicts me at every turn! This is hardly the beginning of a brilliant reign!"

He laughed. "I never contradicted your sister, Tsarina, for even someone as hotheaded as me could see it would do no good. But you are another matter entirely."

"So you wanted me in her place because you think I am more malleable than she was?" She tried to say it lightly, like a joke, but the accusation was plain enough, too.

"No, Tsarina. I think you are wiser. Worthier. And most of all, kinder. You are kind to everyone, even those of us who don't deserve it. And that is why I will never waver. Not about you, and not about…the child you are said to bear. The father is not here, is he?"

"No," she confessed in a small voice. "And I don't know if he ever will be."

"Well. I am sorry, Tsarina. But your daughter, if she has the good fortune to be born, will never want for any care, any service, any protection a father could offer."

"I…I am glad to hear it, Boleslav Vlasiyevich." Her attempt to put an imperial tone back into her voice was stymied by another mortifying bout of sniffling that his words had brought on. "I'm sorry that I have troubled you with my foolish weakness," she said, and instead of stopping there like she should have, she carried on stupidly, "I didn't think it would affect me so, but it did! I'm sorry that you had to see that. You…I presumed too much upon your kindness, but I couldn't stop myself! I'm sorry."

"Any other Empress would have already had me put to death for what I did today, Tsarina," he said. "Once again, you…once again you have shown me more kindness than I deserve. You could never presume too much upon my own kindness, paltry as it is. But, Tsarina?"

"Yes?"

"I wouldn't go around saying 'I'm sorry' to too many others, if I were you. People like a good strong Empress, whether they'll admit it or not. But if you're ever in need of a secret shoulder to cry on—well," he suddenly smiled, "you know where I live."

This made Slava laugh through her sniffling. "That would be quite a sight!" she said. "The Empress coming into the barracks to sob on a guard's shoulder!" She grinned, feeling her sniffling retreat for good. "I fear it would do nothing for my hard-won dignity, however."

He grinned back. "Well, I could always come to you, Tsarina, if you prefer," he said.

Slava blushed, scandalizing herself and thanking the gods that the light from the single candle was not enough to show her face. She thought she knew well enough what he was offering, but a member of her own guard! And her carrying another man's child! It would be, it would be...well, quite in line with what many of her foremothers had done, but that was neither here nor there.

And...a small part of her had to admit that there might be healing in that, in finding solace in someone who wore a guard's uniform, in someone who could help her come full circle and—not undo, not erase, but heal over the dreadful hurt that had been inflicted upon her, by her own kinswomen, when she was barely more than a child. And maybe there would be healing in it for him, too.

"I thank you for your loyalty, Boleslav Vlasiyevich," she said. She meant to say it formally and distantly, but she could hear the laughter bubbling out with it, and so, by the look in his eyes, which now she could read very well, could he. Slava could sense that, whether she wished it or not, the intimacy that Boleslav Vlasiyevich had always seemed to believe was between them did, in fact, exist.

For what seemed like the first time in her life, and perhaps was, she was certain, as certain as she could be, that the sympathy that she sensed for him was reciprocated, and that he saw her as clearly as she saw him, maybe more so, he saw her as herself, strangely enough, and not just what he wanted her to be. He saw her as a kindred soul just as (and how strange, how unexpected, how inexplicable this was, given how different they were) she did him. The only question was what she was going to do about it.

The memory of him kneeling before her popped back into her head, bringing with it another blush, one that started in her stomach and made her scalp prickle so that she was sure her hair must be standing on end. Luckily, at that moment Masha and Manya came bustling in, or the gods alone knew what she might have done.

"I will leave you to your evening, Tsarina," he said. Something about the set of his mouth made her sure that he was recalling the same memory, and it was having the same effect on him. "Call for me if you need for anything, day or night."

Slava blushed again horribly, but even though Masha and Manya were lighting candles all over the place and filling the room with unwelcome light, neither of them seemed to notice. "Thank you," she said weakly, and told herself she would be glad to see him go. But just as his hand was reaching for the door, her voice said, entirely (she could have sworn) of its own accord, "I have one condition too, Boleslav Vlasiyevich!"

He stopped and waited by the door, looking at her with raised brows. Masha and Manya also stopped, but then, catching Slava's eye, retreated into the bedroom.

"The dungeons," said Slava. "You will not go down there again, do you understand me, Boleslav Vlasiyevich? There will be no 'brutal work' under my reign, by you or anyone else. Especially not by you. Is that clear, Boleslav Vlasiyevich?"

He caught his breath, and something—perhaps joy? Or was it re-gret?—flashed across his face. "Perfectly, Tsarina. I will make it so."

"Anyone serving under me, anyone whom I can trust, must have clean hands. Do I make myself clear, Boleslav Vlasiyevich?"

"You do, Tsarina."

"Once you have proven to me that your hands are no longer sullied by...by what you have done in my kinswomen's service, well...then I will decide how you may best serve *me*. Do you understand?"

Even from across the room, Slava could see how he smiled at her words. She didn't know whether to slap herself in the face for fool-ishness or smile at her triumph, but when he bowed stiffly and left the room with his eyes still fixed on her face, she knew she had won something. At the cost of, well...she told herself not to dwell on it. She would decide what to do about Boleslav Vlasiyevich once he had prov-en that he could have clean hands, just as she had told him.

And, she thought to herself, *with him there will never be any need to put my foot down. I could let him go a thousand times, and he would always come back of his own free will. A gift I can never earn or repay. If...if the future between us unfolds as I sense it will, I will have to spend the rest of my life being grateful to him for his free offering of more than I ever could or would ask from him. I will have to spend the rest of my life trying to deserve that, and not failing him.* As usual, the thought of needing to help some-one else gave her strength, more strength than any attempt to stand up for herself or put her foot down ever could.

After a moment Masha and Manya came bustling back in, laden with food, which was a very welcome sight. They broke out in flutter-ing apologies about their absence, but Slava, having recovered her-self entirely thanks to their relentless desire to serve her, which meant that she must relentlessly try to be the person they thought they were serving, stopped them by saying she was pleased to see they had been down in the kitchens, as she was starving, which prompted them to stop apologizing and start unburdening themselves of their trays.

Just as the food—much more than Slava could have ever possibly eaten by herself—was being set out on the tables in the front room, Olga and Vladislava came in.

"Are we…" said Olga uncertainly.

"No, sit down, sit down," Slava told them. "You're not bothering me at all."

"Was that…?" asked Olga, raising her brows and pointing towards the door to the corridor with her chin."

"We just saw Boleslav Vlasiyevich in the corridor!" Vladislava informed Slava excitedly. "He had the funniest look on his face! Did you chastise him, Tsarinovna?"

"Tsarina!" Olga corrected her sharply.

"Oh yes, Tsarina. Did you chastise him? Will you punish him?"

"No, why?" asked Slava, trying to convince herself that a child's avid desire for cruelty was not shining in Vladislava's eyes at the thought.

"For serving your sister!"

"Serving her was his duty," said Slava. "I wouldn't punish someone for doing their duty."

"And I think he's already served our Tsarina well enough, and is likely to continue to do so," said Olga, raising her brows again. "If I were you, Tsarina, I'd keep a man like that around. He could be useful for…all sorts of things."

"What did he do?" demanded Vladislava.

"He saved us when we were…down there," Olga told her, stroking her hair, much to Vladislava's annoyance.

"He didn't help us at all! Slava was the one who saved us! All he did was fall down!"

"He never hurt us when we were," Olga swallowed and looked Slava in the eye, making sure that she knew what it had been like, "in the dungeons. He made sure we were gently treated, to the best of his ability, and he never hurt us, even though…even though that's his job, isn't it, Tsarina?"

"It *was* his job," Slava told her. "Now it is no one's. Let him think of the defense of the kremlin and my family, and nothing more."

"Well, that's good," said Olga. "After…after being down there, I can't argue with you, even if others might think you've gone soft. Ah, Tsarina, I didn't mean any offense, of course."

"None taken," Slava assured her. "And I am glad to hear what you told me."

"But *Slava* saved us!" insisted Vladislava again. "Not Boleslav Vlasiyevich! He just got out of the way by falling down!"

"Well, sometimes that's the best you can do," Olga said, her natural cheerfulness reasserting itself as the dungeons were pushed into the back corners of her memory. "Anything else would have caused a bloodbath, like as not, so I'm glad to see he had the wit to take the opportunity when it presented itself. I tell you, Tsarina, if it were me, I'd rather have a man who's willing to fall down in the face of danger than, say, run away from it."

"You may be right," Slava told her. "I will think on your words."

"I *know* I'm right, Tsarina." Olga grinned at her. "And who knew you'd be owing your reign to some man's wavering, eh? Now there's a thought to worry over, and no mistake!"

"A piece of irony, indeed," Slava agreed. "Or perhaps it was all the will of the gods." The fact that her reign rested on what some might call masculine treachery and inconstancy *was* an irony not lost on her, and one that was, as Olga had pointed out, rather worrisome. Or perhaps not. Perhaps *this* was what all those aunts and grannies had meant when they had patted her arm and told her, with many a salacious look and leering grin, that she needed to take in a "bit of a man." Perhaps she just needed to act a bit more like a man from time to time, or at least accept the misdeeds of the men she had encountered throughout her life, because without them, without all their thoughtlessness and cruelty, she might not have gained the rule of Zem'.

Perhaps without all the wrongs that had been done her, she would never have been given this opportunity to do right. Perhaps there was a reason for all of it, or, most likely of all, she realized, this was her opportunity to turn all that foolishness and futility into something that was neither foolish nor futile. She could transmute the dross of pain and petty human problems into something more, if she could find the courage to do so.

"The gods make strange choices, then," said Olga. "But handsome ones, eh, Tsarina?"

"Oh, indeed." Slava made herself smile at that. She found she no longer wanted to talk about men, and particularly about Boleslav Vlasiyevich, grateful as she was to have Olga's unexpected support of him. He seemed like unfinished business, to be put away for a time and brought back out when there was breathing room to contemplate the unexpected—problem? No. Gift? Perhaps—that he had given her. Perhaps next year she and Olga could discuss this again, since Olga, strangely enough, seemed like the most trustworthy confidante for something like this.

But then again, Olga had always liked him, for reasons Slava found mysterious. Perhaps her heart, so much blunter and yet so much shrewder than Slava's fearful and circuitous one, had seen something in him that Slava was yet blind to. It was a thought best filed away for later times, Slava told herself again, and, in order to change the subject, she asked, "Where are the others?"

"Resting. Dima and Dunya and the others almost collapsed on our ride—they must have been up all night last night, and then that long cold wait outside while we were down...there...So we came back, but Vladislava wouldn't go to bed without seeing you. But if we're in your way, we'll leave."

"Oh no, certainly not," Slava assured them. "It will be good to have some friendly faces around me before bed. Otherwise who knows what I'd dream."

"I rode the best pony!" Vladislava told her eagerly. "Do you think I could go riding with her tomorrow? It's too bad that our ride was cut so short like that!"

"Of course," said Slava. "She's yours now. What's her name?"

The rest of the dinner was consumed with Vladislava's descriptions of the excellent pony that Slava had just given her, and her plans for daily rides starting tomorrow, despite the bad weather. Sometimes Olga tried to hush her, but Slava always told her to let Vladislava keep talking, as Vladislava's conversation was more refreshing to her than anything else she could imagine.

As soon as they had finished eating, Vladislava started yawning broadly, and Olga and Slava soon began copying her, which caused Olga to announce that it was bedtime for all of them, and to take Vladislava away and leave Slava to the mercy of her maids.

There was a good deal of fuss over getting Slava dressed for bed, but eventually it was over and Slava was left to rest as she saw fit.

Chapter
Twenty-Two

The next day her first order of business was visiting her sister. Prasha sulked, and Vladya stared vaguely at the ceiling and made nonsensical remarks.

"It is to be expected, Tsarina," said the healer.

"I suppose so," said Slava.

"When do you wish them to be sent to Deep Pond, Tsarina?" asked Anna Avdotyevna, who had, as Slava had guessed, spent the night with them. It was a shame that neither Vladya nor Prasha appeared particularly grateful for her exertions on their behalf, although that, too, was to be expected, Slava supposed.

"As soon as it is safe to move them," said Slava.

"It is safe to move them now, Tsarina," said the healer.

"I will make the arrangements myself, Tsarina," said Anna Avdotyevna.

"And will you travel with them?" Slava asked.

"Do you wish it, Tsarina?" asked Anna Avdotyevna, looking, unusually enough, taken aback by Slava's question.

"You should act as you think best," said Slava. "I will have need of you here, but they will have need of you there. You should act as you think best."

"Then I will stay here, Tsarina," said Anna Avdotyevna unhesitatingly.

"You will?" asked Slava, surprised.

"My place is by the side of the Empress," said Anna Avdotyevna. "I have no need of sanctuaries, nor they of me."

"Then you will be welcome," said Slava, and left Anna Avdotyevna and the healer to the business of preparing Vladya and Prasha for the journey. Slava could hear Prasha's angry complaints all the way down the hall. She wished there were something she could do not only to make Prasha see the truth but to reconcile her to it, but if that were possible, then, Slava knew, she would not be sending Prasha away in the first place.

The next order of business was to see that Vladislava, Olga, and the others were being properly cared for. When Slava entered the chambers where they were being housed, Vladislava threw herself at Slava with squeals of unrestrained joy, as if they had been separated for years instead of a single night.

"You came! You came! You came!" she shrieked in Slava's ear. "They said you wouldn't, but you came!"

"Vladislava!" said Olga sharply. "Leave the Tsarina alone!"

"She is not bothering me," said Slava, letting Vladislava cling to her as she made her way into the center of the room. "I am always glad to see her."

"She needs to learn how to comport herself around a Tsarina," said Olga.

"Says the person who mocked my efforts to civilize her on the journey down," said Slava with a smile.

For a moment everyone in the room (except Vladislava, of course) looked nervous, but then Olga realized it was a joke and broke into laughter, and so did the others after her.

"You are being well treated?" Slava asked.

"Very well," Olga assured her.

"Will you go riding with us today?" Vladislava asked.

"If I have time," Slava promised. "First I believe the Princess Council must be called."

Olga shuddered.

"Which you must attend," Slava told her.

Olga shuddered even more.

"It might be exciting," Slava told her. "I have, after all, just usurped my sister's throne."

"You have not!" cried Olga indignantly. "You saved an Imperial ward and our entire land from certain destruction!"

"You see why you must attend," said Slava.

"Oh, I *suppose*," said Olga. She tried to groan, but it came out as more of a grin instead.

"It will be in the afternoon," said Slava. "To give everyone time to gather their strength for quarreling."

Olga made a face.

"It will be over shortly," Slava promised. "I won't let it last past nightfall."

"Well in that case..." said Olga, sighing and smiling at the same time.

"Can *I* come?" asked Vladislava. "I'm a princess too. Well, sort of a princess."

"No, definitely not," said Olga.

"She should come," said Slava.

"Why would you torment a child like that?" asked Olga. "What has she done to deserve such a cruel punishment?"

"She is a princess, as she said," said Slava. "She should see what it means to be a princess. Someday she will have to sit at the Princess Council in her own right."

Olga allowed, after more groaning and grumbling, that this was, unfortunately, the case, and that both she and Vladislava would be there at the appointed time, providing that Vladislava promised to be quiet and still, and Slava promised to wrap the whole thing up before suppertime, because the only thing worse than sitting on the Princess Council would be sitting on the Princess Council on an empty stomach.

Slava promised that all those conditions would be met, and left Olga's chambers in high good humor. This lasted all through the rest of the morning, which Masha and Manya spent dressing her while Yarmila Kseniyevna told her all the latest news about the princesses and how they had reacted to this sudden turn in events.

"But most of them were there yesterday when you...did what you did, Tsarina," she concluded. "They say that most of them are pretty well cowed, so I doubt you'll have any trouble with them."

"Oh good," said Slava, and let herself be led to the Hall of Council.

The princesses were all already assembled when she arrived. They rose from their chairs and bowed in a mixture of confusion and fear as she made her way to the dais. It took them a long time to settle back down into their chairs, as if they feared that the honor Miroslava Praskovyevna had granted so long ago, of allowing her princesses to sit in her presence during the Princess Council, would suddenly be revoked.

It seemed to take a long time for the Princess Council to do its business, although there was nothing unusual about that. What was unusual was the almost complete absence of quarreling or feuding. There was a brief round of self-congratulatory speeches by some of the princesses, apparently perfectly sincere and fueled by a deep belief in the truth of their statements, on how much they had always loved Slava, how they had always been her staunch allies, and how they had always treated her with the upmost kindness and respect, but Slava was so caught off guard by these sentiments that she was unable to prevent herself from staring at the princesses in blank astonishment, and almost laughing out loud.

After that, Slava didn't think she'd ever seen a Princess Council so quiet. She was almost tempted to remark on that fact, but she guessed by the terrified expressions on most of her princesses' faces that such a remark would not go over well, and so held her tongue. She could tell that the silence was the silence of terror and confusion—because in the princesses' minds, they *had* been her staunch allies and benevolent protectors all along—not consideration and contemplation, and so anything she said would most likely just throw them into an even deeper panic. And so she did her best to soothe their hurt feelings as they would never have soothed hers, and cajole and curry them into a frame of mind in which they could do business.

In the end it was decided that, because of her sister's serious and most likely long-lasting indisposition, no one had any opposition to Slava's rule—at least none that they dared express by so much as an eye-twitch—nor to fixing the succession onto Slava's line, rather than Vladya's, nor to sending Vladya and Prasha to Gluboky Prud. If Slava had not been so dazed from the events of the past few days, and so tired from the effects of what the princesses referred to, guardedly, as her "hopes," she would have been surprised at how quickly and easily such monumental decisions were made, and how little attention she paid to the process, and how little she felt about the outcome. But as she was so dazed, she felt very little at all.

The issue of the Stepnaya lands came up in relation to all these questions of succession, but as there had been no decisive outcome to the Stepnaya succession itself, nothing could be decided on Slava's end either, other than her unwillingness to take the lands while the possibility of a legitimate heir still existed. And with that, the Princess Council was dismissed, and Slava made her grateful way back to her chambers.

A maid was waiting for her there on her return, with the message that "Vladislava Vasilisovna had requested the honor of an audience."

"Show her in," said Slava.

Vladislava came bursting impetuously in as soon as the permission had been given. "So that was a Princess Council?" she demanded as soon as she was through the doors. "It was very boring, wasn't it? Aunty Olga and I were very glad to leave. I thought there was going to be more quarreling and fighting."

"So did I," said Slava. "Usually there is."

"Well, that's good. I'd hate for them *all* to be so boring, especially if I have to come to them all the time when I'm a woman grown."

"Yes," said Slava.

"So are you going to go riding with me?"

"It will be dark soon, little princess," objected Masha, and then looked abashed at her boldness.

"Oh," said Vladislava, looking terribly disappointed.

"We can still go riding," Slava promised. "We can take torches, and ride out into the park to watch the sun set in the trees. Give the command for horses to be saddled, Masha. Go change, Vladislava, and I will meet you in the stables shortly."

Vladislava skipped off to change into riding clothes, and Slava let Manya remove her heavy golden gown and replace it with riding clothes.

"It will be dark very soon, Tsarina, and the weather is still cold and raw," objected Manya at one point.

"I know, I just...it seems fitting. I began this adventure with a ride in the park, and I feel I must finish it that way, too."

"Will they be going with you, Tsarina?" asked Manya, nodding at the snow fox and the snow hare, who were curled up on her bed.

Not a chance, said the snow fox.

I have spent more than my fair share of time in the cold, said the snow hare.

"It seems not," said Slava. "Besides, they might hold us back."

!!! said the snow fox, but despite her indignation, she failed even to open her eyes, let alone get off the bed to join Slava as she left the room.

It was indeed almost dark as Slava and Vladislava mounted their horses and made their way towards the park, followed by half-a-dozen unhappy and bewildered guards.

"There's not much of a sunset," pointed out Vladislava, looking off to the West.

"There never is, in Krasnograd," said Slava. "All the buildings get in the way."

"And the clouds," said Vladislava, wrinkling her nose at the sky.

"And the clouds," agreed Slava. "But look at how they move! They will blow away soon enough."

"It's cold," said Vladislava. "It's springtime in the South, and I'm still cold."

"It will warm up soon enough, too," Slava promised.

"Can we trot, now that we're in the park?" asked Vladislava.

"Yes," said Slava, and they picked up a trot, making the torches the guards were carrying flicker and bob.

"Where are we going?" asked Vladislava.

"To the gods," Slava told her.

"In the center of the park? Where the prayer trees are?"

"Yes," said Slava.

It was soon very dark, and the cold wind blowing away the clouds blew Slava's cloak, making it swirl around her and frightening Rozochka, so that she had to stroke her neck and tell her there was nothing to fear as they rode along. Suddenly the torches in front of them came to a stop.

"The prayer trees, Tsarina," called the guard.

"Take Rozochka," Slava told Vladislava, dismounting and trying to hand her the reins, but a guard intervened before Vladislava could take them, taking charge of Slava's reins himself.

"I'll only be a short while," Slava told Vladislava.

"Good, because I don't like it here," said Vladislava. "It's all dark, and the prayer trees look strange. I don't like the way their ribbons flutter in the wind. It's like they're talking to us or something."

"Look, the clouds have broken and the moon has come out," said Slava. "And the stars." She walked away from the others, over to the largest and oldest prayer tree. The wind and the ribbons made it look like a living thing.

I am a living thing, it said.

I know, said Slava. She reached out and took the tip of a long thin branch, and brought it to her lips.

A kiss from the god-mother, said the tree.

I carry no god, of that I am certain, said Slava. *My daughter, should she have the good fortune to be born, will be of the world of women, just as I am.*

Yes, but you are blessed by them nonetheless, said the tree.

And yet they failed to come to my aid when I needed it most, said Slava.

But you did not need it, said the tree. *Others came to your aid instead. It is unwise to question the gods too closely, or demand too much from them.*

True, said Slava.

The cold wind rose up even more strongly, whipping the branches back and forth so that they lashed Slava's face and tore at her clothing.

You are a wise daughter, it said. *We will be watching you.*

The wind suddenly died. Moonlight was pouring down on Slava.

You have passed many tests, it seems, said the tree. *Are your trials done, do you think?*

No, said Slava. *I think many more await me.*

But perhaps the worst is over, said the tree.

I think there is still much suffering to come, said Slava. *I cannot avoid it.*

And how will you face it, Krasnoslava? asked the tree. *You gave up your chance for armor, for the ice of the Midnight Land.*

The Midnight Land will always be with me, said Slava. *It is in all of us. And I have gained its icy armor in the end. That, I think, I will never lose. After all, I forged it on the anvil of my own abandoned dreams. And every time the links start to weaken, I can reforge it anew, for I will always have more dreams that I must deny. The supply seems inexhaustible.*

Yes, said the tree.

I must go now, said Slava. *But I will return.*

I know, said the tree. For a moment its long thin branches curled around Slava, and then it released her, and she turned and walked away.

"Were you praying?" asked Vladislava curiously, once Slava had rejoined the others.

"Yes," said Slava. She took Rozochka's reins, and looked into her eyes. Rozochka looked wisely back at her. Slava could feel her life, and the life of all her companions, and the great swarm of life and death that was Krasnograd, and the chill thin life of the fields and forests beyond the city, and the great expanse that opened all around them, all the way to the Midnight Land and its eternal ice. The ice looked back at her.

"Look!" cried Vladislava. "A shooting star!"

A great star was flying across the sky, breaking into pieces as it fell.

"Is it an omen?" asked Vladislava anxiously.

"It is if we think it is," said Slava. "Look at the stars! The sky is full of omens, Vladislava. The world is full of omens. Let us go back to the kremlin. I'm cold."

"Me too," said Vladislava. "Did the gods speak to you when you were praying?"

"They did," said Slava.

"They did! What did they say?"

"They said the sky is full of omens. The world is full of omens. And wonder, Vladislava, let us not forget that. Breathe in the night air, Vladislava!"

"It reeks of the city," complained Vladislava.

"But beyond that is the steppe! And the taiga! And beyond that is the tundra, and great mountains, and the sea! The world is a vast and wondrous place, Vladislava!"

"Good," said Vladislava. "Because I'm bored here. I want some supper, and then I want to go on a journey. But a better journey, with less cold rain than our journey down from Lesnograd. That was awful. I want a sunny journey."

"Someday," promised Slava. She thought of the dark path the gods had promised for Vladislava. Perhaps she had already passed through the darkest part of it. Perhaps not. "But now let us return to the kremlin and supper."

"Can we gallop in the dark?" asked Vladislava. "I've never been allowed to gallop in the dark!"

"No!" said all the guards simultaneously.

"Let's just trot," said Slava. "It will give us more time to see the stars."

"Well, if we can't gallop..." said Vladislava, and set off at a trot back to the kremlin.

The horses were also feeling the cold, and were eager to return to their warm stable and supper, and soon the trot turned to a canter, which grew faster and faster into what could probably be called a gallop, but somehow no one could or would rein them in. The dark air rushed past Slava's face. The park was large enough that it was easy, just then, to forget that the city surrounded them, and to feel part of all the vastness stretching out in all directions. The stars looked down on Slava, and she could feel their eyes watching her as she went.

End of Part II

*Dear Reader! Thank you for joining in Slava's epic journey. You can find out what happens to Slava's daughter in **The Breathing Sea!***

From the Author

If you're curious about the typefaces used in this edition, the titles are in Luminari and the main body text is in Athelas. Luminari is based on High Middle Ages ornate religious texts. Athelas is inspired by classical British literature and is named after the healing herb in *The Lord of the Rings*.

Want to know how it all began? Keep up with the latest news and get freebies and insider information? You can get a free copy of the prequel collection *Winter of the Gods and Other Stories* and sign up for my newsletter at epclarkauthor.net. Or you can go directly to the book by scanning the QR code below.

And of course, if you feel so moved, reviews are always welcome! In five minutes you can leave a review that will make an author's day :)

Happy reading!
E.P.

About the Author

E.P. Clark's first story was about a ghost in the bushes back in her native Kentucky. Fortunately for all concerned, it has not survived. Since then diverse adventures have happened, many of them unexpectedly involving Russia. Having, much to her surprise, gained the ability to speak Russian, she then went on to complete her Ph.D. in the subject. When she is not writing, she teaches Russian and contemplates the mysteries of poetic form. She is the author of multiple short stories; this her second novel in what is shaping up to be a seven-volume trilogy. She loves to hear from her readers and can be reached at epclark@epclarkauthor.net, or on her website at https://epclarkauthor.net/, Pinterest at http://www.pinterest.com/EPClark-Author/, Facebook at https://www.facebook.com/epclarkauthor/, and Twitter at @EPClarkauthor.

Also by the Author

www.ingramcontent.com/pod-product-compliance
Lightning Source LLC
Chambersburg PA
CBHW030929020726
47498CB00001B/175